SNAKE MOUNTAIN

A NOVEL

BY JERRY CRAVEN

TEXAS CHRISTIAN UNIVERSITY PRESS
Fort Worth

Library of Congress Cataloging-in-Publication Data

Craven, Jerry
Snake Mountain : a novel / by Jerry Craven.
p. cm
ISBN 0-87565-221-2 (alk. paper)
1. College students—Texas—Amarillo—Fiction. 2. Violence—Texas—Amarillo—Fiction. 3. Cowboys—Texas—Amarillo—Fiction. 4. Amarillo (Tex.)—Fiction. I. Title.

PS3553.R275 S64 2000
813'.54—dc21

99-057781

Design by Shadetree Studio

I dedicate this book
to the Texans who helped shape it:

Judy Alter, Jerry Bradley, Kevin Casey,
Nancy Castilla-Jones, David Craven,
Linda Craven, Judy Cross, Kelly Fristoe,
Jim Goodhue, Billy Bob Hill, Bill Hinson,
Bo Holland, Janus Mays, Bell Meek,
Richard Moseley, Debra Munn, Sam Pakan,
John Reeves, Tracy Row, Carroll Wilson

and to the ranchers who once
frequented the old Chuck Wagon Cafe in
Canyon to eat grits and eggs and
to educate me in their
wonderful use of language.

Jason White stood in the back of a ticket line in the Los Angeles International Airport listening to music with headphones and watching a young woman in another line. She seemed to be looking right at him, but it wasn't the eye contact so much that caught Jason's attention as her dark eyes, olive skin and east Indian features—like a young version of my mother, Jason thought. He smiled at her, and she offered him a tiny, qualified smile before looking down.

It was then that her face seemed to fly apart. He heard a snapping sound that, an instant later, he identified as a pistol shot, but it came to him as background noise, indistinct and barely audible over the music coming through his Walkman headphones.

The young woman jerked sideways and fell to the floor. People began screaming and falling, and Jason thought they were all being shot, maybe with a machine gun.

A man put his hand on Jason's shoulder and pushed him. "Down," the man said, "Get down. On the floor."

Jason—hobbled by a newly healed broken leg—dropped his tennis racket and his cane as he fell to the floor. Pain stabbed his leg. Jason snatched the speakers from his ears as he looked around. People on the floor nearby made little sound, but others further away screamed unintelligible words in high, thin voices. The only man standing waved a pistol, staring at the woman he had shot. His face looked puffy, and his eyes had a wild, crazy roundness to them. Something about the man reminded Jason of the Aussie boy responsible for Jason's broken leg.

The gunman looked over his shoulder toward the entrance to the building at security men rushing toward him. He jumped over several people lying on the floor and began running. As the man ran past him, Jason stuck out his cane. He heard the crack of the man's shin against the wood and watched him fall, smashing his head against a luggage cart. The man went limp.

Jason stood, feeling unsteady, using his cane for support. Some people had begun crawling toward the exit, and others scurried off, hunkering down as if there might be bullets flying through the air, just above their heads. No one had seemed to notice what the gunman had tripped on, and Jason was glad for that. He looked at the man, amazed at how large he seemed and at how bizarre he appeared with his pink, freckled skin and Irish-red hair.

Security men surrounded the unconscious man, pointing pistols at him. Jason backed away and leaned against a wall, angry with himself for acting like the old Jason. The new Jason should have swung the cane, he affirmed. He closed his eyes and replayed the scene, this time cracking the man's shins with a solid swing then scrambling to his feet just as the killer raised the pistol to point it at Jason's heart. The man's thick finger began its deadly pull on the trigger as Jason swung again, hitting the killer's wrist an instant before the pistol went off to send a bullet through the hair just above Jason's ear. He heard it. He felt the sting of its heat. And he stepped fast to the prone man, put the end of the cane against his throat to pin him against the luggage cart.

"But all I did was trip him," Jason whispered. He glanced at the dirt on his white trousers and shirt. Airports are filthy places, he thought, and deadly places, now. If I had gotten some sleep, maybe I could have swung the cane. Maybe I would have gotten a start on being the new Jason.

He had been awake, more or less, for nearly forty hours when he arrived at the Los Angeles International Airport. During the first leg of his trip—from Kuala Lumpur to Japan—he felt too much excitement to sleep even if the flight took most of the night. He divided his attention between the in-flight movie, *Fatal Attraction*, and his anxieties over moving from Malaysia to a ranch in West Texas.

During the eight-hour layover at the Narita Airport near Tokyo, he wanted to sleep, but found the noise and the tobacco smoke too distracting to relax. He limped about leaning on his cane, looking without success for a chair built for someone of his height. By the time he got aboard the flight across the Pacific, his leg ached too much for him to rest in the cramped airplane seat.

When he arrived in Los Angeles, Jason felt numb, and he limped through the airport, almost in a daze, while he followed those exiting from the plane. At one desk, the clerk scowled at his passport and said, "Pay attention to the signs. You need to go to the line for U.S. citizens. This one is for foreign passports."

"Yeah," Jason said, looking around in confusion. American, he mumbled to himself, I'm an American. Make it a mantra, chant it to myself like Muslims chant prayers. American.

Later, a customs inspector glanced at Jason in distaste. "Put your bag there," he said in a querulous tone. Jason leaned against the counter, unaware that the inspector had spoken to him. "I said, put the bag right there," the inspector repeated. Jason put his bag on the counter. "How come you're carrying a tennis racket if you're too crippled up to play?" Jason started to explain he was recovering from a simple bone fracture when the agent pulled a paper packet from Jason's bag. "What's this? Drugs?"

"Cheap gemstones."

The customs official unfolded the paper and whistled. "I'll bet those cost plenty. You'll have to pay some tax on those pretties."

"Those are mostly synthetic spinel—a man-made stone." Jason pulled a receipt from his wallet.

"One hundred ringgit. How much is that?"

"About forty dollars. The conversion from Malaysian ringgit to dollars is 5..."

"Fine." The inspector glanced at the line behind Jason. "Go on through."

Jason found a bench, sat and rubbed his leg. He changed tapes in his Walkman, put the earphones in his ears, and adjusted the sound to cut out most of the noise of the airport. Then he joined the line at the ticket counter of the airline for his connecting flight to Amarillo. That was when he had seen the young woman, moments before her death.

If she had been my sister or my lover, Jason thought, I would stand beside her. When the man pulled the pistol, I'd whack him across the face, gouge him in the stomach with my cane. She would be alive.

Jason glanced around at the numerous policemen, at the paramedics coming down the hall with a stretcher, at the frightened faces of the passengers who had, just minutes ago, been standing in what seemed a routine line. He avoided looking at what was left of the woman who had smiled at him, the woman who was not his sister or lover and who was dead. So this is America, he thought. It's a hell of a homecoming.

Sybil Redbear found the dove, dead, hanging by its neck on a strip of green velvet ribbon attached to the branch of an elm just outside her front door. Someone had killed the bird and left it hanging where Sybil would be sure to see it as soon as she looked out the door.

She walked around the bird, disturbed far more, she told herself, than the death of a bird should disturb her. Her cat, Squeek, brought dead birds into the house with some regularity.

But it's Squeek's business to kill birds. Someone murdered this one. Murdered? She chided herself: that's no word to apply to a bird. But by God, it seems to fit in this case. This isn't natural, this hanging of a dove by a velvet ribbon.

She rubbed her palms on her cheeks, trying for calm. This was an act of will, not some cosmic accident, she thought. Someone is trying to scare me again. And it's working.

She looked around, half expecting to see someone watching, but there was no one. The nearest house stood in the morning sun, barricaded behind a cedar picket fence six feet high. Those folks work during the week, Sybil remembered. Nobody is home.

Beside her house she looked toward the creek and the cottonwood grove. Nobody. If there had been, her dogs in the kennel would have set up a howl. Besides, she thought, most people are afraid to get near the beehives under the cottonwoods.

The sheen of early spring leaves gave the cottonwoods a golden glow in the sun. Parker Redbear had bought the house because of that grove, one of the few stands of trees of such height in the entire town of Canyon. She and Parker once shared a love for that grove, admired its seasonal changes from golden-green in the spring to their autumn gold, like the mountain aspen the trees were related to. Even in winter, the cottonwoods had a tall, gray magnificence about them, similar to images from one of Parker's paintings. Birds loved the trees. Mockingbirds with their startling range of cries. Starlings with their clicks and chuckles and single whistles. Doves.

Sybil went back to the hanging dove, resolved to cut it down and bury it, taking a pocketknife from her jeans. As she reached for the strip of ribbon, she saw the tiny scroll tied to the bird's leg, and she jumped back.

A message—that's just another way to scare me, dammit. And it worked. I won't read it. I won't.

But even as she told herself she would have nothing to do with the note, she knew she would read it.

The delivery of the message seemed so perverse—a parody of a love note. Sybil associated green velvet ribbon with romance, though she did not know why. And the dove with the note on its leg had to be a mockery of a messenger bird delivering a note from a lover to his mate. A note attached to a dead leg.

She thought of the pair of doves she and Parker had watched in an aviary somewhere. Where was that? Near Tucson, she thought. The doves reminded her of herself and Parker, the way they rubbed one another in a never-ending show of affection. Doves mate for life, just as Parker and I did—which means somewhere there is a survivor to this dove, searching, singing its pain in the soft moans doves make. Sybil felt her eyes sting.

"No," she said aloud. I'm not mourning the dead bird or its mate. I'm getting back into self-pity, that's what. And that will not do.

On a day such as this, if Parker were still alive, the two of them would have risen early, before first light. She would bake some biscuits, pack them into a backpack, along with some of their homemade plum jelly, while Parker readied his easel and paints for a hike. Then they would go perhaps to Palo Duro Canyon, maybe walk to the lighthouse, or they would drive to Caprock Canyons, or to Buffalo Lake, where Parker would paint in the early morning light that he loved so much, and she would sit and read or work in her poetry notebook. Spring mornings with all the crisp coolness of the air and fresh smelling earth and birdcalls were once the stuff of paradise.

And now? she asked herself. A conspiracy of accidents have led to this, a time for desecration, for grotesque voodoo dolls with pins, for killing a dove and dangling it from velvet. For obscenities plucked from accidents, acted upon by choice.

She cut the bird down and carried it to the rose trellis on the side of the house. "You will become a rose," she said, and immediately felt foolish for the thought, for speaking the thought. On the way to and from the tool shed for a spade, she pretended to consider burying the dove with the note still attached to its leg.

She laid the dove in the ground, snapped the thread binding the scroll to its leg, set the scroll aside, and buried the bird.

Then she unrolled the scroll.

3

Angela pulled the wire tight and tied it with twine to the eaves of the house. "He ain't going to scare me away from my own home," she muttered. "Not this time." She climbed down from the step ladder and turned to face the Chevy pickup as it pulled off the driveway toward the bunkhouse, stirring up a cloud of dust. A dog ran toward the pickup, barking.

"Shut up, Turdy," Angela said.

The dog circled to the driver's side but backed away, growling, when Lint got out. He ignored the dog, hooked his thumbs over his belt buckle and surveyed Angela's work, looking at the wire she had strung from the main building to the bunkhouse. "Looks to me like fourteen gauge."

"If the sheriff catches you out here, you go to jail."

"Ought to be twelve or maybe ten." Lint turned to her with his little boy smile. His cheeks dimpled. Angela breathed a sigh of relief: he had not been drinking. He never seemed to smile when he had been taking some pulls on the bottle he kept in the glove box of his pickup. "Set your house on fire with a tiny gauged wire like that. What happened to the old wire?"

"Got broke in the hail storm. Lint, you just get in that truck and head on out. There's that peace bond, remember?"

"We got some number twelve at the house. You just say the word, and I'll fetch that wire over here. Even hook her up, if you want." He grinned again.

"Thanks, Lint. But I can twist them wires myself. And what I strung is plenty big for just a couple of light bulbs, Hyram says."

"Hyram," Lint said with contempt. He walked to the stepladder. "You brought her right up to the right spot. I'll strip it and tie it in. You got black tape?" He pulled a knife from his pocket, snapped the blade out, and climbed the ladder.

Angela looked at him with some hesitation. The thought of making that connection herself did scare her, even if she would never admit it. Hyram had connected the wire on the other end, and he did so without turning the house current off. "The key is," he had explained, "not to touch more than one wire at a time. You do, and it'll bite you. Could even kill you. Most people, shoot, they don't treat house electricity with respect. But it could kill you, the juice right out of ordinary house wire. Kill you dead." He told Angela to string the wire, if she wanted, but not to make the connection. He would do that when he got back from town.

But Angela had determined she would get the lights going before Hyram got back, however spooky it might be to cut insulation from wire that was alive with house current. She took a roll of tape from her back pocket and handed it to Lint. "Hyram is going to be really pissed if he drives up and finds you here." Angela saw a quick flash of temper cross Lint's face, but he swallowed it back and smiled. Maybe he has been at the bottle, she thought. The idea frightened her.

He scowled. "Don't talk to me about that fat sumbitch."

"Hyram would just as soon shoot your ass off as look at you."

Lint waved his hand and laughed, then got on with the business of removing insulation and tying the wires together.

He got off the ladder and looked at Angela, moving his eyes in a slow, deliberate way from her feet to her breasts, then back down. "I always loved seeing you in them tight blue jeans. You're one helluva beautiful girl."

"No I ain't."

"Angela," Lint stepped up to her and took her arm. "Angela, you know I always thought you was the prettiest girl around."

"I ain't a girl. I'm a woman, Lint. Look at me in the eyes, Lint. You never look at me in the eyes. You afraid you might see a woman? I might have been a girl when you married me, but I grew up. You never noticed, did you?"

"It's them green eyes, Angela. You know that. Only witches got green eyes. Where's your blue contacts?"

"You can look for them in the garbage, if you want." She jerked her arm away and turned toward Hyram's ranch house. Lint grabbed her hair and pulled her back. She screamed. The dog ran up to them, barking.

"You got no call to talk to me that way." Lint's voice was low and angry.

"Bite him. Bite him on the leg, Turdy."

The dog snapped at Lint's boots. He kicked Turdy, and it ran off, howling. "You ain't treated me nice in a long time. How come you never treat me nice no more?"

"You let go of my hair."

"Don't you look at me. Not with them green eyes. And you treat me nice, you hear?" He jerked her to him, wrapped his arm around her and began dragging her toward the door of the bunkhouse.

"You let go of me, you sawed-off bastard."

Lint jerked the screen door so hard the upper hinge came loose. He pulled Angela into the bunkhouse and released her except for his grip on her hair. "Take off your clothes. I'll teach you to treat me like a woman ought to treat her husband."

Angela started to speak, then clamped her mouth shut and struck out at him. She thought she could detect a faint smell of liquor on him, and she knew if he had even a tiny bit of alcohol in him, words would do no good. Fighting wouldn't either, but she determined she would not give in, not this time.

Lint slapped her and jerked her head about. "Fight me, will you?" He laughed. Angela could tell he liked it when she fought because he believed that meant he would win. He slapped her face again and ripped at her shirt, popping off some of the buttons.

Hyram saw Lint's truck when he pulled in the driveway. He turned off the engine and sat for a moment, looking toward the bunkhouse, thinking he ought to go do something. But Angela had been firm: she would handle Lint if he ever came out to the ranch. And he was, after all, her husband. At least until the divorce was final.

Then Hyram noticed the screen door hanging from the bottom hinge. He grabbed the shotgun from the rack behind the seat and ran toward the bunkhouse. When he got close, he could hear the sounds of a struggle. "Damn," he said, wishing he had not left Angela alone. He took some deep breaths, trying to get his wind enough so he could talk.

Lint pinned Angela to the floor. He had her shirt and bra off, and he was pulling at her jeans. "Any time you want to stop fighting and start helping, just be my guest." He laughed.

Hyram kicked what remained of the screen door aside. "Get off her, Lint, or I swear to God I'll kill you."

Lint released Angela and stood up. "This ain't your concern, Hyram." Lint's voice was just a whisper.

"This scatter gun says it is my concern. You get your carcass out of here. Now." Hyram stepped back, letting Lint out the door. "You come on my land again, and I'll open you up with buckshot."

Hyram stood in the doorway, watching Lint drive off fast and hard to throw gravel behind him. "Coward," Hyram said in contempt. He turned to Angela.

She sat on the floor, her hair hanging in her face, her breasts bare. "You okay, honey?" Hyram asked. She tossed her head to get the hair out of her face and looked at him.

They held eye contact for a long moment. "I'm an old man, Angela. There's some things I could no more do than a cow could jump over the moon." Hyram heard his own voice sounding thin and high. "An old man."

He turned and walked to his pickup, the shotgun hanging in the crook of one arm, pointing at the ground.

Police swarmed the area of the murder, uniformed ones and ones in business suits. One man wearing a coat and tie questioned Jason. "It was your cane that tripped him?"

"Yes. I raised it just as he ran by."

"And you say you never saw him before?"

"No. I haven't been in the United States since I was a little kid."

The man took notes. "And you came from Koala what?"

"Kuala Lumpur." Jason spelled it for him. "The capitol of Malaysia."

"Why are you carrying a cane?"

"I'm recovering from a fracture. The cast just came off a few days ago."

"You break it playing tennis?" The man glanced at Jason's racket.

"A guy shoved me, and I fell wrong." That wasn't the precise truth, but Jason couldn't see the relevance of how he broke his leg to the murder in the airport, so he didn't elaborate.

"Is there an address and phone number in Amarillo where we can reach you, in case we need to ask further questions?"

"Not in Amarillo. I'm going to a ranch south of there, close to a little town called Canyon." Jason took Hyram's business card from his wallet. "That's where I'll be, at least for the summer. Maybe longer. In any case, you can contact me there for the next year or so."

Jason's flight had been delayed until the police could complete their work. After the detective finished questioning him, Jason found a seat in a snack bar to wait out the investigation. It took four hours. He called Hyram and explained the delay.

When flights from that part of the airport resumed, Jason moved through the necessary lines in an almost trancelike state. He heard others around him recounting the incident of the murder, but he said nothing. His leg ached, and he gave all the attention he could to the pain, trying to banish the image of the young woman's smile and of the way her head had exploded.

No one sat next to him on the flight to Phoenix, so he propped his leg up on the seats beside him. That helped him concentrate on the pain, but after a while even pain couldn't keep the images at bay.

It's just fatigue, he told himself. And fatigue was the down side of a cycle. A living cycle. He had been out of a cast less than a week, so his muscles still felt weak. But they would recover, he thought, as the girl never would. He made himself remember some of the conversations that he had noted but not thought about while waiting for the plane.

No one seemed to know why the red-headed man killed the pretty young woman. Some speculated that she was his wife. One man standing near Jason had said he thought the killer must be a hit man, hired to kill some rich bitch. Another thought the killer might have escaped from prison or from an insane asylum. "It would take a crazy person to do something that violent," the man said.

Jason wondered if it were true—if violence was the result of insanity. Maybe that had to be it: maybe that big Australian kid, Tom, paid to see a fight to the death because he was insane. If that's true, Jason thought, then I'm trying to make myself into a crazy person. He shook his head. No. I don't want to be violent. Just not passive. Not a victim. I don't want to be like Tom.

Tom had paid the Malay boy forty ringgit to let the mongoose fight the cobra. Jason saw a crowd gathering just off Jalan Masjid India, near the river in Kuala Lumpur, and wandered over to it out of curiosity.

"Twenty ringgit not enough," the Malay boy said. Jason looked at Tom, wondering if he were about to purchase one of the animals the boy had caged.

"Twenty-two, then, and that's flat," Tom said.

"No can. Cerpelai kill ular. Maybe ular tedung kill cerpelai. I lose. Snake cost more. Animal cost more. Twenty-two ringgit, no can."

"Twenty-five, and you keep the dead snake."

"Thirty. Just five more, and I let them fights."

"No deal," Tom said. He started to walk away.

Jason could see the Malay boy come to a decision. "Can do."

"I'll give you twenty-eight ringgit if you will not let the mongoose kill the cobra," Jason said.

"What?" Tom swung around and looked at Jason. "You butt out, you little shit."

"Twenty-eight for no fights?" A sly expression came over the Malay boy's face. "What you say, big man?" He looked at the Australian.

"I say thirty ringgit and I see the mongoose have it out with old fangs there." Tom turned to Jason.

"Thirty-two. Tom, what's the point? The snake will die—and for what? To entertain you?"

"A good enough reason, what? Thirty-five ringgit."

"You pay forty, and no fights," the Malay boy said. Jason took out his wallet and looked in it.

"Thirty-eight?" he offered.

"So you went broke, eh?" Tom laughed. He turned to the Malay boy. "Forty. No more."

The Malay boy looked at Jason, who shrugged, feeling helpless.

Tom paid. The Malay boy turned the animals loose, and the crowd fell back. Jason turned to go, but found himself bound there by some morbid fascination.

It was a black cobra, common in Malaysia, and not a big one. Maybe one meter, Jason estimated. It spread its neck, lifted its head and faced the mongoose. Every time it tried to strike, the crowd roared and moved back. The mongoose leaped aside, avoiding the slow attack. "It isn't even a contest," Jason objected. "The snake doesn't stand a chance."

"True, true," Tom had said, laughing.

Jason shifted his leg on the airplane seat, remembering Tom. The boy had, just days after paying to see the cobra killed, taken delight in beating up Rozak, one of the bus drivers on campus at the International School of Kuala Lumpur.

The bus driver, a gentle Pakistani-Malaysian, told Jason he had called Tom's father to tell of Tom's foul language on the bus. "He speak bad words to my children, many little children."

The next day, Tom found the bus driver and bloodied his nose. Jason saw the attack, and it horrified him. How could anyone strike Rozak, who always treated everyone with such politeness? But there was Tom, punching away, pounding the man's face and body.

Jason reported the incident to the principal, and within an hour, Tom was expelled from the International School of Kuala Lumpur. Permanently.

Until he saw the murder in the airport Jason thought Tom to be the most violent person he would ever meet. He glanced at the clouds through the plane's window and thought again about the woman who smiled at him just seconds before she died. I didn't even get the chance to learn her name, he thought. It seemed monstrous that he did not know her name. "Suppriah," he said aloud. A beautiful name, a fitting name. It felt proper to think of her as having a name, to think of her as Suppriah.

He had seen the name on the back cover of a book by a Malaysian-Indian anthropologist, under her photograph. The writer looked a bit older than the Suppriah in the airport, and she had a red dot in the center of her forehead and a jewel on the side of her nose—but their eyes were much alike: the classical almond-shaped eyes, dark and brooding, of an Indian princess.

How could anyone even consider killing such a magnificent creature as Suppriah? Maybe only an American could do it. In Malaysia, newspapers like *The New Straits Times* reported stories of violence on the streets of American cities, making the United States seem to be a place where killers and drug dealers and thieves filled every park and alley. Friends of Jason at the International School who had never lived in the United States often expressed fear of going there, fear for their personal safety. Jason once scorned facile generalizations that condemned the entire country for the actions of a few violent people. But after seeing a murder with his own eyes, he wasn't so sure the image of America as a jungle of crime wasn't accurate. He lived many places in the last few years—Madrid, Katmandu, Bangkok, Jakarta, Kuala Lumpur—and never witnessed a murder, much less talked with anyone who had.

Murders occurred mainly in America, then. But even as he felt the truth of the observation, he knew it to be false. It just didn't feel false, even when he remembered the violence of Tom pounding on Rozak with fists that could kill—and Tom wasn't an American.

Is that what I want the new Jason to be? he wondered. A violent American? No. Violence has nothing to do with a remake of self, with putting aside Islam, with learning to care about something enough to die for.

That's what had held him in the Muslim community his mother

thrust him into, the willingness of the men to die for what they believed. At the mosque, with face, hands and feet washed in a ritual, he stood beside Uncle Omar, facing Mecca and the Kaaba, muttering the magic words that made all those present into brothers. But he was a child then. By the time he was fourteen he found the words less magical, for he doubted God spoke Arabic. When he was sixteen standing beside Uncle Omar in the mosque beside the Klang river, he moved his lips as in prayer, but the words he mouthed were words of a Willie Nelson song, for he doubted there was a god such as Allah who would order the use of a rattan whip on a Malay couple who dared to make love without benefit of marriage. Two years later he refused to go to the mosque at all—and yet he missed the magic, the sense of being brother to those around him, those who would die for what they believed.

Dying isn't the same thing as killing, Jason told himself. I will never become like the red-haired man who killed Suppriah.

The image of her in the pool of blood came to him again, vivid and overwhelming. "Gone," he whispered. "She's gone. Forever." The fact of Suppriah's death was too enormous, too heavy; it would crush him.

I will go to Snake Mountain, he affirmed, and live in a strange land and my leg will heal. But she will never change. She will stay the same —she will be dead forever.

He tried to grasp the concept, but it seemed too hideous. One day, he thought, I will have children. But she won't. Ever. The man with red hair killed all her children. And all her children's children. Forever. Jason thought of the eggs Suppriah had carried inside her ovaries. None of them would ripen into a child to pass on part of Suppriah to future generations. None. He shut his eyes and tried to imagine the people who could have been born, springing from a thin line attached to Suppriah a hundred years into the future, five hundred years. They stood in groups, dozens at first, then hundreds, thousands.

Jason opened his eyes to banish the images, and he avowed again that he would never learn the American way of violence. Then he remembered tripping the red-headed man, sending him sprawling to strike his head against a luggage cart, remembered wishing he had swung the cane, then pressed it against the killer's throat. "But that's only if Suppriah had been my sister or lover," he muttered, wishing he had a sister or a lover.

The note on the scroll made no sense. It looked like squiggles that a secretary might write in shorthand.

But there was something somehow familiar about the squiggles, though Sybil couldn't pin it down. She put the note in her shirt pocket and went into the house.

How could anyone murder a turtle dove? she wondered, even as she thought of the likely culprit. The same person who left the hand-carved wooden rosary taped to her door. And the same person who tore a page from the Tibetan Book of the Dead and left it in her mailbox. Then there was the quartz crystal in the leather pouch hanging on a nail hammered into the trunk of the elm beside the front door, the chicken feet left on the seat of her car, the voodoo doll with a pin in its groin dangling from the doorknob of her front door. All left by the same person.

Pug. Of course Pug denied doing any of it, but Sybil was almost certain. Pug wants to frighten me, and she's good at it. But why? To get me to move to her apartment? She knows I won't.

My friend Pug has been good to me, Sybil told herself. I must study ways to love her in spite of herself.

Sybil didn't understand why she found the items left in her car and around her house so scary. They just were. The rosary came first, and it sent chills through Sybil's body, even if she was not a Catholic. Then, in succeeding weeks, the other items appeared, each seeming more sinister than the last, the murdered dove the most sinister of all.

The note on the scroll had a bizarre, spooky quality about it that Sybil couldn't identify. She made herself a cup of mint tea and sat in her living room, trying to think about laughter. The hot mint tea helped. It always soothed her.

Sybil once enjoyed laughing. Parker once said it was her ability to laugh at unexpected times that first drew him to her. "I doubt that," she told him, lifting her breasts to draw his attention to them. "I think what first got your attention was my large," she paused to glance again at her breasts, "dark eyes."

And Parker had laughed.

Sybil knew it was not her dark eyes or her large breasts or her love of laughter that drew Parker to her. Those mattered, of course, especially the large breasts—though he later came to feel intimidated by her sexuality. She knew that what drew him to her was her enthusiasm, her dedication to whatever seemed important, be it causes like racial equality or hobbies like keeping bees.

Parker loved art, and he painted in oils with a fervor that matched any enthusiasm Sybil had. She saw in his control of color and light the talent of a great artist, and his talent became part of her enthusiasm. "Your great talent is an accident of nature," she told him. "To choose to use it and share it will be a choice. One we both can make."

It was she who suggested he paint the landscape of his ancestors, that he sign his paintings "Red Bear," that he play to America's love of the myth of the noble savage by seeming to be more the native American than his upbringing could account for. It was she who set up his first one-man shows; it was she who found the New York agent who spread his name enough that his art started selling for staggering amounts. At the time of his death, Red Bear was better known in the art galleries of New York City than he was in Canyon, Texas.

Sybil drank her mint tea and looked at the locked door to the studio. Parker had placed it on the north side of the house for the light. He told the carpenters to reframe the attic to make room for all the skylights the roof would tolerate. It became a magnificent room, one where Parker painted and Sybil wrote. At the time of Parker's death, Sybil had written about a third of a biography of Quanah Parker, the last great Comanche chief, and a man from whom Parker claimed direct linear descent.

Quanah Parker appealed to her for several reasons, not the least being the grand accident of his ancestry—Quanah was a half-breed. His mother was Cynthia Ann Parker, captured in a raid on a white settlement; his father was the chief of the Comanches who roamed the Great Plains of Texas at the time white men were completing the job of taking America from the aborigines of the continent.

Sybil's mother was a white woman from Port Arthur, Texas; her father a Liberian seaman. The pictures Sybil had of her father showed a tall, muscular African who was himself of mixed blood. She knew little of him and even less of his ties to Liberia. Her reading as an adult convinced her that Liberians little understood their own African heritage, for they came to their country as foreigners, as freed slaves of American plantations. For Sybil, childhood was a time of confusion about her identity. Most black people thought she looked white—and many rejected her. She looked black to many whites, who also rejected her.

When Parker told her about his ancestor, the half-breed who struggled all his life for identity, she knew she had to find out more about the man. Her reading led to her researching a biography of Quanah Parker in the Panhandle Plains Museum on the university campus in Canyon. Another six or eight months and she would have completed the project.

But Parker died. Sybil locked the door to the studio on the day of his death. She had stood in the doorway, looking at the half-finished painting on the easel, at Parker's jacket draped across the back of a chair, at the piles of note cards beside the word processor where she wrote while he painted; she looked at the skylights that, during the day, gave the good north light Parker liked to talk about, at the drying rack he had built that still held his last three paintings, at the white throw-rug on the floor where she and Parker sometimes made love; and she drew the door closed, locked it by turning a key in a deadbolt, and walked out into a cold Panhandle night.

Her walk took her to Hunsley Hills Creek, where she stood on the bridge beside the golf course and dropped the key to Parker's studio into murky, nighttime waters.

Pug came over that night and held her while she cried.

Sybil finished her mint tea. How long ago had she turned that key for a final time, she wondered. A year? And how long since she had laughed out loud? The same length of time. Longer.

She looked at the squiggles someone had drawn with seeming care on the scroll sent to her via a dead bird. They still looked familiar.

Ben Lippman saw the nude form of a woman silhouetted against the sky. The sight startled him so much that his pickup drifted off the dirt road and crashed into the fence across from the rise where Angela stood.

Ben knew the nude woman had to be Lint Bodark's wife. No one else in the entire Panhandle of Texas, that he knew of, would dare venture out on an English riding saddle. And that big horse—it had to be the stud that Hyram saved from the knife. Ben put the pickup in reverse and backed away from the fence. Damn. The fence post he hit had cracked and would have to be replaced. "Shit!" he said, looking at the Dr Pepper can he used for spitting tobacco juice into. It had fallen off the dash and lay on the floorboard, spilling dark, stringy fluid. Serves me right, Ben told himself, for looking at that gal instead of the road. But how come she went and got naked like that?

Angela stood downwind from Ghost so he would forget her perfume and leave her alone. Ghost grazed by the fence. The sky, Angela noted, had already begun breaking into morning. She sat down and took off her boots, then stood and began pulling at the snaps on her shirt. She wanted to be ready when the sun spilled into the valley.

After hanging her jeans on the top strand of barbed wire, she removed her lace panties, taking care not to touch them with her feet. The cool morning air rippled her skin, and she shivered with delight. Paradise, she told herself, looking at the dark, angular lines of Snake Mountain to the west, pushing into the sky. Angela admired the boldness of its push upward, even if the sky pushed back with a violence that flattened Snake Mountain into a mesa. They try to squash me like that, she told herself. By "they" she meant Lint and most other men she had known. But they can't do it. Flatten me a bit, maybe—but nobody will keep me down, make me be like any other Texas gal. Not anymore, they won't.

A few stars still hung here and there above the mesa. Angela looked at them with appreciation.

She turned to the east, to the long, horizontal cracks layering up from the valley rim and beginning, as she thought of it, to bleed the sky from darkness into morning. A star above the bleeding lines shimmered and winked out. "Sunset and evening star," she recited in a whisper, "and one clear call for me." She laughed. "Sunrise," she corrected, "sunrise. Morning and the goddess of the dawn." A glance back at Ghost assured her he still gave his attention to the buffalo grass by the fence. She spread her arms to the east, closed her eyes, and watched the growing red through her eyelids.

A moment of perfection, she told herself. No Lint Bodark. No records to post or horses to lead into the sell ring or cigar smoke or boots and jeans and tight shirts—nothing. Especially no men. Just me and the bleeding sky and cool air. She took a breath and let it out with a sigh, knowing while it felt good for there to be no men around, that it also felt lonely. If only one of them would be a bit different. No—a lot different. If only I could stand here beside someone who would share the dawn with me, I might know true happiness for once. For just once.

At that moment, Angela heard Ben Lippman's pickup rumble off the dirt road and slam into the fence post. A glance at the pickup confirmed it was Ben. Annoyed, she turned her back to him. Let him look, she thought. Let him wish he could kiss my ass.

When he drove off and she turned back east, the sun was too bright to look at. "Goddamn men," she muttered, reaching for her panties and jeans. Next time, I'll ride over that rise. I can hang my clothes on a mesquite.

"Come on, Ghost." She sat to put her boots on. Ghost came over and nuzzled her neck, snuffling for the perfume. "Dang it, Ghost." She pushed his head away and stood. "You act more like a man than Hyram does."

When she got back to the corral, she found Odom trimming the hooves on his paint. The horse stood with its nose to the fence, and Turdy sat waiting to eat the hoof trimmings. Hyram leaned against the gate. Odom let the hoof drop and turned to face her. "You keep that outlaw back, now."

"Ghost ain't no outlaw."

"Not to you." He bent to his job again, tapping on the horse's leg. "Come on. Come on. Give it to me." The paint lifted its foot.

"You must have gone out again before sunrise," Hyram said. "You all right, Angela?"

"I'm fine." She dismounted and took the saddle and bridle from Ghost.

Odom trimmed off a piece of hoof; Turdy snapped it up and retreated to chew on it. "She looks good. Hyram, she looks mighty good this morning."

"It ain't no illusion. I am good." Angela shoved Ghost's nose away when he nuzzled at her shirt collar. "Goodern grits. Now get out to the pasture, Ghost."

"You spruce up some, Angela, and come with me into town." Hyram walked toward his pickup.

"Wait up, chief." Angela put her saddle into the tack shed beside the gate. "What's old Hyram up to, Odom?"

"Dogs." Odom didn't look up. Turdy picked up another shaving.

"We got enough dogs with Turdy. What do you mean?"

Odom dropped the paint's foot. "Had a rock in the frog of that hoof." He pointed with his knife. "Gimped him up some. Turdy there, he ain't worth a pile of his own name, Hyram says. You go on with him, see about them dogs in town."

Angela caught up with Hyram by his pickup. "Which town we going to?"

"Canyon. Which town did you think? New York City?"

"You want me to get spruced up for Canyon?"

"Suit yourself." Hyram shrugged. "It don't matter to me that your mama didn't dress you right this morning." He got into the pickup. Angela went to the other side and got in.

"How come you want to go see dogs? And just what's wrong with the way I'm dressed?"

Hyram started the pickup. He grinned at her, dimpling the deeper lines that ran down both sides of his cheeks. "Nothing. Except maybe for the way you snapped up your shirt all wrong."

Angela looked at her shirt. "Damn." She began unsnapping.

"No bra, either."

"I'm surprised you noticed."

"I'm good at looking." He drove on the dirt road toward Canyon.

> "I'm just an old man with an eye
> for a young woman's tit or her thigh—"

"Another limerick, Hyram?"

> "—but wouldn't you know
> that's as far as I go,
> and if you hear I done more, it's a lie."

Hyram laughed, jerking his belly against the steering wheel.

Angela bit her lip. "You're a good man, a man many gals would love to get attention from, and I'm one of them, sometimes. Seems like the wrong men give me the wrong attention, like that damn Lint Bodark. My own fault, I guess. I should never have called him sawed-off. And I looked him right in the eye without my blue contacts on. He bought them blue contacts for me cause he said only witches got green eyes like mine. I chunked them contacts into the garbage when I moved out of the house, and when he asked about them yesterday, I told him. Thing is, I know how he is, and I shouldn't set him off like that."

"You didn't like my poem?"

"I didn't say that. It was a good one, Hyram. Funny." She sighed. But I wish sometimes, she said to herself, that you would be serious. Talk serious to me and not always be a clown.

She watched the landscape flatten as they left the Palo Duro breaks and turned on the blacktop that led to town. When they reached the edge of Canyon, she said, "Odom told me you wanted to see about a dog."

"Shepherd. Mostly shepherd, anyway. Got a black pup picked out for you."

"Don't shepherds grow up mean?"

"Not to them that feeds and pets them. You and me and Odom will romp with this one and scratch its ears and tell it poems. When it gets growed up, any one of us could whip it with a chain, and it wouldn't even bark at us."

"Hyram! Whip it? With a chain?"

"Not that we would, of course. But come a chicken thief, and that black shepherd would chew on him like Turdy chews hoof trimmings."

"You mean a chicken thief like Lint Bodark."

"Be a good time to get a pup, too, with Nathan White's boy coming to live with us. Fact is, I aim to get that dog for Jason. Nathan, he told me his boy loved dogs, but they can't have one over where they live."

"Hyram, you're about as good as Odom at lying, and that ain't no good at all. You just now made up that stuff about getting the dog for Nathan's boy. Besides, I don't need a dog to protect me."

"Hell, don't I know that? I'm getting that dog for Jason to pet and to run off the chicken thieves."

Angela sighed again. Hyram hadn't kept chickens on his ranch for years. Angela knew if anyone else mentioned chickens, Hyram would go off on a tirade about what worthless critters chickens were. When was the last time she knew of chickens around Hyram's place? A long time before Regan was born.

The thought of Regan came unexpected and sudden. She winced and ordered herself to think of something else.

Jason watched the mountain as the plane flew by in its landing pattern for the Albuquerque airport. Something seemed wrong with the trees on the mountain: they looked squat and not close enough together. And the color—green, but not the color of green Jason understood trees to be. The mountain with its bald spots and scruffy-looking vegetation seemed like a parody of the mountains around Ghenting Highlands in Malaysia.

Sitting back with his eyes closed, Jason told himself to envision the mountains of Malaysia. Perhaps that would hold at bay the images of the pretty woman and her shy smile and of her grotesque, bloody death.

Orchids. Jason envisioned them growing out of the ground and out from moss clumps where trees forked—white and purple flowers perched on the ends of green twigs. Bamboo ten meters high. Gigantic rosewood, some wrapped with the killing fingers of strangler figs. Treetops tangled to hide the sun, and lianes dropped downward like ropes. Jason could see the jungle, feel its heat, hear the hum of its insects.

He looked out the window again and wondered if Snake Mountain looked anything like that sham of a mountain beside Albuquerque.

And how long will it take for me to forget the smile and the dying? Jason remembered two years before, lying in the Subang Hospital in the Kuala Lumpur valley, feverish, unable to sleep because he had slept too much, yet unable to read or even think much for the dizziness. A Willie Nelson tune ran through his head then, repeating itself by the hour, the one he had mouthed at the mosque in order to appear to be speaking an Arabic prayer. Before long he came to hate the tune and the words but somehow could not block them from his mind, not until the fever left him. Will I be the same way about the killing? he asked himself. Must I remember it until some sort of American fever leaves me?

When I recover from the fatigue of jetlag, he affirmed, the images that haunt me will slip away. He shifted his leg, aware of the ache from muscles not long out of a cast.

Jason had some help in breaking the leg. Just weeks from the end of the term at the University of Malaya, he had wandered into the old Chinatown district of Kuala Lumpur. It was his favorite area of the city, a place alive with the noise of street hawkers and redolent with odors of food stalls. Jason stopped on the sidewalk in front of the open wall of the Sun Wah Cafe to look at a display of prayer wheels and temple bells from Nepal. The old man sitting by the display looked Nepalese, so Jason greeted him in Nepali.

The man's face changed from an almost scary-looking sternness to a warm smile, and he answered in his own language. "Sorry. I didn't live in Katmandu long enough to learn to understand all that." Jason laughed and offered his hand. "My name is Jason White. What part of Nepal are you from?"

"I am Chander." The man stood and clasped Jason's hand. "I am Grukha tribesman, from near Pokhara. You know Pokhara?"

"On the plains beside Annapurna Mountain. Yes. I have been there." Jason looked at the table beside Chander, noticing for the first time Chander's display of cut gemstones. Just as he bent to look at the stones, Jason felt someone grab his collar.

"So I catch the little brown rat, what?" Tom said. He pushed Jason against the cafe wall. "Remember me from some time back at the International School? It's you that told on me and got me the boot from school. A boot for a boot, I say." Tom kicked Jason's leg, and the pain of it dropped Jason to the floor.

Later, the exact sequence of events blurred in Jason's mind. Chander moved; Jason had been aware of that. But Jason could not remember how the Grukha tribesman had taken Tom down.

When Jason could focus his attention on his surroundings again, he saw Tom lying on his stomach, his nose bleeding, and Chander kneeling with a knee in the middle of the giant Australian's back. Chander twisted Tom's arm behind him. "You kick my friend, Jason. Maybe I break arm?"

"Thanks, Chander," Jason said. "You can let him go, now."

"Friend Jason say let go." Chander thrust his face close to Tom's. "I let go. You hurt friend to Grukha? I break arm. Ribs. Next time. You understand?" Tom, grinding his teeth in pain, said nothing. "You understand?" Chander insisted, applying more pressure to Tom's arm.

"Yes. Yes, for chrissake."

"Then go." Chander stood. His body language looked like that of a young man ready to fight. But his face was that of an old man. Jason looked up at Chander in amazement.

Tom got to his feet and stumbled off, clutching his arm. And Chander turned to help Jason.

A simple fracture, said the Indian doctor at Subang Hospital. Six weeks in a cast, then a few days with a cane. Not a bad injury.

When the cast came off, just before he left Malaysia, Jason went to the Sun Wah and bought gemstones from Chander. He wasn't sure what he would do with the stones; he had bought them out of gratitude.

Jason sat in the plane at the Albuquerque airport and wondered about the purchasing of the stones. Chander broke Tom's nose and nearly broke his arm. In buying the gemstones, I paid the Grukha for doing my violence for me. But it wasn't Tom's violence in striking Rozak or the killer's violence when he fired the bullet into Suppriah's brain. It was proper violence, for I was a victim, a passive victim. But I won't be one again.

The cabin crew explained again about seat belts and exit doors as the plane taxied around the runway, preparing for takeoff. Amarillo would be about an hour away, Jason thought. Then the drive to Snake Mountain. He settled back and drifted into an uneasy sleep.

Sybil handed Pug a cup of coffee and set a coaster on the coffee table in front of her. Beside the coaster lay the velvet ribbon that had been tied around the dove's neck, and beside that the scroll with its bizarre message.

"So you're down to two dogs," Pug said.

"Two puppies. Yes, if that man comes back for the puppy he chose. And it will be none too soon. I can't give those dogs the attention they need, especially on weekends when I'm at work."

"Work. I wish I could choose when to work and when not to. Is volunteer work at the hospital real work?"

Ignore the insult, Sybil told herself: Pug meant no harm by it. Pug sipped her coffee; she sat on the couch opposite Sybil. "At least I can be satisfied that the German shepherd pup goes to a good place. A rancher out east of town says he wants the dog. It will have a good place to run, so it'll be much better off than having to live in the kennel out back. Next I need to find a home for the other two dogs. They might be hard to give away since they're just mongrels."

"You should keep a dog around. At least one. For protection."

"In Canyon? Hardly. You live in Amarillo, where there is some crime, and you don't have a dog."

"I live in an apartment with security guards around. You're isolated out here."

"Which is why Parker and I chose Canyon. For the isolation. Pug, a year ago, someone robbed the cash register at Wendy's here in Canyon, and the local folk thought it was a crime spree. When they caught the thief, he was just a kid wanting money to buy a bicycle. People in this town don't even lock their doors at night."

"But you do, I hope?"

"Yes. Out of habit from living in cities."

"People around here aren't harmless. They might seem that way, but that's just their phony Texas politeness. Because you dare to be different from them, Sybil, some of them are willing to do nasty things to you. Especially the men. The males around here are all like my father. Polite to your face, especially to women—but you do one little thing they disapprove of, and you're a nothing. Worse than a nothing. Then they can treat you however they wish without feeling guilty because you deserve it. Don't you see? You deserve to be knocked around, hurt, humiliated, because you're different. And you are different, Sybil. They probably call you a nigger behind your back."

"Maybe. Maybe not." Sybil went to the bookcase and picked up a brass bell. "You recognize this, don't you?"

"No."

"Funny. I thought I had shown it to you. Parker bought this for me in Nepal over a year ago." She set it on the coffee table beside the scroll. "The handle is supposed to look like a lightning bolt, the one that split the mountains to drain the lake where the sacred lotus blossom bloomed. Do you know the story?"

"No."

"I thought I told it to you. Buddha split the mountain with lightning so the lake would drain and people could come up to worship the divine lotus blossom that floated in the center of the lake. People came to worship, and they built the city of Katmandu. And they chanted the prayer that is written around the edge of the bell: 'I salute the divine lotus blossom in the center of the lake.' The chant sounds like a series of ohms and umms. Those squiggles on the bell, that is the prayer, carved in an ancient alphabet. It looks like a secretary's shorthand."

"The bell is beautiful." Pug's eyes betrayed nothing, but Sybil thought she understood.

"You wrote those squiggles on the note you put on the dove's foot. Why would you kill a dove, Pug? Was it to frighten me or to disgust me? Certainly I was disgusted."

"Dove? Why, Sybil, I'm sure I don't know what you're talking about."

"You have said nothing about the velvet ribbon beside your coffee cup."

"I dislike velvet. Why should I comment on it?"

Sybil shook her head. "Pug, Pug. We can't be friends when we play such odd games with one another."

"Come off of it, Sybil. Is one of your neighbors trying to scare you again? What's all this about dead birds and velvet ribbons and Nepalese chants? Know what I think? I think someone in Canyon understands enough about you to be playing with your mind. Someone is sending you the message that you cannot be safe in this community. The message is brutal and disgusting and true. Did you know that not too many years ago, they put up a sign right beside the city limits sign that said, 'Nigger, don't let the sun set on you in this town'? Canyon is lily white and middle class and racist and rotten to the core."

"Are you trying to get me to move to your place? That won't work. You know that won't work for me."

"The offer stays open." Pug held up her palms. "No, calm down. I said I'd not ask anything of you, and I'm not asking. I'm just telling you about this town and the racist sign it used to have."

"I've heard that story about that same sign told about many small towns. It's just a story. You're wrong about Canyon. There are two black families living here, and they fit well enough into the community. As well as you might expect in a small town in the south. The only thing you're right about is the town's being mostly middle class. That means middle class values, which means little crime, especially the type based on the have-nots victimizing the haves."

"You're being naive again."

"There is no need for insults, Pug." At times, Sybil didn't like Pug. The woman was so certain of herself, of all her opinions. That trait could be attractive, sometimes, Sybil admitted. But, dammit, she doesn't have to disparage my perceptions. Look at her. Smug Pug. One of the prettiest human beings I have ever seen, even if she dresses more like a man than a woman.

Pug had red hair, the kind of red that anyone could look at and know it came from a bottle, even if she was careful never to let undyed roots show. She wore her hair in an androgenous cut, hanging just over her ears. Her clothes came from the only unisex clothing shop in Amarillo. She wore billowy black pants that tightened around her ankles, a wide cloth belt, and a black shirt that might be seen on male or female models in fashion magazines. On her wrist was a black-faced Seiko, square and bulky. Seldom had Sybil seen Pug in anything but black, though she often wore different uniforms. Her most usual one was the sleek, tight clothing fashionable among women who rode motorcycles with bikers.

"I mean no insult. You know that."

"Pug, who in this entire region but you would know about the lotus blossom prayer?"

"Don't forget this is a university town. Many of the people here are smart—not everyone around here is an ignorant cowboy. Some are educated, though that doesn't mean they aren't narrow, mean-spirited people. They don't want you here, Sybil. You had some protection from them when Parker Redbear was alive and you were married to an artist as famous as Canyon's own Carl Smith. But with Parker gone, they look at you as an uppity black woman who dares to live in a house that ought to be the property of an affluent white."

"Look at me. I'm whiter than most Canyonites. Because of my name, people assume I'm part Indian, like Parker."

"Since when is being part Indian less of an offense to Texas rednecks than being part African? You need to move, Sybil. You need to leave Canyon before someone hurts you."

Hyram parked in the narrow strip of a parking lot in front of the Chuck Wagon Cafe. "I'm not hungry," Angela said.

"I am, and you ought to be. You're skinny as a stalk of bear grass."

Inside, they sat in a booth with red plastic seats surrounding a formica-topped table. Hyram sat facing the entrance. "I'm not," Angela said.

Hyram looked at the menu. "Not what?"

“Skinny. I’m not skinny. You want to see skinny? Look at Odom.”

The waitress came to the table. “You want coffee, Hyram?”

“Martha, there’s been only one time in my life when I turned down a cup of coffee, and I wasn’t there when it happened.”

Martha turned over their coffee cups and filled them. “Morning, Hyram,” she said, “Angela.”

“Morning, Martha,” Hyram said. Angela nodded to her. Martha studied Hyram.

“How come you always read the menu? You always order the same thing. Fact is, I done turned in your order, soon as I saw you pull up outside. Scrambled eggs, grits, crisp bacon, a couple of biscuits, cream gravy, and a side dish of green chilies.”

“Good thinking. And for my little cowgirl, here—what did you order for her?”

“Same thing so’s she can nibble at it and you can finish it off.” Martha laughed, exposing teeth stained brown from the minerals in Canyon’s water.

“Keep the coffee coming, and I’ll remember you in my will.”

Angela drummed her fingers on the table. “How come you always wear your Stetson inside restaurants? And how come you read the menu, like Martha said?”

“Look around,” Hyram waved at the men in the other booths. “You see any men without hats?” Angela glanced around, knowing what she would see. A few of the men wore Stetsons; the rest wore caps with feed-store ads on the front. “And this ain’t a restaurant. We go to a restaurant in Amarillo, and I would wear a string tie, black pants, and my lizard boots. In a place like The Big Texan, I would hang my hat on a peg on the wall. This here is a cafe full of old farts like me, some of them farmers, some ranchers. I wear the Stetson so nobody will think I’m a farmer.”

“Ranchers don’t need dogs.”

“Dogs?”

“We didn’t come to town just to eat, did we? We came to get some mean dogs. Right? Dogs that you think will protect me. I don’t need no dogs, and neither do you. Some dogs run the cattle, and you have to end up shooting them.”

“I don’t cotton to stupid, cow-chasing dogs, Angela. Smart dogs, yes. A dog that knows how to run off a coon or bite a coyote’s ass is welcome on my ranch. Turdy don’t bite coyotes.”

“Don’t get me no dogs, Hyram. I can bite my own coyotes.”

"I ain't getting you no dogs. That boy of my old buddy, White, he loves dogs more than a cowboy loves beans. I aim to buy him a dog from a pretty gal named Sybil."

"Hyram, your bulling me again."

"I ain't."

"Then how come you don't let that boy pick his own dog?"

Hyram frowned. "I didn't think about it."

"Sybil? Sybil Redbear? You going to get a dog from her? I bet a dollar to a silk hat it will be a weird dog, Hyram. She dresses funny and gets about on a motorcycle, sometimes. Weird folks raise weird dogs, and that's a fact. I don't want no weird dog on the ranch."

"That Sybil, she might be a tad strange, but she sure is pretty. That dark skin and little bit of kink in her hair and them African eyes, man alive! If I was ninety years younger, I'd be following that widow around, camping out on her doorstep."

"You talk big, Hyram, but you fire blanks. All sound and no bullets. You don't court no one. Probably never have. And you're not old. Not that old. Not too old to see a widow. Or a divorcee." She gave him what she hoped was a significant look, but he didn't seem to notice. Angela sighed. "You don't pay me no attention."

"I do. More than you know." He sipped his coffee, then put the cup down with a rattle, his attention fixed on the door behind Angela.

"What is it, Hyram?"

He squirmed around in the seat, unsnapped the leather pouch hanging on his belt, and put an enormous folded knife on the table. "Hyram?" She turned to look behind her when Lint stepped up to their booth.

"Angela, we need to talk." He held his hat in front of him, rolling the brim. Angela gave her head a tiny shake and looked at Hyram.

"Lint Bodark, you run along and play with your tools at the feed store."

"I swearta God, Angela." Lint didn't look at Hyram. "I'd of never touched you but for drinking."

Hyram picked up his knife and pulled the blade out with a loud snap. "Lint, you ever hear the story about me going off to east Texas for a long visit? Huntsville. All because I took a notion to carve up a pushy cowboy, a man 'bout your size. Or least he was before I commenced to whittle on him. By the time I finished the job, he was reduced considerable. Knife I used looked just like this one."

Martha, who had been looking round-mouthed at Lint and Hyram, scurried over with a pitcher of coffee in her hand. "Lint, how about me pouring you a cup of coffee? To go."

"I could sure enough use a cup, Martha." Lint turned toward the door, then looked back over his shoulder, his face full of remorse. "I mean it, Angela. You know I mean it."

When Lint left, Angela said, "He did mean it, too. He always means it when he tells me how sorry he is for treating me bad. Just like my daddy always did. But both of them would do it again, maybe even the same day they looked so hang-dog sorry about beating me. I always believed, though, like a fool. I always believed until Regan—" Her lip trembled and a tear ran down her cheek.

"I look at the menu ever time on account of the remote possibility that I might see something on it better than grits and eggs." Hyram folded the knife and put it back into the pouch. Martha set their food in front of them. Angela pulled a paper napkin from the dispenser on the table, dabbed her eyes, then blew her nose.

Hyram looked at his plate with appreciation. "Lookit this spread. Them grits look downright edible."

"Did you really go to prison, Hyram? I knew you lit out for a while, but prison?"

"Who? Me?" Hyram dipped a biscuit into the cream gravy, took over half of the biscuit in a single bite, and pushed the food into his cheek so he could talk. "One night I spent a year in Chicago. That might count as time in prison, I suppose. Went up there to look at the stockyards. It was cold enough to freeze the balls off a brass mule. One day, that was enough for sure. I flat bought a truck out of there."

"Hyram, get serious. I mean about what you told Lint. About carving up a cowboy and having to go to Huntsville."

"One day somebody's going to whittle Lint's gizzard right out of him. I'd shake the man's hand that done it, even if it was my own." Hyram clasped his hands. "How 'bout you munching down some on them eggs? You need to fat up worsern a rangy steer in a spring blizzard."

Jason looked in dismay at the prairie as the plane taxied into the Amarillo airport. It's like an ocean, he thought. The land runs flat all the way to the flat horizon, like the South China Sea. No trees. Nothing.

As he emerged at the gate, Jason was amazed to see so many cowboy hats. There had been none at the airport in Los Angeles.

He looked down at the young woman who touched his arm and spoke his name. She seemed like something off the set of a western movie: a perfect miniature clad all in blue—blue boots, jeans and plaid shirt. And so pretty with her long red hair. The one blemish in her beauty was the way her lower lip puffed out, like she had a cotton pad under it. "Yes?" Jason said. Should I offer my hand? Women in Malaysia didn't shake hands, but what about those in Texas? He shifted his cane to his left hand and put his tennis racket under his arm just in case.

"I'm Angela." She held out her hand. Jason took it, gave it a formal pump, and let go. "Hyram sent me to get you. He said to lay it on thick about how sorry he was not to be out here and explain all about the work he has to do to get ready for his next horse auction. And it's the truth, too—that bit about all the work getting ready for the auction. Come on," she took his arm, urging him down the hall, "let's go get your bags."

Jason allowed himself to be led while he worked on figuring out what Angela had said. Something about Hyram and horses. Her twangy accent made her speech sound only marginally like English, as Jason understood the term.

"Are there any trees on Snake Mountain?"

"Mesquite. Scruffy little cedar. You might accuse them of being trees, if you took a notion to stretch the definition some." They rode the escalator to the ground floor while Jason tried to make some sense of what she had said about trees.

"Sit on that bench. When your bag appears, point it out, and I'll get it, seeing as you're all gimped up. Bone fracture, Hyram told me. How long you gotta haul that stick around?"

"I beg your pardon?"

"That stick." Angela pointed at his cane. "How long you gotta use it?" She pulled his arm, urging him to sit on the bench.

"Just a few more days while my leg gets back some strength." He sat and immediately began to stand again. "There. That's my suitcase. The brown leather one with straps."

Angela put her hand on his shoulder, urging him to stay seated. "Take it easy, like I said. I might be a mite little, but I can hoist a dead ton all over creation."

Jason watched her walk toward the luggage. Her jeans fit her so snug that he imagined her painting them on. What had she just said? He resolved to listen with greater care, maybe watch her lips as she spoke.

Outside, the late afternoon sun felt weak to Jason, who was accustomed to the Malaysian sun hitting him like a physical blow. He followed Angela to her pickup and watched in amazement as she heaved his suitcase into the back. She glanced at him, looking amused. "I told you."

It made him feel disoriented when Jason saw the steering wheel was on the wrong side. It wasn't a surprise; he knew Americans drove that way. But knowing and seeing were different, somehow. He got in and looked around for a seatbelt, but found none.

Angela drove to Interstate 40 and turned west. "Thirty minutes and we will be at Hyram's place." She looked at her outside mirror and said, "Shit."

Jason looked back, leaning down to see under the gun rack. When he realized there was a weapon hanging over the seat back, he jerked in surprise.

"The man in the pickup behind us," Angela jerked her thumb toward the back. "Watch him for a few minutes. Tell me if he takes a drink of something."

"Is that a gun?"

"Of course. What would you expect to find on a gun rack?"

"Why?" Jason fumbled for more words but couldn't find them. The idea of being that close to a lethal weapon unnerved him. He closed his eyes, feeling his fatigue and the jangle of his nerves. Again he heard the shots and again saw the image of the young woman as her face flew apart. He shuddered and sank back in the pickup seat.

"For varmints. Skunks and the like. And hunting quail, when they're in season. If you live on a ranch, you gotta have a shotgun. Hey, Jason, how 'bout keeping an eye on that jerk back there, like I asked?"

With some effort, Jason sat up, turned, and peered out the back window again. "What did you say you wanted me to watch him do?"

"Drink. If you see him take a drink of any kind, tell me. That sucker's tailgating me like he's just tied one on."

Jason tried to see the man in the vehicle behind them, but the glare on the windshield made it impossible to make out the man's features. He seemed to be wearing a cowboy hat. "What is he doing to you?"

"Following too close. Is he drinking?"

"No. Wait. He does have something in his hand. Yes. He just took a drink from some sort of decanter. Who is that man?" Jason wondered what Angela had said. Tied one what onto what?

"Lint Bodark. The king of assholes. I aim to lose him with some quick turns." She switched lanes in front of other cars and left the Interstate on an exit ramp. The other drivers hit their brakes and honked. Lint's pickup was boxed in tight so he couldn't follow Angela across the lanes. "There. I foxed that turkey into going on. And from the look on your face, I scared the tar out of you."

"You did indeed frighten me."

Angela laughed. "Anyone ever tell you that you talk funny? Like someone from England or someplace. It ain't easy to understand you, sometimes."

I talk funny? Jason thought: she can say that right after speaking of foxing a turkey?

"I'll take the loop around to South Washington. It'll add about ten minutes to our trip, but it's worth it to shake that drunkard, Lint." She drove south on a two-lane road. "Sorry for the tricks back there on the highway."

Jason sat back and closed his eyes. Who was this crazy woman, anyway? An employee of Hyram's ranch? Hyram's daughter, maybe? He couldn't remember either of his parents mentioning Hyram having a family. He glanced at her and their eyes met for a moment. She appeared scornful.

"Damn," Angela said, looking in the rearview mirror. "Damn."

"What now?"

"Lint. He took a lucky guess and has about caught up with us."

The other pickup was there again, closing in fast. Jason watched as the pickup pulled up within 20 meters or so. Lint put an arm out of his window and pointed at them. When they heard the popping sounds, Jason ducked. "He's shooting at us! Get down!"

"That egg-sucking skunk. Jason, all Lint has is a tiny hand gun. A Saturday night special. The barrel is only this long." She held up a finger and thumb, indicating about fifty millimeters. "He couldn't hit my pickup, much less one of us, even if he was to shoot right-handed. Reach under the seat and get me the box of shells that's under there."

"What?"

"Just do it."

Jason felt around under the seat. What kind of a nightmare place had he come to, he wondered. The murder in California, then that lunatic cowboy shows up to fire bullets at him and this crazy woman Hyram sent. He found a box and put it on the seat. The man behind them fired several more shots.

"Not that one. That's buckshot. I want to spook Lint, not blow him away. There's another box under there." Jason felt around under the seat again and found another box. "That's what I want." She braked and pulled onto the shoulder of the road.

"You're stopping?" Jason's voice went up an octave.

"Just sit tight. Hide, if you want." She came to a complete stop, took the shotgun off the rack, and took two shells from the box Jason had found.

He glanced back, but the glare on the glass of the pickup kept the driver obscured. Lint had stopped behind them. He sat watching, still holding the pistol out the window. Angela broke open the shotgun, inserted a shell, and got out of the pickup.

When she fired the gun, Jason felt his entire body jump. Never had he heard anything so loud.

Angela broke open the gun again and inserted the other shell. The tires of Lint's pickup squealed as he took off backward. Jason watched him go some thirty meters, wheel around, and take off the other direction.

Angela got back into the pickup and put the gun on the rack. She laughed. "I bet it'll cost him most of a paycheck to clean up what my load of bird did to the front of his truck."

Jason stared. "Who are you?" he demanded.

"I done told you that." She started the engine. "Angela. I'm Angela."

"He never expected that." Angela drove on. Jason slumped in the seat, numb, his eyes closed. "I never faced him before. Not like that." She hummed to herself. Jason felt certain he had never been so tired.

After going some miles, Angela said, "Hyram tells me you'll be staying on the ranch for the summer, then enroll in West Texas A&M University. Maybe live at the ranch, maybe move over to Canyon. Said your daddy went there some years back. Studied geology and made money from it, Hyram said, and moved all over the world. You never really been in Texas, except to get born, Hyram said. You like dogs?"

"What?"

"Dogs. Hyram said you like dogs, only I figured he was lying through his teeth so he could get a dog for another reason."

"Do I like dogs? Yes. I had a wonderful dog when we moved to Kuala Lumpur. The police shot it."

"Some dogs need shooting. What did it do? Bite somebody? Chase water buffalo?"

"It did nothing. It was a dog, which is offense enough in an Islamic country. My mother hated it, but it was my dog. My father's actually."

"Cops shoot dogs over there for religious reasons? Jason, you gotta be handing me a line of malarkey."

"They hate dogs. Muslims think of dogs like they do pigs. It got loose, and the police shot it. Enough of that. Yes, I like dogs. Why did you ask?"

"Hyram got you a dog today, or he said he got it for you. A mean one. Only he won't call it that. Says he aims to get you another one, later, a real smart one."

"Why would Hyram do that?"

Angela laughed. "You ask him. I get nothing out of him, when it comes to dogs. We got one, already. Turdy, and a good-for-nothing mutt he is. Harmless, though.

Jason looked at her. Turdy? Is that what she called her dog? Maybe I misunderstood. Maybe I don't understand much of anything in this country. He sighed.

"Hyram says you don't know nothing about Texas, and I can for a fact already vouch for that. He said we gotta introduce you to Texas culture, and he put me in charge of that. First thing is to teach you to talk proper. You go into a bar in Amarillo and talk like you do, especially with them dude clothes on, and like as not some cowboy would punch your lights out. You gotta learn to drawl out the words, not like they do it on television shows from New York when they're playing at being Texan, but like they do it around here, if you want to pick up a proper way of speaking. I'll break you of saying funny things like 'I beg your pardon.' If somebody talks low and you don't hear, you say, 'Do what?' You learn to use ain't with regularity, but not always. And if you're about to do something, you say, 'Hold on there—I'm fixing to do it.' You gotta learn that y'all is a much better word than you.

"That handshake of yours needs some work, too. Your grip was a tad loose, and you let go fast like you grabbed the business end of a rattlesnake. A man in Texas puts the bone crush on you and shakes your hand like pumping a slow well.

"And your clothes. Only house painters wear all white. And that prissy collar and the bug on your shirt got to go. Nobody with any self-respect will wear an alligator or some other bug on his shirt like you got on. We'll get you into Wranglers and a good pair of roper boots to start off with, and a shirt with a button-down collar. By the time fall comes around and you go over to the university, you'll be one of the boys. Shoot, you'll be dipping and have a ring on the back pocket of your jeans, and horse shit on your boots."

Jason looked at Angela in astonishment. He had understood what she said only in general terms. What amazed him was that she could speak about dogs and shaking hands and proper clothing right after having a gun battle. Will I learn to make such fast emotional shifts, he wondered, in becoming a Texan?

"But you already are a Texan," his father had told him. "You were born in Palo Duro Hospital right there in Canyon, up in the middle of the Texas Panhandle."

"No," his mother said. "My son is not a cowboy." She said cowboy as if it were a nasty word. "If a kitten is born in an oven, it isn't a loaf of bread. My son is a Muslim."

"Some Texans are Muslim," his father had said. "But Jason there, he doesn't seem to be so thrilled at being one."

And that, Jason thought, looking at Angela, was an understatement: I'll never go into a mosque again, never again ablute hands, face and feet for entering a domed room to send Arabic prayers in the direction of Mecca.

"When you ain't needing that walking stick anymore, I'll introduce you to riding. You'll love horses. And you gotta learn to get over being squeamish about guns. I'll show you how to shoot a twelve gauge and maybe how to fire Hyram's nine-millimeter pistol."

"I prefer to have nothing to do with weapons for killing."

Angela turned to spit something brown out the window. When she turned back, Jason could see the fury on her face. And her lower lip looked more normal, as if she had just spit out the wad of cotton she had been holding under it. "I don't know how you do it in Indonesia or wherever you're from, but in Texas if a man shoots at you like Lint done, you gotta do more than flip him the finger for it."

"So you try to kill him. That's brilliant."

"You don't know nothing. Dumbern bug shit. Open that glove box."

"I beg your pardon?"

"Do what? Not 'I beg your pardon.'" She pointed at the glove box on the dash. "Open it."

He did as she directed. Inside he saw a pistol.

"That there is Hyram's nine millimeter. Loaded and on safety. If I had wanted to kill Lint, I would have shot his teeth out with that. Or else loaded up the shotgun with buckshot to turn him into a sieve. You saw me get the bird shot, didn't you? That little load from the distance I fired wouldn't do more than bugger up the paint on his pickup. And you thought I was trying to kill Lint. Hell fire. If I'd had killing in mind, Lint would be back there by the side of the road, dead as a skunk."

They rode the rest of the way in silence. When they pulled into the driveway in front of Hyram's ranch, they found Hyram and Odom standing by the house. "Something's wrong," Angela said. They got out of the pickup.

"Hello, Jason. I'm Hyram."

Jason leaned on his cane with his left hand. "Hello." He took Hyram's hand, trying for a firmer grip as Angela had instructed.

"Jason, that there is Odom. Odom, Jason. And look at you. You done growed up. Odom, seeing as he got a gimpy leg, you haul his stuff into the guest room. Jason, pardon me and Angela for a while. Angela, that new German shepherd pup we got this morning? Somebody shot it. And your other dog, Turdy. They shot him, too." Hyram walked toward the corral. Angela hurried to join him.

Odom took the suitcase from the pickup. "You have a good trip over?"

"Fine. The trip was just fine." Jason followed Odom into the house and took his shoes off just inside the door. Odom walked on, tracking dust across the tile in the entryway. Barbarian, Jason thought. Then he remembered. Americans, according to Jason's father, wear their shoes indoors. Odd.

"This here is the room you'll be staying in. You got a east window with a good view of Snake Mountain. Best room in the house, if you ask me. Hyram said like as not you would be dog tired from the trip and want to hit the rack. For a fact, you look like you just pumped a handcar across Texas." He stepped out of the room and touched the brim of his hat. "Good day to you."

"Thank you." Jason had understood almost nothing Odom said. The man whines his words, Jason thought. A nasal whine. I'll never learn to understand him.

The room held a gigantic waterbed boxed in all the way to the top of the mattress, a stuffed chair, a chest of drawers and a vanity with a mirror. Through another door, Jason could see the room had a private bath. He walked to a window, pulled aside the curtain and looked out, finding the skyline dominated by a hill off in the distance, though it was the oddest hill he had ever seen. The top part was flat instead of rising to a peak. The word *mesa* came to Jason's mind. Could that be what Odom called Snake Mountain? Likely. He knew there were no real mountains anywhere around.

Hyram stood beside the wooden fence of the coral, pointing at the ground, and Angela seemed to be doing something with a stick. Jason looked closer and realized she had a shovel. She's digging a grave for the two dogs, he thought, just as I once did for Big Jeff, after the Malay police shot him.

He closed the curtain. The sight of Angela with the shovel depressed him. How, he asked himself, how am I going to learn to fit into this?

The entirety of the United States seemed to Jason like an arena where the mongoose and the cobra face one another in the ritual of killing.

12

In spite of his fatigue, Jason slept little. When he did doze off, he dreamed of Suppriah smiling at him in the airport. Angela shoved him aside, spat some brown juice on the floor, and lifted a shotgun to her shoulder, aiming at Suppriah. He tried to reach the gun to knock it down before Suppriah got shot again, but he moved in slow motion. Angela fired, and Suppriah's face flew apart. "What are you staring at?" Angela demanded of him. "I didn't use buckshot."

He awoke trembling, unsure for a few seconds where he was. In an attempt to banish the images from the dream, he got up and looked out the window. The waterbed sloshed around behind him, and he resolved to try sleeping on the floor. Maybe, he thought, it's the bed that gave me nightmares. The damn thing moved every time he turned, and it felt as if he might fall at any time.

It amazed him to see how much light the moon cast on the landscape. He could see the corral, some fencing and the prairie beyond it. Off in the distance was the high, flat presence of Snake Mountain.

After taking a pillow off the bed, he tried lying on the floor, but sleep remained elusive. Someone had told him that jet lag from flying east was much worse than from flying west. That didn't make much sense to him, but at that moment, he was prepared to believe it.

He thought of how he had responded to Angela in the airport. She seemed a perfectly wrought miniature of a young woman of the American West standing there in her boots, jeans, and plaid shirt, a bandanna tied around her neck. Jason liked her red hair and the scattering of freckles on her cheeks. Her lips had an appealing, sensuous puffiness to them, even if the lower one had protruded too much from what turned out to be tobacco tucked between lip and gum. She had full, high breasts, something he had not seen on many women in the Orient. Without doubt she was beautiful—but moment by moment, she had become less attractive because of her behavior. Her impenetrable speech. Her gun battle with the shadowy figure in the other pickup. Her spitting through the window of the pickup.

Is she a permanent fixture on the ranch? If so, maybe I should get an apartment near the university for the summer, then move into the dormitories when school starts. I can't tolerate being around Angela for long.

The thought startled him, and he examined it. Is it because I find her repulsive or attractive? he asked, then decided an honest answer was that he found her more attractive than anything else. Then why run away from her? Why not explore what he found attractive in her? "Hormones," he muttered. "Male hormones."

But he knew there was more. She was Texan, perhaps quintessentially so, and he liked her for the Texas in her, though what he meant by that eluded him.

At six in the morning, Hyram knocked on his door. "Angela says she got grits and eggs 'bout done. She says to come get it."

While he dressed, Jason worried about how to come to terms with American eating habits. Grits sounded like something that had been rolled in beach sand. And eggs? Jason shook his head. I'll bet they're fried and dripping with grease. No wonder Hyram's belly hangs over his belt. His arteries are probably clogged with cholesterol and he doesn't understand he is committing gastronomic suicide. He probably knows nothing about nutrition.

In the hall, Jason smelled bacon. Father insisted on eating bacon from time to time, Jason remembered, though the reason for it remained a mystery. His Texas upbringing, I guess. But that smell! So strong and so repulsive. How could anyone eat the stuff after smelling it? Blubber fried in its own grease. These people had eating habits worse than the Chinese in Malaysia.

Jason stopped in the doorway to the kitchen and asked himself if worry about nutrition was real reason for recoiling from bacon. Pig, he thought. My mother inside me is saying it's pig and unclean. But she also hated Big Jeff. The Muslim in me is recoiling from Texas food, and I won't allow it. He sat at the breakfast table. Hyram nodded. Angela, busy at the stove, didn't bother to look up.

Hyram ate with an enthusiasm that Jason found amazing. And so much. How could anyone consume that much food at one sitting, most of it grease? Jason pushed the eggs to one side of his plate with a fork. "I like the mush," he offered.

"Mush?" Angela looked startled. She sat at one side of the table, Hyram at the other. Her hair hung in strings from a bun she had rolled it into and shored up with bobby pins. She wore a green plaid shirt and jeans. "What mush?"

"He means the grits. We gotta get used to his tribal language. Jason, far as I can see, you got raised in a different tribe, learned some different ways of looking at the world. And different always looks weird to most folks. We got another word for that stuff you called mush. We call it grits."

Jason looked at Hyram with renewed interest. A different tribe—that was a bit of insight that could prove useful. Hyram and Angela are of the Texas tribe. The cowboy tribe. I'm—what? International? That's too vague. I'll work that out later. "I like that metaphor. So we come from different tribes. Yes."

"Mush?" Angela laughed. "Mush sounds so gross, like what you get when you sit on a banana. But I guess grits ain't such a fine word for the likes of you, either. How come you don't eat your eggs?"

Jason looked at his plate, embarrassed.

"Like as not, that boy is allergic to eggs. That right?"

"Not exactly." He smiled at Hyram, grateful for his attempt to help. "I'm sure these are superior eggs. It's just that before coming to Texas I was a vegetarian."

Angela stared in amazement. Hyram glanced at him. "Hindu? You get to be a Hindu over in that part of the world?"

"No. It has nothing to do with religion."

"You mean you don't ever eat meat? Ever?" Angela continued to stare.

"I'm not a fanatic about it, and now that I'm here, I want to change."

"How can you live without meat? Hyram would croak plumb off if he didn't get it two or three times a day. A body's got to have meat to live. Ain't that right, Hyram?"

He struggled with her accent, but Jason thought he understood the gist of what she said.

"It ain't. But don't you go telling anybody I said so. Saying you don't got to eat meat all the time ain't exactly the standard line for a rancher who makes a living off folks who believe they gotta get their amino acids from beef. You can get it from nuts and leafs and twigs and grasses, if you know how to go about it. The eight amino acids a body needs come packed in a bunch of ways from Mother Nature."

Jason admonished himself for the smug way he had assumed Hyram ignorant of nutrition. The man can speak about amino acids. How could that be? Then Jason remembered that his father had known Hyram when they were in college together. Did Hyram get a degree? Had he stayed in college long enough to learn much? Jason couldn't remember what his father had said about Hyram as a scholar. But he was positive Angela had to be the ignorant rural Texan.

"But you gotta have meat. If you don't eat meat, you got nothing to build bones."

"Cows and horses got good bones, and they're the most dedicated vegetarians I know. Worse than Jason, they are."

"I don't know what to think about this. Jason, I never cooked for a veggie vulture before. What can I fix for you?"

"You don't need to cook for me, Angela. No one did back in Malaysia."

"Old White, your pappy, told me he had this woman to cook for him. Called her his amah, as I recall. Didn't you eat her cooking?"

"Not often. She puts too much oil in everything to suit me, and she likes to cook meat. I usually prepared my own food. Or bought it from a street vendor."

Angela laughed, and Jason could tell she didn't believe him. "You cook? You?"

"Why not?"

"Remember what I told you, honey. He comes from a different tribe. Jason, am I to understand that your parents are carnivores?"

"Omnivores. Yes. They treat my food preferences with amused indulgence. They say I'll grow out of it."

"Will you?"

"I think so. I'm only twenty-two."

Angela laughed in a way that sounded mean to Jason. "You ain't that old."

Jason looked at her, trying to decide if she was insulting him or challenging him on a matter of factual information.

"Do you drive?" Hyram asked.

"I did in Malaysia. And I obtained an international driver's license before coming here.

"Don't they drive funny over there? On the wrong side of the road? Seems to me the British made a colony of that place way back when the moon was no bigger than a quarter. Them Brits get everbody to drive funny."

"Yes, they do drive on the other side of the road." Jason kept revising his opinion of Hyram. He sounded like such a bumpkin, but he seemed to know a great deal.

"Angela, she'll give you some lessons in driving proper, the way we do over here. And you can use my white Ford pickup whenever you like. Angela, teach him soon so he can get to the supermarket in Canyon and buy some of the kind of food he eats. Ain't much out here on the ranch but meat and potatoes."

"Meat and potatoes will be fine. I'll learn to eat like a Texan."

"Teach him to drive? What about working on the books?"

"Let them go for now. Shoot, I never had much by way of records till you took over them books, anyway."

"Hyram ran his ranch out of his hip pocket," Angela said. "He even eyeballed the numbers for tallying up his income for Uncle Sam, come tax time. I about broke him of the habit, got him to agree to double-entry bookkeeping on ever' transaction."

"You're an accountant?" The idea seemed absurd to Jason. But then, he told himself, I need to stop assuming these people are ignorant and stupid just because they sound like hicks.

"Shoot no. An accountant? Not by a long shot. I do keep books, though. Taught myself that much."

"She's slick about it, too. Knows all the tricks, and even learned to do it with a pencil and a ledger before I woke up and saw how sharp she was and bought her a computer. She took to it like a hog to slop.

"You teach him to drive, Angela, and start this morning. We're going to Sybil Redbear's to get him a proper dog."

"Lint would shoot it, Hyram. He would. Ain't no sense getting a dog if it's just going to get killed in a day or two."

"That Lint Bodark won't do nothing of the kind. I aim to drop by the feed store and have a little chat with that boy. Explain a thing or two to him about what happens to them that kills critters belonging to somebody else."

"The man you're talking about, Lint—is that the man who shot at us yesterday?"

"Jason, sometimes you talk too much."

"Shot at you?" Hyram's brows knit into a hard, angry frown. "Shot at you?"

"It was nothing, Hyram. He followed us in Amarillo and popped off a few shots in our direction with a little snub-nose. He was real far back, firing out the window."

"He's hitting the bottle again. I can put a stop to that. I can stop a bunch of his horsing around. Nobody fires on my folks without answering to it."

"See, Jason? See? You talk too much. Hyram, you won't do nothing. I can handle Lint Bodark."

13

"This here is the pickup you'll drive." Hyram pointed at a white Ford parked beside the tan pickup Angela had driven from the airport. "That there brown job is Angela's company truck. Me, I drive a cowboy Cadillac that's parked in the garage back yonder."

Leaning on his cane, Jason started toward what he automatically thought of as the passenger side, realized the steering wheel was on that side, and stopped. "Keep going," Angela said. "Hyram says you learn to drive. The only way to do that is to just do it." Jason got in the driver's side.

"Ain't that the truth?" Hyram laughed and climbed in behind Angela, who slid over so her hip touched Jason's. "Gimme that cane and I'll hang her in the gun rack—unless you don't want other drivers to see that you got a walking stick."

"It matters not what other drivers see." Jason handed Hyram his cane.

"It matters not," Angela mimicked Jason's intonation. "It matters not. What kind of talk is that?"

"Give the man a break, Angela. Remember that he talks the lingo of another tribe."

"Tribe, bull. He talks like a wimp."

"Where's the seat belt?" Jason moved so he wouldn't be touching Angela.

"Shoulder strap," Hyram said. "Back there. Might be a good idea to drape it over you, but you don't gotta buckle it, if you ain't of a mind to."

Jason buckled the strap. Why would Hyram say something so strange? Not buckle the shoulder strap? Why not? "Do you wear seat belts?" Jason asked Angela.

"Not unless I drive, and maybe even then I just kind of hang it over me, in case a cop sees me. You get a ticket in Texas these days if you get caught driving without being buckled in."

"Dang government wants to change your diaper and wipe your nose," Hyram said. "Ain't nobody's business if I risk death and mutilation behind the wheel of my own vehicle. But the cops are of a different mind on the matter. Seat belts irritate me. I dropped them buggers behind the seat, except for the one the driver gotta wear on account of the law."

That explains, Jason realized, why I couldn't find a seat belt in Angela's pickup. He drove toward the highway, feeling the strangeness of keeping the pickup on the right side of the road. Stay on the right side, he told himself. Maybe I'd better make a chant of it: the right side, the right side. I'll repeat it, if there is traffic.

"You're doing fine," Hyram said. "Like you been driving here all your life. Like you was a genuine Texan. Your daddy was, for sure. Once a Texan, always a Texan. With one for a daddy, you'll be one before you know it."

I wish it were that easy, Jason thought.

Hyram directed Jason to a house on the south edge of the town of Canyon. The house sat deep on a lot, surrounded by elm trees. An assortment of rocks lined the driveway, among them petrified wood and some chunks of blue stone. Jason wondered if the blue ones might be turquoise. As he turned into the driveway, he thought he saw someone working with beehives among a grove of cottonwoods in back of the house, but he couldn't be sure.

"I saw Sybil out back," Angela said.

"Yeah, playing with them dang bugs of hers. If she got them all stirred up, Angela, I'm sending you out to get her."

"In a pig's eye. You want the dog. You go get her."

"Hear that, Jason? I don't get no respect, and me a senior citizen."

They walked around the house. The figure Jason had seen stood over an open hive, and bees swirled around her. She seemed to glow with a light green color, like a jungle plant in the sun. The hat she wore was dark green and the bee veil floated about her head like a green mist. "I'll be with you in a moment," she said. Jason walked up to the hive and stood beside Sybil, leaning on his cane. Angela and Hyram stayed back.

"That boy's got balls," Hyram said, "or he knows something about bees that I don't."

"What breed of honeybees are they?" Jason asked.

Sybil looked at him. "You surprise me. Most people think bees are bees and have no appreciation for subtlety of breed. Midnight Caucasians. Bred to be gentle. But they will sting. You afraid?"

"No. I'll stand still."

"I must be especially vigilant this time of the year. Bees, like most other animals, have reproducing on their mind in the spring, and if I'm not careful to take out the queen cells, this hive will swarm. Then I would have to catch them and build another hive, and I have plenty as it is." She pulled out a frame of wax and pointed at it. "There's one. Hand me that hive tool."

Jason looked where she indicated and saw something that looked like a miniature crowbar. With exaggerated slowness, he picked it up and gave it to her. She used the sharp end to cut out the queen cell, then replaced the frame in the hive.

"That's enough for now, I guess. I'm Sybil. Sybil Redbear."

"I'm Jason White."

"Did Hyram come about the German shepherd pup I sold him yesterday?"

"No. Someone shot it."

"Shot it? No. Don't tell me about shooting dogs. Have you kept bees?"

"No. But I would like to learn more about them."

"You know more than most people already. Where did you learn to move slow like that when dealing with bees?"

"I read about how bees see movement." Jason tried to look at her face through the veil, but it was no use. He watched her put the top back on the hive. She was tall, he observed—just a few inches shorter than he. And most of that height was legs. Nice ones. And nice hips. But it was her voice that most captivated him—a rich, musical voice, one that would sing alto, if it were in a choir. One that knew how to pronounce words without the twang of a Texas accent. "You're not from here," he observed.

"Nor are you." She took off the bee veil as she and Jason walked toward the house. Her hair fell in thick, tight curls to her shoulders. Jason found himself staring at her.

She seemed to be a mixture of races, though he was uncertain which ones. Her skin tone was about the same as his but creamier, smoother. She had a high forehead, though perhaps it seemed high only because of the way she swept back her hair. Her eyes, set far apart, had an Oriental slant to them. Jason thought he had never seen such lovely eyes. And her lips! So sensual.

Sybil, seeming aware of his scrutiny, glanced at him and smiled. "Well?"

"Well what?"

"Well, where are you from, Jason White?"

"That's hard to say."

"Give it a try. Hello, Hyram."

"'Lo. I suppose you know Angela."

"Good morning, Angela." Sybil shook her hand. Angela accepted the handshake but said nothing. "Are you embarrassed about where you came from, Jason?"

Jason hesitated. "It's just that I've lived so many places that I'm not entirely sure what to call home. The last place I lived was Kuala Lumpur."

Sybil turned to him with renewed interest. Angela crossed her arms.

"Where is Kuala Lumpur? Indonesia?"

"Close. Malaysia."

"You came from Malaysia, then. Are you Malaysian?"

"Yes. In a way. I was born in Texas."

"At Palo Duro Hospital in Canyon," Hyram put in. "I helped his daddy pace around just outside of the grunt room while his mamma was squeezing him out."

"Then you're a Texan."

"No he ain't," Angela said. "It ain't enough to get born here. You got to study up some to be a Texan."

Jason laughed. He glanced at Angela, then returned his attention to Sybil. "She's right. I may have been born in Texas, but I was made in Malaysia. I am Malaysian, for now, but that will change."

Malaysian? Even as he said it, he felt the strangeness of the observation. He wasn't a Texan, not yet, but being Malaysian made little sense. I'm not a Malay he affirmed—not a Muslim, not anymore. Indian, maybe? That didn't feel right either. In Malaysia, that left Chinese or Orang Asli, the aborigines of the peninsula, and he knew he resembled neither of those peoples. He was a racial hodgepodge: his mother came from New Delhi and his father, a European-American-Mexican mixture, came from Texas. In Asia, people thought Jason came from India; in America, people thought he looked Mexican. Malaysia seemed like home to him.

Spain once felt like home, but that was long ago. Then there was a year in Nepal, when his parents taught there. Jason remembered Katmandu as if it had merely been a place they visited. Then they had moved to Kuala Lumpur. He had graduated from the International School there, then studied for a while at the University of Malaya, then worked as a clerk for an American oil firm.

"There's bad news about the shepherd pup you sold me yesterday." Hyram took his hat off.

"Jason told me. Someone killed it."

"It won't happen again, not on my ranch. Jason here, he needs a dog, though. You got any more?"

"I need a dog?"

"White told me what them retarded cops in Malaysia done to Big Jeff. Said you would be glad to get out on the ranch were there was a dog or two, and nobody around that would up and shoot it just for the crime of being a dog."

"Big Jeff. Yes. But Hyram, that was some years ago." He turned again to Sybil. "Malays are Muslim, and they think dogs are filthy animals, as bad or worse than pigs. The police in Kuala Lumpur shoot dogs found on the street."

"Not just for Jason, the dog ain't. I gotta have one on the ranch to keep the field rats under control. You got another?"

"There are two left—two that are barely grown. But they're not German Shepherds. To tell the truth, I'm not sure what they are."

"Don't matter none to me if they're Heinz fifty-seven variety, so long as they're good dogs. What about you, Angela?"

"I done told you. I don't need no dog."

"But you like dogs?"

"Dang it, Hyram. You know I do."

Sybil smiled at Jason. He liked the smile and wanted to see more of it. She seemed to notice his response and found it amusing.

"Where are the dogs?" Hyram asked

"Out in the kennels. If you like them, you may have them as a gift. They would be better off running free on your ranch, Hyram, than locked inside the kennels."

Sybil walked toward the kennels. Jason started after her, but Angela grabbed his arm and drew herself close to his ear.

"Her husband just died," she whispered in a fierce tone.

Jason leaned against his cane, confused by Angela's outburst. Have I broken some local etiquette? he wondered. How?

Angela pushed away from him and took a few quick steps to catch up with Sybil. Jason watched them let two copper-colored dogs out of the kennels. They wagged their tails and jumped around the two women. Angela dropped to one knee and stroked the dogs.

"These are great critters. Both are male, that's good. We don't want bunches of litters of pups out on the ranch."

"You like them?" Hyram asked.

"They're a bit rough and need some training. But yes. Yes, I like them. They got names?"

"Their names are—"

"No matter. They just got new ones. Hyram, come over here and meet the Doobie Brothers."

"Doobie?" Jason frowned.

Hyram laughed. "She named them after country and western singers." He joined Angela. "Look at them jaws. Either of the Doobie Brothers could bite a coyote in half."

"Or kill a chicken thief?" Angela laughed.

Sybil walked back to Jason, and the two stood watching Hyram and Angela and the dogs. "Listen to the way they talk about biting and killing. Those two have to be typical Texans," Jason said.

"In some ways. Maybe in many ways."

"All of the Texans I've met so far are a bit crazy."

"Including me?"

"You are not a Texan. Not at all."

"In some ways I might be."

"May I come see you again? I mean, when being around Texans starts making me crazy, too?"

"No." Sybil turned away from him. "No, Mr. White, you may not."

Jason realized he had offended her, but did not know how to make it right. He started to say something else, but she was already walking away.

She would have preferred to go to Bear Lake on the mountain above Cuchara. But in late May, there would still be snow in the high country of Colorado, some blanketing entire fields, some in drifts six feet deep and more. Parker and Sybil had found such drifts just two years before when they tried riding motorcycles to their favorite mountaintop, and after that, they took spring trips to lakes in Oklahoma, saving the mountains for midsummer.

Around Bear Lake, Sybil would find columbines, blue as the summer sky, and wild strawberry flowers ripening into berries the size of currants, and other flowers too numerous to name. Farther downstream was the beaver pond, alive with trout and ringed with mountain pine. The beaver had cut most of the aspen, even as far as fifty yards up the mountain, opening the field for ground flowers, purple and yellow.

She would have preferred the mountaintop, though she was not at all sure she was ready to see it without Parker. Lake Murray in Oklahoma might be a safer place as a first outing since his death.

With the last of the dogs gone, all she had to do was board Squeek with a vet in Canyon, and she was free to go wherever she wished.

Cypress stood in the cove where she would catch her breakfast. If Parker were here, he would be out on the point, casting for stripers. Sybil looked toward the point, almost expecting to see him standing there, his fishing rod flashing in the early morning sun. Enough of that, she told herself. Enough. I'll catch bluegills, clean and cook them by myself, without having to endure Parker's mockery.

That's it: get hold of the unpleasant memories of Parker, and God knows there are plenty of those.

Sybil was amazed at the realization that she had buried such memories to the point of being unaware of them most of the time. She extended the lengths of her compact casting rod, threaded the monofilament from the reel through the eyes, and attached a fly and a casting bubble.

Parker laughed the first time he saw her do that beside an Oklahoma lake. "That's a mountain trout rig. Nobody uses a rig like that in lowland lakes."

"I do."

"You'll catch nothing." His laugh had a mean edge to it.

She hooked a salmon egg to the fly. Parker had once guffawed over that.

On her first cast, she brought in a bluegill as large as both her hands. Two more, and she would have breakfast. As she threaded the fish onto the stinger, she remembered how Parker wouldn't even try eating the perch she caught, how he seemed to resent it that she enjoyed the meal. He caught nothing, for he insisted on going after bass, and they were elusive in Lake Murray that spring. She cleaned the bluegill and cooked them: plenty for a meal for two. But he ate a peanut butter sandwich, and she had muttered "bastard!" as she watched him eat.

That's it, Sybil told herself, hooking another salmon egg, remember the mean side of him, the legacy of his biker years, as she thought of it. "Bastard," she said aloud, and cast her line toward a cypress knee protruding from the water some twenty feet out. A perch grabbed the fly as soon as it hit the water.

Pug had wanted to come with her, but Sybil said no. "Because I once told you that I don't like camping out?" Pug asked.

"No. Because I must do this myself. I must relearn the pleasures lost to Parker's death. I loved to camp out before I met him. I must not stop living just because he isn't around to share with me."

"I would share with you."

"Thanks, Pug. You're kind. But I must go to Lake Murray alone."

Sybil watched Pug start to protest, bite her lip, and give up. Pug can't do my recovery for me, she told herself. I must recover from grief alone, and in my own ways. Besides, Sybil thought, Pug might want more of me than I can give.

On the way back to her camp with her three bluegill, Sybil walked through a field of rust-orange flowers tipped with yellow. Indian blankets, one of her favorites. In the brush beyond the field stood purple thistles and winecups in bright spots of color, and above them the hum of bumblebees in yellow jackets working the thistle flowers. A bit of paradise, she thought.

Parker would love the scene. He would set up an easel right over there and paint what he saw and what he felt. Her eyes stung. Parker.

He seemed an unlikely candidate for an artist, this man with a dragon tattooed on his back and a skull on his shoulder, riding his Harley chopper, wearing jeans and leather.

On Sybil's advice, he played down the biker image during art shows and played up his American Indian ancestry. She braided his hair like that of Quanah Parker in the famous photos of him, and he signed his paintings "Red Bear," also something Sybil had suggested, the breaking of his name into two words to seem more the genuine Indian artist.

She steamed the perch in a skillet over the blue flame of a Coleman camp stove. Tomorrow, she told herself, I'll ride back to Canyon, do so in a leisurely way. I'll stop and look at those purple flowers growing in such abundance beside the highways.

She couldn't recall seeing them before, and she wanted a name for them. They grew in round balls, then sent a stem up to another round ball, then another above that. Pagoda flowers, she called them, for want of a name.

It would be necessary to get home in order to decide which paintings to show to the agent from New York. He would be there Saturday, something she objected to because she liked to do volunteer work at the hospital on weekends when volunteers were scarce. But he had insisted that Saturday was the only day he could fly to and from Amarillo.

The last time he came, she picked him up at the airport on her motorcycle, and the twenty-mile ride to Canyon frightened him so much his lips looked blue when they arrived. This time, he informed her, he would rent a car. And he wanted to take at least a dozen of Parker's paintings with him. But he would get four. That would be between sixty and eighty thousand dollars on the New York market, and it would have to be enough for him, for now.

She dished the fish onto a paper plate and sat in front of her pup tent to eat. Would Pug have sat here on the ground, picking perch flesh from feathery bones for her breakfast? It didn't seem likely. Then why would she want to come at all, if she claimed to dislike camping and fishing? Sybil asked the question, but she knew the answer.

And why would she leave all those gross things around my house like that dead pigeon? She says she loves me, yet she tries to scare me. Sybil thought again of the night she dropped the key to Parker's studio into Hunsley Creek. When she got home, Pug was there, and that seemed good.

When Sybil cried, Pug held her, rocked her, kissed her. And in the fever of her grief, she gave in to the kisses, for they seemed pure and undemanding, unlike the kisses of men. She gave in to the prompting to remove her clothing, gave in to the embraces that offered comfort and fire to blend grief into passion.

It had been a mistake. She felt disjointed the next morning, confused. Who am I? she kept asking, for never had she before even considered making love with a woman. Who am I? Her answer did not include a lesbian lifestyle. Pug wanted that with her, insisted it was the only way for them to live after such a night. No, Sybil said. No, Pug, it isn't my way. My way is Parker. He's dead, Pug said. Dead.

No, Sybil said. Not yet, he's not. Not to me. Get out. Get out. Get out.

And Pug left Sybil's home, Parker's home. But she returned. I'll be your friend, she said. Nothing more. No demands, and Sybil needed a friend, so she took Pug's word. But should I have trusted her? Can I trust her now?

Sybil thought of the two dogs and the people who had taken them to a ranch, and she was grateful. Not having the dogs allowed her to go on the camping trip. And she thought of the young man who had stared at her and requested to see her again.

The afternoon of her second day at Lake Murray, Sybil hiked to a cove where a stand of cottonwood trees gave her a sense of privacy. She took off her clothes and waded into the cold water, enjoying the rippling of her skin. When the water came above her knees, she dived and swam with long smooth strokes, her hair flowing around her shoulders.

Back on the bank, she sat on a boulder and watched the sun dry water beads on her brown skin. At that moment she knew something about her had changed, but she couldn't say what.

The drive back loomed before her as a risk. She imagined a motorcycle accident, and for the first time since Parker's death, felt a twinge of fear. Fear of accident. It drives my life, she told herself: accident drives my life. But it does not have to control me.

"Can you do the two-step?" Angela pushed a strand of red hair behind her ear and turned to Jason. He leaned against the passenger side door of Hyram's extended cab pickup. Angela sat in the middle, Hyram drove and Odom sat in the back seat.

Jason looked uncertain. He had been on Hyram's ranch only a few days, but he already knew that if he admitted to ignorance of anything, he would draw a look of bemused tolerance from Odom, a laugh from Hyram, or a sneer from Angela. He shrugged. "I don't know."

"That answer's dim-witted as a possum. You know how or you don't."

"It ain't likely he can," Hyram put in. "I'd risk all my egg money on the proposition that them folks over in Malaysia don't exactly make a habit of the two-step on a given Saturday night."

Jason stared at Hyram, then laughed. "You have such a colorful way of talking that I often don't understand."

"Hang on to your buttons and it'll all come to you in time." Hyram looked pleased.

"So do you, or what?"

"He don't, and that's a natural fact. But Angela, honey, it ain't because he's stupid, which he ain't. It's just ignorance born of privation. A body is stuck with stupidity for life. Ignorance is curable, which is how come you're gonna teach him the Texas two-step."

"Can't judge a man by dance steps," Odom said.

So the two-step was a kind of dance, Jason realized. At least now he knew the subject of the conversation. And he knew that the place they said they were going, the Crystal Pistol, had to be a dance hall. When he first heard the name, he thought it sounded like a bordello in a western movie.

Jason considered telling them that he had once taken ballroom dance lessons but decided that would draw laughter. But isn't a waltz something they would understand? He remembered reading about frontier people dancing to waltz music. "I can dance to some kinds of music," he offered.

"That's a start, I guess. Tonight, you learn the two-step from an expert. Me."

"She's right there," Hyram said. "The two-step is her trump suit."

"He'll have ever' cowgirl in the place hot to trot for him soon as they look at the proper way we dressed him. Them that don't fall in love with him right off will do so just as soon as he learns the two-step." Angela laughed.

With a nod Jason accepted the compliment, though he felt less certain about his costume. In Malaysia, anyone seeing him would assume he was going to a masquerade ball dressed as a Hollywood cowboy.

That morning after breakfast, Angela had announced: "Jason, I got you some proper clothes. Here." She took two plastic shopping bags from the pantry and handed them to him.

Jason looked in a bag. "Boots."

"Ropers. Good for walking and good for riding. If you put your foot into a stirrup with them sneakers on, like as not it would slip on through and break your leg again, which would be a shame considering you just now got over walking with a stick. You gotta have heels to ride a horse."

"Thanks, Angela, but—"

"Thank Hyram. He paid for them. All I did was shop for them."

"Hyram, thanks. But how did you know my size, Angela?"

"I looked in your shoes. You leave them by the door all the time, though why you take them off ever' time you come in is beyond me."

"They do that in the Far East," Hyram said. "And it makes sense, too, unless you wear boots. Can you imagine struggling in and out of your boots twenty times a day? You walk in for a drink of water or a cup of coffee and you got to sit down and tug on your boots for thirty minutes. Then you drink for three minutes and go back to wrestling with your boots for another ten minutes or so. A body would get nothing done on a ranch acting like that. But man alive, would he ever have clean floors."

"Blue jeans. You bought some blue jeans, a belt, a shirt and a cowboy hat."

"Ask how she knew what size to get," Hyram said.

"For the hat, I looked in your cap. And the others? I looked in your pants." Angela watched Hyram while she talked. She laughed. "They weren't on you at the time. Did it while you slept. And I looked at the tag in one of your shirts. How come you sleep on the floor instead of the bed?"

"The bed sloshes me around too much. And it's too soft." Jason didn't like it that she had come into his room while he slept. He looked at her with some hostility. She laughed.

"You snore." She seemed to enjoy his being bothered that she had gone into his bedroom. "Loud. Not loud like Hyram, but loud."

"Jason, don't listen to ever' damn thing a woman says or she'll drive you plumb up the wall. She don't know how I snore."

Somehow the whole conversation had become uncomfortable but Jason wasn't sure just why. Something seemed to be going on between Hyram and Angela, but what? Why all the sexual innuendoes? Jason shrugged, got up and mixed some powdered milk. Angela sat and picked at a plate of biscuits and eggs. Hyram wolfed down his food with a ferocity that always startled Jason.

It was later in the day that Jason found out why Hyram and Angela bought the western clothes. They were going to the Crystal Pistol in Amarillo, Hyram said, to introduce Jason to more local culture. When Jason asked what the Crystal Pistol was, Hyram just laughed and quoted a dirty limerick about a cowboy named Chuck who spent Saturday nights doing things that rhymed with the name.

The limerick made the Crystal Pistol seem even more like a bordello. But Jason dismissed the possibility since it seemed unlikely Angela would go to such a place. He decided they were going to a western bar, and he had not risked further ridicule by asking more questions about the place.

Hyram waved a hand at the street. "This is Amarillo Boulevard, once known as North-East Eighth. Part of the old Route 66. Keep an eye out and you'll see some of the local gals. There's two now."

The women he pointed out wore sequined, low-cut blouses, tight shorts, nylon stockings and high heels. They waved at men in trucks, motioning for them to pull over to the curb.

"Them's busybodies," Odom said.

"You can see them infesting the boulevard from St. Anthony's Hospital to the old air force base. Cops crack down from time to time and run the hustling indoors, but them pavement princesses keep coming back, working the truckers and cowboys."

"Hyram, you gonna let on you never had an eye for a fallen angel?" Angela asked.

"I do for a fact. Try this one out:

A flatbacker floozie from Amarillo
hung by her heels from a willow.
She said 'I'd prefer,' to her John
an oak tree or a pecan,
but a willow is better'n a pillow."

Hyram looked pleased with himself.

"So you do have an eye for some of them rental models?"

"An eye, yes—at one time. Back when my teeth weren't wore down much and I was too young to have the sense God gave a goose. But an eye, that's all I had for them. Them painted ladies was interested in other parts of a man's anatomy than his eyeballs, so I weren't too popular with them."

"You're a darn sight more popular with the ladies than you know." Angela nudged Hyram with her elbow, a secret little nudge, Jason concluded, one she tried to hide.

When they drove into the parking lot of the Crystal Pistol, Jason thought it looked like a converted barn, an impression that was reinforced by the appearance of the interior.

"Ain't but a few folks dancing," Hyram said. "But that'll pick up as the night gets on. What do you say we take that table over there? It's got the dance floor on one side for us dancers and the bar on the other for Odom."

"Y'all take the table. I aim to sit on a bar stool and paint my tonsils with some Wild Turkey whiskey. Dance while I spend my time talking to the beer wrangler standing over there on the sober side of the bar."

Hyram pulled out a chair for Angela. Jason sat beside her at a tiny table. A waitress placed a bowl of pretzels and three glasses of ice water on the table. "Draws all around," Hyram told her. "No. Make that two draws, and you ask this cowboy what he wants."

The waitress turned to Jason. "Bottle beer? A mixed drink, maybe?"

"Bring me a cola."

The waitress nodded and left. "Bring me a cola," Angela mocked. "Jason, you gotta do better than that."

Hyram chuckled. "Me, I'm heading for the throne room. You two get out there and work on teaching him the two-step."

"Not yet, Angela. I want to watch first and have you describe what I'm supposed to do."

The band played "Jose Cuervo, You're a Friend of Mine," and two couples danced, moving around the floor with speed and energy. Angela leaned close and described the two-step. While she talked, Jason noticed that a tall man sitting at the bar next to Odom seemed to be staring at them. He clutched a beer mug and slit his eyes in a mean way.

During the next song, the man came over to them, set his beer on the table, and announced, "Pretty woman, you're going to dance this one with me."

Angela glanced at him, then returned her attention to Jason. "No I ain't."

"Come on, sweet pea." The man took her wrist. She struggled to pull back, but he held tight. The man laughed.

"Let go of her." Jason started to stand, but the man's fist caught him just below his left eye before he was on his feet. The blow threw him back into the chair, and the chair fell over backward.

"Now. About that dance."

"I don't dance with drunks." Angela jerked away from him.

Jason, stunned, began getting to his feet. Is this how Rozak felt, he wondered, when the big Australian kid beat him up? Jason watched Odom tap the man on the shoulder. The man turned and looked down at Odom. "What do you want, Pops?"

"Just to learn you some manners." Odom's fist shot out, catching the man in the stomach. Jason heard him expel his breath just before Odom's other fist connected with the man's ribs. Odom hit him twice more as he fell. "You all right, Angela?"

She nodded. Jason picked up his chair. Odom looked with contempt at the man on the floor, picked up the beer he had left on the table, poured it on the man's crotch, then returned to his bar stool. Jason looked around. A few people glanced at the man as he rolled to one side, clutching his stomach, but other than that, people ignored them. Jason sat down. "People act as if that attack was normal."

"It ain't normal. But it also ain't none of their business." Hyram nudged the man with the toe of a boot. "Seems to be awake." He sat across from Jason. "I told the bouncer to lug that sack of pig bones out of here. A man that would cross Odom has the IQ of a cantaloupe. He might look like a skinny little runt, but Odom would fight a buzz saw and give it three turns head start. You doing all right, honey?"

"I'm fine. It was nothing, Hyram. I could have handled the drunk. Odom didn't have to step in like that, fists swinging."

Jason poured ice water on a napkin and dabbed his cheek.

"He tagged you a good one, there," Hyram observed. "That eye will get black as the inside of a coffin. Come tomorrow, me and Odom will show you a few Texas tricks with your feet and fists so next time you can avoid getting pounded like that. But tonight you learn to two-step."

Angela and Hyram leaned toward each other so they could make a show of talking rather than watch Jason holding a wet napkin to his eye.

Jason looked at the man on the floor. Somebody ought to do something for him, Jason thought. But not me. I'm too angry at him.

The bouncer picked the man up by his belt and dragged him toward a side door. "What will he do with the fellow?" Jason asked.

"Dunno. Maybe put him in his pickup. Maybe just toss him out in the alley. Forget him. You ready to have Angela teach you a proper Texas dance?"

Sunday afternoon Jason heard the rattle of Odom's pickup and looked out the window. Odom got out, squatted beside the tack shed and began rolling a smoke. Jason, sitting in Hyram's formal living room, heard Hyram enter. "You got to be the only person ever to use this room, except for when I throw a party."

Hyram looked normal to Jason, which was something of a surprise, considering how much beer the man had drunk the previous evening. It had been necessary for Jason to drive home. Angela went to sleep after climbing into the back seat of the extended cab pickup. Odom and Hyram rode up front, laughing and singing dirty songs about bowlegged women and rolling in the clover.

"Why did Odom just arrive? I thought he didn't come out on Sundays."

"Mostly he don't, except when he needs to do something. Today some of what he needs to do involves you, so how about putting your boots on and joining us out back? By the tack shed." Hyram left without waiting for a response.

Jason eyed his boots with distaste. They had put a blister on one toe and chaffed his feet in a few places. He would have preferred tennis shoes, but Hyram had specified boots. I guess that means he and Odom are going to teach me to ride a horse, Jason thought, trying to work up some enthusiasm for the boots. Hadn't Angela said something about needing boot heels in order to ride?

Before putting the Ropers on, Jason wrapped his blistered toe in a Band-Aid. When he got outside, he found Hyram holding out a can of tobacco for Odom. Both men were stuffing brown wads into their mouths. "Wanna dip?" Hyram offered.

"Thanks. I'll pass for now."

Hyram laughed. "It ain't a prerequisite to be a real cowboy, but it don't hurt a man's image." He put a lid on the can and slipped it into his hip pocket.

"Your eye ain't half bad," Odom said.

"What he means is, that cowboy that knocked you one last night was either dog-shit stupid, thinking he could get by with a friendly punch, or he didn't know nothing about a barroom fight. Odom wants to show you what to do next time somebody takes a notion to hit you like that."

"There won't be a next time."

Odom and Hyram laughed as if Jason had told a good joke. Hyram slapped him on the back. "Odom is a man of few words, but he's a crackerjack with his fists, as you saw last night. He'll show you how to bring a man down in a variety of ways, and I'll tell you when to go about choosing the right way."

"You're going to teach me to brawl?" Jason felt repulsed by the offer, though there was something exciting about learning to fight.

"Basic rule in a bar," Odom said, "is never let a man get close like that cowboy done when I come up to him." Odom moved within inches of Jason. "Like this. Never let a man in like this."

"Jason, right now, Odom is showing you how to lay it on a man so he won't get up for a long spell. Never hit a friend the way he's about to show you."

"If you aim to clean a man's plough, you get in close like this. Say something to him, maybe something that could get took as social, maybe even nice—just to distract him. Hold your arms loose, like this, with your hitting arm up a little high, but don't make a fist. Look him in the eye and hit him while you're talking. Hit him here." Odom set his fist against Jason's ribs. "Hook him hard with your knuckles, then follow up with the other fist, here."

Jason looked in amazement at Odom. Hyram laughed. "A blow like that might well crack a fellow's ribs. Like as not that cowboy Odom laid it on at the Crystal Pistol is nursing busted ribs today. Like I said, hitting like that is something you reserve for somebody you don't mind hurting."

"Two is usually enough, if you go about it right. You might want to stick one or two more on him while he's going down, if he done something bad enough to deserve it." Odom stepped back. "Now come up to me, talking in a casual kind of way, and show me where you would hit me."

"Make like he just walloped Angela, but you let on that you took no notice of it, Jason. You don't want to warn a man of your intentions, or he won't let you get close."

"What do I say? Odom said threatening things last night as he went up to that man."

"But he said them in a nice voice. Besides, most cowboys look at Odom and size him up as harmless, him being skinny and old and not overly tall. But you ain't none of them things, so you gotta talk nice when you move in close. The tone is more important than the words, cause usually the man you aim to bring down is a tad drunk and slow to think on words. Say anything. Say, 'gosh, feller, would you mind if—' and then lay it to him like Odom showed you."

"Come on, now," Odom said.

Jason had no idea that there was an entire etiquette associated with violence. Did the big Australian kid, Tom, speak to Rozak before pummeling him on the grounds of the International School of Kuala Lumpur? Jason didn't remember him doing so. Did the red-headed man speak to Suppriah before shooting her in the head? Maybe. If he did, the music from the Walkman blocked it out. Probably he didn't speak, though, for she showed no awareness of his presence before her face flew apart from the bullet.

Maybe only Texans had rules about talk before beatings. Hyram and Odom had some ethics about violence, Texas ethics, ones Jason couldn't find much to criticize. "Gosh, mister, would you mind if I . . ." Jason stepped close to Odom. "Then I would hit you here and then here."

"Good. But don't swing with your shoulder or you might be in for a real fight. You want to avoid a real fight by ending it right off. Swing with your arm only. Jerk your fist up, keeping your shoulder still. Like this."

Odom had Jason go through the motions several more times, complete with speaking his lines. Jason felt as if he were rehearsing for a play.

"I do believe you got it." Odom looked pleased.

"Remember, Jason, to reserve rib cracking punches for them that needs pain. But if you get into a fight with a friend, you go about it different. Show him, Odom."

"A friend?" Jason felt confused.

"Start off more than arm's length. And you start with words." Odom stood in front of Jason. "Say stuff like this. You dumb sumbitch. You don't got the sense to pour piss out of a boot. Maybe you say some other choice things, and you go to lifting your dukes, only don't ball your fists just yet, cause you gotta let him say some things before you hit him."

"Fight a friend?"

"Odom's right. You go about it different. You might get pissed enough to put on your raking spurs, but you gotta keep everything in perspective. You don't want to break ribs or even lay out a fellow in a fight like that. You both might need to blow off a little steam, so you punch the shoulders and maybe the face. Odom'll show you. Remember the words are important. In a friendly fight, a man who can't cuss is useless as tits on a boar hog."

"But what do I say?" The whole affair seemed so absurd to Jason that he decided he might as well go along with it.

"The word sumbitch is a good one," Hyram said. "Use it when you can't think of nothing else. You might say something like 'your breath would knock a buzzard off a shit wagon.' I'll tell you later more about the fine art of swearing."

"When you're done with words, you want a fellow to feel pain, maybe even bleed some. But you don't put a buddy in the hospital unless he done something that's gonna make him not ever your buddy again. You swing with your shoulder, like this." Odom took an exaggerated swing at Jason. "Swing hard, though, cause if you do connect, the other fellow will be moving back. Chances are you won't hurt him permanent. Now. Show me what you know."

Jason faced Odom. "You half pint of pig livers. Beside a son of a bitch like you, a goat's turd would look both tall and handsome."

Odom flushed and lifted his fists. "You dumb sumbitch," Odom growled. Jason stepped back, startled by the edge in Odom's voice and by the way his eyes hardened, as if the intelligence went out of them, replaced by cold fury. He swung a roundhouse that Jason saw coming from the way Odom moved his shoulders. Jason ducked under it.

Stepping between them, Hyram caught Odom's arm as it launched into another swing. "Don't go to getting snakes in your boots, Odom. The boy's just doing what you taught him." He held Odom's arm a moment.

"I guess." Odom ceased struggling.

Hyram looked at Jason. "Easy on the words during practice, boy. We don't want this to turn into a real fight of any sort. Odom, the boy's good with words, wouldn't you say?" Hyram laughed and Odom struggled to work up a smile.

"Fair to middling. But you gotta say sumbitch proper. Say it."

"Sumbitch. Did I do it right that time?" Jason tried to sound contrite.

"Accent ain't right. But it'll have to do for now." Odom sounded placated.

"Odom, you done good by the boy. We'll call it a day. Later, you can show him what to do if he can't get in close for busting the ribs of a genuine sumbitch, and he finds himself in a real fight that means going to it bucktooth and hangnail."

"Thanks, Odom." Jason felt relief that the lesson was over.

Odom nodded. Hyram pointed toward the house. "Come on, Odom. I want your advice on where to put a barbecue pit when it comes time for my birthday party."

That afternoon, after Odom had left the ranch, Hyram asked Jason: "You ever buy a rubber?"

"Rubber?"

"A condom. Used to buy them myself, when I was about a hundred years younger. Somebody told me the best ones was made from sheep skin and not rubber at all. So I went into Walgreens and found the rubber displays and picked up a package of sheepskins marked 'size large,' me being young and having a notion that I was something of a stud. But come Saturday night, and I couldn't get the thing on. It was too small, and being made out of sheepskin instead of rubber, it didn't stretch none. Dang near ruint my whole night. Next day I went back to Walgreens and discovered what I missed before. There was two other sizes of sheepskins other than large: extra large and extra extra large. The folks that made them condoms figured with some accuracy that no man would buy a size small, so they just jacked up the terminology some, calling small a large and the other sizes degrees of large. Men are sure enough funny when it comes to pecker size."

"That's a good story, Hyram."

"It ain't just a story. It's the unvarnished truth. And there's a lesson in it, for them that looks. Especially for anybody wanting to learn to get along with Texas men. In Texas, you don't mention a man's size if he's a tad short. You can call a big man tiny, if you take a notion, and no harm could come of it. But you got to take care about talking to men who wear pockets low to the ground. Even when you're spoofing with a friend, you take care about naming words that have to do with size. Odom near busted a blood vessel when you called him a half pint and let on as he was smaller than a goat's turd. I got to admit I admired your feel for swearing even if it didn't show good judgment."

"I meant no offense. Is Odom still angry with me?"

"Shoot no. He understood you was just cussing him cause he told you to. It's just that he popped a cork when he heard you imply he might have to jump some to be eye-level with your belly button. He must of figured you knew better, even joshing, but on reflection, he got over being so pissed. Him and me, we discussed the matter some, and he now believes that you learned your lesson about them short words. If you use one again around him, you better count on fighting your first friendly fight."

"Who would even care enough about Parker's dog kennels to set them afire?" Sybil wasn't angry so much as puzzled.

Pug looked sympathetic. "Not Parker's kennels. Yours."

"Meaning?"

"Meaning whoever destroyed the kennels knew you were out of town. They knew that when you came back, you would get the message that next time it might not be something so expendable. It might be your house."

"An attempt to run me out of town? I don't believe it."

"This area is full of rednecks. Believe it. They hate anything different. I think it's the same people who have been terrifying you with all the cute little gifts left around the house—like the dead bird."

Sybil paced around her living room. She stopped by a front window and looked out. Off to her left, barely visible through her elm trees, she could see the houses of the neighbors who had come to see about the smoke, who had met her when she returned from Lake Murray to tell her about the burn on the kennel. The Carters. Both were retired from teaching at the university. Sybil liked them. "Neighbors called the fire department. The kennels were only damaged on one side. The Carters over there, along with the young couple who lived on the other side of them, carried water from the side of my house and had the fire out by the time the fire department came. Does that sound like people who want to scare me away?"

"I never said everyone here was a redneck. But enough are. Sybil, what is there for you here in this tiny town? Leave it. I'll help you find a safe place in Amarillo. You could move in with me until you find what you want. You could stay as long as you like."

Sybil turned from the window. "That's a generous offer. But I need to learn independence, not dependence."

"The offer stands. Think about it."

"I have."

Immediately after Parker's death, Pug had started coming around, offering companionship. The morning after Sybil dropped the key into Hunsley Hills Creek, Pug had suggested that Sybil move to her place. No way, Sybil said. That isn't me. That isn't my kind of life. Later, Pug pressed the matter until Sybil's temper flared. Pug had dropped the matter.

And now, almost a year later, she brought it up again. Sybil looked at Pug, knowing her motives. Certainly Pug was gay, but that didn't stop her from dating men. Sybil had met some of them, had disliked all of them. Several of them had once biked around the state with Parker, years ago before he met Sybil, before he saw his painting as something serious.

"It's been a long day. I need some time alone."

Pug stood. "Of course. There is one other matter. It's what I came over about, though I forgot when you told me the horror story about an arsonist attacking your place. Sybil, my brother Mark is throwing a big party for me, for my birthday. He wants you to be there. So do I."

"When?" Sybil looked out the window at the white Ford pickup stopping beside Pug's car. It took her a moment to recognize the man getting out of it as the one who had accompanied Hyram when he came for the dogs.

"Who is it?"

"A friend." Sybil was glad for the diversion from Pug, who had become wearisome.

When he came in, Sybil made introductions. Jason offered his hand. Pug hesitated, then took it. "Nice to meet you," Jason said.

"Your eye looks terrible." Pug smirked.

"It looks worse than it feels."

Sybil could see that he allowed Pug to see his surprise. She felt certain neither Hyram nor Angela would have commented on Jason's black eye. "Some people like Pug have only about two centimeters between her brain and her mouth." Sybil laughed as if she had told a joke.

"Have you and Sybil been friends long?"

Jason started to answer but Sybil cut him off. "Jason and I are old war buddies."

Pug sat down. Sybil looked at her in disdain. "What were you saying about a party at Mark's?"

"We'll discuss that later, don't you think?"

"I think I'd better be going." Jason turned to the door.

"Nonsense. You just arrived, and it has been a while since we got to visit." Sybil took his arm and led him to a chair. "No, Pug, I think now is a good time to take care of the party business. When will it be?"

"Sunday night." Pug crossed her arms.

"Pug's brother is having a birthday party for her. Isn't that a nice gesture? I knew Mark before I met Pug, actually. Mark was an old friend of my husband's. They once belonged to the same motorcycle club. Jason, are you free to go to the party with me? Pug, what time is the party?"

Pug cleared her throat and crossed her legs. Sybil thought she looked as if she might fall over any moment and assume a complete fetal position. "Eight."

"You can go with me, can't you, Jason?"

He looked from one woman to another. "Sure. I mean, I would love to go with you."

"There you have it then." Sybil stood. "Pug was just leaving when you came up." She opened the door.

As she stood, Pug tried without much success for a smile.

"I'll see you Sunday," Jason said as she passed. She gave him an icy look.

Sybil watched her drive away, then turned to Jason. "Sorry about using you that way, but she had become so annoying."

"Can you let me know what was going on? That woman looked at me with mean eyes."

"Maybe sometime I'll explain. But not now—I don't want to think about her now. What brings you over, Mr. Jason White?"

"Embarrassment. The need to apologize for what I said when we last spoke."

"Oh?" Her eyes teased. "And just what did you say? I can't seem to remember."

"Does it matter now?"

"No. Can I get you something to drink? Lemonade? Herb tea?"

"If you're having anything."

"Tea for a social, then. Come with me, Mr. White?"

"Call me Jason." He followed her into the kitchen.

"Jason, then. Sit there." She pointed at a stool beside the bar separating kitchen from dining area, and set about making tea. "Is that all you came about—to apologize? Or did you become sated with Texas ranchers and need to talk with someone you imagine to be more like you?"

"You do remember my gaffe, and it does matter. All right, I apologize for implying that I wanted to see you just to get away from Hyram and Angela. I grovel with embarrassment over such a faux pas."

"Good. Apology accepted. What have you done to treat that eye?"

"Ice. That's about it."

"Parker claimed that a raw Irish potato, shaved into mush, makes a poultice that draws the hurt from a shiner." She wet a paper towel and leaned across the bar toward him. "Turn this way."

He submitted to her pressing the area under his eye. As she withdrew, he took her hand. She raised her brows. "Are you courting me, Mr. White?"

He dropped her hand. "I'm clumsy about it, aren't I?"

"Perhaps. Perhaps not. How old are you, Mr. White."

"I'm Jason, please. I'm twenty-two."

"So old? I thought you younger, from your looks. Do you know how old I am?"

"No. And it doesn't matter."

"But it does. I am twenty-eight. Six years older, Mr. White."

"Please. Stop calling me that."

"Six years ago you were a mere boy, while I was a woman. It makes a difference. I have been married and widowed, while you are just edging into adulthood. You must not court me, Mr. White. I would like to have you as a friend, a buddy. Nobody can have too many buddies. But nothing more than that. Nothing."

He laughed. "You're so serious. Ease up some. I'll make a deal. I won't presume to court you if you will call me Jason."

They held eye contact for a long moment. Jason raised his brows in a comical way. She turned to the teapot. "How do you like your tea, Jason?"

"Straight. Hot."

"How did you get the black eye?"

"A man in the Crystal Pistol punched me. How long have you been a widow?"

She looked at him with renewed respect. "I stand chastised. Mark my question up on the same chart for crudity as Pug's first statement to you. A year. Parker died a year ago. I'm just now becoming functional again." She set a cup of tea in front of him. "Why did he punch you—the man in the Crystal Pistol?"

She smiled, liking Jason for establishing new rules for asking personal questions. I give something personal, then I can ask you something personal. A kind of game he made up on the spot. Or we made up—she wasn't sure which.

18

Jason awakened in the early morning to the faint rattle of a gate. He stood, feeling stiff from sleeping on the floor, and made his way around the dark shape of the water bed in order to look out the window.

Angela stood by the tack shed. He could see her face and hands, white in the predawn light; the rest of her looked like a moving shadow. She rummaged through the shed and pulled a dark object from it, then vanished from sight and returned leading a horse. He watched her put the dark object on the horse—a blanket, perhaps. It looked too small to be a saddle. Then with a swiftness of movement that astounded him, Angela climbed onto the back of the horse. She rode toward the shadow that was the mesa people called Snake Mountain.

Perhaps, Jason thought, it's time to take a walk toward the looming mesa. He dressed, went outside and headed toward Snake Mountain, toward the red streaks on the horizon above the mesa. The morning had a chill to it colder than any rainy season dawn in Malaysia, and drier, much drier. He quickened his pace to warm himself.

After holding down a strand on a barbed-wire fence and climbing through, Jason found the ground sloping toward an arroyo. He stopped and looked around. The only trees in sight stood by the ranch house, dark against the horizon. East, toward Snake Mountain, the land fell and rose in folds of shadows, the dead prairie grass glistening in predawn light like a blanket of snow. Here and there Jason could see dark spots on the prairie. Mesquite trees, Jason thought, and laughed out loud at the absurdity of walking among a wide scattering of trees that were not trees toward a mountain that wasn't a mountain. The entire place seemed like a hoax, a joke that went on and on without a punch line.

As he climbed a rise, he heard a horse, and he veered off toward it. Then he saw her.

She sat on the ground beside what looked like a TV tray, and she seemed to be doing something with her boots—taking them off? But that didn't make any sense. Her horse stood a few yards away, cropping grass. It startled him when she looked up and saw him. "Jason? What are you doing out so early?"

"Just out for a walk. I didn't mean to disturb you."

"No problem," she said. "Come over here." Jason approached her. She had taken one boot off and was working on the other. "Have you ever greeted the morning sun the way people were meant to greet her?"

"I don't know."

"You say the most comical things, sometimes. Sure you know. And you ain't ever done it. But you're about to. Here. Pull this boot off." She held up her foot. He removed her boot. "Sit down and get out of your boots." She laughed. "Tennis shoes, then. I should have known. Take them off."

He sat and removed his shoes. "Why?"

"Socks, too. Because you got to be dressed right for greeting the sun." She stood and began unbuttoning her blouse. "Get your shirt off." Jason stared in disbelief. "I ain't doing this so you can gape at me. Pay attention to yourself. Get them clothes off. All of them, and put them on this camper stool so they won't get dusty."

"I thought that was a TV tray."

"That would work, too, though it would look a mite odd out here on the prairie. It's a stool for sitting that I leave out here for a clothes rack."

"Do you do this every morning?" He began removing his shirt.

"No. Just sometimes. Jason, I ain't a Baptist, like most around here. A church is just another building to me. But that don't mean I don't feel the need of something bigger than me. Greeting the sun is a powerful experience when it comes busting over Snake Mountain and you're standing facing it dressed in what you was born with."

"This is a religious ritual, then." Jason took off his pants and underwear and set them on his shoes. The morning cool roughened his skin.

"Maybe. You can call it that, if you want. Look." She pointed to the brightening horizon. "It will come any minute now. Take my hand and face it—let the light bathe your face and wash clean down to your feet. Watch it through your eyelids, and don't talk."

Taking her hand he glanced at her, at her high breasts with nipples tight from the cool, at her straight legs. So beautiful, he told himself—like a perfectly carved religious icon standing in the silver light. He turned toward the east and closed his eyes. Similar rituals he had seen in Nepal came to mind, men in robes and sandals, bowing in supplication toward the rising sun there on the plains beside Annapurna Mountain.

He glanced at her again. She stood, lips parted, eyes closed, holding his hand and lifting her other arm into a welcoming embrace for the sun. The sight moved him.

I misjudged her, he told himself, remembering how he had found her behavior repulsive that first day, how he had decided he would tolerate her for Hyram's sake, how he spent the time he had been in Texas ignoring her when he could. Then he thought of her breaking open the shotgun to insert the shell, and he grimaced. Don't think about her darker side now, he commanded. Look toward the east.

Most of what Jason knew about the high plains of Texas came from his reading. The landscape still felt alien and exotic. The evening after Odom and Hyram gave him lessons in fighting, he had walked toward Snake Mountain. Not far from the ranch house, two deer with enormous ears paused to look at him before vanishing beyond a rise. He heard a turkey in the distance make its comical gurgling sound, and he passed a prairie dog village of tiny mounds and scurrying dark shapes that squeaked in alarm at his approach. Among them stood a ground owl watching him, its head swiveling in quick jerks as he passed. A hawk flew overhead. When it got closer, Jason realized that it was too big to be a hawk, too golden in the evening sun. It had to be one of the golden eagles that lived in Palo Duro Canyon. He had stopped and watched the eagle, awed.

Angela, nude, embracing the morning, had to be, he decided, as much a part of nature here as the prairie dogs and the golden eagle.

She squeezed his hand just as the first rays of direct sun flashed from the top of Snake Mountain. He closed his eyes and watched the growing redness of his eyelids, giving himself to the experience with a thrill that ran along his spine. Angela's sigh was the natural music of the morning.

They stood together, facing east until the sun had lifted itself above the mountain, then turned to each other. "Thank you, Jason." She slipped into his arms, their bodies touching from her head against his chest to their feet. For the first time in the encounter, he felt the stir of sexual arousal. She sighed in a pleased kind of way and pushed away.

"Turn your back," she commanded. "And get dressed."

They put their clothes on without speaking. Jason floated through the ritual of dressing, the golden light of morning casting his shadow dark before him, the whistles of prairie birds all around. He identified quail and meadowlark but did not know the source of most of the bird sounds.

When he looked again at Angela, she stood just feet away, tucking her blouse into her jeans. "That was wonderful," he whispered.

"Yes. The best. I never shared greeting the sun with anyone." Her voice sounded lower and softer than he had ever heard it. Then it reverted to normal: "But there ain't no need in talking about it, is there? You go on, now. Go finish your morning walk. I'm getting back to the house to cook breakfast for Hyram."

Without waiting for a response, she mounted her horse and rode away.

Jason walked toward Snake Mountain, listening to the morning sounds of the prairie: bird calls, the occasional flapping of wings, the whir of grasshoppers in flight. On what seemed a high spot, he looked back but could see neither Angela nor the ranch.

19

A rattlesnake, big around as his fist and as long as his leg, crawled along an outcropping of rock ahead of him. He stopped to watch it move its slow coils among the rocks. The diamond patterns along its body struck him as beautiful, just as he had found the gleaming scales of the black cobra beautiful that morning beside the Klang River when Tom had paid the Malay boy to set the mongoose upon it.

The sun burned away the morning chill, and a warm wind came from the southwest. Snake Mountain seemed little closer than it had from the ranch. Jason had decided to turn back when he smelled coffee, a faint but unmistakable odor that came with a shift in the wind, then was gone. He resolved to climb one more high spot to see if he could find the source of the smell.

From the top of the rise, he found a scene directly from a western movie: a cowboy sitting beside a campfire, drinking from a tin cup; a saddled horse stood nearby, its nose in the grass. When Jason walked toward him, the man stood, picked up a rifle and held it in the crook of one arm, pointing it toward the sky. Jason stopped. These people are obsessed with weapons, he thought. He turned to go.

"Come on down here, feller, and have a cup of coffee." The cowboy squatted again and put the rifle on the ground. The wind picked up, and when Jason looked back, he felt the sting of dust blown into his eyes. He shrugged and joined the cowboy.

"I'm Jason White." He offered his hand. The cowboy turned his back and pointed toward the door of a dugout that Jason had not seen until then.

"Get you a can outta that dugout and I'll pour you some coffee." Jason dropped his hand. Was that a deliberate snub? Maybe not. The man had not seemed to see his hand. Jason went to the dugout.

He had to bend down to enter. Inside he found a bunk with some rags on it, a chair, and a table. On the table sat what looked like an empty bean can with the top haggled part way off. He picked up the can.

The cowboy took the can and poured some coffee into it from a blackened pot. He swirled the can a couple of times and emptied it onto the ground. "Gotta clean it some," he explained as he poured more coffee into the can. "Might be sorta hot." He handed the can to Jason. "Better grip it high up."

"Thanks." Jason took a sip that burned his lips and coated his tongue with coffee grounds. The cowboy laughed.

"Let her cool down and settle out some. Grab you a rock and sit a spell." He gestured at a rock beside the fire. Jason sat down. "Heard about your daddy." The cowboy smiled. Jason studied him.

"I beg—" he hesitated. "Do what?" he said.

The cowboy's grin spread, dimpling his cheeks, making his thin mustache look like a smudge of charcoal. He's just a few years older than I am, and a good-looking man, Jason decided, except for the fact that he needs a shave and maybe a bath and except for his brown, uneven teeth. "Your daddy," the cowboy said. "I heard about him. Being old battle buddies with Hyram. Heard you would be a-coming here for the summer, then you go to college at WT. Hold on a minute." He picked up his rifle. "There's one of them sumbitches."

Jason looked the direction the cowboy pointed his rifle and saw a prairie dog standing beside its mound. "Wait," Jason said, just as the rifle spat with a clear, sharp sound. Jason watched in horror as the prairie dog's head seemed to vanish. Its body stood a long moment, then fell as in slow motion and rolled down the mound. "My God," Jason muttered. He turned to the cowboy. "That was a bloody and brutal act."

"Shit." The cowboy stood. "Shit." He kicked the coffee pot, sending it clattering across the ground, coffee and grounds flying. "You one of them eastern city guys wants to snuggle up to every sumbitching thing with fur? Shit." He walked over to the coffee pot and kicked it again.

"Sumbitches followed me around the Canadian breaks last deer season, faggots and women, telling me what brutal and bloody business it is to shoot a deer, like I didn't know things bleed when I shoot them. Scaring the deer away. Couldn't shake them sumbitches. I run, and they run right beside me, the women and the faggots, and who'd figure they could keep up and not even get out of breath? They talk real loud the whole sumbitching time. 'You're scaring the deer clean to Oklahoma,' I says, and one of them sumbitching faggots he says 'yessir,' he says, 'that's how come we're out here. To keep you from shooting the deer.' Shit."

When Jason stood, the cowboy whirled around and pointed the rifle at him. "Sit your ass back down. I ain't through." His face looked puffy and purple. Jason felt a stab of fear. A man who could shoot an animal could just as easily shoot a person, Jason told himself. He sat down. How could I have ever thought him nice looking?

"I come here to shoot some varmints and relax some, and you come up with your high and mighty lip and Yankee talk. I'll tell you what. You come screwing around with me again, and I'll by God shoot your nuts off." He walked over to his horse, mounted, and put the rifle into a leather holder attached to the saddle.

Jason stood again. The cowboy swung the horse around toward him. "You put the fire out," he said, his voice taking on a mocking tone, "Mister Jason White. With the wind getting up, that fire could scatter and burn half the county." He leaned forward in the saddle, jutting out his jaw. "On a day like this, a man up wind from you could throw down a couple of lit matches, and you would be a goner, wouldn't be able to outrun the prairie fire, things been so dry this spring."

He turned his horse, then stopped and looked at Jason again. "Put the fire out," he said. "And one more thing. I catch you messing around with Angela, and I'll for sure shoot your nuts off." He slapped the horse's neck with the reins, and the horse, startled, broke into a run.

20

Jason poured his coffee over the fire, then raked dirt over the smoking ashes. He picked up the battered coffee pot and put it and the bean can on the table in the dugout. As he latched the door, he heard the wind getting stronger and felt sand hit his arms and neck.

The sky above Snake Mountain looked blue and clear, but back toward the ranch, black clouds hung above the horizon, and the air was filled with dust.

He looked at the dead prairie dog. He could mistake it for a rock, had he not seen it as a living creature, seen it crumple and fall from the bullet and roll down the mound.

Maybe I was a bit hasty, he thought, in deciding to become a Texan.

As he walked back toward the ranch, he had to cup his hands over his eyes to keep out the sand. After going no more than a hundred meters, he smelled smoke. He scrambled up an incline and stared with alarm at the grass fire moving toward him in a gigantic half-circle westward. But I put out the fire, he thought, then realized the blaze that came toward him was driven by winds from the opposite direction of the cowboy's campfire. It came from the direction the cowboy had gone.

And he remembered the cowboy's words about a man upwind throwing lighted matches on the prairie. Jason felt the back of his neck prickle. I'm in some real danger, he told himself.

A dog ran by him, away from the fire. Not a dog, he realized: a coyote. He turned back toward Snake Mountain, setting a swift pace. Two rabbits shot past him, one almost running into him. Off to his left he saw a deer pause and look at him.

The smoke became thicker, and he tried running. His leg objected, and he slowed.

When he climbed out of a hollow to a high spot, he looked back at the fire. It had gained on him. He told himself to pick up his pace, though he knew his leg would not tolerate much stress. The muscles simply had not had enough time to recover from being idle in the cast.

Sand stung the back of his neck, and smoke made him cough. The wind increased, and the sky grew dark. He glanced back. This time he could see the fire seeming to leap ahead of itself, starting new patches of flame far into unburned grass.

He thought of what the cowboy said about not being able to outrun a prairie fire, and he felt the fear rise in him, driving him into a limping run. Within minutes his leg felt heavy and sluggish, and it started to throb.

He looked around for a place to rest but found none. Prairie grass seemed to grow everywhere—even the few outcroppings of rock were ringed with grass. When he got back to the dugout, he noticed for the first time that its roof was covered with grass. It might be suicide, he thought, to go into the wooden dugout. Gritting his teeth against the pain in his leg, he forced himself on.

When he got to a place of fewer aberrations in the land, where the prairie flattened, running became easier. But the grass in the flat area grew thicker and taller, promising better, faster fuel for the fire.

He looked back and saw the fire was nearly upon him. When he turned to try running again, a sudden thunderclap jarred him, and the jagged neon flash of lightning struck the ground not far ahead. He looked up for rain clouds, but all he saw was smoke. More claps of thunder came, and lightning danced around him. "Rain!" he said, "rain, for God's sake!"

Coughing, eyes stinging from the smoke, he pushed on, looking only at the ground in front of him. When he came to the edge of the cliff, he almost went over.

The prairie seemed to drop away, to open to a straight fall that would be as fatal as would a fall from the top of a five-story building. Palo Duro Canyon, he told himself—and there's no way down.

Fire crackled just meters away, so close the heat burned him. The flame seemed further from the canyon wall off to his left, so he ran that way, threading with care between the cliff on his right and the fire coming from his left. Smoke stung his eyes with such fury that he felt sure he would be blinded, take a wrong move, and fall to his death.

Stepping through a mesquite, Jason stumbled and fell, grabbing the mesquite as his body went over what looked like another cliff.

Mesquite thorns ripped into his hand. He let go, certain that he would fall into the canyon.

Less than a meter down the slope, he hit something that knocked the wind from him. So it wasn't another cliff, after all, he realized, but one of the gullies that cut its way from the prairie into the canyon. His fall into the gully had been stopped by the trunk of a squat little tree. He lay stunned, looking at the greenery of the tree, identifying it as a juniper, then was amazed that he would bother to name the shrub at such a moment.

He tried to turn for a better grip on the juniper but slipped and rolled farther down the incline, then felt himself falling free in the air.

He landed in water and sank deep into it, surfacing in a pool at the base of a waterfall tumbling from the gully that opened into the canyon. It took only a couple of strokes of swimming for his feet to strike bottom.

When he waded out of the pool, he could see the fire at the top of the canyon and along the edge of the gully that he had fallen into. As he watched, the mesquite that had lacerated his hand burst into flame.

He sat beside the pool and caught his breath. The air felt cool, the rocks he sat upon cool, so cool. And he realized that he was safe. The fire raged above him; it could not reach into the canyon. The lightning had moved further off, and rain began dimpling the surface of the pool.

The waterfall amazed him, for he thought the region too dry to produce it. Not so much a waterfall, he thought, as a water trickle. He had fallen into the gully right where it spilled into the canyon. It was steep, but not so steep that he couldn't climb out.

His hand stung, and he looked at it, amazed to see blood. The lacerations didn't seem serious, though they hurt. In Malaysia, he would be in trouble with such open wounds because of the abundance of malicious tropical microbes. But he figured he would be all right here if he let the cuts go unwashed for an hour or so.

The rain came down harder. And so cold. Thunderstorms in Kuala Lumpur came with the same violence, but the rain always fell in fat, warm drops. Texas rain felt like cold needles. He shivered and moved against the canyon wall, out of the storm.

Across the pool, rising from the tops of trees, stood Snake Mountain. Between him and the mesa were more trees than he thought possible to find on the Texas high plains—real trees that lifted their leaves high into the sky, not bushy little mesquite and juniper. Cottonwoods, he thought: he had read that they grew along creeks in Palo Duro Canyon. What a beautiful place tucked into the harsh plains—and who would guess that this oasis was here, just a few kilometers from the flat sameness of the land around Hyram's ranch? He knew he would return to this place.

The rain stopped, and with it the wind. Thunderclouds moved over Snake Mountain, where they dropped rain and lightning on the top of the mesa. Jason rubbed his leg. It ached, though not so bad as it had during the last hours of the flight from Malaysia.

On the edge of the creek he picked up a twisted-looking stick that would do for a cane, then looked for the best way to climb out of the canyon.

When he finally reached the prairie above the canyon, his hand felt thick and swollen. He hobbled along, looking with astonishment at the wet, blackened landscape. Had the deer escaped? Had the rabbits? The prairie dogs?

Turning toward Snake Mountain, he tried to get a fix on his location in relation to the ranch. But he wasn't sure if he could, so he tried backtracking, guessing about how far he had gone parallel to the canyon wall.

The landscape had an ugly sameness to it, and the burnt smell disgusted him. He trudged along, using the stick for support, unsure he was doing much better than going approximately the right direction.

When he reached the dugout, he saw the prairie dog village and the prairie dogs—still alive and running about over charred ground. They made it, he thought, delighted with them for surviving. When one saw him and gave the alarm, they all ran into their holes.

That was it, then. They burrowed under the ground where fire would be no hazard. "I salute your stubborn hardihood," he said aloud. Then he remembered the one felled by the cowboy's bullet. He looked for it as he climbed down the incline beside the dugout. The wet beneath his feet gave way; he fell and rolled over several times. "Not again!" he whispered, lying still for a moment. With slow, painful movements, he stood and looked at himself. "Damn." He picked up his stick and looked around, spotting the blackened body of the prairie dog. "At least that cowboy didn't kill me like he did you. But he tried. He surely tried."

21

As soon as rain put out the prairie fire, Angela rode out on Ghost to look for Jason. Chances were he had been burned, maybe killed. She thought of greeting the dawn with him and found herself blinking back tears.

When she had seen smoke out toward Snake Mountain, she knew

Jason was in trouble. If he started the fire himself, which seemed likely, he was safe enough because he could go upwind. But if the fire started upwind from him, he might not make it. I would live through a spring fire, she affirmed, but then I know the ways of the prairie, know better than to take off across the prairie on foot with a lightning storm on the way.

Ghost didn't like running on the burnt ground, but he did it. She pushed him hard.

Then she saw Jason, stumping along, looking like a tar baby. Before Ghost came to a complete stop, she leaped to the ground, landing beside Jason. "You burned?"

"No. Good morning again, Angela."

She walked around him, inspecting him from head to foot. "Your hand, lemme see that hand." He held it up. "Mesquite thorns. Bet they burn like fire."

"They sting a little."

Angela burst into laughter. "You are sure enough a sight. Like a monster from a horror movie. How's that leg?"

"It hurts some. I'm a bit impatient with it, I'm afraid. I want it to do things it cannot do so soon after getting out of the plaster cast."

"You need to be riding the rest of the way to the ranch. Old Ghost there won't tolerate nobody but me riding him. I'll get back to the ranch, saddle up a horse for you, and get back here in a jiffy."

"No. I've never been on a horse. I'd better walk."

"Then I'll walk with you and you lean on me. That cedar stick you got ain't much."

"It'll do. If I lean on you, you'll get dirty. Besides, I'm too heavy."

"Hell, gimme your arm." She took Jason's stick and tossed it aside. "Over my shoulder, like that, yeah. I been dirtier than you. And I might be little, but I'm tough as a stump. I told you that at the airport when I took your suitcase to the pickup, remember?"

Jason took an experimental step, leaning on her when he put weight on his bad leg. "You're amazing."

"Yeah, I know."

"What about your horse?"

"Ghost? There ain't a blade of grass left out here to distract him. He'll follow me home like a dog."

They walked toward the ranch. Angela could tell Jason enjoyed the closeness of her, and she liked that. "Soon as we get them thorns outta you and get that leg rested up, I'm going to teach you to ride so you don't have to go out before dawn on foot, like you did this morning."

"So I can go with you to greet the morning sun?"

"I didn't say that. Maybe sometime."

"You're beautiful in the morning light."

She stopped walking and pushed back to look at him. "Get this straight. What you and me did this morning had nothing to do with looking beautiful to one another. If I wanted, I could find lots of places to strip for cowboys to tell me how beautiful I am. And they'd do it, too, hoping to score big. Cowboys seem to all have the same thing on their mind, and it don't matter a lot if the women they drool over wants what they want or not."

"You don't like me telling you that you're beautiful?"

"I didn't say that either. I'm telling you that greeting the sun like this morning has nothing to do with sex, and if you think different, that's your business, and you can go about facing the dawn however you damn well please—but do it on your own."

"No, it wasn't about sex, Angela, even if I happened to notice you in the process."

"I noticed you, too. And I noticed you didn't go to pawing around me like a cowboy would have under the circumstances. You knew what it meant to me out there on the prairie, I could tell. I grew up in these parts, but I always felt different from others around here, and being different is dang hard in West Texas, I can tell you. I learned fast not to let on that I was different in any way. And it has been lonely, Jason. Lonely. Here I am, in my mid-twenties, and this morning was the first time I ever dared share the morning sun the way it feels best to see it. That's why I gave you a hug, even if we were buck naked in front of each other for the first time in our lives. Not to try for getting you interested in sex. For sharing. For letting me feel it's okay to be different. That's why I told you thanks. Now let's get you home and bathed and get that hand looked at." They resumed walking.

"I would like you to teach me to ride."

"And shoot, too. I'll show you how to handle a pistol and a rifle."

Jason stopped walking.

"You okay?"

"Yes. Yes. It's just that, well, I'm afraid of guns."

"That's damn smart of you, I'd say. I'm scared of them, too—anybody with any sense would be. That's why you need to learn to handle them proper."

"Is it necessary for a Texan to know how to shoot a gun?"

"Maybe not for a city Texan, but out here it is. What if you came across a diamondback?"

"A what?"

"Diamondback. Rattler. You know, a snake."

"I saw one this morning, a wonderful creature. You would have shot it, I suppose. But I liked it. I like snakes, Angela."

"You would think different if it came at you, shaking its tail so it buzzed and striking at you with its fangs. You would think different if your horse got snake-bit. After living out here a while, you will go to shooting rattlers. And skunks."

"No, Angela, I will not."

"You got a lot to learn."

They walked on in silence. "I watched a man shoot a prairie dog this morning."

"Yeah? Who?"

"I don't know. A cowboy sitting by an old dugout. He offered me coffee, then he shot the prairie dog. For no reason at all. He just shot it. When I objected, he threatened to shoot me."

"This man—did he have black hair and a skimpy little mustache?"

"Yes. He shot that animal for the pure love of killing, I think."

"Lint. You ran into Lint Bodark out there. He's a dangerous man, Jason. You better study ways to avoid him. He's the one who shot at us on the road coming back from the airport, and like as not he killed my dog and the shepherd puppy Hyram bought for me."

"Why, Angela? Why did he shoot at us? Does he want to kill you?"

"Sometimes, yes, if he's been drinking."

"But why?"

"Long time ago, when I was young and ignorant about men, I married Lint Bodark. He used to treat me nice, back then. But he done too many mean things. I left him. Filed for a divorce. He told me he would never let me divorce him, that he would kill me first. He said it when he was drunk, but he meant it. He meant it." She stopped walking and stepped back from Jason. "He set the fire."

"I think so, yes."

"God. Now he's after you. That man is for sure crazy. Jason, it's a wonder that you're still alive. How did you get away from the fire?"

Angela listened to Jason's account of his running, of falling into a gully, then into a pool in the canyon. She nodded. "You did the right thing. He might still be about, though I doubt it. I better check. Come here, Ghost!"

She got on the horse. "This silly English saddle ain't my idea. But I fixed it up so I could carry this." She pulled a rifle from a leather slot she had attached to the saddle. Before Jason could object, she wheeled the horse about and rode off.

Minutes later, she returned, still carrying the rifle. "Ain't nobody around, but we better get on back." She dismounted and stepped close to take his arm over her shoulder.

This time Jason seemed less fond of being so close to her. He felt stiff and aloof. "Would you shoot a prairie dog?"

"You bet. So would you after you had a horse go down under you from stepping in one of the holes they booby-trap the prairie with. First you would have to shoot the horse for having a broke leg, then you would go to shooting the pesky little critters that made you shoot the horse."

"Someone that could shoot an animal could shoot a person."

"Damn right." Angela felt her neck color. "You're damn right. Anybody with any sense would, if it came down to it. You would shoot Lint, if he happened to come at you with a mind to do you harm and you had a gun handy."

"Have you ever seen a person get shot?"

"No. And neither have you."

"Yes. I saw a murder. When I first arrived in this country."

"Bull."

"In the Los Angeles airport. Angela, if you knew, really knew what it's like to see a person shot to death, you couldn't be so casual in talking about shooting people. You want to hear what it's like to see a person killed by a bullet? You want to hear about the bits of hair and bone landing on the counter, the blood spattering people all around the woman that got shot? You want to hear about the way she lay, her face mostly gone and her brains running out of the skull like bloody globs of tapioca pudding, running through her hair and onto the floor? That's what it would be like to watch someone you shot, Angela—to stand there over that kind of horror, holding the pistol, knowing that you were the cause of what you were seeing. It wouldn't be just a mechanical act, pulling a trigger and seeing your victim close her eyes like she was going to sleep, not like that at all. It would be blood and spilled brains and death. Death."

Jason stopped walking. Angela turned to him. She wiped at the tears streaking through the soot on his cheeks.

22

Jason stopped in the doorway to the kitchen when Hyram began speaking. "A few days with some rain has busted the drought, says here in the *Canyon News*. Anybody that looked outside recently knows that. That burnt grass out toward Snake Mountain seems to be coming back right fast. Ain't it a pleasure reading hot news items in a weekly? Here's another one. Says Texans own enough firearms to give ever' man, woman and child in the state five of them if they was averaged out, though why anyone would give arms to a child is beyond me." Hyram lowered the newspaper and looked at Angela.

She adjusted the flame under a pan sizzling with bacon, then scooped bacon out and set it to drain on a plate covered with paper towels.

"I like seeing how you do that," Hyram said.

"What?"

"That little trick with the spatula and the bacon, turning them out so perfect like that."

"You just like my cooking." She turned to the oven to check the biscuits. Jason went to the cabinet near Angela.

Hyram lifted the newspaper again. "It's more'n that."

"And just what is that supposed to mean?"

"I believe you know. Morning, Jason."

"Good morning Hyram, Angela."

"Don't stand over me like that. I can't abide a man standing over me. Sit at the table. You want bacon and eggs, or what?"

"That boy wants or what, iffn you ask me."

"I didn't. And offering eggs wasn't entirely a joke." Angela put her hands on her hips and turned to Jason. "Well?" she demanded.

"Yes, please, but only two pieces. My system isn't accustomed to so much oil yet." Jason took a bowl from the cabinet. "I'll have some cold cereal, and I can get it. You don't have to wait on me."

"Doubling up, are you? Two pieces. Most you've eaten up until now is one, so I guess that's some progress toward eating real Texas food. You really like to eat them raw oats and twigs in that cereal?"

"He does, for a fact. The boy is a veggie terrian."

"I'm trying to get over it. I drink milk and—"

"Milk!" Hyram coughed. "You call that talcum powder you mix up milk?"

"I eat fish. Sometimes I like fish, if it isn't fried."

"A body shouldn't live without red meat," Angela said.

"I can. I do."

"You going to campus today?" Hyram asked.

"He ain't going."

"I'm not?" Jason, surprised, looked at Angela. She stood over the stove, splashing hot grease over the yellow part of four eggs.

"Nope. Today you learn to ride a horse."

"Yeah?" Hyram said. He folded the newspaper. "You finally teaching him a proper way to get around?"

"Not with him wearing shorts and sneakers."

"Saturday," Hyram said. "Today is Saturday. Angela, you know what that means."

"That we leave for New Mexico early tomorrow morning so you can buy tack for the next auction. I remember. And, yes, I'm packed and ready for the trip."

"That ain't what I had in mind. Feed stores are closed on Saturdays."

"You know I always ride out with my rifle."

"Strap that little pop gun to your belt. And take my nine millimeter."

"Hyram, you'll have me looking like a Mexican bandit."

"You take it, okay?"

"Yeah. Okay. The nine millimeter. Here you go, one Hyram breakfast special." She set a plate of bacon, eggs, biscuits, grits and cream gravy in front of Hyram. "And for you, a saucer with two measly strips of bacon."

"I don't understand," Jason said. Why, he was about to ask, should Angela go out armed like a central American guerrilla?

"Simple," Hyram said. "I grew up on food like this. You try a real meal of it just once, and you'll never go back to eating those twigs and drinking that watery milk."

"No—I mean—"

"He knows what you mean, Jason."

"You teach him to ride. And to shoot, if you can figure out a way to make him pick up a firearm. Blow in his ear, maybe." Hyram laughed.

Angela pushed her plate toward Hyram. "You eat this, Hyram," she said. "I got no appetite."

"How come?"

"Don't know. I feel all jittery and nervous. For no reason."

"Maybe you got reason enough. Reason enough. I remember being young, once." Hyram looked at Jason.

Jason noticed the look. He picked up a piece of bacon and realized that he didn't feel like eating, either, though he thought his problem had to do with all the talk about weapons. But he ate anyway, forcing himself, making it a mechanical act, like filling a car with gas.

After breakfast, he went to his room to change into his western clothes, as Angela insisted. He looked in the mirror, astonished as he had been the night they went to the Crystal Pistol to see himself as a cowboy. "It's an illusion," he said aloud, "just an illusion."

Outside he found Angela wearing a nylon backpack. She was putting a saddle on a swaybacked horse that appeared to ignore her. She cinched up the saddle, waited a moment, then pulled on the cinch again. "You watch this, Jason. Dawg Meat is like most horses. He'll puff up like a toad, hoping to keep you from getting the saddle tied on proper. You watch for that, then wait a bit and pull her tighter. If you don't, like as not the saddle will start slipping when you least want it to, and it could dump you on the ground."

"Dog Meat? That is the name of this horse?"

"Nope. D-A-W-G Meat. Say it right, Jason. Dawg Meat."

"Dawg Meat," Jason said.

Angela laughed. She attached a canteen to the saddle horn.

"You haven't ridden out to greet the dawn since we did it together."

"You been watching out your window every morning?"

"Yes."

"Then you seen the reason of it. Rain. Come here and climb into the saddle. No, no—not from that side. Some horses would bite you for getting on them on that side. Dawg Meat wouldn't, but like as not he would look at you like you was crazy."

"I am crazy for trying to ride a horse. Do you really want me to become a Texan like Lint Bodark?"

"That's it—put your foot right there. You did that like you done it before. And you better not turn out like Lint. How about like Hyram?"

The saddle felt odd to Jason, like sitting on a barrel. "This is a first."

"Dawg Meat knows it, too. Here." She handed him the reins. "From now on, you get a grip on these before you climb on the horse. You guide the horse with these, but don't go to jerking right and left with them. Dawg Meat has a tough mouth and won't mind too much, but some horses will take exception to having that bit jerked around. Just sort of hold the reins on the side of Dawg Meat's neck when you want to turn. Dawg Meat will feel what you're doing and obey. To stop, pull back, but not too hard."

Jason watched Angela get on Ghost, a feat he was certain he could never perform. Ghost was gigantic and more than a little skittery. "Do you always ride such a big horse?"

"Usually. Least ways I have ever since I tamed Ghost. And don't you go to commenting on this funny little pancake of a saddle. I only use it because Ghost won't tolerate the regular kind."

"Where are we going?"

"That depends on how you and Dawg Meat get along. If you can ride him with no problems, we just might go for a picnic on Snake Mountain."

23

Jason watched Angela ride ahead of him. She looked tiny, like a doll perched on the giant horse—and so pretty.

Then he noticed the pistol strapped to one hip. Why hadn't he seen it before? he wondered. Am I becoming immune to their violence or what? With a start, he realized that a rifle butt protruded from a leather slot right in front of his leg. They call that the rifle boot, Jason thought, remembering the term from reading he had done about Texas when he lived in Kuala Lumpur. Back then he assumed that a rifle boot was something of the past, something that vanished with the closing of the frontier and existed these days only in western novels.

But there it was. And there he was, riding across a prairie, armed like an Old West desperado. And Angela, there in front of him—with that pistol on her hip and tucked somewhere among the leather pouches of her saddle Hyram's nine-millimeter pistol. What need had she of such instruments? Did she plan to get into another gun battle with her estranged husband? Would she want him to watch while she shot snakes and coyotes?

Jason thought of the red-headed man in the Los Angeles airport: the man must have been a hunter, spending weekends in the hills outside the cities of California shooting rabbits and hawks and maybe herons and house finches, for all Jason knew—shooting little warm-blooded creatures in preparation for the day when he would destroy a human being by pointing at her head with an iron finger and squeezing the mechanism for death. Thinking about all the blood flowing from the animals and birds that the man no doubt killed, and remembering Suppriah bleeding on the airport floor made Jason dizzy. He caught himself leaning in the saddle.

"You okay?"

"No."

"No?" She laughed. "You look mighty good. Couldn't anybody tell by looking that you ain't a real Texan. And you know what they say. They say appearance is the first step to reality. Maybe, just maybe, what a person appears to be is for a fact what he is, you know, inside."

He rode up beside her so he could see her face. Was this Angela speaking? Did she really think about such matters? But why not, he thought: she did, after all, perform that renewal ritual, nude on the prairie, arms lifted to the rising sun.

"But lookit you, riding like a pro. I say we head on into the canyon, sit a spell by the cottonwoods, and then go on up to Snake Mountain for that picnic."

She turned Ghost toward the barbed-wire fence, dug her heels into his flanks, and leaned low against him while he ran. Jason stared in astonishment as the big horse leaped the gate. Angela rode back to the fence and dismounted. "I'll open the gate for you. Dawg Meat could no more jump like that than he could fly to Venus."

Jason rode through the gate and she closed it behind him. "How did you teach Ghost to do that?"

"I didn't. He taught me. I'll tell you about it when we get down into the canyon."

When they came to the place where they had greeted the rising sun, she reined Ghost to a halt and looked at Jason. "This is one of my favorite places, even if the grass ain't healed up proper from the burn.

"I love it, too. Now."

"I'll confess to being a tad scared you would act the wrong way when I invited you to undress." She lowered her voice to almost a whisper. "Truth is, I respect you for being a gentleman like no other I ever met. You didn't stare at me. Not like old Ben Lippman, who gawked like man at a smoker before he run his truck into the fence."

"Ben Lippman?"

"Forget it. That's a whole different story."

"Angela, this morning at breakfast something almost came to me. I think I know what it was, now. Hyram—he's in love with you, isn't he?"

"No." She urged Ghost on. "Maybe. I don't know. I don't have time for that sort of thing, not now."

"Another thing," Jason urged Dawg Meat to catch up with her, "about the last few days—"

"And look up ahead, how the prairie is starting to green up from the burn that Lint put there. Buffalo grass comes popping back fast if it gets a smattering of rain like we been having."

"Angela, except for the walk back from the prairie fire, you been avoiding me since we met at dawn on the prairie. Even Hyram commented on it."

"Hyram did?"

"You don't volunteer much information, do you?"

"Sometimes. What do you want to know?"

"Since you helped me walk back after the fire, you have avoided being around me. Why?"

"You really don't know, do you?"

"I don't, and that's a natural-born fact."

She laughed. "You got that from Hyram or maybe Odom. Good. You look like a Texan and now are starting to talk like one, even if the accent ain't proper yet. I ought to warn you that there ain't many Texas men would ask a direct question about a girl's feelings like you just done. I been busy. Working with Hyram's books out at the horse auction. Keeping the place from degenerating into the chaos I found when he first hired me."

"That isn't an answer."

"It's all you get for now. Let's get going." She urged Ghost on.

"Wait. There's something else."

"Not now, there ain't." She looked back at him. "Get Dawg Meat moving, cowboy."

She led him to the dugout where he had talked with Lint, then she dismounted. "Get off of Dawg Meat. No, no—get off on the left side. Yeah, like that."

Jason backed away from the horse, looking at it with distrust. It nosed the ground for grass and seemed to have forgotten about him.

Angela took something out of a saddlebag. "Come here."

Jason started toward her, saw what she had in her hand, and stopped. She worked the mechanism of the nine-millimeter pistol and aimed at something.

"Are you going to shoot a prairie dog?"

"Nope. It would take too long for them to get the nerve to come out of their holes. I'm going to teach you to shoot this pistol."

"Do I need to know that?"

She turned to him and took a deep, exasperated breath. "Jason," she spoke with inflection, as to a child, "I ain't planning nothing that would hurt you." He stepped back. "Okay, okay, dang it. You don't even touch the pistol. But at least watch. No harm in that. Watch me get a couple of shots off, then we forget about shooting and move on toward Snake Mountain. Deal?"

Jason bit his lip. "Deal." He stepped closer to her.

"This is the safety. Locked is here. Click it like this to release the safety so the pistol can fire. Then point, like this, like you was just pointing a finger, and squeeze the trigger, gentle like, slow and easy."

The weapon barked and jumped in her hand, and dust flew into the air a few meters away. Jason felt the sound like a blow to his chest, and the image of the woman in the airport came to him, her face distorted in death, then came the image of the prairie dog, headless, toppling from its mound. He put his hands to his temples and bent forward. Angela fired another shot. "It's all simple, really. Just point and squeeze." She fired another shot, then turned to look at Jason.

"Are you finished?"

"Look at you, holding your head like I done something terrible." She snapped the safety on the pistol. "Ghost! You get over here! For your information, Mister Jason, I done nothing but squirt a little lead out of a tube onto the ground. Ghost!"

He watched her walk in a huff over to her horse and put the pistol into a saddlebag. She caught the reins and mounted. "Get on your horse, Mister Jason, and see if you remember how to ride."

Jason caught up with her just as she veered off into an arroyo that cut down toward the canyon. "Just let Dawg Meat have his head," she warned. "He knows the way down. You just hang on and watch him get you where you want to go. Most flat-land horses don't know diddle-dee squat about climbing around hills, but I got Dawg Meat and Ghost trained to it."

He gripped the saddle horn while Dawg Meat went down an impossible incline, edged off to the left around the rim of a drop-off that made Jason's stomach churn, then angled down a rocky path to the edge of the creek beside the canyon wall. Without waiting for instructions, the horse waded across the creek to join Angela and Ghost.

He looked back, trying to trace the path Dawg Meat had taken into the canyon, but it was no use. It didn't look possible that a trail existed among the rocks and juniper bushes on the side of that steep incline. He sighed. Angela laughed. "I understand. First time I rode down that spot, I thought me and the horse would tumble to our deaths for sure."

"What does 'diddle-dee squat' mean?"

"Depends on how you use it."

"Are you still angry?"

"Hell, I never was angry. Whatever made you think that?"

Jason shook his head. "Where to next?"

"To the cottonwood grove." She pointed.

"Will you answer a question now?"

"Nope. Wait till we get to the grove, then we'll negotiate."

They approached the same trees Jason saw after he had fallen into the creek while running from the prairie fire. Beyond the trees stood Snake Mountain, rising orange and brown from the canyon floor.

Angela led the way into some thick brush. "Watch for cactus, and stay on the path."

"Those little purple trees look out of place. What are they?"

"Plums. They are sort of out of place. Got planted here back in the Great Depression by some boys in the tree army, Hyram said. Might be some ripe plums on them a bit later in the summer. People around here call them hog plums. Good for jelly."

"And all those vines look like grape vines.

"Close. Those are currants. Some make jelly out of them, too." Angela vanished around a bend in the trail.

As he moved Dawg Meat into the brush, Jason caught a glimpse of movement off to his left, toward a bend in the creek, something large like a deer—only he knew it wasn't a deer because something about it flashed in the sun, like a metallic gleam. He looked around but saw nothing. Maybe I'm just getting paranoid, living here among all these gun-toting Texans, he thought. Five. Each one of them owns five firearms.

As Dawg Meat moved into the plums and juniper, Jason could see only a few feet in any direction. Branches brushed his legs and arms, and currant vines seemed to cover everything.

He came to a clearing dominated by two giant cottonwoods. One tree trunk, two meters thick, ran along the ground then lifted above the brush. Angela sat on the horizontal part of the tree; Ghost grazed the grass beside the other tree, which grew straight up, throwing spotty shade over the entire clearing.

"Give Dawg Meat a rest and join me up here."

Jason dismounted. He rubbed the insides of his legs, which felt numb. Angela laughed. "You'll toughen up soon enough."

"Do I tie up the horse?"

"Nope. Let it move around for the grass. These horses know better than to wander off. And if they do, why I'll just run them down. See that twig by your foot? Before you climb up here, pick it up for me."

Jason walked up the cottonwood trunk, amazed by its size and the way it grew. He sat beside Angela. She took the twig from him, examined it, then snapped it in two. "Look where I broke it."

In the center of the twig Jason found a perfect five-pointed star. "That's beautiful."

"You break it anywhere, and there's a star. It's easier to break where there's a bumpy spot that looks like a joint. I knew you would like the star, same as I do."

Jason looked at her with appreciation, then turned toward a flutter of red motion. "A cardinal," he pointed. "Male. Red as a drop of blood. Look at it—surely it has to be one of the world's most beautiful birds. And there, the female, more drab, on that other branch."

"You know American birds?"

"Only from books. Listen. A woodpecker. They sound the same the world over. There it is, hopping around the trunk of that tree. Black and white with just a touch of red on its head. On the way over, just above the canyon wall, I saw a pair of Mississippi kites."

"Them hawks that flew over the creek while we entered the canyon?"

"Yes. So magnificent. I love the way they ride the air currents with hardly a flap of their wings."

"Lint used to shoot them. For sport. I guess I never thought much about it, seeing as how they was hawks."

Jason glanced at her. Her face looked intense, focused on the cardinals. "Would you shoot a hawk?"

"Was that your question? Don't ask me that. Yes." She looked at him. "You think less of me now."

"Would you shoot one of those cardinals?"

"No. Don't be ridiculous."

"There it is, then. Hawks and rattlesnakes." Jason fell silent. They watched Ghost and Dawg Meat move to the edge of the clearing where the taller grass grew.

"Explain what you mean by hawks and rattlesnakes. You mean that I would shoot them?"

"Not just that you would kill them, but the reason for it. They're both predators. You hate them for that. In nature, one predator will kill another that comes into its territory, like a tiger in India will kill a lesser cat. Predators do not like or trust one another."

"And I am a predator," Angela whispered.

"The deadliest. But it doesn't have to be that way. Even Texans might learn to see the beauty in other predators."

"Damn." Angela pushed herself off the tree, walked a few steps away and stood with her back to him. "Damn. You asked why I been heading out every morning right after cooking breakfast, why I been avoiding you. That's why. The kind of things you're saying. The way you make me see myself." She turned with a quick motion and looked at Jason. "You see me different, and that makes me have to see the way you see. And I'm somebody who don't look so good. Not so good at all."

24

Angela put a thumb and a finger into the corners of her mouth and whistled. Ghost came to her. "Get Dawg Meat," she told Jason. "We're heading to Snake Mountain. I'll show you the bed rock on top of the mesa." She mounted her horse.

"Bedrock? Don't you mean caprock?" In a matter of seconds Jason had watched Angela shift from almost crying in what he thought of as a feminine way to whistling like a crusty old rancher to call a horse. He sat on the cottonwood, staring. Angela still had a wet glimmer in her eyes, though nothing else about her revealed any softness at all.

Sybil Redbear surprises me, he thought, but she is never anything but a woman. Angela goes from being a woman to being a cowboy, and it's always a shock. He shook his head.

"Move on out, cowboy." Angela gave him a stern look. Jason mounted Dawg Meat and followed Angela through the brush.

At the base of the mesa, they dismounted beside a juniper. Angela took the rifle from the saddle boot. "Don't you say nothing about this here rifle. Watch." She worked the bolt, then held up a cartridge. "I'm carrying this in my pocket. Without it in the firing chamber, this rifle might as well be just a stick of hardwood. You carry that saddlebag and one of the canteens." She turned to the mesa.

Jason took the bag and canteen and followed her. She vanished into some brush and appeared on a ledge about ten feet above him. "Strap them things to your belt so you can use your hands for climbing."

He caught up with her at a place where the path up the mesa vanished. She took an enormous folding knife from her pocket, snapped it open, and began gouging out handholds in the orange dirt of the cliff. "Ain't been here since Regan . . ." she hesitated. "Not for a coon's age. These notches wash out with a few rains, so I have to make new ones. Don't trust them overly because they crumble. Keep your hand on a root or a rock when you put your foot into one." She stepped back, looking at the top of the mesa above them and threw the rifle up to it.

Jason watched her gouge more holes in the cliff as she worked her way to the ledge. She climbed with a fierce determination similar to the attitude Jason cultivated for a tennis match. And, he noted, she was so beautiful.

Then he looked at the white ring on the hip pocket of her jeans, a ring put there from the wear of carrying something in the pocket. He had seen similar rings on the jeans of young men at the university in Canyon when he had gone to campus to practice on the backboard of the tennis courts.

She pulled herself to the top of the mesa and looked back at Jason. "Come on up." She stood and brushed at the dirt on her jeans.

When Jason reached the top, he found himself looking at a barren and flat summit, at prairie grass broken here and there by a mesquite or a bare patch of rock. "Why is this called 'Snake Mountain?' It isn't a mountain, and snakes wouldn't live up here."

"Don't bet on it. I seen a rattler up here one time. But forget that. There," Angela pointed. "The north side of the mesa. Come on." She took his arm and led him to a flat rock near the cliff. "This is what I call the bed rock. Sit down with me."

"Why do you call it that?" He took the canteen and bag from his belt and sat beside her.

"Because ever since I was enough of a grown-up to think about such matters, I thought one day I would make love on this rock. If I ever found the combination of the right man and the right time. But it never happened. Least not to me. I'll bet the Indians did it here, though. On cold days when a blizzard drives in from the north, this spot is maybe twenty degrees warmer because the wind whips up from below and makes a pocket of still air right here. Indians figured that out, them that lived on the plains before this place got settled, and they came up here to ride out the cold spell."

"You never came up here with Lint?"

"I asked him, when we was first dating. But he said only a dang fool would do that much climbing for no reason at all." She laughed. "He didn't know about the bed rock, or his tongue would have been hanging out at the thought of scoring with me up here. I wasn't about to tell him without him climbing up here first. I don't want to talk about Lint."

She dropped her backpack, dug through it and handed Jason a sandwich. "Boiled egg," she said, "with a dab of mustard and a bit of low-fat cream cheese. On whole wheat. Hyram said you won't touch white bread, not yet, anyway, and you treat anything oily like it was edible as bear grass. On my sandwich, I put some mayonnaise, which Hyram claims you won't eat at all, so yours didn't get any."

“Thanks.” Jason looked close at her while she ate. “Did you bring me up here to make love?”

Angela pushed her food into her cheek. “Don't ask that. Ask me something else.” She smiled. He could see a smear of grease on her lower lip, and gobs of white bread stuck like plaster on her teeth. He looked away, surveying the canyon below them.

“Okay. Are you taking birth control pills?”

“Jason White, you cut that out.”

“Sorry. You mentioned down there when we sat on the cottonwood tree that you would tell me a story if we ever got to the top of Snake Mountain.”

“Did I say that? I musta thought you would never survive the climb. But you were a regular billy goat.”

“So what's the story?”

“Ghost. You keep eying that stud and shaking your head. Odom don't like him, either, and Hyram won't go close to him. They call him an outlaw, which he ain't.”

She fell silent. Jason waited, watching her finish her sandwich, then rinse her mouth with a sip from the canteen. She took a beach towel from her backpack and spread it on the rock, stretched out on the towel and propped her head on one arm. “Turn loose a bit. Lie here.” She patted the towel beside her, “Maybe cover your face with your hat. This here's a place to enjoy, a place to get away from Hyram and Odom and the other men who complicate my life. A place to warm up in the sun. Relax, Jason.”

He did as she directed. The rock beneath the towel felt warm. “What about Ghost?” he prompted.

“Luke Davis over at the Davis ranch was about to take a knife to him. I was there with Hyram to buy horses when Luke went to stropping his knife on his boot. I looked at Ghost, standing seventeen hands high, proud as a stud ought to be, and I busted into tears.” She put her head on his shoulder and lay against him.

Jason stroked her face with his fingertips, drew her closer so their lips could touch. She put a leg over him, then pulled herself on top, keeping her lips on his. Her tongue was a tiny, hard knob probing between his lips and teeth; her red hair fell over his face and neck. She pushed herself up, her knees straddling his chest. “You sure enough are beautiful, Jason. Unsnap my blouse.”

As he did so, she unbuttoned his shirt.

25

Jason liked the feeling of the sun on his nude body, liked the way Angela lay against him. It amazed him that they were still lying on the beach towel—except for one of his legs, and it felt comfortable enough on the warm rock. Bed rock, he remembered her calling it, and he smiled.

She had cried out only once, a soft, vocalized catching of her breath. Jason savored the memory. Then he remembered the thing he had glimpsed crawling off to his right, just on the edge of the bed rock. In the passion of the moment, the image had floated on the edge of awareness, then he simply forgot about it.

But afterward, he could identify the image. A spider—and a large one. Jason struggled to sit up. Angela resisted. "What is it, honey?"

"I don't know. I thought I saw a gigantic spider over there."

She sat beside him and pushed a strand of her hair from her face. "How big?"

He held up a thumb and finger, spread wide. She nodded. "A tarantula, then. Probably a female."

"Tarantula?" Jason stood up. Angela laughed.

"You still got a lot to learn. They don't bite, unless you mash one, and even then, like as not you won't get bit."

"Can't a tarantula kill you?"

"Not unless you die mighty easy. I understand it would feel like a wasp sting, though I never talked personal with someone that could vouch for it. Come here." She held up her arms. "And the answer to your question is yes."

"Yes a tarantula can kill you?"

"No, not that question. Yes, I am taking birth control pills." She drew him down to her. "You're a good man, sir. You got something special about you when it comes to loving. Patience. Gentleness. I was afraid it would be over for you in a couple of minutes, but you stayed with me. You're good. Good. Are you a religious man, Jason?"

"That's a hard word, religious. What do you mean?"

"I'm not sure. God, maybe. I once believed in the God the preacher talked about in the church I had to go to as a kid. And you know what he looked like?"

"God? You believe you saw God?"

"Back then, maybe. He looked a lot like my Daddy. Big. Stern. I used to say prayers at night and see God standing up in the clouds with a razor strop in his hand, looking like he was about to whop me with it, if he could reach me, which he couldn't on account of being way up there in the clouds. I didn't like God, but I kept telling myself that I loved him on account of what the preacher said about everybody having to love God. I didn't like my Daddy none, either, even if I didn't admit it to myself. Did you ever have such a vision of God, Jason?"

"No. I remember arguing about God with a neighbor when I was a little kid. He said God could do anything and I said then he could make a rock so big he couldn't pick it up and put it in his pocket, which meant he couldn't do everything."

Angela laughed and brushed the tips of her fingers across Jason's chest. "So you never saw God. But when you thought about God, you did the same as me. You thought he was a man. Well he ain't."

"What do you mean?"

"God ain't a stern man in the clouds holding a razor strop. God ain't a man at all."

"We agree there. I have no use for a personal God."

"Personal, yes. A man, no. God has to be personal. I think you felt God that morning we greeted the sun. God was the sun at that minute, even if God ain't the sun. I felt God here on the bed rock when you made me cry out for joy, and again when you cried out for holding me. God ain't a man or a woman. God is a knowing and a touching and an understanding. You don't think I'm weird, do you?"

"Weird? No. I think you know some things I need to work at learning."

She pulled away from him with a quick jerk. The movement startled Jason. "What is it?"

"Ghost." She picked up the rifle, jumped to her feet and ran to the edge of the cliff they had scaled. "Somebody's down there." Jason thought he had never until then seen such a strange sight: a beautiful woman, nude, looking over the edge of a cliff while she clutched a rifle.

He watched her hurry back to the pile of clothes on the bed rock, pick up her jeans, and take the bullet out of a pocket. She inserted in into the rifle. Jason shook his head in disgust. Why does she assume that anyone who wanders close to her is somebody she ought to take a shot at? She just made love, just talked about God being understanding, and she thinks of shooting someone. He began dressing.

"Hurry with your clothes. We're going down. Something ain't right down there." She set the rifle aside and picked up her clothes.

When they got to the base of Snake Mountain, Angela said, "Somebody took the horses. But how did they manage Ghost?"

"Look." Jason pointed at a pair of boots protruding from behind some rocks. Angela took the pistol from her holster.

"Put that thing back," Jason snapped.

Angela, ignoring him, went to the rocks. "Lint. I hope that sucker is dead. But he ain't."

"Lint?"

Angela laughed. "Looks like he went to messing with Ghost, trying to get aholt of his reins so he could steal him, but Ghost got him, instead. Looks like Ghost kicked him in the head."

Jason looked at Lint. He lay in the sun, unconscious, in a patch of buffalo grass and dandelions, his head resting on a rock. Over one eye was a purple spot and blood from the back of his head stained the rock. He breathed in a labored way.

"Let him lie. Back in Colonel Goodnight's day, we would have slipped a noose around his neck and hanged him from a cottonwood. Wouldn't even bother to wake him up for the ceremony. That's what they did to horse thieves. Let's look for the horses. You go that way, and I'll go this." She left without waiting for a response.

Angela's husband, Jason told himself, kneeling beside the man. And I just made love with her. Damn.

The blood on the rock under Lint's head reminded Jason of the pool of blood around what was left of Suppriah's head there on the floor of the LA airport. He took off his shirt, poured water from the canteen on it, and dabbed at the purple spot over Lint's eye.

In Malaysia, a gash such as the one on the back of Lint's head would already be infected. He lifted Lint's head and looked at the wound.

The blood had coagulated, matting the hair into deep crimson clumps. Jason poured water over the back of Lint's head. Lint groaned and stirred but remained unconscious.

Jason picked him up and carried him to the shade of a juniper. It startled him to find Lint so heavy. He didn't seem like a big man—not like the Aussie who had broken Jason's leg—yet he felt heavy and solid.

Angela returned, riding a horse Jason had not seen before and leading Dawg Meat. "What are you messing around with him for? Let him be."

"He's hurt."

"So? He tried to kill you with that prairie fire, and he just now tried to steal our horses. Let him be. He'll not be thankful for your help."

Jason propped Lint's head so the wound would not be against the ground. "I'd try to help anyone hurt like this. Anyone." Especially, he added to himself, a man whose wife I just had sex with. So I'm helping out of guilt? No matter. Guilt is enough of a reason to behave in a civilized way. For a change.

"Suit yourself. I'm going after Ghost." She dropped Dawg Meat's reins and rode off.

I am suiting myself, Jason thought. But would I have washed the wound on his head and moved him into the shade if Angela and I had not made love? Jason shook his head. Maybe. Maybe.

Lint opened his eyes, but they seemed unfocused. "Are you okay?" Jason asked. Lint turned his head toward Jason, then clamped his eyes shut in pain. When he opened them again, they were fixed on Jason. "Likely you have a mild concussion. You ought to lie still and avoid straining yourself. And you need that scalp wound tended to. I've rinsed it some, but only with water."

Lint stared, his face showing no emotion at all.

Angela returned, riding Ghost. She dismounted, walked up to Lint and kicked the sole of one of his boots. "You miserable asshole."

"The man is hurt, Angela."

"He ain't hurt bad enough, and he ain't much of a man."

"We need to get help for him."

"No we don't. Ain't nothing wrong with him but a couple of bumps on his head. Getting kicked in the head by a horse is part of the life of a cowboy, though usually they don't deserve it like Lint does. Soon as we leave, he will get up and ride out of here like nothing happened. He might take a notion to fire off a few shots at us, but I emptied his rifle and took the cartridges from his saddlebag. You hear that, Lint?" She kicked his boot again. "I done took the bullets, so you might as well go on home like a kicked dog. Which is what you are." She turned to mount Ghost.

Jason watched Lint. His eyes followed Angela, but Jason wasn't sure Lint saw anything he was looking at.

"Get on Dawg Meat," Angela said. "We're leaving."

"You go ahead, Angela. I'll try to get this man to some medical help."

"Why are men so dadburned stubborn about being stupid? Do it, then, but don't come crying to me when he kicks you in the teeth." She turned Ghost and took off at a gallop.

Jason looked around for Lint's horse. Did Angela lead it off somewhere? Could I catch it? Probably not. And if I did find it, would the animal kick me in the head like Ghost did Lint?

After tossing his wet, bloody shirt on a bush, Jason took Dawg Meat's reins. "Let me help you up. Don't strain or you might start the bleeding again. Likely your concussion has your brain swollen some, and you might pass out. We shouldn't even be moving you, but I don't know what else to do." He slid one arm under Lint's back and lifted him to his feet. Lint cooperated in a passive way. "Can you get on the horse? I'll lead it out of the canyon and see about getting you to a hospital."

With urging, Lint put his foot in the stirrup and fumbled his way onto the saddle. Jason took the reins and walked toward the canyon wall. He kept glancing back at Lint, who sat slumped forward, his empty-looking gaze fixed on Jason.

When they reached the creek, Jason looked for a place to cross. He walked along the bank, leading Dawg Meat toward a wide place where the water would be only ankle deep.

He looked back at Lint just in time to see a boot swinging toward his head. Jason jerked to one side, and the toe of Lint's boot caught him on the shoulder, spinning him around, off balance. He fell into the creek.

Jason landed in less than a foot of water, and his hands sank past the wrists in bottom mud. He struggled to his feet and looked at Lint.

Lint's eyes seemed to bore into Jason. "You stupid little pissant." Lint leaned forward and took the reins in a slow, insolent motion, keeping his eyes on Jason.

Muttering something to Dawg Meat, Lint pulled back hard on the reins. Dawg Meat walked backward several steps, then Lint turned the horse as expertly as Jason would turn a car. With one last glare at Jason, he pushed Dawg Meat into a trot.

How did he do that? Jason wondered. How did he make the horse walk backward? Surprised at the irrelevance of the question, Jason bent to wash the mud from his hands.

When he climbed up the bank, he found Angela sitting on Ghost with Lint's horse beside her. She threw her head back and laughed with genuine amusement. "Ain't you a sorry-looking sight."

26

"Lint made a bad trade, riding off on Dawg Meat and leaving Playboy. You get on Playboy, but go about it slow and easy. This horse is a tad skittery." Angela held out the reins.

"I thought you went back to the ranch."

"Are you kidding? And leave you with Lint Bodark? Even after a kick in the head from a horse, that man is more dangerous than anyone I know."

"I'm not afraid of Lint, Angela." Jason took the reins and muttered encouragement to Playboy, as he had seen Angela do with Ghost. He patted the horse on the neck, then climbed onto the saddle.

"You did that like a pro. Shoot, Playboy thinks you're just one of the boys. Maybe he likes half-naked cowboys. I got your shirt off that bush you hung it on, in case you're interested." Angela turned Ghost toward the shallow spot in the creek. "Ride up here beside me, cowboy."

"Why would Lint try to harm someone who was helping him?"

"Listen to you, Jason. You might be learning to ride like a cowboy, but you still talk funny. Say it this way: 'how come Lint kicked me in the crick?' Say it."

"How come Lint kicked me into the creek?"

"In, not into. And say crick proper. Come on. Crick."

"In the crick."

"Better. The drawl ain't right yet, but you're getting the hang of it. Lint didn't figure you was helping him. He figured you was lording it over him that you're strong enough to tote him about. It don't matter that he was knocked silly at the time. Thing is, you're bigger than Lint, and stronger. Which would be all right if you didn't come from someplace foreign. Maybe not all right, but not so bad. I seen Lint dang near hammer a cowboy into the floor just for shoving him aside in a bar. He took special pleasure in it because the cowboy was bigger and stronger. Keep this in mind Jason: a mean cowboy will always beat a strong one. Always. You're strong, but Lint is meaner than a treed bobcat. You ought to be scared of him, if you got good sense. I am."

She's right, Jason told himself. Whatever was I doing, saying I wasn't afraid of Lint? Trying to impress Angela? Myself? As if I needed to act macho, be macho. Jason shook his head in disgust. Some things about becoming a Texan are disgusting. Next I'll own five firearms and. . . . And what? Have sex with a cowboy's wife? "Shit," he said, and dug his heals into Playboy's flanks.

The horse went from a walk into a pounding run. Jason's hat flew off, and he gripped the saddle horn to keep from falling. He pulled the reins to the right, and Playboy crossed the creek, sending water flying. On the other bank, Jason pulled back on the reins and Playboy broke its run and stopped.

Angela picked up Jason's hat and rode up beside him. "Here." She handed him the hat. "Next time, cram it down to your ears before making Playboy run. He starts fast cause he's a quarter horse, bred to run like hell for short stretches. Look at his ears." Jason looked. Playboy's ears stood straight up in a perky way. "He loved it that you gave him his head and let him open up and run. Playboy loves to run. He ain't even breathing hard. Playboy can outrun Ghost for maybe a hundred yards, but over the long haul, there ain't a horse in the county that can beat Ghost."

"Thanks for getting my hat." Jason tried to look nonchalant, to cover up for how surprised and frightened he had been. He had thought to goose the horse into moving a bit faster, not to make it take off like a shot.

"Come on, Jason. We can get out of the canyon right over there." She pointed. "Playboy knows the way. Let the reins hang loose and don't ask him to run, not until we reach the top."

"I'm through running for the day."

"Good judgment, that. You want me to finish telling you what I started up on the bed rock, before something else came up?"

"About God?"

"No. I don't normally talk like that, Jason. But after we, uh, after, uh, oh shit. You know what I mean. So you want to hear about Ghost or what?"

"I do want to hear that story, Angela. But I need to say something first."

"So say it."

"What we did up there on the mesa. It wasn't right. I liked holding you, and what we did was wonderful. At the time. But it was wrong."

"That's pure bull, and you know it. Neither one of us is a Bible-thumper, and we ain't letting nobody tell us what to do with our bodies. Making love ain't evil."

"I didn't say that. I said wrong. Wrong for me. You're a married woman, Angela."

"That's a stack of meadow muffins. Married to Lint? Hell, me and him are finished. Least ways I'm done with him. Marriage is just a slip of paper, and soon enough another slip of paper called a divorce will be final. But my feelings are final right now. Don't you go to feeling guilty. Not about us."

Jason gave Playboy free rein, and the horse began climbing out of the canyon. When he reached the prairie overlooking the creek, Jason reined up until Angela came beside him. "I don't feel bad about you. Just about me. I need to back away from you some while I try to get straight what is going on with me. It's good that you and Hyram are about to take that buying trip into New Mexico tomorrow because that will give us both a little space."

"Don't turn away from me, Jason. Not now. Not after what we did on Snake Mountain."

"We need to cool down."

"Wrong."

"Please understand my position."

"Like you said, I'll be gone a few days. Then we'll talk about us, okay, cowboy?"

"Okay. Tell me about Ghost."

"Yeah. Where was I? Luke and his knife. Luke Davis nearly ruined Ghost. He would have cut him for sure, but when I seen what he was about, I busted into tears, like I told you. Hyram, he never can stand to see a girl cry, so he offered to buy Ghost for me."

While they rode beyond the canyon, Angela continued talking: "Luke laughed in a mean kind of way and allowed as how he would sell the horse on account of it being an outlaw. But he seen my tears and knew Hyram would pay more than he figured the horse was worth, just to please me. Luke got this cagey look on his face and named a real outrageous price for an outlaw horse, and Hyram took to dealing. Can't nobody out-deal Hyram, when it comes to horses."

When she and Hyram took Ghost back to his ranch, Angela decided to see what the horse was good for. "Stay clear of that outlaw," Hyram warned. "He nearly kilt Luke Davis, and he's as good with horses as anyone in the county. Said Ghost wouldn't tolerate a saddle on him when he tried to break the horse's spirit and make him into a usable cow horse."

Angela thought it wrong to break an animal's spirit, especially an animal as magnificent as Ghost. That was Lint's way, she told Jason, the breaking of the spirit. Lint trained horses with a board and a whip. He wanted the horse to obey and he cared nothing for how the horse felt about the matter.

But Angela cared. She put Ghost into the corral, got a sack of oats, and sat down in the center of the corral with the sack between her legs.

Ghost stayed away, but he kept throwing up his head and sniffing. Angela assumed he was smelling the oats. The horse circled her with caution, then came up from behind and put its nose against her neck. Angela sat rock still, thinking that Odom and Hyram would crap if they knew how she was submitting herself to possible danger. But she felt in no danger. What she mainly felt was surprise. Ghost seemed to have no interest in the oats, but he was plenty interested in her neck.

He tugged at her collar with his teeth, pulling her shirt down in the back, then sniffed where the collar had been. It was then that Angela understood. Ghost liked her perfume.

"I figured then and there," she told Jason, "that Ghost had been handled mainly by a woman—a woman who wore perfume. And I knew I had to find out more about Ghost's past so I could handle him better."

Angela took a photograph of the odd brand on Ghost's hip to the American Quarter Horse Association headquarters in Amarillo. Jim Goodhue, in charge of archives, looked at the photograph, then searched through some files. "That brand," he said, "is used only on a German breed of horses called Holstein. They tend to be big animals." He told Angela to call the American Equine Association for information.

A clerk in that organization said only a few registered German Holsteins had been brought to the United States. "Look under the horse's lip for a serial number tattooed on the gums," he said. "With that number, we can get you more information."

Angela found the number, and the Equine Association clerk used it to get the name and phone number of a David Brindle, who lived in St. Louis. Angela called him.

"A ghost from the past," David said in surprise when Angela told him how she had traced the horse to him. "Sure, I'll tell you about him. It's a sad story."

Ghost was a yearling when David bought it for his young wife, Julie. She spent much time training the horse, first to take an English riding saddle, then to jump. "She loved that horse," Brindle said. "And it followed her about like a pet. It did anything she asked of it, and the animal had real talent for jumping. Julie thought she might enter it in the Olympics. But she got cancer."

The disease spread like fire, David said, and as she grew thinner and closer to death, she spent increasing amounts of time with Ghost. "Probably," David told Angela, "her love of the horse extended her life by a few months."

When Julie died, Ghost mourned her absence. It wouldn't let anyone but David close, and it barely tolerated him. "I had to sell Ghost. The grief of the horse was a mirror of my own, and I got to where I couldn't stand to have it around."

"Did Julie wear perfume?" Angela asked.

"Perfume? Yes. Always. She said Ghost liked it."

That day Angela mail-ordered an English riding saddle. "Ghost wouldn't tolerate nothing else," she told Jason. "That's part of the reason he nearly killed Luke Davis, because the turkey kept coming at him with a big old Mexican saddle. And because Luke punched Ghost around, trying to break him to a saddle. All the time he was already saddle broke. To this," she indicated the saddle she sat on.

Angela cultivated the bond between her and Ghost. She always wore plenty of perfume, and she continued to handle Ghost with respect and kindness. "Ghost had to learn to trust again, after being knocked around by cowboys. But once I got that trust, he would do whatever I asked."

One of the things she asked was that Ghost jump fences. "He taught me to jump. I had never done it before, and the first few times really scared me. Odom and Hyram gigged me a bunch about riding on a funny-looking English saddle, but they had to laugh out of the other side of their mouths when me and Ghost jumped over gates they had to open to get their horses through. I would flat dust them whenever we rode out to check the cows."

"I seen you riding in on Lint's horse," Hyram said. Jason sat in the entryway, pulling off his boots. Angela and Odom were out in the corral, taking care of the horses. "You looked like an old west Indian, what with no shirt and that dark skin of yours. 'Cept for the hat and the saddle, of course. An Indian would be barebacked."

"I'm half Indian," Jason said.

"What? Oh, you mean your mama, her being Oriental Indian. I mean real Indian, you know, Comanches. Apaches. You could pass for one, if you shucked your shirt like you done and rode barebacked. And if you tied a rag round your head instead of wearing a hat."

"So I would go from being cowboy to Indian with a change of clothes?"

"You bringing Playboy in tells me that you two got crossed with Lint Bodark. Did Angela shoot him?"

"No." Jason stood up and rubbed the inside of his legs.

"Saddlesore, huh? That Playboy, he's a tough one to ride, especially when you're new to horses. You done good, riding Playboy. Where's Lint?"

"If he has any sense, he's in a doctor's office seeing about a couple of knocks on his head. He rode off on Dawg Meat."

"Dawg Meat. Ain't that the damndest thing. Lint on Dawg Meat. Was he drunk?"

"I doubt it, though he might have been drinking."

"If Lint took one drink, he was drunk. He ain't like ordinary folk, that Lint Bodark. He takes one drink, and he gets meanern a junkyard dog. Beats up on anybody who crosses him and some that don't. He whupped Angela and Regan so bad and so many times that she hauled his ass into the courthouse over in Canyon. The judge ruled that he had to drink this funny stuff that would make him sick as a dog if he hit the bottle that day. Ever' morning, the judge said, Lint has to drink it ever' morning, and in front of a witness. The judge named Ben Lippman the witness on account of Ben owning the feed store where Lint works. Old Ben, he watches Lint drink that stuff ever' morning, 'cept for Saturday and Sunday when the feed store is shut."

Hyram followed Jason into the kitchen. "Have some coffee with me, Hyram?"

"Thanks, yeah. It's strong as a barnyard in the July sun. Been sitting there all morning. I'll take half a cup."

Jason poured coffee for them both. "Who is Regan?"

Hyram looked out the window. "I shouldn't ought to mention that name. Here comes Angela." He turned to Jason and said in a whisper,

"Regan was Angela's baby. Hers and Lint's. Lint beat the kid so much it up and died. But I didn't tell you that, okay?"

"Okay." Jason felt his knees get weak. He sat at the table. Lint killed his own child! Angela's child. It seemed too horrible to be real. No wonder she's willing to fire weapons at him. What would I do if I had a weapon handy and Lint killed my baby in front of me? Would I take up that pistol of Hyram's and shoot him, blow part of his head away? And could I watch him fall and bleed like the man in the airport watched the woman he killed? Could I do that?

He tried to imagine it: Lint killing a child, there by the kitchen counter where the coffeepot sat. But the thought felt too terrible to hold. He gave his head a couple of shakes and made himself look at Hyram.

"I see riding Playboy got you all tuckered out."

Jason shrugged. "Does the chemical Lint has to drink really keep him away from alcohol?"

"You bet your boots it does. Ben told me that the first day Lint drunk it, he had him a beer with his lunch, you know, testing the stuff or thinking maybe it done wore off. Lint, he puked up his toenails and wasn't good for much the rest of the day. Lint has to save his drinking for weekends, which is why I didn't want Angela traipsing off this morning. I figured, though, that between you and my nine millimeter, she was safe enough. She teach you to shoot it?"

"To shoot what?" Angela asked from the door.

"Whatever needs shooting."

"I showed him the use of your pistol, if that's what you mean. He didn't take a cotton to it, though."

"Hell, who would?"

"Odom said he would put Playboy in the trailer and haul him over to Lint's and bring back Dawg Meat. Said he'd do it today. He also told me he thinks the Doobie Brothers been running the calves."

"The Doobie Brothers?" Hyram looked startled. "Why, they ain't nothing but pups."

"We can't have dogs who run the calves."

"Ain't that a fact? But they're just pups. Still, we'll keep an eye on them. Odom, he said he'd come out to the ranch tomorrow, Sunday or no, and keep an eye on ever' thing, including the Doobie Brothers while you and me is in New Mexico."

"Coffee, Angela?" Jason felt he looked at her in a new way, that he could see the pain she held under the surface. He wanted to touch her face, to kiss her forehead.

"Hyram made that. Look at it—strong enough to jump out of the cup and arm wrestle you to the floor. I'll get me some, Jason, so I can water it down to something somebody besides Atilla the Hun and Hyram can drink." Angela looked at Jason as she poured coffee. "How come you're looking at me so funny?"

"I'm sorry. I suppose this has been an odd day."

"Odd, yes." She lowered her voice and looked close at Jason. "But mostly good. Real good."

Jason flushed. He saw Hyram look from one to the other and nod in a knowing way.

28

Before dawn, Jason heard Angela and Hyram in the kitchen. They would be taking time only for drinking coffee before leaving for New Mexico.

Jason lay on the quilt he used for bedding on the floor, wanting to join them for coffee, feeling he should not since the relationship between him and Angela had changed.

She claimed to be finished with Lint, but Jason knew better. She still gave a great deal of emotional energy to Lint, and it mattered little that the energy came in the form of anger. He was important to her, or she wouldn't give so much of herself to being angry. And Lint was far from finished with her.

Jason cursed himself for being drawn into the endgame of their marriage. At the same time, he loved the memory of touching her there on the top of Snake Mountain, of his undressing her, of their bodies coming together, of her crying out in pleasure. Then there was her moving speculation about God, words that Jason felt gave Angela some real depth, attractive depth. He wanted to make love with her again.

But not until she had set her marriage in some safe place in the past. Maybe the ritual of the court hearing and the final divorce decree would do that. Jason hoped so. He didn't know if he had the determination to wait long—especially if somehow he found himself alone with her. He knew he would have to find ways of avoiding such temptation. Also, there was another complication. Sybil. He still wanted to see her, to get to know her.

After Hyram and Angela left, Jason dressed, packed his tennis bag, and drove to the university campus in Canyon. Hitting balls against the wall would, he decided, help get his mind off of Angela and Lint. Besides, he needed to get his timing back for the Canyon Open tennis tournament coming up later in the summer.

By nine o'clock, he was tired of wall practice and found himself wondering if it was too early to go see Sybil. If I went there sweaty and disheveled from tennis practice, she couldn't suspect me of courting her. Which I won't be, he affirmed. She was right when she said a person couldn't have too many buddies. I don't want to consider her a romantic interest. Not now—not after what passed between me and Angela on the mountaintop. But I could use a buddy, someone to talk to about . . .

He laughed at himself. No, there is no way I could tell her about me and Angela. No way. And would I be going to see her at all if Angela had not left town? Yes. If for no other reason than to avoid being around her, avoid being tempted to touch her.

He found Sybil sitting on her front porch, tying something to her ankle. "Jason. You're just in time to help me tax the bees."

"Tax?" He sat beside her. On the porch was an assortment of bee equipment—hat, veil, hive tool, smoke can, a rag, a broad-bristled brush, and a bottle of something with fine print on the label.

"Some people call it 'robbing' them, but I don't like the word. It implies that I do them harm, which I do not. I provide them a home and the means to make more honey than they need, and in exchange, I take some of their produce as a tax for the services they get from me. Would you like to help? You'll have to wear something over your legs. Those tennis shorts won't do."

"I have jeans in the truck that I can put on over these."

"Do it then. I'll get my extra bee helmet and veil. You ought to use gloves, too. I'll bring some." She went into the house.

When she returned, Jason was struggling to pull his jeans on. Her cheeks dimpled. "Are all men such little boys at heart? I used to laugh at Parker for trying to put his pants on over shoes like that. Seem like it would be easier to take your shoes off first."

"It would be. I just don't have any sense."

"Here." She thrust something into the back pocket of his jeans.

"What's that?"

"An index card with my phone number on it, in case you live through taxing the bees and decide to volunteer to help me with them again. It would be nice to have some advance notice about your coming around. And here, put these rubber bands over the ankles of your jeans. They will keep bees from crawling up your leg and stinging you."

After they put on hats and veils, she checked him for places bees could crawl in. "Now let me check you," he offered. She turned while he inspected the way she had tied the veil to her body. "It looks fine. But you look funny. Like you just came home from a moon walk."

"Put these on."

"Gloves? You don't use gloves."

"Trust me. Put them on, Mister Jason White."

"We can't have a working relationship and treat each other with this kind of formality, Miss Sybil Redbear." He thought he saw her smile but couldn't be sure because of the veil.

"Bring that stuff. All of it." Her hand swept toward the porch. "You'll be glad for the gloves when you pick up that rag." She started toward the back of the house.

Jason picked up the equipment. The rag smelled like an oil refinery. When he caught up with her, she was taking a wheelbarrow from a tool shed by the back door. "For the frames," she explained.

"What happened to your kennels? Lightning?"

"Arson. I'll tell you about it sometime."

Beside the beehive, she took the smoke can from Jason, opened it, and dropped in a lighted match. She closed the can and pumped the billows on its side until a thick, white smoke blew from the hole in the top of the can. "This will confuse them." She puffed some smoke into the entrance at the bottom of the hive, then lifted the lid and puffed in more smoke. Jason could hear the alarmed buzzing from within the hive.

"Get the smelly rag." She picked up the bottle with the tiny print on the label. "Lift the lid from the hive and spread the rag over the top."

When he did so, she sprinkled a few drops of liquid from the bottle onto the rag. "Put the lid back on."

Bees came by the thousands out of the hive. "Why?" Jason pointed at the exodus.

"The chemical in the bottle smells like the sewer runoff from a cattle feedlot. Bees hate it worse than we do, and they get out of their house. It's called 'Bee-Go,' and it works, unless you leave the rag on too long and run all bees—even the queen—out of the hive, or unless you use too much and anesthetize them. I did that once."

"If some giant came along and puffed your house full of smoke, then lifted the roof and set down a canvas that smells like a feedlot, you would get outdoors, same as the bees.

Sybil turned to Jason, put her hand on his shoulder. "Yes. That's it exactly. That's it. You just expressed part of what took me years to come to."

"I did?" He liked her touch and found himself trying to understand the implications of what he had said that drew the show of affection.

A voice from the direction of the house startled them. "Sybil?"

She dropped her hand, sighed and spoke in a whisper. "That's Pug. She has the annoying habit of coming over unannounced."

"I've done that. Twice."

"You're different. Besides, you won't do it again, because you now have my phone number."

"Hello, Sybil. Are you robbing the bees?"

"No. Stay back, Pug. The bees don't like red hair."

Pug stopped. "Is it because red is the color of some flowers or. . . ." She heard Jason laugh. "Sybil Redbear! I never know when to take you serious." She came closer.

Sybil held up her palm. "You get too close, and you might get stung. The bees are excited. They know something might be happening to their food supply."

"Then you are robbing them. I thought you just said you weren't."

"We're not. I've explained that to you before, Pug."

"Oh, yeah. I forgot. You're borrowing from then."

"Taxing," Jason said.

Pug glanced at him. "Who's the man beneath the screen?"

"Jason. You met him. He's the one who will escort me to your birthday party tonight."

I will? Jason thought in astonishment. He had dismissed Sybil's invite to Pug's party as a ploy not to have to go.

"Yes, I remember." Pug's voice took on a querulous edge. "But I figured you were kidding about that, him being a newcomer to Canyon, and not a longtime friend, as you let on."

"Pug! Where is your Texas hospitality? Jason and I both come or I stay away. In either case, Jason and I have a date tonight."

He made an effort not to seem startled, then remembered that his veil hid his face. But a date! What is going on here?

"Sorry." Pug didn't sound sorry to Jason, but her voice did soften some. "I just dropped by to see if you wanted me to pick you up this evening."

"Thanks. Jason and I will ride together. Maybe on Parker's chopper."

That information seemed to hit Pug like a physical blow. She took a step back. "Chopper? On Parker's chopper?"

Jason looked at Sybil, seeing only the sun on the screen of her veil. She's toying with Pug, he realized. But why?

"Excuse us, Pug. The Bee-Go needs attention. Jason, take the rag away. If we leave it on too long, it could chase all of the bees out, including the queen. We don't want that."

Jason removed the rag. Sybil used the hive tool for lifting apart the boxes that made up the hive. "Set the top super on the wheelbarrow, Jason." When he had done so, she pried loose the wooden frames that held the honey, took them from the box and held them toward Jason. "Get the brush and brush off the few stubborn bees that are still on the wax." Jason did so, taking care not to injure the bees.

"I would like to help you do that sometime." Pug took a step closer.

"Oh? You said no in a most firm way last time I asked. You'd better stay back."

"I said that? I don't remember." She batted at a bee circling her head.

"Don't wave at the bees, Pug," Jason warned.

Pug glared at him, swatted at a bee, then jumped back. "In my hair! It got in my hair. I hear it. Loud."

"Stay still," Jason warned.

"Jason, do you have a pocket comb? Pug, do as he said. Stay still. Maybe we can comb the bee out before it gets to your scalp."

Pug began shaking her head in a frenzy. Then she screamed and started running toward the house. Several bees gave chase. She screamed and swatted at her neck. "One," Sybil said. Pug screamed again. "Two. Two of them got her on the run. It's amazing how they can fly right by you and leave a stinger in your skin without stopping. Here," she handed Jason the hive tool. "Take the next super off the top and brush the bees from the frames. I'm going to try to help Pug."

When Sybil returned, Jason was putting the lid on the reduced hive. "How's Pug?"

"Pugnacious. Puffy. Pitiful. She got four stings in all. We got the stingers out, and I made a poultice with meat tenderizer that seemed to help. She's gone home. Jason, I have some apologizing to do. And some explaining." She looked around. "You did all the work."

"But not well. Bees keep getting back into the part of the hive I set in the wheelbarrow."

"I forgot to warn you to cover the supers with the newspaper I had in the wheelbarrow. But that doesn't matter. Some always seem to get back into the supers."

"Why do you call the boxes supers?"

"It's beekeeper jargon, probably short for superstructure. It refers to the boxes that stack together to make the hive. Now, Jason, we extract the honey."

Pug drove from Canyon in a white fury. She had some anger for Sybil, but most of it she directed at Jason. That meddling foreign bastard, she thought. I was doing well with Sybil until he came around, had her nearly ready to give up on that place in Canyon and move in with me. Who the hell does he think he is? Does he think he can waltz into something he doesn't know anything about and take over, just because he's a man? He'll find out different. Will he ever find out.

She drove into the heart of Amarillo, turned right on Sixth, and went to Virginia Street. The route felt so familiar, though she had once sworn she would never again go to that house on Virginia, never again seek out Altus.

He sat on his porch, clutching a Dr Pepper can, and stared in disbelief as Pug approached.

Altus wasn't the biggest of Mark's friends, but he was the toughest, and at one time Pug had thought him the best-looking of the bikers that Mark rode with, back when she still thought about men in those terms. Now she thought of him as feral. His eyes were set too close together, and his nose was too long. Besides, it had tufts of thick black hair, like hog bristles, protruding from each nostril. Pug remembered keeping that hair trimmed when she lived with him. His eyebrows grew together, making it appear that he had only one—a black ark over his thin face. Ugly, Pug thought. How did I ever find him even remotely attractive? I'm glad to be rid of him and his greasy body and tobacco breath.

Still, he might be useful. Everyone in Mark's group was a bit afraid of Altus because he had a way of exploding into violence. When he did, he moved with blurring speed, turning into fists and kicks, bloodying those who had drawn his wrath. Lucky for me, Pug thought, that he didn't usually strike women.

Altus looked at her with what Pug knew passed for him as affection. "If it ain't my old lady."

"Wrong. Not any more. And I never did like that phrase, Altus."

"Sit here," he indicated the chair beside him. "You know I never meant nothing by it. It's just biker talk for a fellow's woman."

"Are you going to Mark's party tonight, Altus?"

"He told me that I ain't invited, that it was for your birthday and it would be better if I had my own party."

"You're invited." She sat down.

"Honey—" he reached for her hand. She drew back.

"I didn't come here to get anything going with you again. We parted friends, remember?"

"Yes. But you gotta remember that you can come back anytime."

"I need a favor."

"You got it."

"No strings."

"Did I ever tell you what to do?"

Pug admitted that he never had. Altus gave her a kind of doglike loyalty, and he never forced himself on her. That might have been his best quality, that ability to accept her on her own terms—even when she confessed to him that she experienced a tough time having sex with him. Altus wasn't all that interested in sex, anyway. He thought the lack of interest was due to his having taken so many drugs for so many years. He said it came as a relief to him that he had found a woman who didn't demand he be a sexual athlete.

On one of the few occasions when he tried to initiate sexual touching with her, she stroked his face and held him. Then she explained her refusal. "It isn't you, Altus. It's me. It's the ghosts from my past." She explained how her father sexually abused her from as early as she could remember until she was old enough to attract boys. Since her first date, he had not touched her. If he did, Pug told her father, she would tell, and her boyfriend would take action.

Pug's father, a bully to her, was a timid man when confronted by anyone his size or larger. Pug was still smaller when she made her threat, but her boyfriends were much bigger. He stopped the abuse.

When Altus heard what Pug's father had done to her, he wanted to find the man and beat him senseless. Pug wasn't against Altus doing so, but the problem was that no one knew where the old man lived. Last Pug heard, he moved to Oregon. Altus muttered about hiring a detective to find him, but nothing ever came of it. Altus never worked at one job long enough to afford a detective.

It took Pug two marriages and Altus to come to terms with her dislike of men. She was still in the process of working on her attraction to women. The most attractive woman she had ever met was Sybil Redbear, and Sybil was a tease. Pug understood Sybil didn't mean to be a tease, which made her all the more attractive. Sybil was the one to fill the empty spaces in Pug's life—Pug knew that. But Sybil resisted.

Let her get to know me. Live with me, if she will, Pug had reasoned—then lead her gently back into a loving relationship. It looked to be going well, until Jason appeared.

That's where she figured Altus could be useful.

"No strings," Pug repeated.

"No strings."

"Good. Come to Mark's party. I'll tell him I invited you. Come to the party and I'll introduce you to a man who has offended me."

"He hurt you?" Altus's voice dropped to a growl.

"In a way. He's not one of Mark's friends."

"Wouldn't matter if he was."

"He's a stranger. Looks like a Mexican."

"I got nothing against Mexicans."

"Neither do I, Altus. He looks like a Mexican, but isn't. He talks like somebody from England. I don't like him, Altus, and he needs to be hurt. Nothing permanent. Don't hurt him too bad, you hear?"

Altus's close-set eyes seemed to get closer. "That depends on what he done. Tell me what he done."

"No. It doesn't matter. Don't hurt him bad, Altus. Make his nose bleed. Cut up his cheek the way you do with your knuckles. Make him beg you to stop. But don't hurt him so bad that he can't talk or walk away. Okay?" She stood up. "Okay?"

"Okay." He took her hand.

She gave his hand a squeeze and withdrew. "No strings, remember?"

It seemed unlikely to her that Altus could control himself enough to keep from hurting Jason in some serious way. But what do I care? Sybil will see what a weak, silly man Jason is when confronted with Altus. And if she doesn't, I'll deal with that when the time comes.

30

As Jason pushed the wheelbarrow toward the house, he asked again about the charred place on the kennels.

"Someone wants to scare me, Pug says. Setting fire to the kennels is just the latest in a series of attempts."

"Why would anyone want to scare you?"

"Pug says it's racism, that people in Canyon want me to leave because I'm different. Have you felt any animosity toward you because of the shade of your skin, Jason?"

"Some. Back in Asia."

"I mean here, since you came to Canyon."

"No."

"Pug says that racism is rampant in Canyon, especially among the rednecks—the farmers and ranchers. Do you think it could be true?"

"Do you believe that?"

"Jason, I asked you first." They got to the back door. Sybil took one of the supers from the wheelbarrow. "Hold the door open, then bring in the other super."

Inside, Sybil motioned toward a table covered with newspapers. "Set it there, and welcome to the extraction room. That," she pointed, "might look like a garbage can to you, but it's a centrifugal honey extractor I built. Have you ever seen a honey extractor?"

"No."

"Take off your hat and veil." While they stripped off the bee equipment, Sybil explained the use of the extractor. "We cut the top off the wax with an electric hot knife, put the frames in those slots in the extractor, then spin out the honey."

She set the bee hats and veils on a bench. "So what do you think about Pug's assessment?"

"About rednecks being racist? If Hyram and the man who works for him are representative of area rednecks, then Pug is wrong. I haven't felt the edge of racial hatred at all since coming to this country, even if my parents warned me that I might. They said I look Mexican. I haven't even heard talk of it, or heard a single racist joke. But then, everyone I've seen has been roughly the same color—only a shade lighter than I."

"Americans do tell racist jokes, though. You will find plenty of bigotry here."

"Maybe. People where I have been living, though, invented and perfected racism long before Europeans came to America. Malays and Indians and Chinese all scorn one another, and each group feels superior to the other. Anyway, why would anyone here be biased against you? You're white."

"Mostly. But I carry African blood, and it shows, if you look close."

"Have you sensed racial hatred aimed at you?"

"Not in Canyon. Other places I have. Hand me one of the frames."

Jason removed a frame, heavy with wax and honey, from the hive box Sybil called a super. She stood the frame on end in a shallow pan and poised the electric knife near the top. "Watch how this works." Moving the knife down, she cut off the top layer of wax, exposing honey-laden cells. "Now the other side." She turned the frame around. The wax she removed fell into the pan in wet globs.

"Who would want you to move from here?"

"Pug."

"Why?"

"I would rather not say. Besides, I might be wrong. It might be someone else harassing me." She handed the frame to Jason. "Set this inside one of the slots in the extractor. Put this side toward the wall."

Jason did as directed. Sybil nodded approval. "Now we cut the caps from three more to balance out the extractor cage, then spin out the honey. You want to cut the next one?"

"Carry on, please."

Sybil smiled. "Carry on sounds so British. Hand me another frame, then. Remember what you said out there about how we might leave, too, if someone smoked the house and put Bee-Go on our roof? That gets at the heart of an important issue. If I can understand properly, I will know why Pug does mean things to me, and I will not be angry with her. If, of course, she has been the one doing those things." Sybil cut the caps from the wax. "I was once terrified of bees—even honeybees." She glanced at Jason. "Do you want to hear this?"

"Yes."

She dated her fear of bees from a sting when she was a child. "It had to be pre-verbal. I have no memory of it. Paper wasps lived all around my home in Beaumont."

Then, when she was in the first grade, a paper wasp she had not seen on the seat of a schoolyard swing stung her hand. She cried out and several children on the playground laughed. One said, "A bee stung the nigger."

"A teacher removed the stinger with tweezers, and that probably made the sting hurt worse. Now I know not to pinch a stinger that a bee or wasp leaves in you because doing so pumps more of the foreign protein into you. But that teacher thought she was helping. She also thought she was helping when she warned me about staying away from bees."

Sybil explained that she grew up with only a degree or two worse than normal fear of stinging insects. "One woman from Beaumont became so frightened when a bee flew into her car that she opened the door and got out. The car was going about sixty, so the woman died. I remember reading about that in the *Beaumont Enterprise* when I was sixteen. The headline was something like 'Bee Kills Woman.' I remember accepting the assessment, for I understood how a person would simply get out of a car going that fast if confronted with a bee."

She told Jason how she hiked with Parker up the side of a mountain in Colorado, over a rocky road that followed a stream. "I learned the truth about bees because of a happy accident. Not all accidents are happy ones. Most are painful. This accident was my going to sleep in an odd moment of an odd place."

At one point on their hike, they stopped by a beaver pond to fish. Parker walked around the pond, casting, while she crossed the stream on a fallen tree and sat on the ground among wildflowers. "I thought it was too early in the spring and too high on the mountain for there to be any bees, but I was wrong."

Lying on her back in some clover, she dozed off with the sun on her face and the smell of flowers thick in the air and the sound of the stream tumbling down the mountain, and she dreamed that she sang while gathering strawberries. When she began to awaken, drifting in a delicious state between sleep and wake, she listened to the sound of her own singing. "Mostly I was humming, and I understood it to be a celebration of strawberries, of the sweetness and redness of the fruit, and the song was the song of life and of God."

Then, as awareness came that she was dreaming, she still heard the song, and she willed herself to leave sleep. But she still heard the humming, though it did not come from her. She turned on her side in a slow, fluid way, and saw the source of the singing. Honeybees.

They worked the clover blossoms just inches from her eyes, and they sang in celebration of the gathering of honey. She knew their joy with a conviction that throbbed through her entire being, and she felt the knowledge grow within her. "I cannot put it into words," she told Jason, "for such understanding is beyond words. The bees and I were the same. A bee found a blossom so close to me I could have stroked her wings—and I knew she wouldn't mind if I did, for we were alike. The world around me seemed to vanish—the sound of the mountain stream, the woods beyond the beaver pond, the pond itself. All there was in the universe was a patch of clover, honeybees gathering honey and singing their songs of joy. They sifted through the blossoms, much as I had combed through the strawberry plants in my dream.

"Suddenly I understood why I had always been afraid of bees. I had seen them as foreign, different and threatening. But they were not different. What I learned in that moment was the essential alikeness of all living creatures. That's what God is, Jason—the force that connects all living things. God is also the realization of that connection."

She stood, motionless, the honey knife in her hand, looking at Jason with an intensity that brought a lump to his throat. Then she gave her head a tiny shake and blinked hard. "It must sound a bit silly, I'm afraid."

"Not at all. I envy you the experience."

"But you already knew about such connections. You had no fear of bees. And what you said—"

"I was trying to joke. I knew nothing of the wisdom you just described."

"Maybe. Maybe not. The woman that the newspaper said was killed by a bee? In that moment there on the mountainside in Colorado, I understood the bee's innocence in her death. She died of misunderstanding, of perceiving the bee to be so different from her as to be a monster, and she died as a result of misplaced fear. So I learned the truth about bees by choosing to make an accident help me. An accidental sleep."

Sybil set the fourth frame into her extractor, attached a variable-speed drill motor, and began spinning the cage. "Watch the honey hit the sides of the drum. It will gather in the bottom and drain through that spigot. We'll strain it through cheese cloth as we put the honey into jars."

"It's such a beautiful golden color."

The comment pleased Sybil. She increased the speed of the extractor cage. "When I got back from that trip to the mountains, I went to the library to read about honeybees. Within two weeks, I had ordered a queen and two pounds of workers from a mail-order bee supply house. Parker thought I had gone a bit crazy, but he didn't object to setting a hive in our backyard."

She studied bees by reading about them and by watching them come and go from the hive. The few times she had been stung hurt less than she thought possible. "Understanding why they sting and how the sting works somehow makes it hurt less. That's why I need to understand Pug better, even if I decide to have less and less to do with her."

"Why did you tell her we have a date tonight?"

"Did that bother you?"

"It puzzled me. But I like the idea."

"We don't have a date. Forget that word. We will share an evening as friends. As buddies, remember? Can you live with that? You come over at eight. Don't wear anything that would make you look like a cowboy." She stopped spinning the cage. "Remove the empty frames and put them back into the super. Later we will give them back to the bees, who will repair the damage we did, refill the cells with honey, and recap each cell. That way they spend most of their energy gathering and curing honey instead of making wax."

Jason replaced the frames. "No blue jeans?"

"Jeans are okay. No cowboy boots. No western-cut shirt. That belt buckle will have to go. Get me another frame for the hot knife."

"What kind of shirt is permissible, Mother?" He handed her a frame, and she began removing the caps.

"Can the sarcasm. Permissible has nothing to do with this. A tee shirt will be fine, so long as it doesn't have a collar or an alligator or some such animal sewn on it. A black tee shirt would be best, though a white one would be okay. Of course you wouldn't wear a cowboy hat—but then that's out, anyway because we will go on a motorcycle and you will wear a helmet. Can you drive a bike?"

"Yes. I had a seventy-five cc bike in Kuala Lumpur."

"Seventy-five? I doubt I'd mention that to anyone tonight. I thought we would try the chopper, but that might be a bit of a jump up for you."

He watched her set the frame into the extractor. "Angela worked hard to get me to dress like a cowboy. Now you think it's important for me to look like a biker."

"You won't look like a biker. For that you need long, unkempt hair and a few tattoos scattered over your arms and neck. Maybe an earring. You just won't look like such a foreigner to them."

"Hyram said I came from a different tribe from the cowboys, but if I worked at it, I could pass for a member of the tribe."

Sybil dimpled her cheeks. "Tribe? That's a good insight, for a cowboy. Just listen to me! My own prejudices are showing. Tribe is a good way to put it. Bikers are certainly a tribe unto themselves. A small tribe with limited tolerance for anyone in their midst who is different. They put up with me because Parker once rode with them, and they respected him.

"Maybe, Jason, you should come over at seven thirty so we can work on teaching you to ride a big bike."

Sybil stopped her Sportster in the parking lot of Homeland Supermarket. "You drive from here on." The setting sun threw long shadows across them.

Jason got off the back of the motorcycle. "Why?"

"If we rode up to Mark's house with me driving and you behind me, all those biker friends of his would give us a hard time. Most bikers would never let a woman drive his bike, and none of them would allow a woman to be in control while he rode as a passenger."

"I'm not a biker, so it doesn't matter to me."

"I know that, and it's one of the reasons I like you, Jason White. But when we go to Mark's house, we have to deal with those bikers, and it's easier if we obey their rules. Tribal rules, as Hyram would say."

Jason got on the cycle, his hands going over the controls. "Never have I driven such a large motorcycle. In Malaysia, all the cycles are small."

"You call this large?" Sybil got on behind Jason.

When Jason had arrived at her house, dressed in jeans and a tee shirt, she handed him a helmet. "I think it will fit. Try it."

"Is this one of yours?"

"I guess it is now. It once was Parker's. It looks good on you. How is the fit?"

"Maybe a bit loose. But it will do just fine."

She had taken him into the garage to show him Parker's chopper and asked if he could handle it. He walked around the machine and declared it to be too unbalanced with the front fork extended out so far, and too large for someone with his limited experience. "Then we go on my Sportster. You drive." Again he balked, claiming it to be too dangerous for him to go in traffic without first getting used to her cycle.

"I thought that might be the case—that's why we're starting the evening a bit earlier." She drove them out of Canyon on the VFW road. Just north of town, she stopped, got off and insisted he drive up and down the street a few times while she waited. "If you plan to hang around with me very much, you learn to handle a real motorcycle."

Jason liked the idea of hanging around Sybil, though he doubted if Angela would approve. He decided not to talk to Angela about his being friends with another woman. But she will find out, he warned himself. So let her. She's still married, anyway. Jason realized his reasoning was flawed, but he decided not to worry about Angela right then.

The hardest thing to remember was to be gentle with the throttle. Too much twist and the Sportster would leap forward, lifting the front wheel from the pavement. He eased out of the Homeland parking lot.

Sybil directed him north on Western, up a hill beside a park shadowed with trees, right on Sixth Street, then to a wood framed house on Louisiana Street. Two kegs of beer sat on a porch that ran the entire length of the front of the house. Jason parked the Sportster among the motorcycles on the driveway beside the house. "Sixteen." He took off Parker's helmet.

"What?" Sybil asked.

"Motorcycles. I counted fifteen. Yours makes sixteen. And all of them are gigantic. Do we lock the helmets onto the seat?"

"No. None of Mark's guests would take a helmet, and the petty thieves in the neighborhood are too scared of the bikers to be tempted."

"The bikers are all honest?"

"I didn't say that."

Inside the house, Sybil introduced Jason to Mark, then to a number of men and women whose names came at him too fast to remember. Besides, he thought, they all look alike.

The women wore combinations of jeans and black leather. Few had on makeup and most wore their hair straight and long. Several had marijuana leaves tattooed on their ankles. They stood around, clutching plastic cups of beer, talking loud and laughing too much to suit Jason. He thought they looked like a hard lot, almost as hard as the men.

Mark seemed typical. He wore a black, sleeveless tee shirt, faded jeans tucked into what Jason took to be motorcycle boots. And there were the usual tattoos. The emblem on his arm was a skull smoking a cigar with the word Harley under it. The tattoo running out the neck of his shirt appeared to be a dragon blowing smoke rings.

Mark stood almost a head taller than Jason. Few of the bikers were so tall, though several had what struck Jason as considerable girth. He tried without success to envision one particular man on a motorcycle. He must have weighed over 300 pounds, including about five pounds of ink in the tattoos on his arms.

Altus watched Parker's old lady. So she's dating again, he thought. About time. The dark fellow with her must be the one Pug wants me of hammer on. Better wait until I talk to her, just to make sure.

He spat tobacco juice into a Dr Pepper can and turned back to the women he had been talking with. The blond girl—Ray's old lady—was laughing about something. "No shit?" she said to the other two. "No shit? Altus, what do you think about Pug these days?"

"Lay off of that," one of the other women warned.

"Pug? Me and her are done."

"Cause of her being a dike?"

"Cut the shit." Altus tried to remember Ray's old lady's name. Brenda? Rhonda? He wasn't sure. "I can tell you for a fact that Pug ain't no dike."

The three women exchanged glances and giggled. "Back when you lived with her, maybe," the blond said. "But I hear different these days. Suzie here says she sees Pug going into that gay bar over on Georgia most ever' day. Says Pug hangs out with some dikes that could wrestle you to the mat."

"Bullshit." Altus frowned.

"I told you to lay off of that shit," Suzie told the blond.

"Altus is a big boy. Besides, he done told me he was through with Pug."

"I still say it's bullshit. And if it ain't, then what the fuck does it matter to anybody?" Altus turned from the women, ignoring their laughter. They know how to piss a man off, he thought. Bitches.

Altus had every intention of confronting Pug with what Ray's old lady had told him. He felt she owed it to him to tell him the truth. Most important was whether she was gay when she lived with him. He knew she hadn't left him for another man. If she had, that would have been all right—after Altus had found the bastard and beaten him to a bloody stump. But shit, he thought, to leave me for one of those butch-looking, square bodied women with hair cut up over her ears is more than a man can stand.

When he found Pug, she was talking with Parker's old lady. Altus stood aside and watched. He couldn't hear what they were saying because of the rock music Mark had on his CD, but it seemed clear to Altus that Pug was a bit too fond of touching Parker's old lady and liked to lean in close when she talked, like she was telling a secret. Not only that, but from time to time, Pug shot the Mexican-looking guy a mean look, like she would just as soon be cutting off his gonads as looking at him. "Shit!" Altus muttered.

So she wants me to bend that guy nine ways from up because he's coming on to Parker's old lady and Pug is jealous. Shit. I do that and all them bitches—Ray's old lady and the others—they'll be laughing at how Pug uses me. A dike jerking me around. Crap on that.

Jason eyed the people in Mark's house with increasing alarm. He had overheard several conversations, and all of them seemed to deal with fights or drugs. He turned toward Mark, who was explaining why he kept a loaded pistol on his coffee table. "'Bout ten at night. Them bastards came at me soon as I opened the door, shoving a pistol into my nose. Two of them took me to the floor. Sons of bitches wore ski masks. Kept yelling about where Ray was. I told them, how the hell should I know? Two of them went through the house, like they thought Ray was here, which he wasn't. Then they come back and took my wallet. Lifted nearly $300 from me, the pig fuckers. Course, I couldn't complain, what with that pistol jammed into my nose."

"So where was your old lady?"

"Working. She works all the damn time. Then them bastards made me go out to a car, said I had to direct them to Ray. I got to thinking that these assholes were big time fucked up on coke maybe, and it would be no work to outthink them. Not that they seemed so bright, even if they wasn't fucked up. They kept talking about how Ray took them for some money, and they would show him. Can you imagine anyone pushing Ray around if he knew they was coming for him? I told them I thought I could locate Ray if I could get to a phone. The dumb shits took me to a 7-Eleven. No shit. Parked by the phone and told me not to try anything funny. I got out of the car, went right past the phone and into the 7-Eleven where there was a bunch of people. I made a show of talking to the guys in there and pointing outside, so the dumb shits in the ski masks would think I was talking about them. Which I wasn't. The morons drove off. That's when I went and bought that pistol. If they're stupid enough to hit my house again, they get a taste of what the pistol can deliver."

"Did they find Ray?"

"The next night they did, after I warned him. Found him at home. Ray said he loaded up a sawed-off shotgun with a chunk of lead and waited. You ought to go to his house and see what he done to his front door. Put a hole the size of a quarter in it, and splintered it up bad. About midnight, somebody drove up and went up to the door. Ray heard them whispering about how they should stand aside while one of them knocked, then they would jump him. Ray cut loose with that gun. Ripped a hole through the middle of the door and took a sizeable chunk off the side of the telephone pole across the street, he found out the next morning. No shit. Go by his house and look at that door. After he shot, all he heard was footsteps beating the sidewalk out of there. Them bastards ain't likely to fuck with Ray again. And if they fuck with me, I'm using that pistol."

Those standing around Mark laughed. Jason edged closer to Sybil. As soon as he had the chance, he was going to insist that they leave.

Pug took Altus' arm and smiled. "This is Altus. Altus, you know Sybil. And this is Jason, the man I told you about." Jason offered his hand.

Altus took it. "You're one helluva lucky bastard." He squeezed Jason's hand to show how much muscle he could call on.

"How's that? How is he lucky?" Pug frowned.

That I found out what a bitch you are, Altus thought, in time to decide not to pound him into the floor. He laughed. "To be the first to ride out with Parker's widow."

Giving Jason's hand another crunch, Altus dropped it and turned away. Pug followed, working her way through the crowd in the living room.

She caught up with him by the door, drew close and said in a fierce whisper, "You can make him bleed any time you want."

Altus looked at her with open malevolence. "You make him bleed, bitch."

Jason put his lips close to Sybil's ear. "Do you normally hang out with these people?"

"These are Parker's friends. I haven't been in this neighborhood since before his death. We came for Pug, remember?"

Jason felt relieved. He was about to suggest they leave when people near the door began turning toward Pug and laughing. Others in the house crowded around, straining to see. Sybil and Jason caught a glimpse of Pug turning up a bottle. The crowd roared with laughter.

Sybil caught a woman's arm. "What's going on, Suzie?"

The woman turned, eager to tell what she had seen. "Altus called his old lady a bitch and walked outside. Pug, she just stood there looking like somebody run over her in a Peterbuilt truck, then got Ray to give her his bottle of Ancient Age. She went to drinking it like it was water. And look at her now. Just look at that!"

Pug stood, her head tilted up, a bottle to her lips, swallowing. "The whole bottle," someone shouted, "drink that whole bottle, woman." Others began clapping and cheering Pug to keep drinking the whiskey.

Altus looked through the screen door as Pug started on the booze. Disgusting. But it serves the bitch right, he thought. He would have liked to hit her with his fist, but he knew the guys in there wouldn't stand for that. He looked back through the screen door at Pug spilling whiskey on the floor. Man, will Mark ever be pissed.

Moths flew around the porch light beside the door. Altus swatted one fluttering close to his face, then noticed a stranger coming up the sidewalk, carrying a case of beer. "Who the fuck is that, Larry?" Altus demanded of a man drawing a beer from one of the kegs on the porch.

"A neighbor of Mark's. Wants to be friends with bikers, Mark said, so he is all the time bringing beer over. What's going on inside?"

"Go see. I don't like the looks of that fucker with the beer." Altus stepped off the porch in front of Mark's neighbor. "So you want to buy us with beer?"

"Hello." The man smiled, shifted the case of beer on his shoulder and offered a hand. "I'm Keith."

Altus stared at the hand. "So you want to meet me, do you?" He slammed a fist into Keith's face. "Altus. My name is Altus."

Keith dropped the beer and staggered back. Altus stepped into him, hit him in the stomach and again in the face. Keith fell without making a sound. "Did you get the name? Altus. Altus."

When Keith got to his hands and knees, Altus kicked his leg. "Remember it, shithead. Altus."

People came out of the house to watch. As Sybil and Jason emerged, pushing through the crowd on the porch, Altus stood over Keith, shouting "Remember Altus! Remember Altus!" He kicked the prone body each time he said his name.

Sybil broke free of the crowd. "You're killing him. Stop." She tried to take Altus' arm. He back-handed her across the face without bothering to see who it was he hit.

"Altus! Altus!" he shouted, delivering more kicks. Sybil lay on the grass, her hand to a bleeding lip.

Jason stepped close to Altus from one side. Good God! he thought, I'll be Tom the Australian. Tom. Beating Rozak. Jason had to concentrate to keep his voice steady. "Altus, Pug said you forgot something."

Altus turned to see who spoke. As he did, Jason jerked a fist into the man's stomach, then hooked his other fist hard into Altus' ribs. As Altus doubled over, expelling breath with an audible whistle, Jason hit him again in the ribs and delivered a blow to his face as he fell.

The crowd roared its approval. Some began urging Altus to get up, but he remained on the ground, fighting for breath, holding his ribs.

Pug staggered into the yard. "You asshole," she said to Jason, then knelt by Altus. He lay doubled up, his nose bleeding. "You okay, honey?"

Pug put a hand on Altus' cheek, then looked at Sybil. Jason had just helped her to stand up. "Sybil, lookit what that asshole did. Blindsided him, the little shit." She returned her attention to Altus.

Mark looked at Sybil to see if she was hurt. "You're a brave little fucker," he said to Jason. "And a lot tougher than I would have figured. Altus is a mean dude, and you took him down fast and hard. Two things keep the guys from stringing your ass all over the street. One is the balls you showed in standing up to Altus, something not many of them would do. The other is that Altus had it coming when he hit your old lady. But they like Altus and you're a stranger, so the goodwill won't last. You and Sybil better beat it on out of here."

"We were just leaving."

"Smart. Keep moving." Mark turned his back. "Suzie, see about Keith. We can't have nobody dying at our party."

Jason looked close at Sybil's face. "Just a cut lip," he said. "Nothing serious."

"Asshole!" Pug shouted, her voice thick from alcohol. The crowd laughed when she started to stand, slipped and fell on Altus. "Poor Altus, poor bunny." Altus groaned and tried to sit up.

Sybil and Jason went to the Sportster. "You drive," he told her.

"But—"

"Do it. I don't give a damn about them. We're not bikers. You drive. I want them to watch how we don't care about their rules."

Sybil looked at Jason. He could imagine what she saw. A red face. Maybe some flakes of spital in the corners of his mouth. Eyes round and maybe wild looking. Like the red-headed man in the Los Angeles Airport. Yet she looked pleased. "Okay. I drive. Jason, you're beautiful."

"I'm not." He got on the back of the Sportster and began putting on Parker's helmet.

The bikers in Mark's yard hooted and laughed as Sybil drove off with Jason behind her.

She took a right on Sixth Street, drove across Western, and turned right on what Jason thought was a private driveway. It led to a parking lot, darkened beneath shadows of elm trees. At the end of the lot, Jason could see a building, dimly lit, and the dark shapes of more buildings farther on. To the right and left were dim wooded areas. "Where are we?"

"The Amarillo Country Club. Don't talk." She opened a case on the back of her bike, took something out, then took Jason's hand and led him into the trees. Light from the moon winked through leaves above them, and a few points of neon, distant and dim, flickered from street lights in the distance, beyond the wooded area. In a dark pool of shadows from a tree, Sybil spread something on the ground, sat on it, and drew Jason down to her. She took his hand and pressed it to her cheek. "You may kiss me. Be easy where Altus hit me."

Her open-mouthed, moist kisses excited Jason. When he put his tongue against hers, he found a faint taste of salt from the blood of her wound. The night had a cool deliciousness about it, and the mat she had spread felt to Jason more comfortable, softer than a bed. He lay against her, stroking her face and hair, pressing his mouth against hers for what might have been hours for all he knew. "Will anyone come out here?"

"No. And so what if someone does?" She sat up and began removing her clothes.

33

As they dressed, Jason looked around. The shadows of the trees had shifted and he could see that they were on the putting green of a golf course.

He watched Sybil move like a shadow in the dim light. "You're beautiful. And so passionate." Never had he made love with a woman who vocalized so much, and never had he experienced what she urged him to do. She came again and again in tiny explosive bursts, for what seemed an impossibly long time, moaning with each contraction; then her body stiffened and she inhaled in shallow gasps while her whole body quivered. She lay quiet and limp for only a few minutes before urging him to touch her again, repeating the cycle time and again.

"Yes. I am passionate. But, Jason, I'm no more so than you—you stayed right with me. Come. We need to talk." She folded the beach towel. He followed her in silence through the woods to her Sportster, got on behind her.

In a booth in Denny's just off the Interstate, Sybil looked at Jason in a steady, cool way. "I had no intention of doing that."

A waitress brought them iced tea. Jason squeezed a lemon twist into his and stirred it. "What about the beach towel?"

"Not planned. I always keep that with the Sportster. Don't be so smug. I had no intention of doing that. But I did it."

"We did."

"Yes. We. Listen to me, Jason. I'm afraid of you in many ways. Your youth. Your tendency to be romantic. Your beauty. Your passion. Do you realize we made love for over two hours, and we could have gone on longer? Listen to me. I like you. I like you. But I do not love you. I don't want to love you or anyone else. Have you read Blake?"

"No."

"No matter. In writing about love, Blake said, 'He caught me in his silken net, and shut me in his golden cage.' That's what love does. It binds and holds and makes promises and then leaves you alone and empty. Do not love me, Jason White. I'll not allow that. Never again. Love can be seductive and attractive—the cage is a golden one. But it's still a cage. Do you understand what I'm saying?"

"Mainly. I hear you saying that you've been hurt."

"Yes. I am a wounded woman. The wounds seem to hurt less and less, but maybe they will never heal. It has been too long since I felt the touch of a man. That's why we stayed at it so long. It was connection, Jason, and union and God. But it was also like a feeding frenzy for us both. But you must remember that what we did there on the golf course was not something lasting. It was what it was. No more. You have no hold on me. No control of any kind over me. I want you to understand that."

"Why should I want to control you?"

She shrugged. "Men seem to want that. I don't know. Do you have anything you want to tell me or ask me?"

"No. Yes. For a moment there, I wondered about birth control, then assumed you are on the pill. Is that correct?"

"No."

"Then you might become pregnant?"

"Not likely, from where the moon now stands."

"If you do—"

"If I do, it's no concern of yours."

"Sybil." He put his hand on hers, feeling both anger and tenderness for her.

She withdrew her hand. "I mean no offense. You have no hold over me, Jason. None."

"I'll concede that. I don't want to control anyone. I don't even know how to live my own life—why should I want to control anyone else's?"

"Well said. Anything else?"

"May I see you again?"

"I don't know. Maybe sometime. How can I know tonight? Tonight I want to see you again, to hold your body to mine. I want connection again, and I want another feeding frenzy. But I'm not sure it would be right for me. I just don't know.

"That's a terrible answer."

"It's all I have. Don't ask me again, Jason White. It would feel like pressure, and I will not tolerate pressure. Not now, not ever. I have a question for you, now. It might seem a little crass, but in the age of AIDS, I have to ask it. How sexually active are you?"

"Not very."

"I'm not at all. For years there was Parker, no one else. Then no one at all. Jason, not very is a spooky answer. Be straight with me. I know men will lie about their other women."

"What do you want me to say?"

"How many women have you been with in the last two years?"

"Three. I used condoms."

"Every time?"

Jason hesitated. He had not used a condom on top of Snake Mountain. "For two of them. The other time was not necessary."

"How do you know?"

"How did I know tonight?" He felt his face flush with anger. "Will you stop the interrogation now?"

"And with that little cowgirl that Hyram keeps around?"

"Don't ask that. Please."

"So you are involved with her. I knew it, I suppose. That complicates matters, knowing about you and Angela. Are you finished with your tea?"

"No."

"I am." She stood.

When they left Denny's, Sybil didn't offer to allow Jason to drive. As she drove into the night, he remembered with a start the incident at Mark's house. He was amazed at himself for getting into a fight, but even more for forgetting about it for so long. It was Sybil, there on the golf green, he thought. She was so wonderful in her passion that all else in the world just faded, even the fact that I hit a man.

It pleased him to think that he had won, though he felt ashamed for being pleased. Damn Odom, he thought—if he hadn't given me lessons in how to talk smooth and move in close and then punch in a way that ended a fight before it could get underway, I wouldn't have hit Altus.

But that's bull, and you know it, Jason White. I can't blame anyone else for what I became in that moment. It was my decision to use what I knew. But Altus hit Sybil—I had to step in. Jason shook his head, feeling the helmet move against his neck, becoming aware of the cool night air on his face. That's bull, too, he affirmed. She wasn't hurt. What I did makes me more of a Texan. And that's what I wanted. Isn't it?

Sybil handled the controls of the cycle with confidence, weaving among trucks on the highway to Canyon. Jason liked the way she sat in front of him, liked his legs touching her. He felt a stir of arousal and wanted to touch her as he had on the golf course.

The golf course! It was another amazing thing Jason felt he had to sort through. Making love in a public place, outdoors—what a strange thing to do, and maybe part of my transition to belonging here, to becoming Texan? I made love with Angela outdoors.

Sure. On top of Snake Mountain. Hardly a public place. Sybil knew what she was doing when she took me into the Amarillo Country Club, knew where to go for a private spot. She jerked me around like I was a puppet. There, Jason, fight that man. Here, Jason, screw me on the ground under this tree. Now that the fighting and screwing are over, Jason, don't call me. The fight got her ready, got her hot for—what had she called it? A feeding frenzy, and once sated, she sets me aside. What a bitch.

Even as he felt anger flushing his neck and temples, he knew that what they had done wasn't just screwing, and he wanted to lie with her again. But I won't ask to see her, he affirmed. She said not to ask. She doesn't want me. Jerk me around, use me, then cast me aside. I will not ask.

She took him back to her house, parked the Harley inside her garage and looked out at the pickup Jason had left in the front. She waited.

Jason understood. She expected him to leave. He removed the helmet, handed it to her and affirmed again that he would not ask. "When may I come see you?" He winced as the words came out.

"Mister Jason White, do you remember what I said?"

"Yes. I didn't want to ask. It just came out." He turned away, furious with himself.

"Don't come to see me for a while."

"How long is a while? Can't we just be friends?" Why am I asking her, like a beggar, he wanted to know. What hold can she have over me?

"You asked again. And no, I doubt it's possible to be mere friends after what we did tonight. It might be easy to go from friends to lovers, but it's nearly impossible to go from being lovers to being just friends. Don't be pushy, Mister White."

Jason felt anger like a lump against his diaphragm. What does she expect of me? "I hate games like this. I'll not come." Perhaps ever, he added to himself.

Angela and Hyram drove to the auction barn just before midnight, unloaded the horses and tack he had purchased. They unhitched the horse trailer and took the pickup the three miles from the barn to the ranch house.

As he parked, Hyram turned to Angela. "You come sleep in the main house tonight. In the extra room."

"Not likely. I got a bunkhouse that suits me just fine."

Hyram nodded. "Maybe not in the extra room, if you happened to wander into mine. You got a key. Use it sometime other than to let yourself in to fix breakfast."

"Hyram! What are you proposing?"

"I got nothing to propose, being near on to a hundred years old and not up to nothing. I like being with you, though."

"I've wanted that invite. A month ago I would have taken you up on it and who knows? Next month might be the same. Don't give up on me, Hyram."

"Never. I like that boy, too, you know. You go after him, if he suits you."

Inside the bunkhouse, Angela drew the curtains, tucked her red hair into a shower cap, bathed, then stepped outside into the night air to enjoy the breeze on her skin. As she finished drying, she looked at Hyram's home. No lights. That meant Hyram collapsed in bed without bathing. No lights from Jason's window, either. But then he was a morning person—she liked that about him.

Back inside the bunkhouse, Angela pulled boots onto her bare feet, took a key from a nail by the door, and went to the main house. In the entryway, she took the boots off, making as little noise as possible, and went to Jason's room.

He lay where she expected to find him: on the floor beside the water bed. She lifted his sheet and moved against him. He shifted, put his hand on her and awoke with a start.

"It's okay, it's okay." She pressed her hand on his chest to keep him from sitting up.

"Angela?"

"Were you expecting someone else?" She snuggled against him.

"But you're nude."

"You ain't exactly dressed for dancing." She giggled. "No, you keep your arm right there. Here. Give me your other hand. There. Go back to sleep, cowboy."

"Go to sleep? Now?"

"Now. It's on the sunrise side of midnight, and I'm so tired I could sleep on a barbed wire fence. Not that you feel even like a remote cousin to barbed wire. Just go to sleep, Jason."

When she awakened him by touching his face, faint morning light silvered the window of the bedroom. Jason drew her to him, and they made love with quick intensity.

Angela stood up. She could tell the suddenness of her movement startled him, and she laughed. "Get dressed. Meet me out by the tack shed. If we push it, we'll just have time to greet the sun." She left the room still nude, found her boots by the door, and slipped them on.

On the way to her bunkhouse, she wondered if Odom had slept over, if he might be watching her. So what if he is? She laughed out loud at the thought of Odom's face if he were to see her heading toward the bunkhouse dressed only in boots.

When Jason got to the tack shed, Angela was already there, dressed and leading Ghost from the pasture. She put the English riding saddle on the horse, then watched as Jason cinched his saddle on Dawg Meat. "You done that like a pro. You been practicing while I was gone."

"A few times."

His response pleased her. She rode out on Ghost, encouraging him into a run toward the gate, loving the feeling of flying on his back when he jumped over it. By the time Dawg Meat got to the gate, Angela had dismounted and opened it. "If we hurry, we got time to get to the edge of the canyon. Won't that be grand, standing there at the edge of Palo Duro, greeting the sun as it comes busting up above Snake Mountain?"

"Angela, we need to talk."

"Wrong. We need to ride. Get moving, cowboy."

She rode ahead, amused at the consternation on Jason's face. He seems to get that befuddled look ever' time I call him cowboy. Reason enough to keep calling him that, she decided.

They undressed at the edge of the cliff, folding their clothes and laying them on their boots. Then they turned to each other. Angela shook the red hair out of her eyes and laughed. "We made it, partner. Look." She pointed east at the streaks of light burning in thin clouds close to the horizon. "Turn to it. Hold your arms out to it."

Angela stood, arms spread and feet apart, and watched the sun burning into the sky beyond her closed eyelids. A breeze from the canyon tickled the hair against her neck; the caprock pressed its cool and grit against her feet; the odor of trees came to her from the cottonwoods and plums across the creek at the bottom of the canyon. She took in the morning air, savoring its fragrance and remembered the feel of Jason on the floor beside the water bed, remembered his weight pressing her against the bed rock on top of Snake Mountain.

She turned to him. He stood, arms out, eyes closed against the rising sun, and she touched his arm. "I sure do like the way you look with the light of morning on your brown body."

He looked at her, and she imagined herself as he saw her—pink in the early light, with a scattering of freckles, the sun illuminating golden, blond and red strands in her hair. He dropped his eyes to her breasts, and she caught her breath, pleased. "Last time we done this, you had desire in your eyes, same as now. I could see it, but I didn't want you to touch me, not then. This is now." She put her arms around him. "Someday soon I want you to go with me in the evening to Snake Mountain. We'll climb to the top and spend the night. We can make love under the stars. You've never seen stars like you can see from the canyon at night. Then in the morning, we can greet the sun like the Indians done a hundred years ago, standing on the top of the mountain. Won't that be grand?"

35

From her window, Sybil watched the postman stop beside the mailbox and stare at it. A tree blocked her view, so she could not see what made him pause. He backed up and drove down her driveway to the house, got out and knocked.

Sybil opened the door. "Good morning, Mr. Hargrave. Do you have a package for me today?"

"Good morning, Miss Redbear. No package. Just regular mail. I would have left it in the box, but someone tied a snake to it. A live snake, and a big one. Probably kids trying to be funny. But it ain't funny to me. Here's your mail."

"Thanks."

After putting on shoes, Sybil walked to the mailbox. As she neared, she could hear a buzzing and see something moving on the pipe that held the box.

The largest rattlesnake Sybil had ever seen was wrapped around the pipe, secured to it with many twists of wire. The snake squirmed and writhed but to no avail. Sybil made clicking sounds with her tongue. "You poor snake." In several places, the snake had struggled against the wire until it had chafed its skin enough to bleed.

Sybil ran back to her house, determined to call someone to free the snake. But who? She considered the fire department, the police, nixing both. Those guys would just kill the snake, and she didn't want that. Besides, she distrusted police, something she had gotten from years of living with Parker.

She called the animal shelter and talked with a polite young woman. "We have no one to send out," the woman said. "Perhaps you can call a vet?"

It had not occurred to her to call a vet. She flipped through her Rolodex for Mendy Wiggins, who owned the clinic where Sybil had boarded her cat Squeek when she went to Lake Murray.

"A rattlesnake?" Mendy sounded doubtful. "Wired to your mailbox?"

"I know. It sounds like a hoax. But it isn't, and if the snake doesn't get help soon, it will kill itself trying to escape."

"I'll be right out."

While she waited, Sybil considered who would do such a cruel thing to a snake. Pug? It seemed likely. Pug had never admitted to leaving the other items around Sybil's home—had, in fact, been almost convincing in claiming innocence.

Altus? Sybil doubted he would get close enough to a snake to capture it alive. But then, she thought, I don't know him well enough to say that, do I? He would be mad about being humiliated in front of his friends by what Jason did to him. But he would be going after Jason, not me.

And what about Jason? He left in a snit, like a little boy who had been insulted. But he wouldn't do such a thing to an animal. Would he?

She admitted that she didn't know, though she felt sure he wouldn't mistreat any animal in that way. Besides, she thought, he wasn't even in the country when someone began trying to frighten me by leaving scary things around my home.

That left Pug.

Sybil tried calling Pug, only to get a recorded message saying the number was no longer in service. So she called information. "Pug Littlejohn?" The operator said. "Let me check. The computer shows that she has an unlisted number."

"How long has she had it?"

"I'm sorry, but I cannot give that information."

Mendy, a short woman with stringy hair and a nose that had been sunburned and peeled, then sunburned again, arrived with a cage, leather gloves, and a box of tools. She secured the snake's head with a leather strap on the end of a stick. "Hold this." She gave the stick to Sybil, then began cutting the wire. "These," she held up the wire cutters, "were my father's. I used them when I was a kid and helped him repair the fences around his ranch. Never thought I would ever use them again, especially not to help a rattlesnake."

As she freed the snake, it writhed, but without enthusiasm, and it made only feeble attempts to shake the rattles on its tail. Sybil felt sorry for it. "Do you think it will survive?"

"That's hard to say. My guess is that someone stunned the snake with some blows to its head. Maybe drugged it. If the person who did it didn't do too much damage, the snake will survive." Mendy cut the final wire and turned to Sybil. "I wouldn't have come out here if you hadn't expressed concern for the snake. Most people would want me to kill it."

"I might have, once. But look at it. It's too magnificent to kill."

"I agree." Mendy took the snake in a gloved hand, untied the leather she had secured to its head, and set the snake into a cage. "I'll release it on my father's ranch. My ranch, now. Dad tried to kill all the rattlers on his land. That was a mistake, but he wouldn't hear it from me."

Sybil tried to pay the vet, but she refused to take anything. "If I can get the animal to live, that will be payment enough."

The next afternoon, when Sybil came back from Taylor and Sons Supermarket, she found a pile of white gravel in her yard. Taped to her door was a bill from Randall County Landscape for 2,350 pounds of crushed limestone. Someone had written across the bottom of the bill, "Mrs. Redbear—you asked how much one yard of 3/4 inch stone would cover. It will spread 2 inches deep over 162 square feet. Thanks, Randy." The bill was for $40.

When she reached Randy on the phone, he said, "Yes, Mrs. Redbear. Do you like the decorative stone you ordered?"

"I didn't order it."

Randy was silent for a moment. "A prank, then?"

"Yes. And not a funny one."

"Then you don't want the limestone. I'll have a crew out to pick it up tomorrow. Shall I report this to the police?"

"I'll take care of that. Thanks."

But Sybil did not report the incident. The next morning, she found a dead prairie dog wired to the elm beside her front door.

Hyram opened the *Canyon Sunday News* on the table. Angela drained the bacon on paper towels and began cooking eggs. "Births, deaths and church news," Hyram said.

"You going with me to see Jason in the tennis finals?" Angela asked.

"Here's a piece says the city landfill won't last but thirty more years. Now that's what I call a live wire of a news story."

"How come you never listen to me in the morning?"

"Sunny side up. I'll take them sunny side up."

"That ain't what I asked."

"Three of them, then. Three eggs." Hyram looked up from the paper.

Angela stood, arms folded, glaring. "Four biscuits? No, don't tell me. Crisp. I want my bacon crisp."

"Hyram!"

"Black. I like my coffee black. Saucer and blow it if you have the notion, but keep it black. Angela, honey, you know you got fire in your eyes? I slept well, since you asked, thank you. Like a toad in the sun. That weren't it? No hints. It's coming to me. I remember now. You asked what the headlines of the Sunday news said." He looked at the paper.

Angela turned back to the stove. "Lint Bodark, he never listened to me, either. But I think he got the message that he ain't welcome here. He ain't been around."

"Nope. Not since I went by the feedstore and laid it on him about trespassing on my land. Made him understand I take a dim view of anyone that would do the things he done. Shooting dogs. Starting fires. Taking horses from my people. Of course, there was no way in hell he would own up to doing them things, but he seemed to understand that my part of the canyon, including Snake Mountain, is off limits to the likes of him."

"He shot the shepherd puppy and he shot Turdy, regardless of what he said. Hyram, nobody but Lint would go and shoot dogs for no reason. He done it not long after you talked about going to Huntsville for knifing a man."

"Maybe. Says here in the paper that the tennis tournament took a real funny turn with a couple of top players being knocked out by a kid from Malaysia. And yes, I will go with you today to watch Jason play ball with the other little boys."

Angela shot him a quick glance. "Hyram, you drive me crazy sometimes."

"Yeah." He laughed. "And you love every minute of it." He rattled the paper, pretending to read. "You let on to me like you don't like that kid, but you do."

"You jealous?"

"Not so long as you get the eggs juicy and the bacon crisp."

"What about your invite for me to wander into your room?"

"It still stands, and if I change my mind, I'll let you know. But that ain't likely. My warning still stands, too."

"Warning?"

"About my being old and used plumb up."

"That ain't true. I could show you that ain't true." Angela chewed on her lip. "Forget I said that, Hyram. That part about showing you. But it ain't true what you said about being too old."

Hyram waved his hand. "Jason, he'll be here soon as you finish cooking the gravy, and he might even eat a bit of it. He's on his way to real manhood, something that Lint Bodark never achieved."

"Lint knows about the nine millimeter pistol I keep handy. He knows I could have killed him down in the canyon if I took a notion to. Thing is, I never fought back, not once, back when we lived together. But he went too far, shooting at me with that little pop gun on the highway, then shooting my new puppy. He went too far trying to steal Ghost."

"I'll get us another shepherd. Rule number two in life is you get another dog iffn somebody up and shoots your German Shepherd."

"No more dogs, Hyram. We been through all that. The Doobie Brothers are enough. More than enough if they're running the cows. And if that's rule number two, what is rule number one?"

"Rule number one in life stays constant. It's rule two that you change when you have a mind to. Rule number one is that you never piss against the wind."

Angela made an impatient gesture. "That's a dadburned man's joke. And you forget about getting another dog. Remember we got them mongrels, the Doobie Brothers."

"The Doobie Brothers—they been running the calves this week?"

"I suspect they have, even if I haven't caught them at it. They better wish I don't. And good morning to you, Jason."

Jason paused in the doorway. It seemed to him that he was walking in on something that was better left between Angela and Hyram. But it felt awkward to back out after just walking into the kitchen. "Good morning, Angela. Hyram. You sleep well?"

"Like a toad in the sun. You young folks got plans for Saturday week?"

"Next Saturday? I don't. Do you, Angela?

"How 'bout Saturday week?"

"Hyram means Saturday after next."

"No plans."

"And you, Angela? Any plans?"

"Hyram, you know I don't plan nothing much more than two days in advance these days. But I see you got something going. What?"

"You might not believe it to look at my manly figure," Hyram patted his tummy, "but my sixty-fifth birthday is coming up. I'm thinking we're going to have a real wing-ding of a barbecue. Invite all the neighbors. Throw a goat-roast that they'll talk about for years. What do you think, Angela?"

"Your birthday, Hyram? You never told me that. In two weeks. You ain't as old as you say, but yeah, I think we ought to do it up big. Get a band here, a good one like The Last Train South. Have Odom cobble up a dance floor so's we can all do the two-step. Get a couple of kegs. Dig a real barbecue pit and pick out a steer to dress out—"

"Slow down there, honey." Hyram grinned. "It's just a retirement party, not a ball for the governor. Besides, I done got Odom working on a place to dance outside."

"Retirement? For you? Come on, Hyram. You ain't retiring."

"Didn't say I was. I ought to go and do it, though, seeing as how old I'm getting. I ought to."

"Hyram loves to mess with your mind, Jason. But he's got a heart, somewhere. Matter of fact, he just told me he would drive us all to campus this morning for your game."

"Says here you made the finals." Hyram picked up the paper. "Says you knocked out some tough men. Seasoned players not used to losing to just a kid. Says your serve goes a hundred miles an hour, then bounces crazy. Says you're gonna lose in the finals to that lawyer from Amarillo who always wins the local tournaments, when the high school coach is out of town."

"That last part proves the reporter don't know nothing," Angela said. "Can't nobody in the Panhandle of Texas beat Jason."

"I've watched the lawyer play. Malcolm Roddy. He's a better tennis player than I am. But he makes bad judgments, and he has a temper. If I can shake his confidence, I might win."

"He ain't better," Angela said. "I know it."

"Been watching Jason play, have you?"

"Yup."

"Having some people in the stands pulling for me helps. It makes me play harder." Jason had been pleased that Angela went to the matches. Sometimes he wished Sybil would come, but he knew that was foolishness. He had seen Lint there, standing just beyond the gate, skulking around by the little building that housed the university police. To Jason, it looked as if Lint ignored the tennis matches. He kept his attention on Angela. And he took a few drinks from a flask that he pulled from his hip pocket.

When Jason saw Lint do that, it unnerved him, and he double-faulted twice. So he walked around on the court, bouncing the ball, telling himself that Lint Bodark would do nothing to Angela with all those people around, and with the university police coming and going right beside him. Then Jason had stolen a glance at Angela and served an ace.

Jason watched Hyram eat breakfast, awed that the man could consume so much grease and not get ill. Hyram kept a running monolog going, managing to say little but to say it in comical ways. Angela said nothing. She glanced at Jason from time to time in a shy way.

When he had talked to her out on the prairie, the two of them nude in the morning sun, he expected her to object to what he had to say. He told her they would have to be formal with one another until she and Lint were through with their marriage. She laughed, took his hand as if they were just being introduced and gave it a formal shake. Then, standing on the edge of the canyon, she put her clothes on. Since then, when they were alone together she had acted as if they had never been lovers. She treated him as if they were best friends, though when Hyram was around, she was distant, almost cool. Jason had watched her from his window several mornings as she prepared to ride out to greet the dawn. She seemed aware of his watching, but neither spoke of it.

After breakfast, Jason brought his tennis bag to the front door. He sat on the floor and put his shoes on. Would Sybil come to the match, he wondered. I hope not. Why should she, anyway? She hadn't come to any of the earlier matches in the tournament. Face it, he told himself, she doesn't want to see you. Ever.

The thought gave him a flash of anger, and he jerked at a shoelace.

"Careful. You'll break it that way." Angela handed him an enormous red-checkered Thermos bottle. "Ice water for the court."

"Thanks," Jason had a canteen of water in the bag already, but he said nothing about it.

Outside, Odom squatted beside a grid of two-by-fours, nailing pine flooring on them. Hyram stopped. "It's Sunday, Odom. You ought to be over in Canyon at the First Baptist Church, dropping money into the plate to pay the preacher."

"You pay him." Odom bent the nail he was driving, cursed and pulled the nail. "I ain't paying no preacher nothing."

"Then knock off and go fishing. Even the Lord didn't work on the seventh day."

"The Lord didn't live on a ranch. And he had no use for a good dance floor. You lay off of me, Hyram, or I'll build this floor crooked so you and the little gals you dance with come Saturday week can't two-step without falling on each other."

As Hyram, Jason, and Angela drove off in Hyram's pickup, Angela said, "Odom's looking forward to your party."

"Yeah. To the keg of beer and watching the fillies dance. It's against his religion to do much that ain't work, 'cept for drinking beer and thinking about the gals. He don't like to talk with them or dance or nothing like that. But he likes to look. I bet by the time we get home, Odom has the floor finished, has a respectable barbecue hole dug out and is chopping mesquite for the fire. And the party ain't due for a long spell."

Angela looked back at the ranch. "I would have invited him to come with us, but I know he thinks tennis is a waste of time."

"It is, for a fact. No offense, Jason, but I never could see the reason for it. You bat a little ball with a stiff-looking fish net, then run like hell so you can bat it again. It's a dumber game than golf, and that's going some. Golfers are a case. Hit the ball, chase it. Hit the ball, chase it. It must feel good to them that does it, cause they is all the time out there on that Hunsley Hills course, trooping around with their shiny sticks and funny-looking hats, scratching around on the ground to find the balls they hit."

"Tennis is just a game. For me, it's a way to have fun and stay in shape, and to get a scholarship to the university in Canyon."

"I don't see the reason for it. No offense. Maybe I got raised all wrong. Or growed wrong in my mama's womb—got my eyeball nerve crossed up with an asshole nerve, so I got me a case of ocular rectitus. For sure I got a crappy outlook when it comes to tennis and golf."

"Hyram!" Angela slapped his leg. "You say the grossest things."

"But you love it. You pure-dee love it, all them gross things I say." Hyram laughed.

Jason liked Hyram but was puzzled by him. Was he always the clown? Or was he serious sometimes in his clowning? The only time Jason could remember Hyram being serious was when he told about Lint killing Regan.

It had taken Jason weeks of close listening and watching Hyram's mouth just to understand the literal meaning of the words the man spoke, and still sometimes it was a strain. I now, Jason thought, understand Texan. As a language. But how do I read the meaning behind all that strange way of talking, when it comes to someone like Hyram? Does he really hate sports? Then why come to see me play? Why does he read the sports page of the paper?

Hryam parked by the tennis courts. "That there is Lint Bodark's pickup. What's he doing at a tennis match?"

"He came yesterday, but he didn't watch tennis. He watched Angela. And he left before the match was over."

"There he is," Hyram pointed. "He's watching the tennis now. And looks like he's got a drink in his hand."

Lint sat on the lower part of the bleachers. When Hyram, Jason and Angela approached, he stood up and grinned. "Great day for tennis, ain't it?" He held up a can. "Dr Pepper. I see you folks looking at it. I done give up drinking ever' thing but soft stuff like this."

"Lint Bodark," Angela demanded, "what the hell are you doing here?"

"I come to watch the tennis, Angie. I'm a real sports fan."

"I'd call you a regular athletic supporter," Hyram said. "You like tennis about as much as Odom likes rattlesnakes. I happen to be of the opinion that you need to get in your truck and clear out of here."

"Come on, Hyram. This here's a free country. I came same as you, to watch this boy play in the finals." Lint sat down.

"Let's sit right up there. Jason, you get on out there and warm up. Angela, you don't happen to have a nail file, do you? I need to clean my fingernails."

"Hyram, have you ever seen me use a nail file?"

"Then I just gotta use my knife, I suppose." Hyram unsnapped the leather pouch on his belt and took out his lock-back knife. He bent down in front of Lint and unfolded the knife. "Course, I gotta be right careful with this, seeing that it's sharp as my grandpa's razor. I could slip and cut somebody's throat with it." He gave Lint a hard look.

Lint laughed. "They'll report it in the *Canyon News*. 'Man cuts his own throat while cleaning fingernails.' Just sit down, Hyram, and enjoy the match. These girls playing right now, why they're worth watching.

One of them got real pretty eyes, big and brown as the eyes of a two-day-old heifer. And the other girl is cute as a cottontail." To Jason's surprise, Hyram laughed with what sounded like real amusement.

Jason went to a back court to stretch and hit a few shots. If it isn't guns, Jason thought, it's knives. He shook his head. It's a wonder the cowboys in Texas haven't become extinct from killing each other off.

Then he remembered punching Altus, and his cheeks flushed. He tried a serve but hit the ball into the net. You've got to concentrate, he told himself. Concentrate on tennis, not on Lint or Angela or Hyram. Tennis. Clear your mind of everything but tennis.

He bounced the ball several times, imagining that nothing existed in the world except for him and the tennis court. Then he hit a serve that would be a winner in any game.

When match time came, Jason felt centered, ready to play his best. He shook hands across the net with Malcolm and smiled. Malcolm narrowed his eyes. He's far too serious, Jason thought. He gripped Malcolm's hand tighter, then released it. "Be careful," Jason told him, "or you might wind up having fun when we play."

"Jesus," Malcolm muttered. "You nuts or what?" Jason went behind the baseline to receive serve.

Malcolm looked long and hard at Jason before serving, scowling in a mean-looking way. The first serve went out by inches. Malcolm didn't slow the second serve down at all, and it bounced good for a winner. The crowd on the bleachers applauded. Malcolm sneered at Jason.

He's showing me he doesn't have to worry about a double-fault, Jason thought. He's trying to get me rattled. And it's working.

Jason felt his palm begin to sweat. He looked toward the bleachers and saw Lint spitting into his Dr Pepper can. That man tried to murder me with a prairie fire, Jason thought; and now Malcolm is trying to kill me on the tennis court.

An image of a putting green came to Jason's mind. Sybil sat near the flag, nude. He wondered if anyone had ever come to the university tennis courts in the middle of the night to strip and make love, on the add court, maybe, close to where Malcolm stood, scowling. Maybe they made it on a towel brought there in a motorcycle saddlebag.

Malcolm served an ace and the crowd applauded again. Jason shook his head to banish the image of a couple copulating in a pool of moonlight there on the tennis court. He glanced at the audience. Lint clapped like an avid fan; Angela and Hyram looked glum. Jason took a deep breath. The cobra and the mongoose, he thought. And it's my luck to be the slow-moving, doomed cobra.

The way Malcolm served out the game looked easy. He ran Jason from one side of the court to the other, toying with him, laughing when Jason lost each point.

In the second game, Jason double-faulted twice. His hand seemed to sweat more than it ever did in the tropical heat of Malaysia, and he mishit his ground strokes.

The first set went to Malcolm, six to love. Jason leaned his racket against the net, picked up the Thermos Angela had given him, took off the lid, and found a note taped to the stopper. He unfolded the note. "Malcolm Roddy is the dumbest name I ever heard, even for a lawyer. Beat him, Jason."

Jason looked up at the bleachers. Angela stood up and cupped her hands around her mouth. "You can do it. You know you can do it. Remember what you said."

What did I say? Jason wondered. He picked up his towel and wiped his hands and forehead. Then he remembered.

He walked to the back of the service line and crouched, waiting for the serve. Malcolm looked startled, then laughed. Some people in the crowd laughed, and a few whistled derision at Jason. "Get further back, kid," one man yelled.

Malcolm tried for his strongest boomer serve. It went out by over a meter.

Jason held up a thumb and finger to show that the serve was close. The crowd laughed again, this time at Malcolm. His face got red, and he tried for another boomer serve. It went out by nearly two meters. Malcolm struck the court with his racket and cursed. Jason laughed without humor but loud so Malcolm would hear.

He tried for another sneer right before his serve, but when he saw Jason standing inside the service line, the expression turned to pure rage. He served the ball into the net.

For the next serve, Jason retreated to the base line. Malcolm patty-caked in a blooper of a serve, then rushed the net. Jason hit a shot past him, and the crowd roared its approval.

Malcolm's next serve went wide, and the second serve bounced so high that Jason smashed it for an easy win.

As they walked past each other changing courts, Jason whispered, "I told you that you could have fun playing if you tried."

"Asshole!" Malcolm snapped. The crowd heard him and booed.

Jason served two aces, then rushed the net on serve and volleyed for a winner. He put heavy topspin on the next serve so it bounced high, and Malcolm hit it with the edge of his racket, losing the point and the game. He smashed his racket against the court and the strings broke. The crowd booed.

Malcolm got another racket from his bag. He served without looking at Jason, concentrating better on his shots. But he made repeated mistakes in judgment—lobbing at the wrong time, rushing the net on shallow serves. Jason won the next two sets six-two, six-four.

After winning match point, Jason went to the net to shake hands. Malcolm looked at Jason's hand and walked off the court. The crowd booed him one final time.

Angela ran onto the court and hugged Jason. "I'm sweaty," he warned. "You'll get wet."

"I don't care. You were great, Jason. Great." She pressed against him.

Jason patted her back and looked toward the bleachers. Lint Bodark stood by the fence, Dr Pepper can in hand. His eyes met Jason's. Lint lifted a lip in a snarl then turned and spat on the ground.

A thunderstorm drifted up from the southwest during the night and dropped nearly two inches of rain on Canyon. Sybil awoke to the sound of hail pelting the roof. She sat by a bedroom window and watched lightning light up the meadow behind her house, watched pea-sized hail bounce in the neon flashes; then rain come in sharp, cold needles.

In the morning, she decided to check the bees to make sure their hive had not been damaged. Going out in the damp barefooted appealed to her. She wanted to feel the wet grass under her feet, maybe wade in a puddle, if she could find one that wasn't too muddy. She put on a tee shirt and white jeans, rolling up the legs for the wet.

Water stood here and there, puddling mud upon the path from her back door beyond the burnt kennels to the hive among the cottonwood trees. The bees seemed to take no notice of the water. Their flight pattern buzzed loud around the hive entrance. A western king bird sat high in one of the cottonwoods, watching. Sybil saw it swoop into the flight pattern, snap a bee in its beak, and dart back for the high branch. Bees followed the bird, and one stung it, causing the bird to squawk. It lit on the branch, becoming rock still, and bees flew around it several times before going back toward the hive. The bird jerked its head, crunching the bee in its beak. Sybil wondered how it felt to swallow a bee whole, stinger and all.

"Good work," she told the bird. As far as she was concerned, it could eat all the bees it had the nerve to catch, for there were plenty in the hive to spare a few for bird meals: out of some 80,000, as she estimated, a dozen or so made no difference. Besides, she admired the bird for having the nerve to make its living catching bees.

As Sybil turned back toward the house, she saw Pug coming toward her, a figure in black striding with determined steps. Sybil stood on a grassy spot beside the muddy path and waited.

"Good Morning, Sybil." Pug held her brows knit into a half frown.

"Pug."

"You look good. Have you been doing well?"

"Yes. No thanks to you and your dirty tricks."

"Whatever are you talking about?"

"That rattlesnake, for starters. A truck load of white gravel. The other things—you remember. And, of course, the phone calls."

"Snakes? Gravel? I'm sure I don't know what you're talking about."

"I would have talked with you about stopping the harassment, but you were clever enough to get an unlisted phone number."

"You look so upset. Yes, I changed my number. Someone started making obscene phone calls, so I got an unlisted number. Of course I'll give it to you. Have your Canyon neighbors been bothering you again? Sybil, why not just move in with me? The only harassment I have experienced in Amarillo has been those phone calls, and I solved that problem."

Sybil studied Pug. The woman seemed so hard. Her lips compressed into a tight line, and she squinted her eyes so that lines creased the corners. "So you want me to live with you?"

"I'm offering you a room in my apartment, yes. As one friend to another."

"As a friend, Pug? I might have believed that, once. But your friends are folk I want nothing to do with."

"And just what is that supposed to mean?"

"I guess I mean your taste in men. Morons like Altus that you like to keep dangling to suit your purpose. I don't understand what you want with me, Pug. I am not your kind."

Pug's frown deepened. "I want to be your friend."

"I'm afraid that somewhere inside you is a desire for more of me than that. Might you like me just a bit too much, Pug? I mean, is it possible that you want me in some unusual ways, ones I'm not capable of handling, so you get angry at me? Pug, I'm not like you—I prefer men to women."

"You mean that you like Jason. What can he do for you, Sybil? He's little more than a child."

"Some parts of him are full grown, Pug. Right after you pulled those cute stunts at your birthday party, Jason showed me what a man he could be."

Pug let out a tiny groan and leaped at Sybil, grabbing her hair, kicking. Startled, Sybil stepped back, tripped and fell to the wet grass with Pug on top of her. "Bitch! Bitch!" Pug spat the words low and angry while she jerked Sybil's head this way and that with the grip she had on her hair.

Sybil put a hand on Pug's face and heaved to one side, rolling over on top of Pug, tumbling her from the grass into the muddy water on the path. Pug held tight to Sybil's hair and grunted as Sybil came on top of her.

Grasping one of Pug's hands, Sybil bent a thumb, tightened her grip and pressed until Pug cried out, releasing Sybil's hair. She tried to get the nails of her other hand into Sybil's eyes. Sybil drew back, knocked the hand from her face, and pressed harder on Pug's thumb. "Bitch, bitch, bitch!" Pug repeated and tried again to rake Sybil's face.

"Stop it, Pug. Stop it now." Sybil straddled Pug's body, pinning her into the mud puddle. Pug kept struggling, so Sybil took her hair, twisted her head to one side, and held her face into the water, then lifted her nose out of it. Pug flailed about with her free hand, sputtered and fought for air. "Enough?" Sybil pressed Pug's face toward the water again.

"Yes, for godsake. Enough!"

"I'm going to let you up, Pug. But you have to promise you'll not jump on me again like that. Okay?" When she got no immediate answer, she pressed Pug's face toward the water.

"Okay! Okay!"

Sybil stood up. Pug remained prone on her back in the mud while Sybil stood over her. Theatrics, Sybil thought, but she said nothing.

Pug made a show of finding it difficult to stand. When she got to her feet, she did so with her back to Sybil, took several steps, then turned, dripping and muddy, to look with venom at Sybil.

"You are a sick, sick woman, Pug. And I'm not talking about your preferences in bed. I'm talking about the meanness of your spirit. I would feel sorry for you but for all the mean tricks you've pulled. Go away, now. Stay away. You have no reason to keep trying to scare me out of my home, not now that it's clear to us both that I will never in my wildest nightmare consider living in your apartment."

Pug's face hardened. She ran her eyes from Sybil's face to her feet and back, then she spun around and walked away, her black blouse and pants gray with mud. Sybil thought she had never seen anyone so angry.

I'll have to soak my jeans in bleach, Sybil thought, looking down at herself. Her wet tee shirt clung to her breasts, revealing their fullness and both nipples standing hard and firm.

She thought of Jason. If he saw me fighting Pug, wrestling around in the mud like that, he would be appalled. She imagined his face if he had stood beneath the cottonwood, watching her fight. It would be filled with disgust, that brown, lovely face, and he would label me a barbarian, lump me along with the cowboys he saw in the Crystal Pistol. He would despise me. And I've earned it, haven't I? Earned the animosity of one who abhors violence. It wasn't necessary to bait Pug like that, making her explode. I became as violent as she. More so.

Sybil's cheeks burned with humiliation, and she hated Jason for making her see herself as a wild harpy. She walked toward her back door, staying on the mud path, kicking the brown stuff, splattering more of it on her clothes.

At least, she thought, at least I'll be rid of all the bothersome harassment around here, what with Pug gone for good.

But that night the phone calls resumed, and the next day a delivery man arrived with thirty pounds of chicken livers.

39

After Jason watched Angela ride toward the first streaks of morning light, he dressed and wandered into the kitchen to make a pot of coffee. He heard Hyram turn on the shower just as the phone rang. Jason let it ring several times, then answered.

"Jason? Jason, are you all right?"

"Mom? Are you calling from Kuala Lumpur?"

"Yes," Jason's father said, "And me, on the phone downstairs. How's life in West Texas?"

"Fine. Strange, though. Hyram is as comical a person as I have ever met. He has a woman who keeps books and cooks—"

"Jason, are you all right?"

"Yes. I'm fine."

"I mean your leg. Did it heal without any problems?"

"It healed fine. I'm playing tennis on it."

"Already? Jason, you listen to me. You take it easy on that leg."

"I've been out of the cast a long time, now. Dad, I won the Canyon Tennis Open yesterday. The championship. That probably means a tennis scholarship this fall."

"The championship? Great. But, Jason, you don't need a scholarship. You should spend your time studying. You need to be able to go to school without distractions."

Jason held the phone away and sighed. They still treat me like a child, he thought. "I know, Dad. And I appreciate your saying that. It's important to me to pay for as much of my own education as I can. And I want the scholarship for recreation, to help me keep in shape. And for the travel to tournaments. I haven't seen much of this country."

"Just don't let it interfere with your studies," his mother said.

"Is Hyram there? Can I talk with him?"

"He's taking a shower, Dad."

"I'll talk with him later, then. Do you like him, Jason?"

"Yes. I do. He gives me everything. His guest room. A pickup to run around in. He even bought me some western clothes. He came to watch me win the tennis finals, and he was supportive, even if he said some strange things. Did you know his sixty-fifth birthday is coming up this week?"

"No. Sixty-five? No, that's not right, Jason. He and I were in the army together, remember? Stationed in Fort Hood, right there in Texas. We were best buddies. After our hitch in the army, we went to West Texas State together—"

"I know, Dad."

"Yes. Well, the point is, I know Hyram's age. He's six years older than I am, which would make him fifty-five. Not sixty-five."

"No kidding?"

"Jason," his mother said, "Did you know you talk with a Texas accent?"

"I do?"

"You have picked it up a bit, Jason." His father laughed. "But that happens to anyone. Anyone."

"In some ways I've worked at being a Texan," Jason said. "But I thought I'd never pick up their way of speaking."

"He told you he would be sixty-five? That's just like him. Always joking."

"You look young, Dad. Hyram looks old. Really old."

"Ranchers get wrinkled at an early age, son. They're out in the sun all the time. Back when we were fresh graduates from West Texas State University, he looked younger than me."

"It's called West Texas A&M now."

"Yeah. I keep forgetting."

"Are you saying Hyram has a university degree? Did he really graduate?"

"He did. Hyram plays a game about being an ignorant country boy, Jason. But he was an honors student at the university."

"Honors? I believe that. Hyram does seem to know a lot more than you would expect. But, Dad, he talks like an ignorant hick. Why would an educated person talk like that?"

"Hyram might be a country hick, but he is far from ignorant. He always did use colorful language, even when he talked to teachers in the classes we had together. Hyram would often make the highest grade in class on an exam, but he never admitted it. He got a degree in agriculture or agricultural business or something. And he played on the tennis team. Did he tell you that?"

"On the tennis team? Dad, Hyram hates sports, especially tennis. And you ought to see him. I could wrap his belt around me at least three times."

"He always did tend to carry a little extra weight, even as a young man. If he told you he hates tennis, he was kidding in his odd, West

Texas way. Ask him about the top tennis players today. He'll know them. He practically memorizes the sports pages of the paper. Or he used to. Ask him."

"Jason," his mother said, "You plan on flying home for the Christmas holidays, all right? The three of us will go to Bali for two weeks. Spend some time on the beach."

"I can't afford the airfare."

"I'll send you the tickets, son."

"No. I'm a grown man now. It's time for you to stop spending money on me like I still lived in your home."

His mother sighed in a theatrical way. "I knew you would say that. I knew it. Tell me the truth, Jason, do you need any money?"

"No, Mom. Nothing out here costs me anything. Hyram—"

"You do sound like a cowboy, Jason." His father laughed.

"Have you decided about living in the dorm? It might be quieter to live on Hyram's ranch."

"Probably the dorm. I don't know yet."

"You call us if you need anything?"

"Yes, Mom. Thanks." Jason said goodbye and hung up.

Hyram came into the kitchen. "Morning, Jason. Where's Angela?"

"She's out greeting the sun."

"Greeting the sun?" Hyram sounded puzzled.

So, Jason thought, Angela has never told him about her morning ritual. The realization pleased him. "You're up early."

"Is that a fact? The early bird gets the worm, they say. Which is why I don't always get up as early as you young folk. I don't want the worm."

"Mom and Dad called. Dad said you were on the tennis team when you were in college."

"Your dad said that? Well I'll be dogged. Jason, you tell Angela not to bother cooking eggs this morning. I got some business in Canyon, so I'll just run on over there and grab me some breakfast at the Chuck Wagon. You want to go? I'm going to a little nothing of a horse auction north of Canyon. Heard there's a roan going into the sell ring, one I been wanting."

Jason hesitated. He wanted to see a horse auction, but he had agreed to go to Amarillo with Angela to shop for a birthday gift for Hyram. Jason had suggested getting one of the gems he bought from Malaysia set in a ring or a belt buckle. Angela said she was of the opinion that the stones were all too pretty for an old cowboy like Hyram, though she did find a blue topaz among the stones that might be all right, if the jeweler, Janus, approved.

"Thanks, Hyram. Any other day but today, and I'd go with you. I have some errands myself. In Amarillo."

"Some other time, then. And you gotta make it to my auction coming up. Biggest one from Snake Mountain clean to Prairie Dog Creek. You'll learn something about dealing horses. Last time we done one, you was all gimped up, so I didn't say nothing about it. You recovered right proper, though, seeing as you whipped everbody in two counties in tennis. Jason, you're one helluva tennis player, not to mention being a fox at gamesmanship. Better than old Malcolm. He can look right mean when he serves. Right mean."

"The mean-looking one at the tennis courts was Lint Bodark. Did you see him when Angela hugged me after the match?"

"I did for a fact. In his case, Jason, he ain't bluffing. He is mean. I let him be when I shoulda run the bastard off. Thing is, he can be a likable cuss and make you forget for a minute or two that he's such a dadburned jackass. You get to thinking that he might mend his ways when he talks up a good job of reforming. But you gotta keep reminding yourself about rule number two in life. That rule says you can't polish a turd." Hyram held his belly and laughed. "Nosir, you just can't polish a turd." He left the kitchen, laughing.

When Angela returned, Jason met her at the corral. "Prickly pears have red fruit on them. Ripe ones." She stripped Ghost and turned him into the pasture.

"Hyram went to town." Jason watched her put the English riding saddle into the tack shed. "He said to tell you—"

"That he would eat at the Chuck Wagon. Yeah." She rubbed her hands on her jeans, then took Jason's arm. "You ever eat cactus fruit?"

"No." They walked toward the house. Odom worked in the yard, doing something with mesquite logs. He waved.

"Morning, Odom. Never tried them, Jason? Then you got to ride out with me, come Saturday. Today is beautiful. You should have been out there on the prairie with me. The love grass has come back where Lint put the burn, and there are ground flowers. You need to be out again at sunrise, when everything is fresh and covered with dew. The sun comes up over Snake Mountain, and the little drops of water on the flowers and grass look like diamonds and the yucca look slicked down and green from the morning wet."

"I read that the yucca is sometimes called the desert lily."

"Not around here, it ain't. Cowboys call it bear grass. Jason, remember what I said about always wanting to meet the morning sun on top of Snake Mountain? But it would mean riding out mighty early, maybe carrying lights. That or spending the night on top of the mountain." She stopped walking and turned to him, standing close, looking up at his face. "Will you do that with me sometime, Jason? Will you stand with me on top of Snake Mountain in the first rays of morning?"

Jason thought he had never seen her so intense and so beautiful. He imagined them standing together, nude, on the bed rock, facing east, saying nothing but being aware of touching arms and maybe legs as the sun came lemon-yellow and crimson, staining the horizon with new light.

Angela gripped his arm and pulled him to her. He thought he should kiss her. "Will you go?" she demanded.

"It would be like heaven." He leaned toward her. She released his arm and stepped back.

"You want to kiss me," she said. "And I want that, too—more than you know. But not now. Not now. You was right about what you said that last time we greeted the sun." She turned and set a quick pace toward her bunkhouse.

Angela came to the main house to announce it was time to go see Janus about Hyram's birthday present. She seemed not to remember what had passed between them that morning. When they got into the pickup, she said, "I put Hyram's nine millimeter in the glove box."

Jason said nothing. Carrying a pistol seemed so absurd—as if he could ever use it. As if he could be like the red-headed man in the airport, pointing the pistol at Suppriah, firing. He thought of Lint's murderous look when Angela hugged him on the tennis court the previous day. Maybe, he thought, Angela would need that pistol, if Lint Bodark sees us together.

Need it? Jason was amazed that he had such a thought. Need it? Did anyone need such a weapon? Maybe Angela thought she did, but he sure didn't. He decided he would take it out of the pickup later if Angela did not.

She sat so close that their legs touched. "You can't buckle your seat belt sitting there," Jason said.

"I don't like seat belts. You just drive and let me worry about where to sit."

When they left the dirt road and drove onto the blacktop, Angela put her head on Jason's shoulder and sighed. Then she moved to the other side of pickup.

Jason glanced at her. "What's the heavy sigh about?"

"It's about Lint Bodark, that bastard. He's got friends all over the place, and if one sees us cozied up and tells him, he's liable to come after you. Lint's meaner than an acre of rattlesnakes, even if his friends don't know that. You'd think a man like Lint would have no friends, but he does. He's a charmer, that Lint, unless you live with him. Then you learn different."

At Janus' Jewels in Amarillo, Janus looked at Jason's gemstones and drew the corners of her mouth down. "You want me to make something for a rancher?"

"Yes. For what he says is his sixty-fifth birthday, even if he is only fifty-five years old."

"I could make something for him from one of these, but I doubt an old rancher would have much to do with it."

"I thought these rocks was a tad prissy," Angela said.

Prissy? The word startled Jason. Such a word certainly didn't occur to him in Kuala Lumpur when he bought the stones from the Grukha tribesman who had knocked Tom to the floor. What was his name? Jason groped for the name, then shrugged.

"How about a bolo? I could put a nugget of some kind on a bolo string tie. I'll bet a rancher would go for that. How about something like this?" She produced a tray of polished stones. Each reflected light like a rainbow.

"What are these?"

"Fire agates?" Angela picked one up. "These are the prettiest rocks I ever saw."

Chander, Jason remembered. The Grukha's name was Chander. He wondered that such details, so important to him once, could be slipping away.

"Yes, from Pima, Arizona. Really fine fire agates, the best I have ever bought. Does this rancher wear string ties?"

"Sometimes," Angela said. "If he wears a tie, you can bet it's a string. He's got only one—an ugly thing with a scorpion stuck inside of some clear plastic. What would this one cost set in a tie?" She picked up the largest of the agates.

Janus weighed the stone, then did some scribbling on a pad of paper. Angela turned to Jason. "What was that about Hyram being only fifty-five?"

"My father told me on the phone how old Hyram really is. Why would Hyram tell us he's ten years older than he is?"

"You can bet he has his reasons."

Janus looked up from her scribbling. "You picked the most expensive one. I'm afraid that stone set into a bolo would be nearly $200. One hundred eighty seven to be exact."

"Well forget that." Angela waved her hand.

"No. Make the bolo for me."

"Jason! that's too much money for a rock tied to a string."

"Not if Hyram would enjoy it. Angela, Hyram is so generous with me, and what do I do for him? Nothing. It would give me pleasure to get something nice for him."

They left Janus' Jewels and went to Boots N Jeans, where Angela bought an enormous shirt for Hyram. On their way back to the ranch, Angela said, "You should of got Hyram a hat. You could buy a fine Stetson for less than you paid for that rock."

Jason said nothing. He kept glancing at her, trying to determine what was going on. Was Angela angry that he bought the fire agate? Why should she be? It wasn't her money. He shrugged.

Angela directed him out of Amarillo on South Washington. Jason recognized the street as the one where, only a short time ago, Lint Bodark had fired at them with a pistol, and Angela had fired back with a shotgun. He remembered thinking at the time that he wanted nothing more to do with Angela.

And look at us now, Jason thought.

As he approached the turnoff from the blacktop, Angela slid across the seat and put her head on Jason's shoulder. "I'm glad you done it," she said.

"Glad I done what? Did. Did what?"

"I'm glad you bought that fire agate for Hyram. He will love it. Mind you, though, he just might make fun of it for being so pretty. But he'll love it."

Jason parked beside Hyram's house. "Lookit Odom," Angela said. "He's chunking something."

"He's what?"

"Chunking rocks at something. Ain't that just like Odom, to chunk rocks instead of using something better." She got out of the pickup and headed toward her bunkhouse. Odom picked up a stone and threw it toward a herd of cows in the pasture beyond the fence.

Jason joined Odom. "Howdy, Jason." Odom threw another rock.

"Hello, Odom." Jason looked at the cattle. They were agitated and moving around. Then Jason saw the dogs—the Doobie Brothers—nipping at the flanks of a calf. The calf scrambled into the herd, and one cow charged the dogs, her horns low to the ground. The dogs ran around her after the calf.

"Dang dogs." Odom threw another stone. "They'll worry that calf plumb to death. Get! Doobie, you get, now! Get!"

Jason watched the dogs chase the calf through the herd, then cut it off from the other cattle and run it out across the prairie. Then he saw Angela.

She rested a rifle on top of a fence post and sighted down it toward the Doobie Brothers. "No!" Jason yelled, but his voice was drowned out by the report of the rifle. One of the dogs fell. Jason watched in horror as it tried to get up. Another bullet smashed into it; the dog jerked and lay still.

"No Angela," Jason called out. He ran toward her. She glanced up at him, then sighted down the rifle again and squeezed the trigger.

The other dog tumbled and rolled, leaving a puff of dust hanging over it. The calf kept running.

Angela pushed a strand of barbed wire down and climbed through the fence. Jason followed her. As he went between the wires, he felt a barb grab his shirt and tear into his back. But he pushed on through, hearing the shirt rip. He took a few quick steps to catch up with her. She strode up to the first dog.

"Look at it, Angela. It's little more than a puppy. Look at it."

"I am. It shouldn't have took me two shots. I got the other dog with one."

"But why? Why, Angela?" He stared at the dead dog. Blood spilled from its side, and part of its snout had been shot away. "Why?"

Angela walked on to look at the other dog. When she came back, Jason still stood staring in horror at the dead animal. "Come on," she said. "Come on, now. You get into the house. Odom and I will bury the dogs. Come on." She took his arm.

Jason looked at her hand on his arm, then met her eyes. He pulled away.

"Shit. You act like I enjoyed shooting the Doobie Brothers. They weren't much, far as dogs go, but I liked them, Jason. I sure didn't want to shoot them. But they was running the calves. You saw that."

"But to kill them! Angela, you could have given them away. Or taken them to the pound. You didn't have to kill them."

"You can't give a dog to a neighbor if it runs cows. They won't stop doing it. All you can do is shoot them. At the pound in Canyon or Amarillo, they'd just gas them, so why go to the bother of hauling them to town?"

Jason stared at Angela. She seemed like a stranger standing there with the rifle in her hands, like someone he was looking at for the first time. He tried to see her as she was that morning when he had leaned toward her, offering a kiss.

But it was no use. He looked again at the corpse of the dog, shook his head, and started walking toward the pickup.

41

Jason drove to Canyon, not having any destination in mind. He parked by the university tennis courts, then cursed himself for not thinking to bring his tennis gear. It would feel good, he thought, to hit a few balls, maybe run some laps around the track. Exercise might banish the image of Angela standing with a rifle over the dog, its nose shot away.

Then he remembered the nine millimeter and opened the glove box to see if it were indeed there. It was. And beside it an index card with something written on it.

Sybil's phone number. He had forgotten she gave it to him—slipped it into his pocket the day they taxed the bees. The day he had punched Altus. The day that led to them making love on a golf course. He took the card from the glove box and stared at the number for several minutes, then got out of the pickup and walked to the pay phone beside the entry to the university police station.

When the phone clicked with a mechanical sound, he knew he had managed only to reach an answering machine. Sybil's recorded voice said, "This is the number you just dialed, and this is the beep."

"Hello, Sybil. I just called to. . . ."

The phone clicked and Sybil said, "Jason? Hold on a moment. Let me turn the machine off. Sorry about that, but I use it these days to screen calls."

"These days?" His voice took on a hostile edge. "Since we went to the bikers' party, do you mean? Since we went to the Amarillo Country Club?"

"Don't be so defensive, Jason. No. The answering machine has nothing to do with you. In fact, I was hoping you would call. Or come by."

"You were?"

"Someone is pulling some mean tricks on me. Meaner than leaving a dead pigeon with a cryptic note. Meaner than burning my kennels. This morning was the meanest trick yet."

"Sybil, what is going on?"

"Where are you, Jason? Can you come over?"

"Now?"

"Yes. Right now. I managed to deal with the rattlesnake and the dead prairie dog and the chicken livers and the quartz crystals. But this last trick has me strung tight enough to snap."

"I'm at the tennis center. It should take me less than ten minutes to get there."

On the way over, Jason wished he had not called her. So here I am, he thought, trying to sort through what I just saw Angela do to the Doobie Brothers, and what do I do? I get involved with a woman who has even more problems than I. Anyway, she doesn't want to see me—she just wants a distraction from her problems. Just as she used me to get Pug to leave her house, and just as she used me out there on the golf course. So when I serve my purpose, out I'll go, given the boot. Why do I set myself up this way? Crap.

When he got to Sybil's driveway, he found a hand-lettered sign taped to her mailbox: "Notice to Delivery men: If you have something for this address, I did not order it. Leave nothing here. Please take one of these sheets for an explanation." Attached to the sign was a sheaf of paper.

Sybil met him on the driveway. She got into the pickup. "Take me somewhere." Her voice seemed strained and thin.

Jason backed into the street. "Where?"

"Anywhere. Just drive."

"I saw your sign. What does your note say?"

"That someone is victimizing me and the merchants who are asked to deliver merchandise to my home."

Jason headed toward Fourth Avenue, thinking he might drive toward Palo Duro Canyon State Park. "Merchandise? I thought you mentioned a snake and a dead prairie dog and chicken livers."

"Not everything around my house these days is the result of commercial deliverymen." She told him about the rattlesnake on the mailbox, about a prairie dog wired to the elm, about the load of decorative stones. "And there's more. Twenty bags of bat guano arrived a few days ago. I got the idea for the sign from a man who was supposed to leave a barrel of quartz crystals from a mine in Arkansas. He had an order on official-looking letterhead paper from Redbear Rock Shop ordering the crystals. The letterhead gave my address as the place of business. Jason, someone is putting out a great deal of energy and money to annoy me. And then there's the phone calls." Sybil slumped in the seat, looking exhausted.

"Have you called the police?"

"No. I do not deal with cops."

"Were the phone calls threatening ones or obscene calls?"

"I would call them both. At all hours of the night. I sure am low on energy. What time is it?"

"Just after noon."

"Have you had lunch? I just realized that I haven't eaten since yesterday morning."

"Lunch sounds good to me." Jason turned toward The Rail Road Crossing Restaurant. "So someone is harassing you on the phone."

"Yes. Breathers. Males saying nasty things. Females saying nasty things. I thought hanging up would discourage them, but it did not. So I bought an answering machine. They leave messages, sometimes in an electronically distorted voice, sometimes in what sounds like a computer-simulated voice. Weird messages."

"Weird? Like what?"

"Like 'You will surrender Singapore or we will cut off your water supply.' That came in the night. In the morning, I discovered that someone had turned off my water at the meter. It was easy to turn back on, but an annoyance. The worst thing they did, though, happened sometime during the night."

"You alluded to that on the phone when I called. What happened?"

"Two days ago, I got a dog. One that would make some real noise. A pit bull, nearly grown. She was beautiful. I always thought pit bulls would look like frogs—you know, with that broad head and underslung jaw that you associate with a bull dog. But I was wrong. I answered an ad in the *Amarillo Globe* for a good guard dog and found a pit bull. It was a normal-looking dog, shaped up almost like a Dalmatian, only solid brown instead of spotted. Rupita. She was beautiful, and she did her job. That first night, someone came to my bedroom window, and Rupita tore up the Venetian blinds trying to get at the prowler. She growled and barked something fierce. Nothing happened the next night. Then last night, when she growled and barked at the back door, I let her out. That was the last time I saw her."

Jason parked beside The Rail Road Crossing. "Does this sound okay for lunch?"

Sybil nodded. On the way in, she took his arm. Jason almost withdrew, as she had done from him in Denny's, but he didn't. You're being used again, he warned himself. Don't allow it. Be friendly. Stay distant. Stay wary.

Inside, he asked to be seated in the non-smoking section. As the hostess led them toward the back, he asked her, "Why do you put the smokers up front so the non-smokers must walk through a cloud of nasty smoke? Why not reverse that? Put the smokers in the back?"

"This is your table. Your waitress will be with you shortly."

Jason and Sybil sat on opposite sides of a booth and the hostess placed menus in front of them. Jason tried to make eye contact with the hostess, but she would not. "That's all the answer I'll get?" he asked. The hostess walked away. "Thanks for the friendly service," he called after her.

Sybil looked solemn. "Do you practice being sarcastic?"

"She deserved it."

"True. But you didn't deserve to have to stoop to it."

"Thanks."

"There you go again, being sarcastic."

"Are you baiting me?"

"No. I'm asking you to loosen up."

"You're asking me? You? Have you heard the stress in your own voice, Sybil?"

"Yes. I shouldn't be here. I don't need your anger on top of everything else." Sybil stood. "I can walk home."

"No. I'm sorry. Please. Sit and have some food. The salad bar looked wonderful."

She hesitated, then sat down and picked up a menu.

Jason studied her. "So what happened to her?"

"To who?"

"Rupita. Your pit bull."

"I don't know. This morning I called and called. She's just gone."

"Is that the terrible thing that happened today? Someone took your dog?"

"No. Let's eat right now and get to the disgusting topics later, okay?"

Jason started the pickup. "Back to your place now?"

"I guess. No, not just yet, please. Go down this street—Fourteenth Avenue. At the end of it is a town park. Let's go there and walk around.

He parked beside some children's playground equipment. They walked beyond it, over a basketball court, toward a pond edged with cattails. Jason noticed some tennis courts off to the right, just west of a series of cement ponds surrounded by a fence. A circular brush-looking device picked up the water in one pond, stirring it. Wind blew from the south, and when they got just north of the fenced-in ponds, they felt a fine mist of water blown from the stirring device.

"Is that what I think it is?" Jason pointed south.

"What? Oh. The sewer treatment plant. Yes, if that's what you meant."

"This is sewer water on us? Gross." He took her arm and went back toward the pickup.

"I guess I'm so out of it that I didn't notice. Yes, this is sewer mist in the air. Jason, let's walk that way—around the road that circles the marshy pond. The mist will not reach us that far away." She turned and set a swift pace without waiting for an answer.

Jason caught up with her, glancing at her from time to time. The farther they walked, the more lively she seemed. By the time they had gone all the way around the park, she looked to be the Sybil he had come to like the day they had traded turns asking and giving personal information.

When they got near the pickup, she put her hand on his shoulder. "Thanks, Jason." He stood, not moving, offering no return touch. "That walk helped me. That and the food. Thanks. Now I'm up to showing you what they left for me behind my house."

They got into the pickup. "They?"

"Whoever. I don't know. Whoever is out to torment me."

Back at Sybil's house, they found her sign gone from the mailbox and a truck load of something brown in the yard. Sybil wrinkled her nose. "I hope that isn't what it appears to be."

Jason parked in the driveway and sniffed. "Bad news. It is. What's that white thing?" Even as he asked, he recognized it.

"A cow's skull. Someone killed a cow just to spook me?"

"No." He got out of the pickup, waited for her to come around beside him. "That cow died long ago. Look at how bleached out the skull is."

"This is scaring me."

"A cow's skull on a pile of manure scares you?"

"No. Don't be deliberately dense. It scares me that someone is watching me close enough to zip in here when I'm out for lunch, remove my sign, and have a load of crap delivered." She looked toward the street.

Jason glanced around. The nearest neighbor's houses stood nearly a block away to the north. To the south were the cottonwoods where Sybil kept her bees, and beyond that the land dipped through a meadow toward a wet-weather creek, land too subject to flooding for the town to grow in that direction. Jason saw no one. He looked back at the brown pile. "That crap smells terrible."

"I guess that's the reason someone ordered it for me. Look—there's a note on my door. That will be the bill. Good. I can call whoever delivered the stuff and have it hauled away.

Inside her house, Sybil began closing windows. "Ordinarily I prefer the ceiling fans. But today we get air conditioning, at least until the smell is gone." She disappeared into the back of the house to close windows.

Jason heard her make a all, explain the prank of having fertilizer delivered, ask that it be removed. When she returned, she looked tired again. "This is getting to me. Maybe I really should move away."

"Do you still want to tell me the worst thing the tricksters have done to you?"

"I'll show you." She sighed, deep and loud. "Let's go out the back way."

As they approached the cottonwoods, Jason sensed something wrong. Then he understood. "No bees. But there's the hive. Don't tell me they killed your bees."

"Yes. Someone sprayed them a few nights ago. About 80,000 bees murdered. That was bad, Jason. I cried when I saw it."

"Are you saying that killing the bees isn't the worst thing yet?"

"No. Not the worst. Come around here, behind this tree." She pointed, directing his attention to the high branches.

The horse's head was suspended from a chord that pierced its nose. From the severed neck hung threads of coagulated blood. Flies swarmed on the exposed neck muscles that protruded, black and stringy. A breeze ruffled the cottonwood leaves, and the severed head swung like a pendulum, twisting on the chord. Jason stepped close to Sybil, needing the touch, keeping his eyes turned up, staring at the horror in the tree.

Sybil felt rigid. He looked at her, found her eyes fixed on the ground beneath the head. She began trembling. "Rupita. Rupita." She stretched out her arm, pointing a quivering finger. "Rupita."

The dog lay on the ground where blood had dripped and puddled. Its skull had been crushed. One eye, popped from the socket, seemed to stare in a cold, glassy way, and Rupita's tongue lolled out over exposed teeth. Insects hung in a tiny black cloud above the ruined head, and flies walked in quick jerks over the dog's tongue and gums.

Sybil dropped her arm. "She wasn't there this morning. Someone put her there while we were out."

Jason closed his eyes. "I hate this place. Hate it."

"Yes. It needs hating. Jason, let's go inside."

She walked in front of him back to her house. Jason could see her shoulders shaking as she cried. It seemed to him that he should be offering her comfort, but he felt numb.

She sat on the couch in the living room. Jason started to sit in a chair opposite her, but she said, "No. Sit here."

He sat beside her and put his palms over his eyes. "This is a terrible day. First the Doobie Brothers, then the horse and your dog, Rupita. A terrible day."

"What do you mean, 'first the Doobie Brothers'? Did someone shoot them like they did the German Shepherd?"

"Yes. Angela, for Chrissake. Angela shot them."

"Why?"

"For chasing a calf. I watched her, tried to stop her. But it was no use." Jason sat back and looked at his hands. "Three quick shots with her rifle, and the dogs were gone. Like the prairie dog. Like Suppriah."

Sybil sat on the edge of the couch, leaning toward Jason. "When did this happen? When did Angela murder the dogs?"

"Today. Just before I drove to town and called you."

"Oh, Jason. And all I did was pour out my own misery. I'm so sorry. There I was, caught up in my own problems, and you call, needing to talk. But I didn't allow it." She stood on her knees on the couch, took Jason's head to her chest and stroked his hair.

He liked the comfort of it and nuzzled closer, rubbing his cheek against her breasts. Sybil unbuttoned her blouse, unsnapped a hook on the front of her bra, and bared her breasts, then took his cheeks in her hands and guided his mouth to a nipple.

Somehow her offering him comfort turned into a desperate clutching of bodies. Twice Sybil's passion dissolved into tears, and she held Jason to her while sobs shook her entire body. He thought she must be crying about something far more deep the loss of a dog. Then she became still for a while, moving only her fingers in his hair, drawing his lips toward hers. And they resumed the motions of loving each other, Sybil becoming vocal in her passion.

They lay on the floor, limp with exhaustion, her head on his chest. "Did you hear a truck?" she asked.

"Truck? Maybe. I thought I heard something."

She sat up and straightened her dark hair. Jason stared. "I like your breasts, especially when you lift your arms."

"I like you looking at them." She stood up beside the window. "It's gone. So I did hear a truck. They picked up the dung heap."

Jason sat on the couch. "Don't send me away again."

"Don't leave in a huff."

"You want me around?"

She sat beside him. "What do you think?"

"Say it. I think I want you to say it."

"I want you around." She raised her brows.

"I see a but coming. You want me around you but. But what?"

"But there are problems. You've been with Angela for some time now."

"Yes and no. I told her we would be formal with one another until her divorce is final. And by that I didn't mean the legal paperwork. I meant until she and he had settled it that they were finished with each other."

"Then, Jason, you understand. I must tell you the same thing. Settle your feelings about Angela. Then come to me, for I will not share you with another woman. Do I make sense?"

"Yes. But I am settled about Angela. Seeing her shoot the Doobie Brothers did that. I'm through with her."

"Oh? And did you stay formal with her after you told her that you must?"

Jason hesitated. "Not at first."

"You aren't finished with her."

"I am."

"Be sure. Until then, we'll be just friends."

Jason looked at her nude body. "Friends? I thought you said we couldn't do that—go from being lovers to being just friends."

"Call me, then. We'll relate over the phone." She began putting on her clothes.

"The phone? Relate over the phone? No."

"Yes. That or nothing. You felt some of my pain while we made love. You saw the intensity of how I suffer from loss. I want you Jason, but I will not risk what's left of me until I have some better guarantee that you will not turn away. To Angela."

"Sybil, there are no guarantees in life."

"I know. But I want them, anyway. Put your clothes on, Jason. You will go back to that ranch and settle what you must settle. Don't think you can do it in one day, either. It took more than a day to get where you are with her, and it will take longer to untangle—or to decide not to untangle, as the case may be. I don't want to know what you do or how you do it. If you want me when you finish out there, call, and I might be here."

"Might?"

"Might. There are no guarantees in life."

"And when I come to you? What then?"

"Then we'll see. The odds are against us. I know that, and it terrifies me. But there are no odds at all right now."

"Sybil, don't do this to me. Let me stay here and not ever go back to that terrible ranch."

"Don't pressure me. I warned you already about that. And after seeing the manure in my yard, seeing the dead hive and the head in the tree and Rupita's crushed skull, you think this place is any less terrible than the ranch?"

"But I need to stay here. You need me to stay. Look at the violent things that are going on around here. With me here, that might stop."

"Jason, stop being a stupid male for a moment. I don't need your protection. Do you think I'm helpless? A poor sweet Penelope being tied to a train track by some dastardly villain, screaming for her handsome hero to come to the rescue? I don't need rescuing, Jason White. Just because I cry when I hurt doesn't mean I can't take care of myself. Just because I want you doesn't mean I need you to protect me. Understood?"

"You're angry at me again."

"No. I'm angry at the male behavior you seem to insist on. When you come to me—if you come to me—it will be as an equal. As an equal, Jason White, or I'll not have you."

Before he left, Jason wanted to urge her to call the police about the killing of her dog and the horror hanging from the tree in her backyard, but he was afraid to offer advice that might be taken as an attempt to protect her.

On the way back toward Snake Mountain, Jason decided he would force himself to stay through Hyram's birthday party. Then he would move to Canyon—to Sybil's or to an apartment.

On Hyram's birthday, the band arrived well before dark. Jason watched them unload instruments from a van that had "The Last Train South" painted on the side.

Odom showed the musicians where to set up. He had strung wire for amplifiers and placed lights on top of several poles near one end of the dance floor. "So the pickers and fiddlers can see what they're a-doing," he had explained to Jason.

Heavy clouds swept across the prairie to the north, and Odom eyed them with apprehension. "The weatherman on TV says it ain't going to rain in these here parts today," he told Jason, "but I don't trust that sucker. Clouds like that can pour down a real turd floater, and before you can even run for cover it can be raining like a wet dream. Might even hail, this time of year."

Jason thought of his parents saying he talked like a Texan and shook his head in amazement. They don't know what a Texan sounds like, he decided. They've lived abroad for too long to remember.

Hyram had hired two cowboys to cook a side of beef in the pit Odom prepared. The smell of cooking meat hung heavy in the air, and it attracted what to Jason was staggering quantities of flies. Odom battled the swarms by hanging pest strips from the light poles and by swearing. "God had no business making a fly," he told Jason. "They breed in the cow shit, which is sure enough plentiful in Texas, and they make a good effort to wrestle your food away from you if you take a notion to eat outside. But at night, they freeze up, so we won't have to put up with them but till the sun goes down. If it comes a toad choker of a rain, nobody'll be getting grub outside, noways."

Angela looked out the kitchen window at Jason, Odom, and the band members of The Last Train South, and she felt excitement rise in her over the coming party—even if Jason had acted like a snot most of the week, avoiding her and speaking little when they were together. And all for what? Shooting couple of damn calf-chasing dogs that needed killing? To hell with him, she thought, at least for tonight. Tonight I'll dance and drink and live it up some. Enjoy myself for a goddam change.

She had spent the morning making potato salad and baked beans. Hyram loved her baked beans and claimed nobody could make them like she could—which was nonsense to her. All they were was canned pork and beans to which she added heaps of brown sugar and ham hocks. Hell, anybody could do that. Potato salad was different, though. Not many people knew the secret of using more pickle juice than mayonnaise. Hyram said to be sure to keep the potato salad on ice, or it would grow salmonella. "What's that?" she had asked.

"Little critters that will give you the galloping two-step."

"Salmonella cause food poisoning," Jason said. She thought he said it like he was talking down to her, and she thought well screw you and the horse you rode in on. But she didn't say it.

And look at him out there, jawing with Odom and the boys in the band like he thought he was a native son. He might look cowboy in the hat, boots, jeans and shirt I picked out for him, but he ain't. Not even close. You can see it in the way he moves, not like a cowboy at all, leastways not like one I ever seen. Maybe I'd do better with him acting so high and mighty if he weren't so dang pretty.

She thought about that word, pretty, and decided it fit him. Handsome wasn't right, most of the time. It fit when he took her on the bed rock up on Snake Mountain. And when he had stood beside her on the rim of the canyon, nude in the morning light. And maybe when he was beating Malcolm Roddy in tennis. But on a regular basis, especially in the last few days when he was so cold and aloof and acted so confounded superior in a snotty way, the word handsome was the wrong one.

She saw Hyram drive up with the beer and went out to help unload it.

In the back of Hyram's pickup was a stack of cases of Lone Star longnecks, two aluminum kegs and many bags of ice. "Them cold?" she asked, pointing at the longnecks.

"Grab one and give her a try," Hyram said. "I told the man at Buffalo Chip Liquors they better be four degrees cooler than cold or I'd have my boys come after him with a rope."

"Jason," Angela said, "get that ice into the tubs Odom put out. Shove in a case for every bag of ice, and cover the bottles good and proper."

Jason was staggered by the amount of beer in Hyram's truck. "How many people are coming tonight?" he asked.

Hyram shrugged. "Fifty, maybe."

"That's," Jason did some quick calculation, "nearly ten beers each. And I'm not even counting the kegs." Hyram must have made a mistake in getting so much.

"You reckon that will be enough?" Odom asked. He took a bottle from the truck and opened it with his teeth.

"Enough?" Jason stared. "Enough?"

"I got two cases inside in the fridge," Hyram said, "in the event that we run out."

Angela helped Jason put beer and ice into one of the wash tubs. She lifted a tentative hand and straightened his collar. "How about us pretending we're friends, just for the evening. For Hyram's sake. It is his sixty-fifth birthday, after all."

"Fifty-fifth."

"You ain't giving nothing, are you? You don't need to be a shit, not tonight."

Jason looked at her, startled by her language. He was even more startled to see that she was fighting back tears. "No. No, I don't. I'm sorry, Angela."

She sniffed and smiled. "Friends, then?" She held out her hand across the tub. Lightning crackled on the horizon behind her, and Jason looked from Angela to the dark presence of the distant thunderhead.

"Friends." He took her hand. But not lovers, he added to himself, not lovers.

Her hand had a firmness to it that put him in mind of how she had used it in making love, and he felt a stir of desire for her. Damn, he thought. I can't even think such thoughts, not when I'm waiting out Sybil, biding time out here on the ranch until she can believe I'm through with Angela. And I am through with her. Through.

Angela withdrew her hand, brushing his fingertips with hers. She sniffed again. "Thanks for that, Jason. It's tough on me to see you so cold and hard, and me wanting you the way I do. But I didn't mean to say that." She turned away and with an impatient gesture wiped away a tear, then raised her voice: "Odom, help me fetch some folding chairs."

Jason watched the way she moved in her tight jeans as she walked away. Sybil thinks I'm not finished with her, he thought. But all that's left is normal male lust. She does look good. But then, he admitted, she probably looked good while she bent over her rifle, catching the Doobie Brothers in her sights, and I didn't look at her hips then.

The guests began arriving before all the beer was iced. They came mainly in pickup trucks, though a few rode up on horses.

The young men wore starched, white shirts, jeans and dark brown cowboy hats. The older men wore the same uniform, but most had on white hats. "Why the difference?" Jason asked Angela. "I thought bad guys wore black hats and good guys wore white ones."

"Not black usually. Dark. And not entirely white. I don't know why dark is for young men. Maybe being a young man and being a bad guy is the same thing."

The guests did a great deal of handshaking and back pounding, even, Jason noted, the women.

Most of the women wore jeans and plaid blouses; some wore denim skirts. The older women had hair teased out into bubbles. "Beehives," Angela whispered to Jason. "Young girls don't do that to their hair anymore." But Jason saw a number of younger women with the puffy hairstyle.

Everyone drank amazing amounts of beer. One man opened a beer and handed it to Jason. "You look mighty dry," he said.

"But. . . ."

"Take it," Angela said. When the man wandered off, a beer in each hand, she said, "Just walk around holding it, or somebody will hand you another. You don't have to drink, but you better look like you're drinking."

Jason held the beer under his nose and sniffed. Nasty, he thought. Like rotten yeast. But I could get used to the smell. If drinking a beer is required of Texans, then maybe I should make an effort, even if they shoot dogs.

Like the Malays, he realized with a start. Like the Malay police shooting Big Jeff. But the Malays mixed religion into their dog killing, and Texans didn't. Angela killed the Doobie Brothers for a practical reason, and practical is better, Jason told himself. He took a sip of the beer, then helped Angela and Odom bring the potato salad and beans out to tables Odom had set up. The cowboys who cooked the beef brought huge aluminum trays of meat to the tables. They served people with one hand and waved at flies with the other.

Members of the band went through the line first. When they had finished eating and began playing music, some people were still going through the serving line.

Jason took a small portion of the meat. He filled his plate with beans and got a dab of potato salad. It seemed impossible to keep flies off his food, so he went indoors. But there were nearly as many flies in there. He found that one bite of the beans was enough. They tasted as if they had been candied.

A cowboy offered him a beer. "But I still have one," he protested, picking up the beer he had set aside.

"You're still working on your first one?" the cowboy asked.

"Yes."

"Good gawd, boy. You're falling behind. Here." He thrust a bottle into Jason's other hand. "You better two-fist it, boy, till you catch up some."

"Thanks," Jason said. When no one was looking, he emptied one beer into the sink and put water into the bottle. He wandered back outside.

"Jason," Odom said, his jaw full of food. "Get the grits and throw some on the dance floor. People is starting to want to dance."

"Grits?"

"Cornmeal." Odom leaned close to stare at him. "You already two-fisting it, boy? You drunk already?"

"Two-fisting it?" Jason held up the bottles. He took a drink from one. "Yep. But I ain't drunk. Not yet."

"Slow her down. Eat some more meat—get you some of them slabs of fat to coat your stomach so's you won't get wasted early on. Mind you," Odom laughed, and it was then that Jason realized the man was drunk. "Mind you, I ain't taking my own advice so good. Which is why I'm asking you to grit the floor. 'Nother four or five beers, and I won't be good for much around here, and somebody's gotta keep the cornmeal on the floor so's people can slide their boots proper when they dance, especially with it growing on to dark. You grit the floor, you hear?"

Jason went into the kitchen and looked through the food pantry until he found a box of corn flour. He opened it and poured some into his hand. How could this powder keep the floor slick? he wondered. He took it outside and threw a handful on the dance platform. As soon as people saw him scattering the powder, several began to dance. Angela grabbed Hyram's arm. "Come on," she said. "Let's do the two-step."

"Wait a cotton-picking minute." Hyram took the last bite from his plate, licked his fingers, and tossed the plate toward a table but missed. "Now, pretty little woman, we can dance." He wobbled and Angela steadied him.

She took only a few steps before she stopped, bent down and looked at the dance floor. "There ain't nothing there but some powder. It don't skid." She rubbed her foot around on the boards. "Jason, lemme see what you threw on the floor."

He handed her the box. "Flour? Gawd all mighty." She punched Hyram and showed him the box. "Corn flour. That's what we're trying to dance with. Flour!" She and Hyram laughed.

"It made no sense to me, either. But that's what Odom told me to put on the floor."

"Grits, Jason," Angela said. "Cornmeal. It's ground up rough so it rolls around under your boots like little balls. You better get some out here before somebody breaks a leg."

"Get me another beer," Hyram told Angela. "And one for you, too."

Another beer, Jason said to himself. They were already drunker than he had ever seen anyone get, except for in movies. He went inside to look for cornmeal.

When he came back out, he found Odom turning on the lights he had strung on top of a number of poles. Jason scattered cornmeal on the dance floor, and he could hear the immediate gritty scrape of boots sliding with the meal over the boards.

He looked around at the guests. Most had finished eating; all held beer bottles or plastic cups filled from the kegs. Angela came up to him. "Jason, I'm sorry I laughed at you." She pressed her breasts against his side and leaned against him. "Dance with me, Jason."

"I'm still not so good at it."

"No matter. Just hold me and move around." She pulled him toward the dance floor.

"Angela," Odom came up, out of breath, his face puffy and red. "Angela, Lint Bodark just drove up with a bunch of his buddies. That stupid shit. I oughta draw down on him."

"No. Odom, no. This here is Hyram's birthday party. Nobody's going to ruin it by shooting a skunk, not even one named Lint Bodark." She turned to Jason. "We better not dance, not just now." She sighed.

"Angela," Lint called from across the yard. "Angela!" He walked over to her. His four friends, Jason noticed, headed for one of the kegs.

"You ain't supposed to be here, Lint. Remember the court order barring you from being on these premises or looking me up?"

"I couldn't miss Hyram's birthday, now could I?"

"You come on Hyram's property, rip the door off a bunkhouse, pull my hair, and next thing I know you're burning up the prairie grass, trying to get Jason."

"Burning? I ain't burned nothing."

"You shoot my dogs and try to steal my horses—Lint you got your nerve coming around here after all the stunts you pulled."

"Angela, you know if I done anything bad, it was on account of drinking. And look," he held up a Dr Pepper can, "I don't touch the hard stuff, or even beer, not no more. I swearta God, Angela." He turned to Jason. "The tennis player. Howdy. You're one hell of a tiger on the court, whipping Malcolm like you done, and him being stud duck of the tennis players for years around here."

"Why did you kick me into the crick when I was trying to help you?" Jason was surprised at the amount of hostility he felt in asking the question.

"Kick? In the crick? I don't rightly recall doing that. I went up to Angela's big horse to see if it would make friends with me, and that bastard reared up and knocked me one good. Next thing I remember, I'm nearly home, riding Dawg Meat. You say I kicked you?" Lint looked puzzled, then grinned. "In the crick. Well I'll be a bandy-legged mule."

Jason noticed Odom clutching Hyram's arm, leaning close and whispering in a fierce way. Hyram looked up and saw Lint. He patted Odom on the shoulder, and shuffled over. "Lint Bodark," he said.

"Hyram. Happy birthday to you." Lint held up his Dr Pepper can in a toast.

"You ain't got the sense God gave a goose, coming here. But you look like you're behaving civil enough. Keep it up. Dance a dance or two. Then clear out. You got it?"

"Got it."

Jason decided it was time for him to be elsewhere. He wandered over near the band to watch them perform.

The guitar picker sang about loose women and truck stops. He sounded to Jason a bit like Willie Nelson but more polished. Still, Jason thought, you polish up Willie Nelson, and you still have country music.

The only ones who looked sober to Jason were the members of the band. Some people still danced, but they seemed to stagger more than dance. As he watched them, Angela and Lint stepped onto the dance floor. Why would she dance with him, Jason wondered. All these people are crazy, every last one of them.

Lint drew Angela close to him, and she offered no resistance. She put her cheek against his, clasped her hands behind his back, and dragged her feet in heavy, slow motions around the floor, out of time to the music. Lint hooked a thumb into her hip pocket and let his fingers rest on her rump. In his other hand, he still clutched a Dr Pepper can. He moved her about the dance floor as if he held a giant rag doll.

Lint saw Jason watching. He made a show of patting Angela's bottom, then thrust out his middle finger from the Dr Pepper can and mouthed something.

Something obscene, Jason thought. He went into the house, paused at the door, thought about taking his boots off, and said, "To hell with them." He went to his room.

When he turned on the light, he found two people on the water bed, a woman with her blouse pulled up and her bra off, and a cowboy with his pants pulled down around his hips. Both had passed out. "Tribal mating rituals," Jason said, turning the light off. He went to the closet, pulled a string for the light, and looked for his Walkman. Those two, he thought, looking back at the sprawled forms on the bed, are more crude than the Iban headhunters in Sarawak.

A year before, Jason and his father had taken a boat trip up the Skrang River in Borneo. They hired a guide to take them to spend a night in an Iban longhouse far into the jungles of Sarawak. Jason had read a book, *Into the Heart of Borneo*, in which he discovered it was customary to bring gifts to the head man of the longhouse you visited. His father brought several cartons of cigarettes; Jason brought a lock-back pocketknife and a file.

The head man of the longhouse opened the knife, then couldn't close it. Jason showed him the trick of it. He had to communicate through gestures for their guide understood little Iban. While Jason struggled to explain the use of the file—an implement that puzzled the head man—a beautiful bare-breasted girl watched. She was, the guide said, daughter of the head man.

Later that evening, the girl came to Jason, took his hand, and pointed at the partition to the dwelling of the head man. In the window was a lighted candle. She drew Jason's hand up to her cheek. "What's going on?" Jason asked the guide.

"She is inviting you to spend the night with her. She finds you attractive, and wants to mate with you."

"Mate?" Jason was amazed. Among the Iban, the guide explained, a girl of marrying age never takes a young man from her own longhouse as husband. When a boy visits, she lets him know of her interest by lighting a candle in the window, and he understands he can spend the night with her. "But she doesn't even know me," Jason protested.

"Apparently she knows enough," his father joked. Yes, the guide said. She knows she likes what she sees.

"Well, I'm not doing it. Will she be insulted?"

The guide said she would not, but urged Jason to go with her. "Iban women very juicy."

Women? Jason looked at her. She was just a girl — maybe fifteen years old. "What if one of the boys makes her pregnant?"

"Then she must marry," the guide said. She picks the boy she most liked and tells her father he was the one who fathered the child she carries. She then marries and moves into his longhouse. In the old days, the guide explained, the boy had to bring a head to hang in the longhouse before he was deemed man enough to take a wife.

Jason eyed the ancient skulls hanging in baskets from the ceiling of the common room in the longhouse. Bits of flesh and hair still clung to the bone. "Japanese," the guide said. "Iban took heads of Japanese during war. No take heads no more."

Jason's father found the entire event comical, and he had ribbed Jason about the offer for the rest of their stay in the longhouse. "If you go to her," he said, "You'll have to borrow the lock-back knife from the head man so you can take a head for the lady."

"It isn't funny, Dad," Jason had snapped.

He found his Walkman in the closet, selected a rock tape, and turned again to the couple on his bed. "They got too drunk to mate," he muttered. A closer look at the girl on the bed told him she wasn't much older than the Iban who lighted the candle for him.

Outside, Jason found a crowd around the dance floor. People muttered in angry tones. "Let's beat the living shit out of him," someone said, and others said, "Yeah."

Angela stood to one side, crying. "What happened?" Jason asked her.

"Lint," she said. "That bastard." She rubbed her jeans with a red bandanna. "He gave me a drink from his Dr Pepper can. And you know what was in it. You know. Tobacco juice. I been spitting and gargling with beer. The bastard."

Several women in the crowd began calling for blood, and it became a chant: "Let's see some blood, blood, blood. Let's see some blood. . . ."

Jason didn't see who threw the first punch, but he saw Lint fall to the dance floor, and Lint's friends began swinging.

Two men fell at Jason's feet, kicking and gouging. Women screamed and men cursed, and everywhere Jason looked men seemed to be punching each other, swinging in broad, drunken-looking ways, doing little real damage when they connected. Jason retreated into the house and watched from the kitchen window.

Members of the band took their instruments and vanished into the darkness. The crowd broke up into little groups of men who slugged and kicked and rolled around on the ground, clawing and punching. Jason could make no sense of who fought with whom.

It wasn't a battle between Lint's friends and Hyram's. Every man out there appeared to be determined to hit every other one.

It seemed to Jason that the melee went on forever, though he glanced at his watch and estimated that within five minutes the fight was over. Most of the men were prone or sat on the ground, looking dizzy.

Two men who had wrestled on the ground helped each other to their feet. One of them drew two beers from a keg. He took a long drink from one and handed the other to the man with whom he had just fought. "Holy Buddha," Jason muttered.

He turned on his Walkman, put the earphones on and went back outside. Beside the door, a woman with a beehive hairstyle knelt to dab her handkerchief on the bloody nose of a man lying on the ground. Jason stepped over another man, who looked like one of Lint's friends. Lint himself lay sprawled on the dance floor.

As men struggled to their feet, other men and some women filled cups with beer and handed them around. The band reappeared from the darkness, assembled near the dance floor, and began playing a bluegrass piece. Jason turned off his Walkman to listen to the fiddling and banjo playing. The musicians played with somber determination, glancing from their instruments to the cowboys scattered about.

Jason saw Odom get a beer, take it over to Lint, and pour it into his face. Lint sputtered and rolled over; Odom stumbled off for more beer.

A young woman with glazed-looking eyes thrust a cup of beer into Jason's hands. "Drink it and cool down, cowboy," she said. "We got more partying to do."

"Good to see you hitting the suds," Hyram said. Jason turned to him, noting he had a bruise over one eye that ran a tiny trickle of blood. His string tie set with Janus' fire agate had been ripped nearly off. "Jason, my friend, how about getting them two cases of longnecks out of the fridge. Looks like most of them tubs got nothing but ice water in them, and the kegs won't hold out much longer." He turned away and held his beer up in salute to the guests. "Wah-hoo," he yelled. "That was one wing-ding of a fight. Now let's get on with the party!"

"Jesus Christ," Jason muttered. He went into the house for the beer.

When he got back out, he saw Lint pouring liquid from a pocket-sized flask into a beer cup. He filled the cup the rest of the way with beer, drank it down and poured more from his decanter.

Jason put the longnecks into a tub. He stood from the task to find Lint standing beside him. "You been screwing my wife." Lint's voice was slurred from drinking. He tried to hit Jason.

Jason side stepped the punch. Lint tried again in a slow, drunken way, and Jason ducked. "Stand still, you piece of shit." Lint tried another punch. Jason moved aside, and Lint stumbled. Hyram came up from one side, swung his fist in a wide arc and landed a blow in the center of Lint's face.

Jason heard the blow hit like a wet towel slapping against a wall. Lint fell to his knees, and Hyram hit him on the side of his head. "You shouldn't ought to have come out here." Hyram rubbed his knuckles. Lint lay facedown, unmoving. "I done told you that. I done told you."

When Sybil heard someone driving up her driveway, she considered going to the bedroom for her Webley-Vickers pistol. If it were daytime, she suspected that a delivery man was coming with a load of something no one in her right mind would want. She had discovered that people hired to deliver merchandise had a kind of tenacious stubbornness about them. They would read her sign about not leaving anything at her house, knock on her door to make sure the sign was accurate, then try to get her to sign for the delivery.

But this time it was after working hours. The sun sat on the canyon rim just west of town, throwing long shafts of light through the elm trees into the living room windows. Too late for a delivery man. Sybil started for the the pistol. Then she recognized the sound as Jason's pickup.

The day she and Jason had found Rupita's body under the cottonwood, Sybil had gone to a pawn shop in Amarillo, just across Polk Street from *The Friendly News*. A clerk in the shop acted as if her request for a pistol was routine. He produced several, extolling the virtues of each. Sybil had selected the Webley-Vickers because it looked so intimidating and because when she cocked it, the sound came out a scary "snick-snick," something sure to frighten anyone.

As Jason turned into the driveway, Altus and Pug stopped up the street on Altus' Harley. He pointed. "Is that the prick who caught me off guard at Mark's party?"

"That's Jason. Yes. But, Altus, this isn't the time to get him." Pug patted his shoulder.

"The hell it ain't. You stopped me from doing that little job for too long to suit me."

Pug bit her lip. She had bought his help in part by claiming that Jason lived with Sybil and by saying that the time would come when he could beat on Jason after he had suffered in some other ways. That was after taking Altus to bed to convince him she wasn't gay.

Pug considered Altus' idea about dead shrimp. He had suggested making Sybil and Jason learn to live with a stink they couldn't find. "I done in my English teacher back when I was in Palo Duro High School." He had laughed, savoring the memory. "Done it with only twelve shrimp. Put three of them mothers in each of her hubcaps. That dumb biddy washed her car a hundred times, even took out her seats looking for the smell. Never did find it. Nothing can stink like dead shrimp."

Pug thought the dead shrimp a good idea, though the timing wasn't right. Not then.

"Altus?" She tried to make her voice soft, soothing. "Remember your idea about using shrimp? How about if we go find some shrimp and come back. By then it'll be dark and we can give Jason's pickup the treatment it deserves."

"I don't know. I'd like to pound on that chicken shit bastard."

"You will, honey, and soon enough. Do you know where we can buy some shrimp?"

"Yeah. At the supermarket just down the road. Take us ten, maybe fifteen minutes. But what about that pit bull you told me Sybil got? We go to stuffing shrimp into the caps on the pickup, and that dog comes out, he'll bite my ass off. Friggen pit bulls got jaws like a bear trap."

"Don't worry about the dog. She got rid of it. Trust me. Now, what about those shrimp?"

"I'd rather go grind that fucker's face into the floor. But if you want, we'll go for the shrimp." He twisted the throttle on the Harley and turned up the street.

Jason feared that Sybil wouldn't even let him into her house. Hadn't she made it clear that they were not to see each other for a while? He didn't like her stand at all. When would she declare he was through with Angela and stop sending him away? He stood for a moment in the mottled light from the elms filtering the setting sun into patterns on Sybil's front door. Then he knocked.

To his surprise, she greeted him with a smile and stepped aside for him to enter. "Sit down."

Jason sat on the couch. Sybil nodded. "Good. You sit there, and I'll take this chair. For now we need to stay at least six feet away from one another lest we begin activities that are better left undone." She spoke with such charm that Jason almost smiled in spite of the message.

She seemed amused by his presence. Or maybe just pleased that he was there—he couldn't tell which. "You look terrible," she said.

"Thanks."

"Ease up, Jason. I've warned you about sarcasm. I'm trying to make a joke. You do for a fact look out of sorts. That worry line across your brow. The way you keep your chin close to your chest. What brings you back here so soon?"

"I'm through with Hyram's ranch. With Angela." He held up his hands when she started to interrupt. "I know, I know. You don't believe me. But that's beside the point. I'm not here to ask you for anything. Just to tell you that I'm moving into town. In fact I've spent much of the day looking for a place."

"You and Angela have a spat?"

"That's unfair. You don't know what happened."

"I apologize. Okay, so tell me what happened."

Jason wasn't sure where to begin. "Hyram's birthday party—it was the strangest affair I've ever witnessed. It was all that beer everybody kept putting away that bothered me at first. I don't know. Last night—the whole evening. Crazy. Those cowboys are beyond comprehension."

"Try me. What happened last night?"

First he told her about the way everyone at the party seemed determined to make him get drunk. She smiled at that. "Jason, at any party where people are drinking, those with booze in their hand distrust those who won't drink, so they pressure them to drink. It's not just in the cowboy culture. Did they get you to drink?"

"No. But I carried around a bottle in self defense. Sybil, did you know they scatter ground corn on their dance floors? Ground corn."

Sybil laughed. "Yes."

"Cowboys drink themselves into a state of stumbling stupidity. And then they like to fight. They all love to punch and pummel each other until they're half senseless. When everyone is properly punched around, they pound one another on the back like long-lost buddies at a reunion and they share more beer."

He told about the arrival of Lint Bodark, about the fight and the way it ended. When he finished his account, she laughed. He stared. "It wasn't funny."

"Maybe not then. But now it's hilarious. Come on, Jason. Where's your sense of the absurd?"

"The absurd isn't always funny. Sometimes it's depressing."

He stood up. "I shouldn't have come."

"Maybe not." She moved between him and the door. "But you're here now, and I'm glad you came."

"You think I'm pretty goddamn funny."

"Not you. Those cowboys and their ritualistic brawl. Not you, Jason—though what you just said sounds much like the way a cowboy would talk."

Altus parked his chopper up the street in the shadow of a cedar fence. He and Pug walked to Sybil's driveway. "They're both still there," he said. "Least there's a light on in the front room."

"Can you pop off the hubcaps without making any noise?"

"You kidding? How do you think I made cigarette money all through high school?" Altus pulled an enormous folding knife from a pocket. He snapped out a blade. "This here is honed down to the best screwdriver and hubcap popper in the Panhandle of Texas. Gimme them shrimp."

Pug handed him a sack. "No more talking, now. You get on with your business, and I'll peek in the window to make sure they're not coming out."

When she stepped on the porch, one of the boards creaked but not loud. Pug stopped to make sure no one inside responded. She heard snatches of muffled conversation through the door, then heard nothing. Maybe, she thought, they went into the kitchen.

She stood by a window and leaned with care until she could see inside.

From the darkness behind her came faint scrapings of Altus' boots on the driveway and the rattle of a paper bag. So he got one of the hubcaps off already, Pug thought.

Jason and Sybil were less than four feet from the window. He stood with his fists clinched. Sybil rubbed herself against him in a feline way, kissing his cheek.

As Pug watched, the stiffness went out of Jason's arms, and the couple embraced in a kiss that lasted, in Pug's mind, long enough to be downright silly. Sybil unbuttoned the two top buttons of his shirt and kissed his chest and the two of them began a slow dance across the living room toward the couch. When they got there, Sybil's blouse was unbuttoned, Pug realized with a sudden shock. She stepped back from the window. "Animals!" she said aloud.

The word surprised Altus, and he stood up beside the truck. "What's that?" he whispered.

"Altus, I think you were right. Now is the perfect time for you to go in there and get Jason for what he did to you at Mark's party."

"Now?"

Pug moved into the dark shadows of an elm. "Yes. Now." Her voice had the harsh sound of a cat hissing, and she knew Altus would be glad that the anger in that sound wasn't aimed at him.

Altus dropped three shrimp into the hubcap and knocked it back on the wheel, not bothering to muffle the sound. He frowned and told himself again that Pug confused him. Is she jerking me around somehow? He didn't know, but it seemed likely.

He stood, wiped his hands on his jeans, and looked at the door to Parker's house. Not Parker, he reminded himself. Jason. The asshole who sneaked up on me.

At the door, he hesitated. Should I knock? He glanced toward Pug for instructions, but couldn't locate her in the shadows. Did Jason knock when he came up to me? Shit no. He came in swinging.

The doorknob wouldn't turn. Locked. Altus smiled at the notion that such a pissant lock would stop anyone. He stepped back and drove the side of his body against the door. Wood splintered, and he stepped into the living room.

Parker's old lady and Jason were going at it on the couch. They sat up. "Altus?" Sybil cried.

Jason stood and Altus stepped into him, fists swinging. "One to the head, one to the stomach," Altus muttered as he struck Jason. Another to the head and one to the back, he told himself. But don't finish it—not yet. I want him moving some. I want him to watch me take him apart.

"Get up you goat fucking cowboy."

Jason struggled to stand. Altus looked around for Sybil, but she had vanished. Let her hide he thought. My truck is with this dog prick.

He looked back in time to see Jason lunge. The attack surprised him for the way Jason came in with his head, driving into Altus' midsection. Something cracked and pain spun Altus around. Jason swung wide, and Altus stepped back. He clutched his side, knowing he had at least one broken rib. The knowledge enraged him.

He gripped his side with one hand and swung a fist in a clumsy way. Jason batted it away and struck again at Altus' ribs. "Damn," Altus muttered and shuffled back, clutching himself, trying to keep more blows from landing. But it was no use. His back hit the wall, and he slid down, one arm over his face and one over his side. A fucking naked cowboy, he said to himself, a fucking cowboy beat me up. Shit.

"Stop it, Jason. Move back." Sybil's voice came to Altus low and muffled as through a wall. "If he gets up, I'll put a bullet in him."

It took a moment for the meaning of her words to sunk in. Altus turned his palms out. "You don't need no pistol," he said.

Jason glanced at Sybil—now wearing a house robe—glanced at the weapon she waved around, and he remembered Suppriah's smile before the red-headed man shot her. He looked at his clinched fists, looked at the crumpled heap that was Altus.

Altus breathed in shallow gulps. "Sybil," he whispered, "you point that cannon away from me, just in case it goes off without you wanting it to."

"So you're the one who has been harassing me. And now you've hurt someone important to me. Really important. Jason, you okay?"

"Fine. I'm fine." The lie came easy, too easy Jason thought. His face throbbed where Altus hit him, and his stomach hurt. He picked up his jeans and put them on.

Altus struggled to his feet. "How about pointing at my legs. I could live with a bullet in a leg."

Sybil lowered the pistol a bit. "All the phone calls. The delivery men. Then you killed that horse and hung its head in the elm. And my dog." She swung the pistol back up. "You killed Rupita."

"Dog? Horse? Goddammit, Sybil, I ain't had nothing to do with them." He turned his head toward the splintered door and raised his voice. "Pug, get your bitchy ass in here."

"She's out there? I should have known."

When Altus moved toward the door, Jason could see something was wrong with him. The way he held his side and bent over said he had some serious injury to his ribs. Good. Jason touched his throbbing cheek and fought the urge to smile.

"Pug. You get in here. You got some talking to do. Goddammit."

Jason watched Sybil catch the hammer of the pistol, uncocking it.

When Pug appeared in the doorway, Jason thought he was seeing her shadow until he realized she was dressed in black. She stood by the door and looked from Altus to Sybil.

"You killed her dog, Goddammit, and her horse. I told you not to do animals. Bitch."

"The horse isn't hers, and it was already dead." Pug's voice had a high-pitched quiver to it.

"Look, Sybil, I come to bust Jason for what he done to me at Mark's party. Look at him, about half busted up, and that's that. I ain't hanging around here no more. The rest is something ugly between you and Pug, and I got nothing to do with it. Sybil, I never done no horse and no dog. I like dogs. I'm leaving now, and you can shoot me if you don't like me going." Altus turned to Pug. "You and me is through. You come around my place again and I'll set my dog on you."

"Altus, honey, let me explain—"

"Don't you honey me none. You jerked me around the last time. Walk back to Amarillo." He vanished into the night.

Jason watched Pug fold her arms and glare.

"I'm leaving."

She turned, then froze when she heard the snick-snick of Sybil cocking the pistol.

From somewhere near the street came the sound of Altus' motorcycle. Pug muttered something about Altus abandoning her.

"You go on, Pug. But if you come around here again, I'll not have a dog waiting. I'm not near as nice as Altus. I'll have this pistol loaded and waiting. You know I'll use it. And if you send any more delivery men or pull any more rotten tricks around here, I'll come looking for you."

Pug, her back still to Sybil, nodded and left. Sybil turned on the porch light and stood in the doorway a moment.

Jason sat on the couch. Sybil sat beside him. "How did you like the little Texas drama?"

"Would you have shot him, Sybil?"

She laughed. "Guess."

"Maybe. I don't know. Would you have?"

"Look." She broke open the pistol to show the empty chambers. "I played a dangerous bluff. Never do that, Jason. If you point a weapon at a man like Altus, you better be ready to put a bullet in him, because he might attack. I was lucky. But I also knew you were here just in case."

She leaned back and looked at him. "I do believe you have another black eye, Mister White."

"Yeah? You ought to see the other guy."

"I did. He'll be wearing a wrap on his ribs long after you have recovered. I'd better get some ice on that eye. Seems like I've done a good bit of doctoring your punched-up eyes, Mister White. Come on." She stood and pulled him to his feet.

He sat on a stool by the breakfast bar in the kitchen. She wrapped an ice cube in a wash cloth and dabbed his eye. "Hold still. You're just like the rest of them, Mister White."

"You can call me that now. And how am I like the rest of them. The rest of who?"

"Men. You all suffer from testosterone poisoning. One punched out another for slapping around his woman. Then the one that got punched had to come sniffing around, waiting for the chance to punch back. Men."

"You were the one with the pistol. Pug was the one who killed the dog. Women."

"And just why do you no longer object to my calling you Mister White?"

"Good. Change the subject when I have you on the run. Smart. Just like a woman."

"Watch it."

"Before when you got formal and called me 'mister' it was a way to distance us. You didn't like me much back then. But now I know better. I can take some distancing when I know I'm important to you. Very important."

Sybil leaned close, bringing her lips to his. She laughed. "Don't believe everything you hear, even when I'm the one talking."

"Sybil, I'm finished with that ranch. Finished. I'm going back to explain to Hyram and to get my clothes. Then I'm moving into town." He half expected her to order him to remain on the ranch.

"Not tonight. Tonight you're staying here so I can watch that hurt eye."

"I'll go in the morning, then."

"No. In the morning, you're taking me to Buffalo Lake for a picnic. I might find time to let you talk to Hyram tomorrow afternoon."

"I'll need some clean clothes."

"I have some things that might fit you. Parker's clothes. I left all his stuff in his closet. You look to be about his size." Her voice grew soft. "But of course you will do what you want to do in spite of my bossiness. So I'm asking now. Will you stay with me tonight?"

At the entrance to Buffalo Lake Wildlife Refuge, Sybil waited for the question. She watched his face as Jason drove to the rim of the canyon and stopped the pickup. "So where's the lake?"

"It used to be right out there."

"No lake? Then what's that dead fish smell?"

"I smelled it when we first got into the pickup. Maybe you have a dead bird lodged in the grill? Anyway, about the lake. This is West Texas. In dry years, lakes vanish and weeds grow. Then grass fires sweep the area where there was once water."

"Lakes catch fire, then. What a loony world we live in, Sybil. Lakes that aren't lakes, mountains that are flat as a plate. Will I ever get used to it?"

"That depends on how long you hang around."

"I'll stay however long it takes."

"And just what does that mean?"

"It means I want to belong somewhere. I didn't belong in Malaysia, not for a long time. The mosques, Sybil, I used to try going to them with my Uncle Othar. Mom wanted me to be a Muslim, and I tried, but it didn't work, and I felt like a fraud doing all that prayer among people who mumbled toward Mecca. I'm working hard at becoming a Texan. It isn't easy. Not all of it, anyway. Last night was easy. I want more nights like last night. More mornings like this morning. We slept like spoons. Spoons."

"Good metaphor. Yes, like spoons. I like your body close to mine, Jason. Drive on, now. Go there, to the bottom of the canyon. We'll picnic at a table near the lake's edge. Or where the lake would be if there were any water in it."

Jason drove on. "You did it again."

"Did what?"

"Changed the subject when I get us to talking about any kind of future together."

"Do we have one, Jason?"

"We do if I have anything to say about it."

"Maybe you don't. Maybe I don't, either. I want you, Jason, but not on any terms that come along. I want you on my terms. And your terms."

"What does that mean? We set our own terms."

"Maybe. Sometimes events run our lives for us. Sometimes all we can do is say yes or no to the choices that come our way. Accident rules our lives, Jason. I know, I know—you don't believe that. But you're still young and have some learning to do. Accident took Parker away from me. Accident brought you to me. Accident might take you away or bring you to me somehow that feels more like pain than it ought. Stop over there, by that cottonwood. We'll walk down to the cement table for lunch."

"I chose to come to you last night. You chose to let me into your house." He pulled the truck into a pool of shade beneath the tree.

"You came to me because of a host of accidents, events you had no control over. And yes, I chose to let you close again. You'll go back to the ranch this evening, and who knows what will happen?"

"I know, that's who." He set the brake and opened his door. "I like your picnic basket."

"You'll like the food in it even better." They walked to the cement table.

"I'll explain to Hyram about deciding to move into town, gather my clothes and move out."

"In Hyram's truck?"

"He'll loan it to me until I can get some wheels of my own. I need to do a thorough cleaning job on this truck. It has a rank smell about it."

"What about Angela?"

"What about her?"

"Easy, Jason. Don't snap at me. Your temper tells me you aren't finished with her yet."

"I am. You know I am. After last night—after this morning, how can you even think I would have any interest in anyone but you?"

"You didn't. You don't now. But tonight, who knows what can happen. I don't."

"I do."

"Good. Hang on to that knowledge." She took his arm and drew him to her. "Just remember, Jason, that I know you might come back tonight, and you might not. I also know that you might come back in such a way that one of us will say no to the other. I don't want that, but I don't control the wild accidents that drive our lives."

"That's silly."

"Yes. Silly."

As Ghost climbed out of Palo Duro Canyon, Angela looked back at the cottonwoods along the creek. Yucca stalks drying to gray sticks dotted the canyon among the yellow flowers that caused people to name the Texas high plains "the great golden spread."

From the top of Snake Mountain the view had been even more spectacular. She considered stripping and lying nude to the sun and wind on the bed rock, and would have done so but for finding a tarantula sunning itself there. She had killed it with a stick before sitting down to eat her lunch.

Ghost drifted toward a knot of juniper growing near the place where she and Jason once stood on the canyon rim to greet the sun. The memory made her eyes sting. Why he had soured on her was a mystery to Angela.

In the two days since Hyram's party, she had not seen Jason. Neither had Hyram. "You ain't his mama," Hyram told her the third time she asked. "We made that boy into a cowboy, so when he goes to moving around like one, you don't need to act like you dropped a bucket down the well and drawed up a skunk. He's off tomcatting around, like a cowboy ought to do. But you're a powerful draw, and sure as ducks on a pond he'll be setting down here when he's ready."

Angela wasn't so sure. Jason had acted about half bent out of shape even before some of the stunts she pulled at the party. Most of that evening seemed like a haze, and parts of it she had no recollection of at all. But some images stood out clear. Like her unbuttoning Jason's shirt and kissing his chest right before announcing it was time for her to get to bed. "And I'm so twisted that I ain't sure I can make it to the bunkhouse without help," she had said. She felt color come to her cheeks at the memory, and she jerked at the bridle in a way that surprised Ghost.

She liked it that Jason had not taken the hint. Hint hell, she thought. Invitation, it was, put up in neon lights. I might have thought I was being subtle, but that thinking was straight out of a beer bottle. Many beer bottles. And now he thinks I'm some kind of cheap, low-class bitch. Shit. I ain't never going to drink again, least ways not around Jason. Not that I'll get the chance, what with him nowhere to be found for nigh on to two days.

Angela turned in the saddle for one last, long look at the canyon. She wished she could take Jason up to Snake Mountain once more—take him at a time when he cared for her, like he did the morning they went into Amarillo and he bought the fire agate for Hyram. She sighed and patted Ghost on the neck. "Take us home."

Jason hadn't even ridden out with her to see the Indian blankets in bloom, and it wasn't likely that he would now. Not since he watched her shoot the Doobie Brothers. He won't go with me, she thought, not after the way I acted at Hyram's party. "It was the alcohol," she said aloud, then: "God, I'm sounding like Lint."

When she approached the barbed wire fence, she noticed Ghost's ears prick up, and he stepped a little faster. She patted his neck. "Want to jump it, do you? Then let's do it." The big horse broke into a run.

Ghost jumped and Angela leaned low against him, loving the feel of his power. He came down with his front feet in a patch of sand, skidded and went down.

Angela felt the weight of the animal pinch her leg, and then felt a stabbing pain. Ghost cried out and tried to struggle to his feet, only to fall again. "Easy Ghost, easy boy," she said over and over.

The horse lay upright, on his belly, quivering in his effort to stand. She could see that he probably had injured one of his front legs, that she would have to get off and walk to the ranch for help.

But she couldn't put any weight on her own leg. "Damn! Ghost, looks like I got a broke leg. You'll have to get me home." She patted and soothed the animal, calming it, then urged him to get up.

It took several tries, but Ghost responded to her demands and stood. "Now let's get home." Ghost staggered and hobbled along without using one of his front legs.

Twice on the way back to the ranch, Ghost screamed in pain. He jerked, lurching this way and that, like a three-legged dog, Angela thought. By the time he arrived at the ranch house, he was covered in sweat.

She could see Odom standing near the front door, watching her approach. He ran into the house just as Jason turned up the driveway. Ghost screamed again, though he struggled to get her to the house. Odom and Hyram came outside. Ghost kicked at Odom.

He jumped back. "Jeez! How come you're a-riding that outlaw with him hurt? Lookit that leg. He's hurt bad."

Angela urged the horse closer to the porch. "Get back, all of you. I think I got a broke leg, and this horse has to get me as close to the house as possible. Easy there. Easy boy."

She could see the wild look in the horse's eyes. Ghost struck out at Jason, and Angela jerked on the reins, trying for control.

Hyram moved in from the side. "I'll catch the reins."

Ghost reared up and whinnied, kicking at Hyram. He moved back. "It's got a broke leg, looks like."

"Mine's broke, too," Angela said. "I got to have help getting down."

Hyram circled the big horse. It moved around, refusing to let him near. "That horse is plumb loco with pain. I'm gonna have to shoot it to get you off of it."

"Shoot Ghost?" Jason said. "No. There has to be another way."

"Jason," Angela said, "there ain't. Not this time. Hyram, get your pistol."

"No." Jason approached the horse. It swung around, hitting Jason with its shoulder and knocking him to the ground. He scrambled out of the way just in time to keep Ghost from trampling him.

"Jason, you stay back," Hyram said. "I'll get the nine millimeter." He started into the house.

"It's in the glove box of my pickup. But there's got to be another way."

Hyram got the pistol and approached Ghost from the side. Angela shook her head. "No! Hyram, I got to do it myself. Throw the pistol to me."

Hyram set the pistol on safety and tossed it to Angela. She caught it just as Ghost jerked around to face Hyram. He moved back. "Do it! Do it fast!"

She felt the tears on her cheeks as she took the safety off. "Oh, God, Ghost. I'm so sorry." She put the barrel to the back of the horse's head and fired.

Ghost jerked, then became still for a horrible moment before collapsing in what to Angela felt like slow motion. He fell forward on his knees, then on his belly. As Ghost tumbled to one side, Angela got off, standing on her good leg. Hyram and Jason rushed to her.

"No." She pushed Hyram's arm away from her. "Give me just a minute." She lowered herself against the side of the horse, whimpering in pain as she moved her left leg. "It ain't fair. It just ain't fair." She put her face against Ghost and cried, her whole body shaking.

"A simple fracture." Dr. Ryan pointed to the X ray he had clipped to the light panel. "Right here. We'll put a cast on her, and tomorrow afternoon you bring her in to be fitted with crutches. There's little swelling, and the break is just a hairline with no movement of the bone. There should be little pain, though I want her to keep the leg elevated most of the time."

"Six weeks in the cast," Jason said, thinking about his fracture. Was Sybil right about weird accidents running our lives? He shook his head, not believing. The unexpected trip to town to see about Angela's leg delayed my leaving the ranch, he affirmed. It won't stop me from going.

"Six. Yes, that's right." Dr. Ryan turned to Hyram. "She says there's no pain, yet she keeps crying. Something isn't right."

"Her horse. It broke a leg, and she had to shoot it. She sure enough loved that horse."

Dr. Ryan nodded. "I understand losing a favorite horse. The nurse and I will put her lower leg and much of her foot into a plaster cast. No one needs to shoot this little filly." He laughed.

By the time Hyram, Jason, and Angela returned to the ranch, it was getting dark. "You stay in the main house," Hyram said.

"Hyram, we done been through all that. I live in the bunkhouse. That's where all my stuff is, and that's where I'm most comfortable."

"Suit yourself." Hyram knit his brows into a heavy frown and twisted his hands on the steering wheel.

When they arrived at the bunkhouse, Jason carried Angela inside. "Catch the light switch by the door," she said. "Put me there on the bed. Hyram, you come talk with me some."

Jason set her on a twin bed, stood and looked around. The building seemed like a tiny box. A metal-walled shower stall sat in one corner; beside it, hanging on the wall, was a lavatory. Beside that hung a floral curtain. Beneath the curtain, Jason could see the lower part of a porcelain commode.

Hardwood in uneven widths covered the floor, and the walls were plastered sheetrock. The one window had blinds hanging over it, and on one wall hung a black velvet painting of a bullfighter stabbing a bull through a red cape. Shelves lined another wall; on them were red coffee cans, cooking pots, some pillows covered with stained ticking and a stack of blankets.

Hyram moved a wooden crate close to the bed and sat on it. Jason heard the crate creak and noted that the boards along the side bowed out from Hyram's weight. Hyram took Angela's hand and looked at her with sad eyes.

"You just cut that out and go back to being your old joking self," Angela said. "Jason, before you go, would you prop me up with a couple of them pillows?" She pointed to one of the shelves.

Jason got the pillows. Angela sat up and put them behind her back. "I'll check on you before going to bed," Jason said.

"Thanks." She turned to Hyram. "Tell me a joke. Or one of them dirty limericks."

Hyram took a deep breath and said without enthusiasm: "There was a young lady named Rose who had erogenous zones in her toes—"

It seemed to Jason that he had been dismissed, so he left. On his way to the ranch house, he met Odom. "How's Angela?"

Jason told him about the fracture and the cast. Odom nodded. "That horse was too dang big and too dang mean to suit me, especially with her treating it like a pet dog. I'm glad that sucker's gone, even if I feel sorry for Angela over it."

"What did you do with Ghost?"

"Had a stock removal company come and get him. They'll turn him into dog food and fertilizer. Had to threaten them sumbitches to make them get out here right away. They was reluctant, but they done it. I didn't want her a-seeing that horse again, if you know what I mean."

As soon as he got inside, Jason called Sybil's number. After the fourth ring, Sybil's recorded voice said, "This is one of those annoying answer machines, and here comes the annoying beep."

Jason sighed and waited for the beep. "There's been a crazy accident. I'll tell you about it when I get back, which won't be long. Hyram will be in soon, and I'll visit with him about my decision, then I'll be there. And, Sybil, I know you're listening to this while it gets recorded, and I understand." Jason hung up the phone and went to his room to pack.

As he carried a suitcase to the front door, Hyram came in. Jason set the luggage down. "Is she feeling better?"

"She's got the miseries. She sure was attached to that outlaw horse. But to my thinking, that ain't entirely what's got her so down in the dumps."

"What's going on with her?"

"Seems like you ought to know better than me. Jason, she said to make sure you came to check on her. Said to tell you as long as you could see a light in the window, it would be all right for you to go out there. And there's one other thing." Hyram hesitated.

"One other thing?"

"She told me not to tell you this. So I didn't, okay? Seems to me she's like a little girl. Like a little girl. Don't want to be alone, but won't come into this house. Jason, she wants you to stay the night with her. Out there in the bunkhouse. But I ain't said nothing."

"I don't think it would be a good idea for me go spend the night with her."

"Maybe. Maybe not. I'm telling you because I can't stand to see her cry like she's been doing."

"I don't think I should do it. But if I did, would you be bothered?"

"Me? Shoot no. Long as you and she didn't noise it around. Even to Odom. He stuck his head in, by the way, and told her good night. I heard his truck leaving, heading home. He won't be back till tomorrow round eight, and you can clear out before then."

"I ought to at least go check on her, as I told her I would."

"Yes. Then you heading somewhere?" Hyram gestured toward the suitcase.

"I need to stay in town a while, Hyram. This might look ungrateful of me, but it isn't. It's just that—"

"A man's gotta do what he's gotta do, Jason. No need apologizing to me or nobody else. I do sorely wish, though, that you'd hang around a bit longer, after what happened. But I ain't asking. Just stating an opinion."

Hyram looked older and more tired than Jason had ever seen him, and, at that moment, Jason couldn't remember why it was so important that he leave the ranch. He set the suitcase down. "I'll go check on her."

Outside a full moon hung just above Snake Mountain, and on the horizon to the northwest, rain clouds loomed, looking like mountain peaks in the distance. The wind came from the direction of the clouds, and Jason thought it had a heavy, wet feel to it. He looked at the ground where Ghost had died.

Odom had covered the spot with dirt. It must have taken several wheelbarrows of earth, Jason thought, considering the gigantic red stain around Ghost's head, puddling here and there and leaving the buffalo grass the color of a Burmese ruby.

Jason thought of Suppriah in the airport, of the prairie dog Lint shot, of the Doobie Brothers, of Ghost toppling like a giant. "So much blood," he whispered to the night. "So much killing and dying." He looked at the lighted window of the bunkhouse and thought of the Iban girl, her bare nipples like the noses of puppies; he thought of how she had taken his hand and gestured toward the candle in the window of her father's dwelling. And he thought of the heads in the baskets, heads taken, perhaps, by young men who killed in order to mate with girls like the pretty Iban.

He looked again at the light in the window, realizing that he wanted to go to her, to soothe her, to touch her cheek. And he knew that he should not go.

Lint Bodark sat in the Chuck Wagon Cafe, eating a chicken-fried steak, when Dr. Ryan entered and sat at the next table.

"Dang gristle," Lint sawed on the steak. Angela would never serve him chicken-fried steak cut out of industrial grade beef. She was a good little wife, Lint remembered. Always kept the place clean, always had his supper on the table when he came in. She seemed to like doing that kind of thing back when they lived together, before Regan. . . . Lint felt a tightness in his throat.

Regan. She was a sweet little baby and so pretty. But dumb. God that kid was dumb. Not as dumb as Angela let on, but she weren't normal. Had a sixth sense, that kid—she always knew when me and Angela was tumbling in the sack, and she'd go to whimpering and carrying on, and when nobody come, she went to blubbering then hollering like she was hurt.

Lint gave up on chewing a piece of the steak, took it out of his mouth, and laid it on the edge of his plate.

And would Angela let the spoilt brat just lay there and yell? Hell no. She'd up and leave like nothing was going on, and go get that kid and rock her. And if I come into the room, that little sumbitch would look up at me and grin a shitty little grin like she was saying, 'I won, I won, I won.' Not even two years old, and already a ball-busting bitch.

Lint clinched his fist. Goddam steak. He sawed off another piece, picked it up with the point of his knife, and put it into his mouth.

But I shouldn't of hit her. Lint closed his eyes, not wanting to remember that night, but it was no use.

He thought Angela was loving it more than usual when Regan started her whimpering, and Lint went into a rage. "I'll take care of the little shit," he said.

"No, Lint. I'll do it." She shoved him off of her and started to get up.

"Like hell, you will." Lint hit her with the flat of his hand. Some part of him warned him to try for control, and he got still for a moment, struggling. And I might of made it, too, Lint thought. I might of got aholt of myself, if Angela had the sense to let me be. But did she? Did she? Hell no. She had to push.

Angela tried to duck around him and get out the door, and something inside seemed to break open and let loose a flood of something red and hot that ran all through him until his hands didn't seem to be his anymore. It was like someone else made one hand shoot out at Angela. She screamed, and the sound made the red tide worse. His hands bunched into fists and hit her again and again while he yelled, "You do what I say. Do what I say!"

He went into Regan's room and found the child standing in its crib. When she saw him she got quiet and grinned. The grin made the red tide hotter and fuller. "So you won again, huh?" he heard his voice say in a growl, low and angry, like they weren't words at all but the sound an animal would make.

Lint gave up on the steak. It just wasn't edible. He shoved it aside and poured cream gravy over his fried potatoes. All I intended to do was to teach her a lesson, Lint thought. He had not meant to strike the child. But somehow his arm flew out and he saw that the back of his hand hit Regan in the face. As soon as he saw how her neck jerked back and heard the sound it made, he knew he was in trouble.

The red tide seemed to flow out of him, and in its place came fear, cold and heavy. He felt for a pulse, but found none. Angela was still in the other room, crying. He didn't want her coming in and seeing what he had done.

He picked up the child and dropped it on the floor, then he called to Angela. She didn't come right away, so he called again, this time telling her that something happened to the baby.

That brought her in fast. He said he picked the baby up, but she squirmed out of his hands, and he dropped her. "She landed funny," Lint said over and over. "She landed funny."

Angela went wild with grief, and Lint had to let her cry some before he could get her to listen to what they had to do.

They had to get into the pickup and go drive off the road somewhere in a ditch so it looked like the baby got killed in a car wreck. Angela gave him no argument. She looked at him with fear and did just what he said.

Later, the police seemed suspicious about the nature of the wreck, but they had to accept Lint's story. All Angela would say was, "Just ask Lint. Ask Lint." And she would cry.

With a start, Lint noticed all his French fries were gone. He had no memory of eating them, but he could feel their heaviness in his stomach, and there was gravy on his fingers.

I shouldn't of hit that kid, Lint told himself. I just shouldn't of done it. He licked the gravy from his fingers.

Dr. Ryan leaned over and touched Lint's shoulder. "How's the little woman's leg?"

"Leg?" Lint grinned. Is the doc making some sort of nasty joke? he wondered.

"You haven't been home yet today. Have you?"

"Home? No."

"I had to meet Angela at the clinic this evening. Hyram and some Mexican-looking kid brought her in. She had a bone fracture in her leg.

It seems she got it when her horse fell on her. Hyram said she had to shoot the horse."

"She shot Ghost?" Lint said with astonishment.

"Angela's break wasn't a bad one. I put her leg in a cast. You bring her out tomorrow, first thing in the morning if there is much swelling. If it looks just a little puffy, get her to keep her foot elevated, like I told Hyram, and come in the afternoon to get her fitted for crutches."

"Doc," Lint said, "me and Angela, we sort of broke up some time back. She filed for a divorce on me."

"I'm sorry to hear that."

Lint thought that Dr. Ryan didn't look sorry at all. The doc, Lint remembered, had taken care of her face a time or two after she begged for a beating at the wrong time. Doc, he even lectured me once. The meddling old bastard.

Lint stood, fumbled a dollar from his pocket and dropped it on the table. He didn't want to discuss personal things with the doctor.

At the cash register, he remembered how tough the steak was and regretted leaving a tip. He glanced back at the doctor, who sat staring at him. People seemed to do that a lot right after Regan died in that wreck, and Lint hated the stares. He paid and got out of the Chuck Wagon as fast as he could.

Lint drove down Fourth Avenue, past the Varsity Theater, past the museum, and he told himself that he wondered where he was going.

But he knew. He was going out to check on Angela, because things were looking up for them. She danced with me, he remembered. And snuggled up tight, like she used to do—and she done it right in front of that wet-back kid who plays tennis. She done it like she was telling him to butt out on account of her wanting her husband to come back to her. Yeah. With a broke leg, she'll need me around. She'll want me around.

Maybe she'll let me spend the night. But I won't ask. I won't. I'll just wait for the invite, then take her slow and easy, being careful on account of her broke leg.

Lint smiled at the thought of making love to her. It seemed impossible to him that Angela would want anything else that night.

Jason stepped with hesitation into the bunkhouse.

Angela smiled. "I didn't think you would really come tonight."

"Neither did I." He sat on the crate by her bed. "Does it hurt?"

"The leg? Nah. I been knocked around a lot worse than this. A broke bone is nothing. Nothing."

"Hyram said you've been crying."

"Hyram talks a mite too much. Yes I've been crying, but not on account of my leg. Jason, I loved that horse. He bonded with me—do you know what that means, to have a horse bond with you?"

"No."

"A horse that bonds with you will do anything you ask of it. Anything. Ghost even got up and took me home with him hurting so bad he couldn't see straight." She squirmed around on the bed, shifting her leg and pulling at her jeans above the cast.

"I did that a lot," Jason said. "When I had my leg in a cast, I was constantly moving the leg about, trying to find a comfortable position. There wasn't one."

"None of us thought about how I was going to get out of my Wranglers when the Doc put the cast on. I ain't going to wear the same jeans for six weeks."

"I guess you'll have to cut them off."

"Yeah. Maybe. Too bad, Jason, you never had a horse bond with you. There ain't nothing like it. A lot of the cowboys I know say it's bad to get a horse that attached to one person, but I'm of a different mind on the matter. Lint, he would make fun of me for taking a good cutting horse and making a pet of it. His way was to whip a horse into line. He's good with horses, I got to hand him that. But they was scared of him, all of his horses, and none of them loved him. A horse will perform out of fear, but it'll do even better out of love. Look what Ghost did for me. Some of the boys Hyram hired temporary for a roundup, they teased me about Ghost. One time, I was out patting Ghost on the neck and giving him a lump or two of sugar, and he just laid down on the ground. A horse will do that, sometimes—lay down to sun itself. So I laid there beside it and propped myself against Ghost's stomach, you know, laid my head on him. And danged if the two of us didn't go to sleep. The boys drove up and found us like that, and I thought I'd never hear the end of it. They laughed like fools over the way I treated that animal." Her eyes filled with tears. "And then I had to go and shoot him."

"You had no choice. It isn't your fault Ghost is dead." Is that true? he wondered. No matter. It's done, and there's no bringing the moment back to look for an alternative.

"I know I had to do it. Jason, did you know you can tell how a man treats his woman by watching how he treats his horse?"

"You talk like a man can own a woman, the same as owning an animal."

"No. I don't mean that. You know what I mean. If you see a man controlling his horse with sharp words and spurs and he don't say a kind word to the horse at all, you can bet he treats his woman the same way. Most cowboys are like that. They go for control. Of horses and women."

"How do I treat a horse?"

Jason thought Angela looked at him as if she were measuring something about him. "With respect. I've never met a man like you. I heard they exist, but you're the first I ever met. And it's just my luck that you don't seem destined for me. I'm starting to believe that I'm destined to end up with a much older man, and that ain't all that bad." She pulled at her jeans again. "Jason, get those scissors off that shelf and help me with these Wranglers."

He got the scissors and offered them to her. "Will you do it? Sit there on the end of the bunk. Yeah, like that, only don't be afraid you'll hurt me. Like I told you, my leg ain't all that bad. I've had worse things wrong with me. Kind of snip up to the knee of the jeans."

Jason did as she directed. "Is that enough?"

"Snip just a little higher. There. Now help me get these things off." She unsnapped and unzipped the jeans.

"You better do that after I leave. I'm not sure we can stay objective if we take them off as a joint project."

"Hell, Jason. If you think I got anything on my mind after breaking a bone in my leg then you got another think coming. Here, help me with these. I don't think I can do it by myself." She pulled her jeans over her hips and lifted herself on her hands so he could take the jeans the rest of the way off.

Lint stopped his truck back from the driveway to Hyram's ranch. If Hyram hears me, Lint thought, that fat old bastard will like as not come out to check with a shotgun. I better walk to the bunkhouse. When he got close, Lint heard Angela talking to someone, so he went up to the screen door and looked in. He saw Jason sitting on his wife's bed, pulling Angela's jeans down. At first Lint just stood there, not wanting to believe what he was seeing. But there it was. Angela twitching her butt around so that kid could undress her. The bitch. I ought to kill her on the spot.

Control, control, he warned himself as the red tide threatened to wash over him. Remember what getting out of control did to Regan. When his hand took the screen door knob, he watched it like it belonged to someone else. The hand jerked the screen door open, and Lint stepped across the threshold. Inside him, the red thing seemed to swell and push against its bounds, like it was about to break through.

"What the hell you think you're doing?" he demanded.

Jason, startled, looked at Lint. "I'm helping her get her jeans off—"

"I can see that, asshole. You shut up. Angela, how could you do this?"

"It ain't what you think, Lint."

"How goddam stupid do you think I am?"

"Now just a minute." Jason stood up. Lint looked at him, at how tall he was, at the way he seemed to offer a challenge, and the hot, red tide inside him broke loose and flooded through his entire body. Even his vision seemed to cloud with red.

Lint held his right hand out toward Angela as a distraction, and his left shot out hard into Jason's stomach. Jason doubled forward and Lint brought his knee into his face.

"Stop it, Lint! Stop!" Angela screamed. Lint grabbed Jason's shirt and pulled him around, away from the bed, and shoved him to the wall. He took Jason by the hair and jerked his head against the sheetrock.

As Jason went limp, Angela picked up the scissors and threw them at Lint. The point caught him in the small of the back, and the scissors fell to the floor. "Sheee-it!" Lint ran his hand to his back and looked at his fingers. "Blood. Lookit that, Angela. Blood." He wiped his hand on his jeans. "Look at you, laying there with your pants down around your knees. How come Doc Ryan told me you got a broke leg? Shit, there ain't nothing wrong with your legs, 'cept that you was about to wrap them around that wetback. If I'd come a minute later, he'd have you naked. You bitch."

He lifted her by the front of her blouse. "My leg! Lint!" Angela cried. "My leg!"

"You lying bitch." He threw her to the floor. She screamed and tried to dodge aside, but he straddled her with his knees and pinned her down. "Bitch, bitch, bitch!" he growled, taking her hair in both hands and slamming her head against the floor.

Angela quit screaming and went limp. Lint kept hitting her head to the floor until he saw blood puddle on the hardwood. He let go and stared at the blood. The red tide that had flooded him seemed to recede. "Angela?" he whispered. He stood and looked at her. "Angela, Goddammit!" He kicked her leg and felt something hard under the jeans. "Angela, say something!"

He kicked her leg again, then knelt to examine what felt so hard against his boot. "A cast! Well I'll be a sumbitch!" He saw how the jeans had been cut, and he looked at the scissors on the floor. Maybe that kid wasn't about to mount her. Bull he wasn't. Since when would a cast stop a man from doing it? Any man with any sand would cut away those jeans and go right to it. And that bitch probably begged him to. He looked at her again, at the way her hair looked orange against the red puddle of blood. Was she breathing? He started to feel for a pulse when he heard the door to the ranch house slam. That would be Hyram. And he would come with his shotgun. Lint stepped to the door and turned off the light.

"Jason?" Hyram called. "I thought I heard Angela screaming. Is she all right?"

Lint slipped out the door and ran into the darkness.

Jason became aware of a droning sound that had a soothing, faraway feel about it. Familiar. It seemed so familiar, yet he couldn't identify it.

Then it came to him: rain. He loved the falling of rain against the bedroom window in his house in Kuala Lumpur, a cleansing and steady sound that he heard every day during the monsoon. After the downpour, sometimes monkeys from the big rain trees across the street would come into his yard to climb among the oleander and frangipani blossoms, to chatter at each other and shake themselves, throwing a mist from their fur into the sun.

Another sound seemed to demand his attention, one he didn't want to listen to, not when there were the monkeys and the drooping frangipani flowers, and birds, so many birds. Someone put a hand on his shoulder and shook him. "Jason, Jason," a small, faraway voice said. It became louder. "Jason! Come on, boy, you gotta help me."

Jason opened his eyes, finding it hard to focus. Then he saw Hyram, bent over him. "Jason, you got to get up. You got to."

"Hyram?" The man seemed grossly out of place. Jason could still hear the rain.

"Angela, she's in awful shape. Can you get up, Jason?"

"Yes." He sat up and felt pain shoot through his head and his vision clouded.

"Jason?"

"Yes. I can get up. I can." He opened his eyes to find Hyram's face next to his.

"Here, boy, I'll help you." Hyram lifted Jason to his feet.

"Angela!" Jason said. The memory of Lint entering the bunkhouse came to him with sudden clarity. "Where's Angela?"

"There on the floor. Jason, you got to get to the house and call an ambulance. I'm scared to move her and I'm scared to leave her."

Jason steadied himself on Hyram, then looked beyond him to the figure on the floor. Angela lay on her back with her head in a pool of blood. A shotgun lay on the floor beside her. "He shot her!" Jason said. "With that gun!" The memory of the woman in the airport flooded through him, and he saw her, not Angela, lying in the blood.

"No. She ain't shot. But she's hurt pretty bad. That there is my gun."

"Not shot?" Jason moved around Hyram and knelt beside a woman with red hair. It was Angela, after all, and not Suppriah.

She breathed in a rough, troubled way, but Jason could see no wounds. Yet there was all that blood. "Where. . . ?"

"The back of her head. Looks like she got hit there right hard. Lint Bodark done that." Hyram's voice had a thin, dangerous edge to it. "Go, Jason. Go call an ambulance."

Jason nodded and stood up. His head hurt plenty, but the dizziness seemed to have receded. He went outside. Rain hit him in cold needles. Lightning forked across the sky, illuminating the ranch house. Jason ran toward it, his head throbbing with each step.

When the paramedics put Angela on the gurney, Hyram climbed inside the ambulance. "You can't ride in here," one of them said.

"Piss off," Hyram snapped. "Jason, you follow in the white pickup so's we'll have wheels at the hospital. Put on the blinkers and speed right behind us." As the paramedics drew the door closed, Hyram added, "Put the shotgun on your rack."

Jason stood in the rain, watching the driver get into the ambulance. Shotgun? He didn't want to do that. But Hyram said . . . and what about Lint? I've got to move fast or not be able to follow them. He looked into the bunkhouse at the weapon lying beside a puddle of blood. "Shit!" he said aloud, and went inside.

The shotgun had an unpleasant oily smell to it and it weighed more than he expected. He ran through the darkness and rain, holding the gun away from him. It seemed to him that the odor of gun oil made his headache worse.

It took some fast driving to catch up with the ambulance, and the bumps in the road jarred and rattled the pickup so much that he feared the gun could go off. The back of his neck tingled from the nearness to the stock of the weapon on the rack behind him. A shiver ran through his whole body. Is that fear, he asked, or just from being wet and cold?

Lightning danced across the prairie, and thunder crashed like cannons. The inside of the windshield clouded up, and Jason had to divide his attention between what little of the road he could see in the driving rain and the levers on the dash until he found the controls for the defogger.

Lights on the ambulance blurred in the water on the windshield, and rain fell in crystal waves. At times Jason wondered if he would be able to distinguish the road from the prairie if it weren't for following the vehicle in front of him.

His head pounded. This is like the fever dreams I had when I was a child, he thought: the cold, the fear, the pain. This drive is a nightmare, this terrible drive with Angela up there, maybe dying.

A tight feeling of self blame—that was a part of those childhood fever dreams. I did something terrible, and I'm no good, Jason used to hear in the half sleep following a fever dream. Once he awakened, the feeling of worthlessness lingered, sometimes for hours; and he never understood what terrible thing he had done.

The old familiar sense of uneasy guilt washed over him like the water splashing on the hood of the pickup. He tightened his grip on the steering wheel.

Jason parked near the emergency receiving center of Northwest Texas Hospital and ran through rain to the ambulance. He followed

Hyram and the paramedics inside. They wheeled Angela into a curtained-off area.

A woman with close-cropped red hair pushed the curtains aside and looked at Angela. "What happened?"

"She needs a doctor," Hyram said.

"I am a doctor. What happened?"

"She was attacked," one of the paramedics said. "Hit on the back of the head."

"Get these two men out." The doctor gestured toward Hyram and Jason.

"You have some papers to fill out," one of the paramedics said. He escorted them to a waiting area and pointed to a desk. "That lady there has the forms."

Jason sat down while Hyram took care of the paper work. When he finished, he went to Jason and said, "Dr. Brynko sent Angela to intensive care."

"How is she?"

"They don't tell much around here, just that we can go sit in the waiting room until somebody takes a notion to come out and tells us how she's doing."

Outside the intensive care unit, people gathered in groups, some whispering, some just staring at the floor. Hyram drew Jason to an isolated corner to sit. "She's gotta be all right," Hyram said in a fierce whisper. He sighed and shook his head. Tears filled his eyes and spilled onto his cheeks, but he seemed not to notice.

"She'll be fine." Jason rubbed his temples. It seemed to him that he owed it to Hyram to confess his role in Lint's anger. There had been a moment of sexual titillation when Jason helped Angela with her jeans. Lint's jealousy wasn't so far off the mark.

Hyram took Jason's arm. "Angela." His voice faltered. "Angela, she's got it for you, you know. In love. And that's all right. You understand?" His grip tightened on Jason's arm. "You understand?"

"No." Jason felt the pain in his head increase. Hyram knows, he told himself. He knows. Guilt as from a fever dream spread through him like he had swallowed something hot.

"You been talking about moving into Canyon, but Angela, she don't want that. It's a plumb bad idea, iffn you ask me. A bad one. You stay on the ranch, Jason, when you go to college in Canyon, like me and your daddy agreed. Me and Angela, when she gets outta this place, we'll get married so she can feel okay about living in the main house with me, only she can do like she dang well pleases, if you know what I mean." He let go of Jason's arm.

"Married?" Jason looked at Hyram in astonishment. "Married?"

"Angela, she'll be my third wife. Third one. I won't ask nothing of her that she don't want to give, long as she understands she's getting an old coot for a husband. She can't expect much outta me, seeing as I'm an old man. But she don't need to worry none about how the house is set up, long as ever' thing is kept, you know, private. I'm a dried-up old man. She knows that. Old. Still, I can give her lots of things, help her out, you know. She won't have to worry about that Lint Bodark. Or about being poor. You understand?"

Jason shook his head. The room seemed to tilt. "Have you proposed to her?"

"Not as of this minute, but I will. I will. I got to study the matter some and study the right words so she'll know what I mean when I ask her. We would be married right proper, only it wouldn't be a regular kind of marriage arrangement that the preacher at the First Baptist Church would expect. You know what I mean, don't you?"

"No. What do you mean?"

"You know." Hyram glanced around the room and lowered his voice. "It's just that, well, out here in West Texas folks get all bent out of shape if they think you ain't just like them. So what the hell, who needs to know what ain't their business? With you around, I think she would be okay, you know, marrying me. I don't expect her to move into my room, seeing as I'm old and not up to much. You and she can . . . well, I don't get jealous. You know what I mean?"

Jason stared. The pain in his head seemed to spread down the back of his neck and into his shoulders.

Did Hyram mean all that? And if so, he wondered, what do I do about it? I must tell him about me and Sybil. No way can I stay around the ranch. But when is a good time to bring up Sybil?

All these questions could wait, he decided. Angela had to recover so Hyram could put the odd proposition to her. She would say no, Jason told himself, and I won't have to worry about how to tell Hyram about me and Sybil.

Jason looked at the tears on Hyram's face and concluded that for now, he shouldn't talk about Sybil or even about leaving the ranch. For now, he would stay with Hyram and help him however he could.

Jason found a phone in the lobby of the hospital and called Sybil. A recording of her voice said, "You know what to do and when to do it." Then came a beep.

Jason sighed. "What you said about accidents is true. Today, out there beside Buffalo Lake that isn't a lake. Good God, that was just today. Seems like longer ago. I'm at Northwest Texas Hospital in Amarillo."

Sybil picked up the phone. "Jason? Just a second while I turn the machine off. There. Are you hurt?"

"I'm okay. It's Angela. Her horse . . . never mind. Her husband beat her senseless and she's in a coma. Right now she's in the intensive care unit and I'm with Hyram. He's in bad shape and I'm staying with him."

"Can I help?"

"It was my fault Lint beat Angela. He knocked me out, too, but that was no big deal. The big deal is Angela's injury. And Hyram. He wants to marry her. Can you imagine? We don't even know if she will live."

"You aren't making much sense. Are you all right, Jason?"

"It's hard to concentrate on anything. Sybil, I thought nothing could keep me from you tonight. I was trying to help, then in came Lint. What a world."

"You said it was an accident. I understand accidents."

"I did? An accident? Only that Lint came in when he did—that was the accident. I was stupid, unbelievably stupid. Look, Sybil, I better check on Hyram."

"Call me?"

"Yeah." Jason hung up and stared at the phone for a few seconds before turning away.

He had difficulty understanding time. It seemed to operate by different laws in the waiting room and in the hall outside the Intensive Care Unit. People wandered about, hugged one another, then sat and looked at their hands. Sometimes they talked, though they said little of substance, so far as Jason could tell. Hyram paced in the hall, peering through the windows in the doors to the ICU. Jason stood beside him as an orderly wheeled a gurney out. When the doors opened, he caught a glimpse of Angela in a glassed-in room; she lay still and white, wearing a turban of bandages and tubes running from her nose.

From Hyram's sudden intake of breath, Jason knew Hyram had also seen her. When the doors hissed shut, Jason took Hyram's arm. "Come sit down."

Hyram looked at his watch. "They'll let us in there come ten o'clock." He let Jason lead him into the waiting room. "Ten o'clock, the doc said. After that, there ain't no way to get in again until morning."

When Sybil arrived, it seemed to Jason that he had just gotten off the phone to her. She bent and put her cheek to his, then sat beside him and took his hand. "I do volunteer work at this hospital," she said. "Sometimes I sit at that desk and talk to people who come to this waiting room."

At ten o'clock, they stood in the hall, waiting to be allowed to see Angela. Sybil explained that only family could visit patients in the ICU.

"I'm Angela's husband," Hyram said when a nurse approached. The nurse escorted him in, talking to him in low tones.

Jason squeezed Sybil's hand. "I expect he will want to stay the night in the waiting room, just in case there is a change in her condition. I'll stay with him."

"And I'll stay with you."

Sybil sat beside Jason, who kept most of his attention focused on Hyram throughout the night. Hyram alternated between slumping in a waiting-room chair and pacing the hall. The medical staff allowed him into the ICU every two hours beginning at eight in the morning, and each time he came out after five minutes looking worried and shaking his head.

When he returned from his last visit for the day, after Dr. Brynko assured him that she would call if there were a change in Angela's condition, Hyram gave in to Jason's offer to drive him home.

"I came on the Harley," Sybil said. "If you don't mind, I'd like to follow you to the ranch."

Hyram looked at Jason. "Your face is terrible, cowboy, if you'll pardon my saying so."

"Yeah. You look pretty tired yourself."

"Tired? Maybe. But I ain't beat-up looking. That eye needs some attention, which it's going to get soon as we get back to my place. That goat-kissing toad licker of a scumbag Lint will pay for tagging you with that shiner after I work him over for what he done to Angela."

Jason's hand went to his eye. "This is a souvenir from a biker named Altus, not from Lint."

"A biker? You do get around these days."

Sybil took Hyram's arm and escorted him down the hall toward the parking lot. "Altus is in much worse condition than Jason," she said. "I think he has several broken ribs."

"Then the schooling from me and Odom took, and Jason now knows the difference between a real fight and a friendly one. You're a good man, Jason."

When they reached the ranch, Hyram watched Sybil park the Harley beside the pickup. "You know what I said about you living here to be around Angela? Forget I said any of that stuff. I didn't realize about you and Sybil. Go to her, cowboy. She's more woman than I've ever had. Get on that hog of a bike with her and get some sleep at her place. Tell her to put some ice on that eye."

"Accidents determine most events in the universe." Sybil said.

They took off their helmets, hung them on the rearview mirrors of the Harley, and went into Sybil's house.

"I'm too tired to think about such matters," Jason said. "But maybe cause-and-effect rules the universe. Angela is in the hospital because she shot Ghost and the other events followed because of bad timing." He sat on the couch.

"Not there. You come into the bedroom with me."

"The bedroom?"

"To sleep. You need sleep worse than anything."

"I needed that invitation worse than anything."

"I'll hold you while you sleep, then." She held out her hand.

Jason took it and stood. "You know I'll resist going when you try to send me away again."

"I won't. And if I do, I want you to resist going. It would be fine with me if we found a way never to spend another night apart. We will, of course, given how the world operates, but maybe we can choose to be together as much as possible. Do you want that?"

"Yes I want that. But what's changed to cause you to say such things?"

"I'm not sure. You. Watching you take care of Hyram, maybe."

Two days later Dr. Brynko transferred Angela to the Bivins Rehabilitation unit at High Plains Hospital, where Jason saw Angela up close for the first time since that rainy night in the emergency receiving center. Sybil had gone home to shower and sleep.

Angela lay motionless except for her eyes. She watched Hyram move around the room, but she said nothing.

"Does she even know we're here?" Jason asked Laura LeVitus, the counselor at Bivins Rehabilitation Center.

"On some level, perhaps she has some awareness. But does she know who is here or why? Probably not."

Angela had the back of her head bandaged, and she rested on a special pillow to keep pressure off the wound. Other than appearing pale, she looked normal. When Jason watched her move her eyes around the room, he could almost believe that she was all right. Almost.

Laura LeVitus led him and Hyram to her office where she told them that Angela might never recover. Hyram put his face in his hands and cried. "But she might?" Jason asked.

"It's possible that she will regain awareness of her surroundings. We have no way of knowing. Look, you two need to get some rest. Angela needs you to be healthy and well. Go home. I'll call you immediately if there is any change."

Jason excused himself so the counselor could talk with Hyram.

Beyond the door to the hospital, he saw a roadrunner standing in the shade of a locust tree. Two grackles who had a nest in the tree dived and fussed at the roadrunner. It endured their noise, then hopped on the sidewalk and walked up to the building, turning its head to eye Jason. Roadrunners eat snakes, Jason remembered. But that one looked tame as a chicken, domesticated, incapable of killing anything. Did roadrunners often become tame like that, he wondered. Maybe I can ask Angela before long. "And," he said aloud, "maybe not." He felt his eyes sting with tears.

Over dinner at The King and I restaurant, he asked Hyram, "Will you be going to the auction on Saturday?"

Hyram looked long and hard at his iced tea. "You learned to eat all these noodle dishes in Indonesia?"

"Malaysia. Yes. Do you like the pad Thai?"

"That what you call this dried up chicken noodle soup with peanuts? It'll do until some real food comes along. Hell, a cowboy can learn to eat anything. You ever read *Lonesome Dove*? Them cowboys on the trail, they sure enough ate grasshoppers. And liked them, they did."

"Did you ever eat a grasshopper?"

Hyram looked out the window, his eyes seeming unfocused. Then he turned back to Jason. "I'll be at that auction come Saturday. It won't be the same without Angela." He blinked and cleared his throat.

"I'll go with you, if that's okay."

"I'd like that, Jason. But you might ought to go be with Sybil."

"I'm going to the auction with you."

Saturday morning Jason got up before dawn to drive to the ranch. Sybil made a tentative offer to accompany him, then withdrew it when she saw how distracted he seemed. "You go on," she said. "Cook breakfast for Hyram and go to that auction with him. It will be good for both of you."

When he arrived at the ranch, he half expected to see Angela saddling up Ghost for her ride out to the prairie where she would greet the rising sun.

But Ghost is dead, he thought. Dead. And Angela might be—who could know?

Jason looked at Snake Mountain, dark against the predawn sky, then went inside to attempt to cook a Texas country breakfast.

He took a can of biscuits from the refrigerator, peeled a layer off the cover, and rapped the can against the edge of the table. These biscuits I can make, he thought. He had bought them at Taylor and Son's Supermarket in Canyon, along with frozen hashbrowns. At the checkout counter, he asked the clerk how to make cream gravy. She gave him a startled look, laughed and told him. Jason took out a pen and a pad of paper and took notes, aware that people behind him in line watched with amusement.

When Hyram came into the kitchen, he looked with appreciation at the meal. "You shouldn't ought to go to all the trouble. But I am grateful."

"The gravy looks a bit thin." Jason paused. "A tad thin," he corrected. Hyram laughed, a sound Jason had not heard all week.

"It looks goodern grits to me."

"And I broke the yolk of one of the eggs. I don't know how Angela turns them without breaking even one yolk."

"Yeah. Ain't she good, that Angela? Can't nobody cook like her. She'll be back at it soon. Real soon. I'm thinking I just might bring her home, you know, hire a nurse for when we gotta be out. Could be that she'll wake up better here cause ever' thing is familiar to her. I heard that happens sometimes. A Canyon kid hurt like she was, only from being knocked down by a car—this kid stayed in a hospital forever and never saw nothing he looked at. Same as Angela. Then his folks took him home for a spell. He was lying on the couch in his living room one Sunday where his family was watching a football game, when of a sudden he turned to his mama and said, 'Can I have a Coke?' like he been watching the football game all along. Happened right over there in Canyon. I know the kid's daddy."

"Today's the auction."

"Yeah. Angela, she always loved the auction, especially when I did that fast talking. But I ain't up to it, not today. Hired Ben Lippman to do it, and he's as good a auctioneer as anyone in the county. I'll help Odom get the horses into the sell ring and kind of stay out of the way." He ate in silence.

Hyram asked Jason to drive the two of them to the auction barn. "Drive the white Ford," he said, "since you're used to it. On the way maybe we can figure out why it smells worse than a feed lot in July. You sure you didn't run over a skunk?"

"The smell mystifies me, too. So far as I know I haven't hit an animal. I've washed the truck inside and out. But the smell still lingers."

"We'll find what causes it or it will wear off. But what's a little stench to a couple of old cowboys like us, anyway? I'll get the shotgun out of my pickup and put it on the rack in the Ford. On account of Lint still being out there somewhere. It would put a grin on my face to locate the sumbitch."

"No need for the shotgun. Remember you put the nine millimeter pistol in my glove box?"

The day after Angela was injured, Hyram had objected when Jason wanted to take the shotgun out of the Ford. "Lint ain't been picked up by the cops. Which means that snake is still around somewhere. If he takes a notion to come after you, you'll need that gun."

Jason argued that he would not need it, that he didn't like it behind his neck there on the gun rack. "Then," Hyram said, "I'll take that shotgun out, but only if you let me put the nine millimeter in the glove box in case you need it." Jason sighed and said yes, put it there. He figured he could ignore its presence better than he could the shotgun. And if it gave Hyram comfort, then why not let him put his pistol wherever he wanted it?

When they got into the pickup to go to the auction, Hyram looked in the glove box just to make sure the weapon was still there.

Outside the auction barn men moved in small groups along a rail fence, looking at horses. I'm in the middle of a whole tribe of cowboys, Jason thought.

They wore almost identical costumes—boots, jeans, plaid shirts and cowboy hats. Most had faded round spots on their hip pockets where they carried tins of chewing tobacco or snuff. Several wore leather chaps.

The barn stood over two stories high and covered a substantial piece of prairie. The structure was angular and ugly, sided with corrugated sheet metal. "Angela said you own this building."

"Yup. Pull in over yonder, by that horse trailer."

"Do you own all those horses?" Jason parked the pickup.

"Nope. Most of them I'll sell for a commission. The owners bring them and I sell them." Hyram opened the pickup door, then turned to Jason before getting out. "Just hang around and watch and listen. Selling horses is an art, and my crew is as good at it as anyone. I got to go do some big-shotting with the buyers. They expect it. You just watch and learn, but don't get involved in nothing." Hyram joined a group of men who leaned against the fence, pointing and talking. Jason wandered along the fence to look at the horses in the pens.

A black colt came up to him and sniffed his hand. Behind him, a cowboy said, "Lookit that. Somebody done spoilt that critter. Look at it nosing around for sugar."

"Sure is a pretty little thing, though," another said.

"You call that pretty? Look at them bandy legs. And that critter got a head like a jug of whiskey."

Jason patted the colt. Its head looked fine to him, and he could see nothing wrong with its legs. But then, he told himself, I don't know much about horses.

He liked the black colt, liked how it nosed around on his shirt, sniffing his pockets. If I stay in this part of the world, he thought, maybe I'll buy a young horse like this one and raise it myself. I could learn what Angela meant by bonding with a horse.

When he heard Hyram's voice among a group of men, Jason moved closer to listen. "For sure you're right about that stallion being old," Hyram was saying, "but look at him. A thoroughbred, he is, and one time he was the fastest thing around. Won the Belmont, he did. Big money. You buy a horse like that for a stud, and he'll pay for himself in no time at all."

"But he's over twenty years old," one man objected.

"Close. Going on near to seventeen years. But a horse ain't like a man. The human male got only one quart of jism for his entire lifetime, and when it's gone, that's that. An old man can no more be of real service than a cow can jump over the moon. But nature gave a horse fifty gallons. This fellow won't run dry in his old age. He's good for a bunch more years of stud service."

"What about that paint standing over there?" one of the men asked.

"What about it?"

"How high you starting the bidding?"

"Don't you go quoting me on this, cause Ben Lippman's got the exact figures, but I think that one starts somewhere around four hundred."

"Four hundred! Ain't that high for a horse that got a limp?"

"Limp?" Hyram leaned on the fence and looked at the paint. "It sure enough is favoring that front foot some. But hell fire, that little buggered-up spot on its foot is a long distance from its heart. That there is a healthy animal."

When the men started drifting into the auction barn, Jason followed. They registered at an office just inside the door, each taking a piece of cardboard with a number written on it. Some then went to a concession stand; others went to the bleachers. It looked to Jason like a sporting arena of some kind. The bleachers faced what Hyram had referred to as the "sell ring," though it didn't look much like a ring to Jason. It was a rectangular area of bare dirt with gates on both ends. Behind it stood a platform where the auctioneer and a record keeper sat, facing the bleachers. That must be Ben Lippman, Jason thought. Hyram had mentioned him, but where else have I heard that name? From Angela. Yeah. She once told me that Ben saw her out on the prairie, beside a dirt road, when she was performing her meditation before the rising sun. Didn't she say he drove off the road when he saw her greeting the sun?

Jason looked at the craggy face of the old rancher and decided that the man would indeed be startled to find a nymph out on the prairie, naked in the early morning light.

The image of Angela lying in her hospital room, damaged and unresponsive, came to Jason. He shook his head and forced his attention into the present.

"Everbody got a number?" Ben Lippman said into a microphone. "Iffn you ain't got one, then get it quick, 'cause we're about to start with the tack."

Hyram had warned Jason about the tack sale. "It'll go on long enough for you to grow a beard, long enough for your dog to get arthritis and your grandpappy to lose his teeth. Just when you think we'll never get to selling horses, the boys will start running them into the sell ring."

At first, Jason found the tack sale interesting. Two spotters, dressed in outrageous cowboy outfits, stood under the auctioneer's platform to hold up brass items with leather dangling from them while Ben talked nonsense into the microphone. "Gotta bidda dolla, who'll bidda bidda two, two, two, three now, gimme three, bidda three bidda bidda—"

His voice went on and on while the spotters surveyed the men on the bleachers. When someone held up a number to bid, a spotter would shout "Hah!" and point at the bidder, and the record keeper beside Ben would scribble something.

Jason remembered his first encounter with Texas English in the Amarillo airport when Angela came up to him. He had thought at the time that no one could talk in such an incomprehensible way and still be speaking English. I was wrong, he thought. Angela became understandable soon enough, or at least her speech did. But what Ben is shouting into the microphone, Jason thought, has a grammar and a vocabulary all its own. His speech is some sort of ritual.

Jason looked around, struck with a sudden realization. It was all a ritual, all of it. The ceremonial dress of the buyers and sellers, the vestments of the acolytes in the sell ring, the chanting of the high priest. A cowboy tribal ritual.

By the time the first horse entered the sell ring, the men in the bleachers were as ready to be done with tack as was Jason. Odom rode a paint from one end of the ring to the other, then turned the horse to face the buyers.

Ben Lippman cleared his throat, loud and raspy over the loudspeaker. "The owner of this here horse says the bidding gotta start at four hundred. Look at him, gentlemen. That's as good a paint as you will find on the high plains of Texas. Okay, here we go and four hundred, four, four, who'll bidda bidda bidda four, yeah bidda bidda gimme four. . . ."

After cajoling the buyers several more times in his slow drawl, then launching into the ritualized, fast-paced nonsense, Ben gave up. "Ain't nobody going to go for four. Where's the owner?"

A man in the bleachers waved. "Will you go for less? No? The man says four is the bottom dollar. Take him out. Any of you want to look at this fine horse later can go out to the corral. Just four hundred will get you the best dang paint between Muleshoe and Kansas City."

The next horse brought into the sell ring got three people interested, and the bidding escalated, mainly, Jason thought, because of the skill Ben had in getting them to bid against one another.

"Next," Ben said, "we got a fine colt, a black one that's as pretty a thing as you'll find this side of the Canadian River."

Jason watched two men drive the colt through the gate. Its eyes were wild with fear, and as the gate swung shut, the colt shied to one side. The latch rod on the gate hit it on the neck, and the colt jerked in pain. Jason saw blood spurt from the wound. "Two hundred bidda bidda two who'll bidda two bidda. . . ." Ben was saying. The people in the bleachers shifted and began talking and pointing. Ben fell silent and looked at the colt.

It stood, trembling, while blood gushed in rhythmic pulses from its neck. "That there's a dead colt," Ben said. "Looks like the bolt on the gate pierced its jugular. Who's the owner? Can I sell him as dog meat? Yes? A good-sized piece of meat it is, yes sir, who'll bidda twenty bucks, twenty bidda bidda, fifteen gimme fifteen fifteen for the body bidda bidda bidda fifteen."

Jason stood, gripping the rail above the sell ring, watching the colt. One of the spotters shoved it to one side as soon as it had been sold.

The black colt stood with its head down, its eyes glazed with pain, while blood poured onto the dirt floor. Ben went on with auctioning the next horse. Two cowboys had to work at controlling it because it stamped and reared when it smelled the blood from the colt.

Jason looked around in disbelief. No one except him showed any concern for the suffering of the colt. "Who bought it?" Jason demanded of a man standing next to him.

"That feller up there with the red bandanna on his neck," the man pointed. "He owns a processing plant."

Jason climbed the bleachers to the man. "That colt is suffering," he said.

The man looked surprised, then set his jaw and looked with deliberate slowness at Jason from head to foot. "So what?"

"So you have to do something for it."

"I don't gotta do nothing for nobody. That colt will lay down and die of its own accord when it's ready. You got a big mouth, boy. You run on and leave me alone."

Jason looked back at the colt, then surveyed the people at the auction. Ben chanted bidda bidda into the microphone, and everyone looked at the skittery horse in the center of the sell ring. Hyram, Jason thought — Hyram wouldn't stand for this. But Hyram was nowhere in sight.

Jason got off the bleachers as fast as he could and ran outside to the pickup. The stink of the truck hit him as he opened the door. He took the nine millimeter pistol from the glove box and ran back into the auction barn.

He climbed to the spot above the sell ring where the colt stood dying. Ben's chant continued, and the crowd of cowboys gave their attention to the bidding. Jason released the safety, as he had seen Angela do that day on the prairie where Lint had once killed a prairie dog. Leaning over the rail, Jason put the barrel of the pistol close to the back of the colt's head and pulled the trigger.

The pistol jumped and the sound of it filled the auction barn. Jason watched the colt fall into the pool of blood that had drained from the wound in its neck. Angela shot Ghost, Jason thought. She shot Ghost. Then she cried.

He clicked the safety back on, put the pistol into his belt, and took another look at the dead colt. The way it lay with its head in the pool of blood reminded Jason of the grotesque horse's head hanging from the tree in Sybil's backyard.

He walked out of the barn. Men moved aside for him. A part of Jason noted the silence and the surprised stares, but he gave little attention to the people around him. Of more concern was the oily sensation in his stomach. As he went out the door, he heard Ben's voice announcing it was time to get on with the sale. Jason thought he would vomit, but he did not, though his stomach convulsed and he gagged several times. He leaned against the white Ford pickup, feeling sick and dizzy. What am I becoming? he asked over and over.

52

"Okay, boy," a voice said, "gimme the gun."

Jason looked at the man pointing a rifle at him. Two others stood off to one side, both aiming pistols at him. "Who are you?" Jason demanded.

"Police."

Jason shook his head. "You're not police. Not even in Texas would a policeman dress like that. You're a cowboy. Point that rifle somewhere else."

"The pistol. Give me the pistol. Those two are security police," he nodded at the other two men, "hired by the owner of this place. I'm a deputy sheriff for Randall County. I'm off duty, but I got the power to arrest you for firing a weapon in a public place. That gun you got under your belt. Come on, now, give it to me."

"Point that rifle somewhere else. And tell those cowboys to do the same with their pistols. Then we talk about Hyram's nine millimeter."

"No deals. Take that pistol out of your belt with your thumb and only one finger. Move right slow."

Jason shrugged and did as the man asked.

When Hyram walked up, Jason's hands were cuffed behind him and the deputy was pushing him toward a brown pickup. "Now hold on there, Lantz," Hyram said, "you turn my nephew loose."

"Nephew?" The deputy looked puzzled. "Hyram, this Mexican ain't your nephew."

"He is, for a fact. And he ain't no Mexican. Not that being one would make a big goddam."

"The cuffs hurt," Jason said. "You put them on too tight."

"Let the boy go," Hyram said.

"Can't do that, Hyram. You know I can't. I'm running him in for firing a gun in a public place and for malicious destruction of property. I got to do it."

"Like thunder you do. Dammit Lantz. . . ."

"Hyram," one of the security men said, "the boy did kill that wounded colt, right there in the middle of the auction. That colt needed killing, for a fact, but the kid showed mighty bad judgment going about it like he did. Lantz is right. He's gotta take the boy in. Lantz, you loosen them cuffs."

“You ain’t telling me how to do my job.”

“To me, you’re off duty. You hurt that boy with them cuffs, and I will take it personal. Loosen them.”

“Awe, shit, Hank, you think you’re a real cop when you ain’t nothing but a hired guard. You stay outta my official business.”

“Right now, I’m just plain old Hank, and I’m working up a real mad about how you put them cuffs on Hyram’s nephew.” Hank took a menacing step toward Lantz.

“All right, Hank. Don’t you go to getting your panties all in a wad over nothing.” The deputy loosened the cuffs.

“Thanks,” Jason said.

“You shut up,” Lantz said.

“Lantz,” Hank said, “he ain’t a criminal. He’s just a kid that wishes he was a cowboy bad enough to up and shoot a hurt horse. You done that yourself, once. Treat him nice, you hear?”

“I’m sorry, Jason,” Hyram said. “I’ll come get you away from the police station soon as the auction is over. That’ll be about two more hours.”

Lantz drove Jason to the county jail on the corner of the square in downtown Canyon. On the way, Lantz asked, “You really old man Hyram’s nephew?”

“No. He and my father were best friends when they were in the army. But he treats me as if he were my uncle.”

“You talk funny. You ain’t from around here.” Lantz said it like an accusation, then remained silent until they went into the booking room at the jail.

Jason tried not to think about the colt, but the images were too vivid in his mind: the way it came up to him before the auction, the fear in its eyes when it entered the sell ring, the way it stood dying before Jason fired the bullet into its brain. I did that, Jason said to himself: I used Hyram’s nine millimeter to kill a young horse. Didn’t I once say that a man who would kill an animal could kill a human being? Didn’t I believe that?

He studied Lantz as they drove into town. The man looked like a larger version of Lint Bodark. This deputy and the man he called Hank, Jason thought—they’re a real pair. They nearly got in a fight over my handcuffs. And the man who bought the colt for dog meat is like the rest of these cowboys. I think he would have punched me if I had said much more to him. I don’t understand these people. And yet—and yet, here I am, dressed like a member of the tribe.

He had once heard Hyram say, "If it looks like a duck, walks like a duck, and sounds like a duck, then by golly the critter is a duck." And hadn't Angela said something about how appearance was the first step to reality? So maybe it was true. Maybe he had finally become a Texan. He sighed and squirmed around in the seat of the pickup. It is true that I'm being arrested for shooting an animal with a pistol.

When they walked into the booking room, Lantz pointed at a bench. "Sit there. I got some paperwork to do."

Jason found it awkward to sit with his hands cuffed behind him, but the worst thing about all this, he thought, is how ashamed I feel. But ashamed of what? I had to kill that colt. So maybe the shame comes from wearing the cuffs, from being dragged into jail, from being treated like a criminal. I sure look like one right now—which would be enough to make me one, to Angela's way of thinking.

With deliberate effort, he forced his attention from himself to the booking room. Something seemed to be missing. The walls were stark white, as were the floors. The bench he sat on, a couch across from him, and the two chairs in the room all looked alike. All were made with steel frames and black plastic cushions. The desk Lantz stood beside was black and gray, and behind the desk sat a woman dressed in a black-and-white uniform staring at a colorless computer screen.

Color, Jason thought. There is no color in the room—that's what's missing.

A uniformed policeman came in leading two men who looked to be Jason's age. Both were handcuffed. The police officer shoved them toward the couch. "Sit and keep it quiet."

One had been crying. He looked around, wide eyed. The other looked bored. "You don't need to be scared," the bored one said.

"But I ain't never been to jail before."

Join the club, Jason thought. I've been in the United States just a few months, and here I am, being thrust into an American jail like a common criminal. The feeling of shame washed over him again.

"You call this place a jail?" the bored one said. "Shit. This place is like a goddam motel. You know what they call the Randall County Jail? They call it the Randall County Hilton. This place is clean and nice. You want to see a real jail, get yourself picked up in Amarillo and sit in the city jail for a while. They put you in the bull pen, everybody in one big room, and that's where you stay. Lessen you're drunk, then they put you in the tank that's nothing but cement and steel so's they can hose the place out if you barf. In the bull pen, there's a pisser that don't never work, so the smell is bad as a barnyard. The floor is so grimy that when you walk, your feet kind of stick with ever' step you take. Bunks are nothing but iron slabs hanging by chains on the walls, and on each one is a mattress that's so old it's all split and leaking cotton from the holes —and smell! You oughta smell them mattresses. Can't nobody but bums with a dead nose sleep on one. You throw it off on the floor, when it comes time to sleep. Not that you can get any rest on a slab of iron and what with the bright lights they keep on all the time and all the noise of everbody talking ever' hour of the day or night. That Amarillo city jail, now that's what I call a real jail. This here place, shoot, they let you watch television, right there in the day room. The pissers flush and don't smell to high heaven. At night, they put you in a clean cell that has a bunk a body can get comfortable on, and they turn down the lights so you can get some sleep. You ain't in a real jail, not here."

After the booking, Lantz left and uniformed police officers took over. One had Jason remove his clothing and put on bright orange coveralls. Then he was taken to the day room.

A commode with no partition around it sat beside one wall. Built into another wall was a television. Six men sat in various places in the room, all dressed, Jason thought, like carrots. Aside from the flicker on the television screen, the orange jumpsuits provided the only color in the room.

Jason eyed the commode and thought about the indignity of having to use it in front of other people. This is the Randall County Hilton? he said to himself.

An unshaven, balding man came up to Jason. "Do you know anything about God?" the man demanded.

"Not much, but I'm learning."

"It is my Christian duty to witness to you, young man. Do you walk hand-in-hand with God?" The man held his eyelids too high to suit Jason. He could see the whites all around the cloudy blue. The bushes the man wore for eyebrows twitched up in a wild sort of way.

"God doesn't have hands. God is not a man." Jason wondered why he bothered to prolong such an odd discussion.

The man looked pleased in a mean sort of way. "My name is Brother Noah, and I can see that God sent me to this den of thieves to witness for Him, to show you the way and the light. God is a man, but he is much more than a man. He is Jesus Christ—"

"And," Jason interjected, "he is the Lord Krishna, the spirit of the universe incarnate. A lot of people say that. Some say he is enlightenment, like the Buddha. I like that vision of God, though I think he isn't a he at all. God is an understanding. God is naked bodies exchanging pleasure and love. God appears on mountains and golf courses, in sunrises and bedrooms. God is the connection we feel with a wasp. God is the mercy in killing a suffering Ghost or shooting a dying colt."

Brother Noah backed away from Jason. "You are in deep darkness. I see the Devil sitting on your shoulders."

"I'll be glad to bend down some and let old Nick climb onto your shoulders for a while." Jason leaned toward Noah. "I believe in sharing my demons."

The man's eyebrows twitched in alarm. Jason was so caught up in watching those brows that he didn't see the fist until it was too late. Noah's blow caught him just below the eye, staggering him.

"You stay away from me. Get thee behind me, Satan." Brother Noah rubbed his knuckles and backed away. Others in the room laughed as Noah fled to the other side of the day room.

Later, an officer took Jason through a grim corridor, down an elevator, and into a narrow room that was partitioned in the middle with a long desk and glass. Hyram entered on the other side of the glass. "Go to the first unit," the police officer told Jason, pointing. "Use the phone."

Jason sat on a stool and picked up a phone. Hyram sat across from him, picking up the phone on his side. "You sure do look funny in that monkey suit. And that eye. You had a black one from that biker you told me about, and now you got two of them. Lord-a-mercy, but you already got into something in the jail. Did one of the cops do that, Jason?"

"No. A religious fanatic punched me, another inmate. I hate this place, Hyram. How long will I be here?"

"I could get you out today."

"Do it. I don't want to spend the night in here."

"Jason, I did some talking with one of the boys here who used to work for me out at the ranch. He said it weren't good judgment to pay bail today. He said the booking officers are of the opinion that you need a lesson in West Texas manners and that a night or two in jail would do the trick. If I get you out, they'll file the papers that will get some serious charges against you. If I make you stay, like as not you'll be turned loose come Monday morning, and nobody needs to know if you don't want them to know. What do you say?"

"You mean these policemen set themselves up as judge and jury?"

"You could see it that way, I guess. What about it? You want out bad enough to have to face criminal charges? They could be downright embarrassing to you and your family."

"Two nights? And then they just let me walk out?" Jason considered it. "I don't think I could stand it, Hyram."

"Stand it? Shit fire and save matches, boy. I been longer in places a bunch worse than this. Down in Pecos. That place was bad, real bad. And in Port Arthur—shit you shoulda seen them roaches crawling on the floor and the walls. Big as a mouse they was, and they could fly like a bird. Them sumbitches would light on you when you was asleep and bite the tar outta you. The Randall County Jail, shoot, it's better than camping out on the prairie."

"But being in here is so dehumanizing, so embarrassing."

"Yeah? Then a couple of nights here might be real good for you. Stick your courage to the screwing place, boy. Think about how you got the opportunity to get over being squeamish. From the looks of that eye, you got a jump-start on the learning. And consider how being here will get you outta legal trouble that could be a real hassle. If I know old Nathan White, he'd be here on the next plane, soon as he heard his boy was in trouble with the Texas law. And your mama, she would have technicolored bowel movements the minute she heard you was in a Texas jail."

Jason felt numb. What Hyram said about his parents was true. It would be hard to face them—even though I've done nothing wrong. Jason sighed. Would they believe that? They might not, not completely, anyway. "Okay," he said. "Okay, I'll stay."

"Kind of figured you would. I went to talking around them cops about how you was a good kid but needed a kick in the butt, and that I was gonna tell you that you deserved to have your happy ass in jail. They liked that kind of talk."

"Was what I did so wrong, Hyram?"

"I weren't in the auction barn to see what you done, but I heard plenty about it. Everybody there, when they talk in groups, is all blustery and pissed off with you for firing a pistol around all them people. I get them off one-on-one and some of them sing a different song. Mind you they is still pissed, but in a different way. They say you did right, that the colt needed killing, and that somebody should of done it. But you ain't one of them, see, and they take it as an insult that you come in here, a stranger, and have the unmitigated gall to lesson them in proper conduct for a cowboy when it comes to a hurt horse."

"You mean that if one of the local men had shot that horse, it would have been all right?"

"That's what I'm saying."

"It isn't fair."

"Nope. You remember me telling you not to get involved in nothing? Remember that—right as we got outta the pickup by the auction barn?"

"Yes. But I didn't understand what you meant."

"It takes a while for folks to get used to you around here. I know folks who won't do business with anybody they ain't known for at least ten years. But never mind all that. You're going to find this little stay in jail a real education in itself, something you'll remember for the rest of your life. Try looking at the positive side of it."

"How can there be anything positive about staying here?"

"Hell's bells, Jason. Spending a couple of nights in jail is part of growing up male in West Texas. Ever' body does it. Your time just came a tad later in life. Used to be, though, you could at least get something to read in jail—them that liked to read could, anyway. I always got me a Zane Grey novel to while away the long hours. On the way over here, I stopped at the drugstore and got you this." He took a paperback from his hip pocket. "Louis L'Amour. One of his Sackett books, and a good one, I know. I read them all. But when I tried to get the cop in there to take it to you, he said no dice. Said reading material ain't permitted in jail on account of this being a place for punishment. Said you could have your personal Bible in your cell, if somebody brought it to you, but nothing else. Said you would find a Bible in ever' cell, put there free of charge."

"But they have a television in the day room for everyone to watch. They will allow television and not books?"

"Like I said, they think this is a place to get punished. You watch much daytime TV and that's sure enough punishment.

"And there's something else. I aim to bring Angela home tomorrow. I got it mostly set up. Hired me a nurse for when we can't be with her and for taking care of that catheter and such like."

"I didn't know."

"No reason for you to, I figured. At Bivins they said they can't do more for her unless she takes a notion to wake up. They even agreed with me that she just might come around better at home than in a hospital room. Word I got from a cop here is that you'll be sprung come

Monday. By that time, Angela will be set up at home in one of them crank-up beds. I aim to put a television in her room.

"One more thing. I called Sybil on your account. She said to tell you to sit tight and not let the pigs bother you, that she'll try to overcome her aversion to cops and come here to visit and that she will pick you up on Monday."

"No. Please. Call her and ask her not to come. I don't want her to see me like this."

"Not even to pick you up?"

"Not even for that."

"Suit yourself. I'll have Odom come get you."

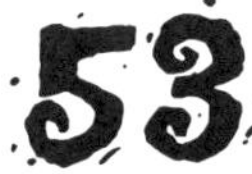

Monday morning a uniformed policeman gave Jason the clothes he had worn to the auction. It surprised him that he was free to go.

As soon as he left the Randall County Jail, he hurried across the street to the town square, stepping fast as though being close to the building put him in danger of some kind. Jason imagined the structure and its contents as a single living entity, like a beehive, imagined those who lived inside catching him in the entryway or just beyond the exit and mumbling something about a mistake being made in letting him go, imagined being thrust back into orange coveralls and put back into the day room with all the weekend drunks and petty thieves.

He felt soiled from the jail, though it had looked clean enough inside, and he found himself taking deep breaths to exhale as much of the jail air as he could from his lungs. A shower, he kept telling himself: I want a shower.

He didn't want to see Sybil yet—not until he got cleaned up. From a phone in the office of the *Canyon News*, he called Hyram. "This is Jason," he said. "How is Angela?"

"About the same, I reckon. Jason, I brought her home yesterday. Put her in the front bedroom, where I tried to get her to stay ever since she moved into the bunkhouse. You get outta the slammer?"

"They did just like you said, Hyram. The booking officer lectured me about proper use of firearms, and they turned me loose. What about the man who hurt Angela? Have the police caught Lint?"

"No. I think that weasel hotfooted it out of state. New Mexico, most likely. He'll come back, though, and when he does, some good Texas citizen is liable to use him for target practice. You wait by the courthouse on the square for Odom to pick you up. That Odom, he sure enough is working a buttonhole to get me out to look at a dead calf in the pasture toward Snake Mountain."

After he talked with Hyram, Jason called Sybil's number. "Today," Sybil's voice said, "the blue sky and the golden sun proclaim it too beautiful to be indoors with a telephone. So leave a message after the beep."

"Hello, Sybil. I just got out of jail, of all things. Jail. I'll be heading for the ranch as soon as Odom gets here. I need a bath. Then I'll come right home." He hung up feeling a bit foolish.

After he left the *Canyon News* building, Jason toured the town square, looking into windows of local merchants. Except for the names on the signs and the modern cars parked along the streets, the center of Canyon, Jason thought, must look as it did fifty years ago. A hundred, maybe.

He paused on Fourth Avenue to look east and west at what he could see of the rest of the town. It wasn't much. The street ran flat and straight, right out to the treeless horizon, and Jason imagined himself standing in an oasis, a small settlement of people in the middle of the vast desert of the Texas High Plains.

When Odom drove up in the pickup, Jason thought he looked like a stranger. His face was familiar enough, but the familiarity was shallow in time. Remove the last few months, Jason thought, and how would I see Odom? As a ruddy little cowboy, a man who might have stepped off a billboard advertising cigarettes, a tough little guy with lines carved in his face by sun and dry wind. The pickup with the gun on the rack fit him, though a horse with a rifle boot and a lariat would be better. Jason imagined Odom riding a horse across the prairie, pausing from time to time to lift a rifle stock to his cheek and squeeze off some shots at coyotes, prairie dogs or snakes, killing some, kicking up dust on the prairie with missed shots, cursing—"I get you next time, you sumbitch"—then he would spit a stream of tobacco juice onto the buffalo grass before taking a drink from his canteen.

Odious Odom, Jason thought, a man who fits in this oasis on the high plains as I never can.

Or do I? Who went into the bunkhouse to help a cowgirl take her jeans off? Who just spent two nights in a place called The Randall County Jail? Who wanted to be a Texan?

Besides, Odom isn't odious, is he? I like him, Jason thought. Don't I?

"You hungry?" Odom asked as Jason got into the pickup. "As I recollect, jailhouse food ain't worth a coyote turd. I'd sure enough take you to the Chuck Wagon Cafe for a bellyful of grits and eggs."

"Thanks. I'm doing fine, though. It might be best to get back to the ranch." Just listen to yourself, he thought: get back to the ranch. I'm just a step away from being a candidate for Odom's sidekick in a cigarette ad or riding the prairie with him, maybe handing him a carton of shells when he needs to reload so he can shoot another prairie dog.

But dammit, I do want to get back to the ranch. "How's Angela?"

Odom started to speak but found his voice so thin that it threatened to break. He cleared his throat several times and blinked hard. "She ain't so good, to my way of thinking. Hyram, he's of a different mind. He says she looks at you like she's about to say something any minute now. But she don't ever say nothing, and when you look in her eyes you can tell there ain't nobody home." Odom cleared his throat again.

As they drove out of Canyon, Odom said, "I found the stink in the white pickup. It caught a nail in the front tire, and when I changed the flat, I found shrimp hulls in the hubcap. Shrimp! Don't that beat all? Found hulls in the other hubcaps, too."

The absurdity of shrimp finding their way into the hubcaps of a pickup struck Jason as appropriate for West Texas, as fitting in with the many other absurdities of the region.

Jason let the rest of the trip pass in silence. He watched the fields of wheat and sorghum flow past, watched the landscape turn into grassland, watched the land drop away into canyon and saw Snake Mountain appear on the horizon.

When he entered Hyram's house, he resisted the impulse to pause in the entryway and take off his boots. He and Odom went into the front bedroom where Hyram sat in a rocking chair beside Angela. She fixed her eyes on Jason when he entered.

"Howdy, boys," Hyram said. "Angela is glad to see you. Look at that, her looking at Jason. She's glad you're here, you can tell."

"Hello, Hyram." Jason went to the side of the bed and took Angela's hand. "Hello, Angela," he whispered. She held eye contact with him, and Jason thought maybe she was about to say something. But she remained solemn and silent, and her hand did not respond to his touch.

"Hyram," Odom said, "about that critter out in the meadow, you know, that I told you about. . . ?"

"Okay, okay," Hyram said. He stood up. "Jason, Odom here won't let me alone till I go have a look at some dead calf. I'll leave you to keep an eye on Angela. You don't gotta be in here all the time—just look in ever' once in a while."

Jason watched Angela's eyes follow Hyram and Odom from the room, then return to him. In the other room Hyram said, "Now what the Sam hill is all the fuss about one dead calf? Couldn't you just set out some bait for the coyotes?"

"That's what I want you to see about," Odom said. "It don't look like no coyote kilt that calf. It looks like somebody done it, then carved some steaks off of it, then tried to make the kill look like the work of coyotes. I want to see what you think when we get out there."

Jason heard the front door close. "Angela," he said. "Angela." She looked at him in silence. Jason sighed. He released her hand and looked around the room. "Hyram brought you flowers," he observed. "Do you know they're here?"

She seemed to tire of looking at him. Her gaze fixed on nothing at all, and for the first time Jason thought her face looked empty, as if there were no awareness behind her sight. "I'll bet if you were speaking, you would tell me to go take a bath. Surely you could smell how sour I am after being in that jail without bathing for a couple of days. But who could take a bath there in the open, with everyone watching? I sure couldn't. I'll do it now, Angela. I'll go shower."

She didn't respond to his voice, but when he moved to the door, she watched. "I'll be right back, Angela."

When he left the room, he felt himself crying.

Lint got off of Playboy and climbed out of the gully. He shifted the pistol holster on his belt, then settled behind a yucca and looked at Hyram's ranch house through field glasses.

Angela was in there, he knew that. Sunday afternoon he had sat on that same spot and watched some men take her out of an ambulance and carry her into the house. He could see that she still had her leg in a cast, but other than that, she looked just fine.

It relieved him that she seemed all right, considering the last report he had heard.

After that Mexican tennis player tried to get into Angela's pants, with her help, and Lint found it necessary to hammer on the kid and slap that slut around some, Lint had gone home, thinking maybe he had accidentally killed Angela. He strapped on a pistol, threw some food and a bottle of whiskey into a sack, got a pocket radio and his binoculars, saddled up Playboy, and headed out across the prairie so the cops wouldn't get their hands on him.

Later that night, Lint was sitting on a rock at the base of Snake Mountain, taking some sips from the whiskey bottle, when he heard on his radio that Angela had been beaten bad enough to get put into the intensive care unit. There was a warrant out for the arrest of her estranged husband, the report said. The newscaster quoted the sheriff as saying that if Angela died, he would go after the husband with a warrant for murder.

Murder? That word got Lint's attention. He looked at the glint of moonlight on the bottle in his hand. "It's this sumbitching whiskey." He stood and heaved the bottle into the night. It landed with a crash of shattering glass.

The next day, he had regretted the impulse to throw away the whiskey. It was, after all, the bitch's own fault he slapped her around. Hell, he told himself, I'd a done what I done anytime I found some Mescan kid taking my wife's pants off, whiskey or no whiskey. There's some things a man can't help doing, not if he's a man.

Lint rode to the dugout on Hyram's ranch each night, and every morning before sunup, he retreated into Palo Duro Canyon. Twice each day, he rode through the arroyos and gullies close enough to get a good look at Hyram's house to see if there were any sign that Angela had returned.

He heard no more news reports on her, then sometime during his second day out, the batteries in the radio died. Two days after that, he ran out of food and had to shoot a jackrabbit with his pistol.

It wasn't easy to get a rabbit. He wasted most of his shells before he rigged up a forked branch to steady the pistol and made himself lie still for what seemed forever, waiting for a rabbit to get close enough. It wasn't worth the effort, he decided, for a little tad of stringy meat, a conviction that had driven him to kill one of Hyram's calves.

Lint surveyed the ranch and the outbuildings with his binoculars. Odom's truck was there. So was Hyram's. And there's them sumbitches now, he thought, watching Odom and Hyram leave the house, heading to the corral. They saddled up and rode toward Snake Mountain. Gone to see about the calf I killed, Lint thought. That leaves Angela alone in the house. Good. I can go talk to her, maybe get her to call the sheriff or somebody to lift that warrant. Maybe make her see how I didn't mean to hurt her none.

Where had that kid gone, he wondered—the one who caused all the trouble. The kid left on Saturday and never showed up again, not after driving off with Hyram Saturday morning. Good thing for him he ain't around no more, Lint decided, or I'd of rode down there and shot the sumbitch.

Lint slid down into the gully and mounted Playboy. "Come on, now," he said. "Let's get down there so I can talk to my girl."

In the entryway of Hyram's house, Lint paused. "Angela?" he said. He could smell the faint aroma of bacon from Hyram's breakfast, and it made him aware of how empty his stomach felt. She's probably asleep, he told himself, and went into the kitchen.

In the refrigerator he found a box from Colonel Sanders that had a couple of pieces of fried chicken in it. They tasted old and dried up, but better than rabbit cooked on a stick over a campfire. Better by a long shot. Sure could use some coffee, he thought. He looked around the kitchen, but found no coffee made.

After tossing the chicken bones onto the table and wiping his hands on his jeans, he decided it was time to find Angela.

She lay in bed in the first room Lint looked into. "Hello, Angela. I'm right pleased to see you looking so good. I been keeping up with you, best I could, but what with that warrant out on me, I thought it best not to come by. Been up to Snake Mountain." He laughed. "You remember how you all the time tried to get me up there? And I all the time said no on account of not seeing any profit in doing all that climbing? Well you sure enough was right. I been going up to the top dang near ever' day. You can see forever from up there, maybe clean to New Mexico. I should of gone up there with you back when you was pestering me to make the climb. I should of done it."

It unnerved him that she stared in silence. But it also irritated him that she looked at him with green eyes. Where's them blue contacts she used to wear to cover up them witch's eyes? he wondered. Did she say a while back that she threw them away? He struggled not to show his irritation.

"So how you been? I hope you been fine, Angela. I went plumb crazy with jealousy when I seen that Mescan kid pulling down your pants, plumb crazy. I had no business knocking you around, I know. But I went plumb crazy. Angela?" He stepped up to the bed and peered close at her face. "Angela? How come you don't talk to me? It's me, Lint. But shit, you know that. You're looking right at me. Angela, goddammit, you say something to me."

She looked away, and it infuriated him that she did so. "Look at me when I'm talking to you, you bitch." His hand shot out and he slapped her a sharp blow across the face. Angela turned her head and whimpered, then looked at him.

"You sure enough know how to get to me, don't you?" He struggled to control his anger. Shouldn't ought to hit her, he told himself. Shouldn't ought to do that. Not when I need her to call off the cops.

He forced himself to look remorseful. "I'm sorry I done that. But you know how I get sometimes. I ain't going to do that again. I ain't. Come on, now, you gotta get up and get to the phone. Call the sheriff and tell him it weren't me that hurt you last week. I know you got a broke leg. I'll help you get into the other room for the phone. Come on." He stood for a long moment, looking at her. "Here," he said, leaning over her, "I'll carry you into the kitchen so you can use the phone, okay?"

He put one arm under her back, the other under her knees. When she made no move to help him at all, he had to control the anger that rose up in him, the red tide that threatened to take over. "Shit," he mumbled, then, louder: "Angela, come on, honey. Come on. I'll get you into the other room. Come on."

He picked her up and stepped away from the bed. Something under the sheet seemed to snag, and Angela made a low moaning sound. He pulled her further from the bed and saw a clear plastic tube fall away from her. The word catheter came to Lint. How come she would need that? he wondered. All she got is a broke leg. He looked at the cast on her leg. It's just a little pissant of a cast, so the break can't be all that bad. "Shit fire," Lint said. "I had worse breaks than that, and no doctor ever rammed one of them catheters into me."

He carried her into the kitchen. Now what? he wondered. He looked out the window at Hyram's pickup. I bet, Lint thought, Hyram leaves his keys in the ignition. The fat sumbitch got no sense. And if the keys ain't there, why I can hot-wire that thing. I can take Angela home, pet on her some, get her to talking to me, and then maybe she'll call about that warrant.

Jason got out of the shower and was drying when he heard the front door close. He opened the bathroom door and said, "Hyram?" When he got no answer, he went to the window. Holy Krishna, he said to himself. Lint Bodark! And he's carrying Angela.

Jason grabbed his pants and ran through the house toward the front door. Pausing only long enough to pull on the jeans, he opened the door and ran toward Lint and Angela. "Put her down, Lint." Jason shouted. "You put her down."

Lint turned, a startled look on his face. He dropped Angela and pulled the pistol from the holster on his hip. As he brought his arm up to fire, Jason hit him.

The pistol went off, and a part of Jason was aware of the sound of the bullet striking the house. His headlong run into Lint knocked the man to the ground, and Jason fell on top of him. Lint tried to bring the pistol up again. Jason slapped the hand, knocking the weapon from him, and Lint punched Jason's ribs. The blow took away Jason's breath, but he managed to smash Lint in the face with a fist. His head snapped back against the ground, and Jason swung again.

Lint twisted, throwing Jason off of him. As Lint scrambled to his feet, he hit Jason again, sending him reeling off to one side. He landed on top of the pistol. Lint took a knife from his pocket and snapped it open just as Jason sat up with the pistol in his hand.

"So you think you're gonna shoot me? You ain't got the guts." He circled.

Jason glanced at Angela, lying just a few feet away. She seemed to be trying to sit up, though she wasn't looking at him or Lint.

"Move back," Jason warned. He followed Lint's movements with the barrel of the pistol. Can I do it? he wondered, and thought of the red-headed man in the Los Angeles airport, of Suppriah in a pool of blood. He felt his grip on the pistol falter. What was it Altus had said to Sybil? That he could live with a bullet in his leg—that's it. I could shoot him in the leg. Jason firmed his grip on the pistol and lowered the barrel so it pointed at Lint's legs.

Lint laughed. He angled a bit closer, just as someone on a motorcycle pulled off the road toward the ranch house. When Jason glanced behind him toward the sound of the engine, Lint dived toward him.

Jason saw the knife coming at him, and he felt the pistol jump in his hand, heard the report sharp and clear, then heard another shot though the pistol didn't jump. Lint jerked and his face showed more surprise than pain as he fell forward.

Two shots, Jason thought. He stood over Lint, pointing the pistol at the place on his shoulder where blood darkened his shirt. But I tried for a leg, for a leg. Jason glanced at Lint's legs, saw that one of them was bleeding.

He heard the horses and saw Hyram and Odom. Hyram held a rifle. "Good shooting," Odom said, "especially from a saddle."

The other shot, Jason thought, the bullet that hit his shoulder—Hyram fired it. Did he kill Lint? Jason dropped the pistol, bent to look, and saw with relief that Lint was breathing.

"Hyram?" Angela said. "Hyram?" She sat gazing toward Snake Mountain.

Jason went to her. "Angela," he said. "You talked!" He knelt beside her.

Sybil kicked down the stand on the motorcycle. She slid off the seat and headed toward Jason.

"Hyram, go with me." Angela pointed at Snake Mountain. "Go there with me, there, to the top of the mountain. Will you do that? Will you?"

Sybil touched Jason's shoulder. He took her hand and looked around. Odom stood over Lint, nudging him with the toe of a boot. Hyram stared at Angela. He gripped his rifle to his breast, and Jason could see him blinking back tears. Hyram nudged the horse closer to Angela.

She fixed her attention on Snake Mountain. "You'll go with me, Hyram? To the top of the mountain?"

"Yes," Hyram said. "Yes."

Jason stood and leaned against Sybil.

Hyram sat on the bed and watched Angela dress for the party. She took off her shower cap and let her red hair cascade to her shoulders. Hyram knew she pretended not to know he was watching, but he saw the small grin and the way she cut her eyes toward where he sat on the bed.

She stumbled a bit putting on her bikini panties—always to that left side, Hyram noted. Doc said she like as not would have a game left arm and would favor her left leg. Hyram sighed. At least she's up and around and is near back to her old self.

She turned to Hyram with a pleased expression. "I like to hear you sigh like that when there ain't much cloth covering me." She looked at her breasts. "You like them?"

"Them's the finest blue undies between Amarillo and Post."

"I know what you for a fact mean, and it's got nothing to do with blue nor underwear."

"You been a long time catching on to codes. You know I ain't much on being direct."

"That was direct."

> "A man who points straight and direct
> might get his pecker in check.
> It's best to tell jokes
> about eggs with no yolks
> than be a man with no head and no neck."

"That's better. Indirect. Except I didn't quite catch on to that poem, Hyram."

"Hells bells, Angela. It's a poem for chrissake. Didn't you learn in high school that nobody but the wizard up in front of the class is supposed to catch on to a poem, unless it happens to be a bad one?"

"Good, Hyram. That's good." She sat on the bed beside him. "I think I can live with your speaking in code if you can live with me asking a question real direct ever' once in a while. Not often. I won't push it often. But, dangit Hyram, I'm a woman, and I gotta hear it once in a while. Get aholt of yourself cause here it comes. Do you for a fact love me?"

Hyram felt his throat get tight and his eyes become moist. He coughed and cleared his throat. "I hope I show how I feel cause showing counts more than words. And I hope you can live with the ways I show it."

"Come on, Hyram. That ain't direct." Her voice was soft, and she wiped a tear that ran down one of his leathery cheeks.

He coughed again, a slight, unnecessary cough. Then he stood and took his eggshell Stetson from a peg on the wall. Angela's hair fell across her face. She shook it aside and looked up at him, then down at her bare breasts.

He stood in the doorway to the bedroom, rolling the brim of his hat. "Yes. And I like looking. Yes."

"You like more than looking, and you're dang good at what a man needs to be dang good at doing for his woman. And, Hyram, thanks. I know that was hard. I'll try not to be a pushy bitch and ask hard questions. Leastwise not too often."

He nodded, jammed his hat on, and left.

Outside, his hired boys iced down some beer. Odom, carrying a stepladder, grumped something about them sumbitching lights around the dance floor. Guests had been arriving for half an hour, and all had asked about Angela. Hyram had been telling them that she was a tad slow getting ready, but she would be out.

And she would, too. He knew she would.

When Jason and Sybil arrived, they came on a big Harley. Jason drove. He wore jeans, a shirt with snaps and cowboy boots, and he looked like no biker Hyram had ever seen. He stood by the beer kegs and motioned them over.

"You look like two kinds of Texan, Mister White." Hyram looked at him from head to foot. "Once you step away from that Hog, a person might think you just got off a horse. All you need is a black string tie with a black widow spider set in plastic on it, and you will be almost a true cowboy. You'll be lacking only one thing to be the genuine article."

"And what might that be, Hyram?" Sybil asked.

"A lobotomy." Hyram laughed. "And you, the lovely lady Sybil, you're sure enough an eyeball pleaser all decked out in black. Looks like you caught yourself a biker cowboy. But look, yonder comes Angela." He lowered his voice. "Jason told me some about all them mean things somebody been doing to you, Sybil. Is that stopped now?"

"Yes. Pug moved to Dallas and Altus is in jail. They were the ones harassing me."

Hyram nodded sharp and curt. "You and Jason is a mighty fine and handsome couple."

Angela slipped up to Hyram and hooked a thumb in one of his belt loops. He put an arm around her. "Howdy Sybil," she said. "Evening, Jason. Has Hyram told you about us yet?"

"Ain't told nobody. The boys ain't all set up yet. They'll do it after they finish icing the beer."

"Set up for what?"

"For making the cow jump over the moon. I aim to set off fireworks to light up the sky at the precise moment after I make the big announcement. Have a drink, folks."

"Hyram, you know I can't drink nothing. Doc said folks who got head injured got to stay away from hooch. That includes beer. I don't like that none, and folks tonight are going to be looking at me funny, but I can't drink."

Jason took a plastic cup from beside a beer keg. "Take one of these, Angela, and fill it with water. Carry it around, and no one will be pushing a drink on you."

Sybil picked up another cup. "Let's go get us both some water, Angela. I don't like to drink alcohol, either."

"Didn't say I don't like it. I said I can't." Angela gave Hyram a hug. "We're getting married. That's the big announcement that's coming up. Me and Hyram here, we'll be flying high. Come next week, I aim to teach Hyram the proper way to greet the sunrise. Come on, let's go for that water."

Hyram and Jason watched the two women walk toward the house. "I figured as much," Jason said. "Congratulations, Hyram. I believe you two will be a good match."

"Yeah. Flying high. Did you hear the one about the skywriter? It goes like this:

A love-struck skywriter named Sherm
Jumped out with his chute long and firm.
With a jerk and a spasm
He had an orgasm
And wrote out 'I love you' in sperm."

"That's great, Hyram. That just might be your best one. I like it because it's dang funny and because it says something about your self-confidence in certain matters."

Hyram cleared his throat and filled a cup with beer. "What the hell, Jason, we're falling behind all them other sumbitches here that been hitting the suds." He thrust the cup into Jason's hands.

"Thanks, Hyram. I think I'll drink this one and maybe a few others. That way I'll be ready for the friendly fight when it starts."

Hyram clapped Jason on the back. "Ain't going to be no fight this time. Lint can't start one—seeing as how he's in the Randall County Hilton, and from the look of things, he's gonna be studying bars for some years to come. This here is a party where I personally will take it amiss if some stupid cowboy starts a fight of any kind." He drew himself a beer, held it out and blew the suds onto the ground. "Here's to you and me both flying high, Jason. Flying high."